DOWN SALEM WAY

A LOVING HUSBAND STORY

MEREDITH ALLARD

Copperfield
PRESS

Copperfield Press

ISBN: 9780578500645

Cover design by LFD

Down Salem Way/Meredith Allard – 1st paperback edition

{1. Historical—Fiction. 2. Salem Witch Trials—Fiction. 3. Colonial Ameria—Fiction. 4. Massachusetts Bay Colony—Fiction. 5. Paranormal—Fiction. 6. Literary—Fiction} I. Title

"To My Dear and Loving Husband" and "A Letter to Her Husband, Absent Upon Publick Employment" by Anne Bradstreet are in the public domain.

MY BELOVED LIZZIE

How have we come to this?

If you can feel the shaking of my hand in these unsteady words, know tis because I tremble with the loss of you. I know not how I breathe without you, knowing where you are, feeling how you suffer. My whole being aches. My arms are empty without you.

I cannot eat. I cannot sleep. I cannot sit. I am anxious and my legs tremble and I must move. Then I cannot walk steadily and others watch as though I'm afflicted. I do not know what else to do so I sit here at my desk under the window. I write, and I write, and I know that one day we shall be together again.

Oh, my God, Lizzie. What has happened? What Evil has come to Salem that has you and our Grace languishing in that foul-stenched Hell? I cannot stand to be here whilst you are there. Stay strong this much longer, my love, a few more days at best, and I shall see you out of there and we shall escape, together, to where no one shall hurt you again. I shall never stop until you are warm and safe with me where you belong.

And I ask again...how have we come to this?

10 JANUARY 1691, MONDAY

*T*he winters are colder here, I'm certain of it. I feel it so in my bones, which feel brittle, as though they shall shatter like icicles against a hammer. The sky looks nearly as it does in England, gradations of gray from near-black to tinder-slate that shed wind, sleet, or snow depending on its mood. Whilst England grows cold enough in the sunless months, in Salem the sky disappears beneath a woolen blanket. I cannot step one foot outside without feeling liquid ice in my veins, but such is life in Massachusetts in January.

This morn Lizzie laughed as I piled on layers of clothing in an attempt to stay warm: my woolen flannel underdrawers, my linen shirt, my thickest worsted leggings, perhaps not the most fashionable, but they are my warmest; my woolen suit of doublet, jerkin, and breeches, and my heavy coat, the deep blue one Lizzie says matches my eyes, though what matters my eyes when I cannot see for the blizzard? Lizzie pulled my coat close to my ears and knotted my scarf near my throat so I might keep whatever warmth I take with me. I would cover myself in ten coats if I could without looking ridiculous. Even as I was, Lizzie could not stifle her giggles.

"Good heavens, James. You look like a blue onion ready for the peeling."

"And shall you peel my layers away?"

She blushed in that way I love, red-hot along her jaw. She pushed me toward the door as though she could not be rid of me soon enough.

"Perhaps when you return home. If you're lucky."

I pulled my dark-haired, dark-eyed beauty closer and basked in her warmth. I ran my lips along her red-stained cheeks. "I have been lucky thus far. I cannot imagine that my luck shall not continue."

Lizzie tugged my coat closer round my neck, then opened the door and pushed me toward it. She shivered in the cold, kissed my lips, and pressed me outside.

"Go. Father waits for you."

"Shall you wait for me?"

"What other man might I wait for who is tall and strong with hair the color of spun gold and eyes like the bluest, brightest jewels?"

I stepped into the unfriendly gloom and the door shut behind me. I had lost the battle to Lizzie, which is as it usually goes.

I quivered in my boots as I walked toward the shore, warming my mind with thoughts of Lizzie, her wondering dark eyes, her dark hair, her luscious, berry-like lips. I needed something else to occupy my mind, but there was nothing. I'm still struck by how sparse tis in Massachusetts.

"They call this a town?" I said aloud, to no one. I struggle to think of this place as civilized. Salem Town grows livelier toward the harbor since tis the hub for shipbuilding and the merchant trade. Tis even more provincial at the Farms. There is so little of everything here, and tis still a shock to walk amongst nothing but seashore to one side, farmland on the other, and wilderness all round.

"Is this all there is?" I said, again to no one. A seagull cawed overhead, but then I doubted what I heard since even seabirds must know to stay away from Salem in winter.

I shook myself as far as the sea and stood at the edge of the white-gray bay, the tips of my boots licked by the lapping waves, the ocean spray splattering my exposed face with bitter water-like pinpricks along my cheeks. Again, I thought the cold in England was not ever this cold. I squinted into the expanse of water, slapping my forehead when I realized I left my spectacles at home. What a confounded fool I can be. Twas an excuse to return home to Lizzie, I knew, but Father waited for me at the wharf so I pressed forward. If I concentrated enough, so that my temples squeezed, I could see well enough. If I pinched my brain that much tighter, I thought, I could see past the ocean to England, and home.

A sharp spray of salt water brought me back to myself. The air is even colder at land's end. With my hat pulled over my eyes and my face turned from the wind, I bumped into a man in a leather coat, a fisherman, I think. The man's Monmouth cap fell to the ground, his leather pouch flung from his shoulder, and he grimaced with severity.

"My apologies," I said. "I did not see you there."

"Blind, are you?" The man spat in my direction. "A Pox on you!" With a hmph! he skittered away, his gray doublet and breeches blending into the slate of sea and sky. Indeed, I am blind. I cannot see my own hand before my face without my spectacles, which were at home with Lizzie, where it was warm, where she was warm, her embrace warmest of all. I wanted to be in my cushioned chair before the hearth reading Samuel Pepys' *Memoirs of the Navy* with Lizzie beside me knitting, mending, or chatting to me about her day, but instead I was there near an unforgiving shore whipped by the angry weather like a thief in the stocks. Still, I pressed forward. I stared into the distance, struggling to make out Father's short, slight shape. Then I had a fright brought on by one word: "Pox."

I did not need that ill-tempered man to remind me of the Pox running rampant along the shore. There has been another outbreak, and those living closest to the port suffer most. I pulled my scarf closer to my mouth, as though the meager movement would keep the Pox where it belonged, over there, away from me and mine.

My head ached with the clinking of nails hammered into wood and the grunts of strong-backed men in heavy coats hauling barrels on their shoulders. The woody scent of fresh-made lumber, salt, and fish lingered everywhere. I stopped near the port, squinting into the distance, still searching for Father, until I thought my head would burst into a star-like pattern from the effort. With some struggle, I saw a vague outline of men and guessed Father was amongst them.

The closer I came to the dock the more I heard the haggling of sailors and the lapping of waves. Father was indeed amongst the huddled men, and I heard his hearty stage actor's laugh before I saw him. Something about his infectious mirth makes him appear taller, as though he fills any space he enters. I laughed as well, only my amusement was centered on the round hat Father wore. The long flaps fell over his mouth and ears.

Father lifted the front flap so he could see me better. "Do you like the hat, Son? It keeps what is left of my brain from freezing." His slanted blue eyes brightened. "You see, friends, here he is. My James. What better son could any father wish for?" The men murmured in agreement.

"You look worried, Father," I said. "Can you see trouble with the ships from here?"

"Tis a troublesome time for the ships, Son. The waiting could kill you. Tis all too easy to lose goods and good men. One bad decision, or one bad wind, and everything and everyone disappears to the depths of the ocean."

"And the profits disappear as well." I recognized Mr. Sanderson by his voice since he stood too far for me to see. He stepped closer and peered into the horizon as though he could make out trouble in the distance. I thought to loan him my spectacles, then remembered I did not have them.

I looked down the narrow expanse of rocky shoreline, across to the tall wooden squares used as warehouses. Then I followed Father's gaze toward the bay and the ocean beyond. Twas, I thought, not unlike a wake for ships not yet sunk or sailors not yet lost. Despite the somber tone of their meeting, the men, including Father, were well dressed in their finely fitting, jewel-toned fabrics, flashing their rings here or their jewel-encrusted walking sticks there. The merchants are not so overdressed as to be ostentatious since there are those here who would call them sinful for their vanity. The merchants wear enough for others to see that they can afford that ruby ring, that sapphire-studded walking stick, that finely tailored suit.

Father clasped my shoulder more firmly and brought me closer to the circle of men. The sweet smell of rum hovered on their breaths since Father often provides free samples of his wares. Mr. Smithers offered me the bottle but I shook my head.

"Mr. Wentworth the Younger," Mr. Boxley said. "How good to see you again." He poked me in the ribs with his elbow. Boxley is a short-statured, rounded man with three chins. He stares at everyone as though searching to see what their true motive might be, so much so that at times I think he has four eyes. In fact, he has the normal two, and I felt the pinch as both bore into me. The man shivered into his fur-collared robe whilst blowing into his gold-glittered fingers, which flashed like lightning. He grabbed my arm, and I turned away to avoid intoxication by the rum-induced fumes. "We have not seen you this month past. Keeping close with that pretty little wife of yours, eh?"

Rude-sounding words popped into my ice-hard brain. I was about to speak them when Father stepped in front of me. "Now, George. You know James has been married but a month."

George Boxley slapped his hands together. "Aye, indeed. What else should your boy be doing these days, and nights for that matter?" The men laughed. "The bliss of early married days is sweet. But they pass, young man. They pass. Enjoy them whilst you can."

"My wife and I are quite content together, I assure you," I said.

"But weren't we all content when we first married?" Each man nodded as though this were quite serious. "There is joy in the early months of marriage, but then, before you know it, tis gone. As I say, enjoy it whilst you can."

"And as much as you can!" said a scrannel-like man whose name I do not care to remember.

"Hush!" Father squinted as though searching for spies amongst us. "If the farmers from the Village hear you they will cite you for vulgarity. Perhaps they shall set you in the stocks and throw stones at your head for your sin!" Raucous laughter filled the air.

"Where are Hathorne and Corwin?" asked the scrannel-looking man. "They would be the first to tie you to the whipping post."

"Fortunately, they are not here," Father said.

"The Villagers can go to the Devil, if they have not already," said Mr. Davies. "That is what happens when you have no proper education. You are too easily manipulated to the bidding of others."

"They have no thoughts other than that which their Reverend tells them to have," said Mr. Stevens.

"I'm not sure that's fair," Father said. "They are well educated. They began Harvard College. They set great store in literacy."

"So they can read the Bible," said Mr. Stevens. "Thomas Oliver says Parris speaks of nothing but the spread of the Devil's black magick. Tis no surprise Parris' own family suffers."

"They are simple folk," said Mr. Smithers. Smithers' white-shirted stomach pressed his coat aside as though it only meant to stretch halfway round his waist. "Tis like living down the road from a field of cattle who allow themselves to be led wherever someone else decides they should be."

I exhaled, watching the cold smoke linger before my face. "I'm afeared you are not quite correct about the Villagers," I said. "My wife lived in the Village after her family arrived from England. There are intelligent, perceptive people amongst them. They sound like no fools to me. They fight firmly and forever if they believe they are in the right."

"What do they have to fight about?" asked Mr. Smithers. "Someone stole their livestock? Someone borrowed their plow without asking?"

"That, and who has the deeds to which lands and who legally inherited those lands and who has too much land and who has lost too many children." Mr. Davies looked me in the eye as if to emphasize his point. "Even amongst themselves they argue about Parris. Some want him heading the Village Church and others cannot wait to see him gone."

"Some of these families have been arguing amongst each other for two generations," Mr. Boxley said. "Tis hard to make sense of the lack of civility they display toward anyone or anything they do not understand. What rude, intolerant people."

"When you, of course, have always shown the utmost tolerance." Father smiled. The men laughed, thinking he teased.

As though in afterthought, Mr. Davies said to me, a glint in his narrow eyes, "Your wife is from the Village? My blessings on you, young man."

"Fear not, young Mr. Wentworth," the scrannel-looking man said. "We shall not speak of Goody Wentworth as we speak of others in the Village. She must be a worthy woman if a successful young man such as yourself married her."

"Mistress Wentworth," I said. "She may have been born a

farmer's daughter but she is now my wife and is due the respect of her proper place."

My fuming heart wanted to continue telling off the oaf, but I silenced myself. I need not have worried. Father, as always, took my side though doing so could have cost him several business associates and quite some profit.

"My son is right. My daughter-in-law is entitled to her place as are your wives."

"We meant no offense to your son or his bride," said Mr. Davies.

"Besides," Father continued, "we cannot make generalizations about those in the Village any more than they can make generalizations of us here in the Town."

"Ha!" Mr. Boxley poked Father in the ribs. "They make many proclamations about us. We are sinful. We are wrong. We are bound for Hell. They cannot bear to be in our Church because they cannot stand the proximity to us. They believe themselves to be too Godly for our kind of people."

"Ignorant farmers, the lot of them," the scrannel-looking man said. "When the new Charter arrives and we are a people under law again, we shall put them in their place."

Father shook his head. "True, with the loss of the Charter, they lost their ability to make laws. But that frightens them. When people are frightened they become even more far-reaching in their demands." Father bowed toward the other men. "Now I am afeared I must move along, gentlemen. I shall meet up with you Monday next. As always."

Father bowed toward the men, and they returned the gesture. He pointed me away from the shore, leaving behind the hammering of the shipbuilders and the shouts of the fish sellers and the rum-filled laughter of the merchants still scanning the ocean as though waiting for news of their ships. The smell of dried codfish lingered whilst the fishermen rowed toward the bay. I wondered how they kept their stomachs in place jostling against the waves. The further inland Father and I walked the faster our steps became.

"Those merchants are insufferable fools," Father said. "You would think they were children, the way they speak." He removed his hat and scratched his balding head under its wrap.

"And yet you keep company with them," I said.

"We do what we must to keep the business moving forward, James."

"Did you hear them? Did you hear how they spoke of Lizzie? Goody Wentworth they called her, as though she were some fisherwoman or farmer's wife."

We neared the road where farmers from the Village carted their flour, salt beef, pork, firewood, and cider to market.

"What is wrong with fishwomen or farmer's wives? My father was a sailor, so your grandmother was a sailor's wife. Lizzie is a farmer's daughter, so her mother was a farmer's wife. Don't point fingers, Son, and never be prideful. Judge not lest ye be judged. We are not all of us cut out for university as you are. Some of us do the best we can with what we have. Let those foolish men be hanged by their own conceit. Let us stand apart and watch them fall."

The hammering of the shipbuilders still rattled my brain. "What were they saying about the Reverend Mr. Parris?"

Father smiled. His love for gossip contributes to the easy friendships he makes. "The Reverend Mr. Parris' daughter and niece have had a turn, they say. The girls have been overcome with fits. Some say tis the work of Witchcraft. I know you do not believe in Witchcraft, though you realize you are the odd one out on that matter."

"I prefer demons I can see," I said.

"Aye. But be careful what you wish for. Demons you can see may not be any better than those you cannot. If you can see them, you know they are coming."

"If you say so, Father."

Father winked at me. "Did you know that Prudence has cast her eye your way?"

"Prudence?"

"Aye, James. Prudence." Father poked me hard in the ribs. "Prudence Connor? My helping-girl? The sister of Patience Connor, your helping-girl?"

"Ah." I thought of wispy Patience, thankful for how much help she has been to Lizzie. I struggled to picture her sister in Father's house, but all I could recall was the sound of pots being scrubbed, floors being swept, and the swish of fast-moving skirts.

"Ah," Father said, mimicking my careless attitude. "Prudence asks after you frequently, wondering aloud when you'll be back, making your favorite lobster stew when she knows you are coming, patting her hair under her coif when she sees you through the window. Whenever you are there she cannot turn her head from you. Thank God you are halo-haired and sky-eyed like your mother. We would not want you short and bald like me." He laughed at himself.

"You know I'm married, Father. You helped arrange it all. You were the one who asked Silas for permission for me to pay my respects to Lizzie."

"Old Silas did not need much convincing, did he? He knows you and I are upstanding members of Salem Town Society."

"Better yet, he knows you have money, a lot of it. You told him you would build a house for Lizzie and me. You told him you would give us the land on which to build that house. I have never seen someone fuss the way you did over every detail inside and out. And that was you at our wedding fussing over the Indian pudding, was it not?" I glanced sideways at Father. He was enjoying my agitation, I could tell. "Your helping-girl knows I'm married, I hope."

"Prudence knows you are spoken for, but she does not care. She still thinks of you as the most eligible bachelor in Salem. I lost count of the well-to-do fathers and mothers pushing their daughters in your direction. And not one of those so-called suitable girls caught your eye." Father laughed so hard he shuddered. "My son does not make a match with a merchant's daughter or a governor's daughter. He falls in love with a farmer's daughter."

"You said you do not mind that Lizzie is a farmer's daughter."

"I do not mind, Son. I know you made a perfect match with Elizabeth, as I made a perfect match with your mother. There are no coins, no jewels, no gold that can replace what Elizabeth has brought to your marriage—her heart, as you have brought yours. Tis a father's dearest wish that his son find a help-meet worthy of him, and you have. Never mind what those dotards by the shore say. Your task is to follow your heart."

"Which I did," I said. "There is no one for me but Lizzie. But can your helping-girl not find a husband of her own?"

"I think she would if she could, Son, but it appears all the men of marriageable age in these parts are spoken for. She could have Old Man Pemberley, I reckon, but I do not imagine she would want him, broken down and without a shilling to his name. She has found someone else's husband to her liking. I'm simply letting you know you have an admirer."

"The only admiration I need is from Lizzie." Speaking Lizzie's name made me long to return home so I changed the subject. "With the Reverend Mr. Parris at the helm of the Church in the Village, do you still believe tis best to allow the Village to have their own Church? They are still petitioning the Town to be let free. Since you are a Selectman you have a say in the matter."

Father shook his head. "I say let them have their own Church. Let them show their long, humorless faces to each other. I cannot stand to look upon them."

I looked sideways at Father as the lines etched deeper round his mouth. "A moment ago you said we should not judge. That was you, was it not?"

Father sighed. "You are right, James. Tis my frustration with Parris that makes me speak so. I fear he is creating a divide amongst us. I'm not the only one unhappy with him. Tis the Villagers' own folly for allowing someone as insufferable as Parris to head their Church. What an unlikable man. Fool!"

Father said that last word as though he spat a foul taste from his mouth, slapping his hand in the air as though swatting at Parris himself.

"You do realize that we are members of the Church in Salem Town," I said. "For all intents and purposes, our Anglicanism has been set aside."

Father looked aghast. "Nay! We joined the Church to become a part of the community, to…"

"Make a profit?" I said. Father looked serious, his slanted eyes now slits, his lips pulled into his mouth. "And all it took was some false piety before the Congregation claiming we found God."

"That was no false piety. You have found God, James, have you not?"

We neared Father's house. After some thought, I said, "I do not know that I have found God. You know God better than I do, and I know you do not believe in the Puritans' doctrine."

"I lived under Puritan rule in England with Cromwell's Roundheads after they disposed of the King. I liked it not. Twas 11 years until the new King was restored."

"Yet here you bend to their doctrine willingly. We could have accepted the Half-Way Covenant. Many here do so."

"We could have. But we did not. Sometimes we must make sacrifices. You'll learn that for yourself one day."

Twas fully dark by then and I no longer cared about Kings or Commonwealths or hard-believing Sinners. I bid Father good night and made my way home. I have never been a night person and always prefer to be home before the sun falls.

Yet tis still odd when I am at home and realize I feel awkward at times near Lizzie. We are still learning each other, still understanding one another. In one moment I feel as though we have been married all our lives. In the next tis as if we are strangers in close proximity.

After our evening meal, Lizzie and I sat in our chairs before the hearth, Lizzie sewing whilst I read. Suddenly, I felt an urge to feel her skin against mine so I took her hand. She smiled as I did so, which gave me courage. I leaned my face close to hers and pressed my lips to her temple. Lizzie leaned into me and my blood drained away at the sight of those full berry-like lips. I thought I should say something, start some conversation, but words left me. Finally, I thought to tell her what I heard of Reverend Parris.

"Did you know them when you lived on the Farms?" I asked. "The Parrises?"

"A little." Lizzie resumed her sewing. "Now that I live in the Town I hardly see them except perhaps when I visit Pa and Mary Grace." Lizzie stared into the red-gold glow of the fire. "Perhaps I should check on them, the girls."

"I heard tis an odd illness. Tis not contagious, do you think?"

"Are the Reverend and his wife ill?"

"Not as I have heard."

Lizzie looked thoughtful as she considered. "Then I would not expect so."

"Strange that the girls are so ill but no one else in the household is."

"Sometimes illnesses are odd. Sometimes they cannot be explained."

I basked in Lizzie's peach-like glow. How tender she is, how considerate to be worried about sickly girls she hardly knows. I spent the next hour gazing into the deep night of her dark eyes.

11 JANUARY 1691, TUESDAY

*C*ows. I live down the road from cows. I traveled all the way from England expecting the Promised Land, as Father said it would be. He made it sound like a place where gold grew from trees and silver was ripe for the plucking. Instead, I find myself keeping company with kine. In truth, I do not mind them since they make for good, quiet neighbors who spend their days grazing languidly in the boundless fields. Occasionally, one will low, a melancholy sound, but I nod, understanding the lament. I have come to enjoy watching the cows through my window, the animals chewing the cud carefully, one mouthful at a time, looking content with their lot as the long grass slips between their teeth.

My dearest dream is to take Lizzie, commandeer one of Father's ships, and sail for England where I can return to my studies. This merchant life does not come naturally to me. Tis Father with the business sense, Father who can talk to anyone, buy anyone ale at the public house, Father who understands how to get what he needs. But one day I shall take Lizzie home. I shall stay awhile yet to help Father, and then I shall take Lizzie and go to where we can be free to live our own lives.

In truth, I'm tired of working with Father's ledgers. I'm tired of puzzling out loss or profit for Father's various importing and exporting ventures. Tis an odd job for me, I reckon. I understand words. I know figures, too, but I do not enjoy their company as well. Figures have to work out correctly. Sums and differences and percentages are simple enough to calculate, yet it causes problems when the numbers do not meet up as they should. I prefer words, reading and reflecting, to maths, multiplying and dividing. With words I can decide for myself what I believe. Tis difficult to have deep, considerate thoughts about a numerical fraction, but then I am no Newton or Descartes.

I must write down a conversation between Father and myself that occurred this afternoon before it slips from my memory.

I have asked Father about my grandfather on countless occasions, and on countless occasions I have been rebuffed, which is unlike him. Father is a chatty man if ever I met one. Father and I were at his house sitting at the table before the hearth, I calculating figures as per usual, Father grumbling about a Royal Navy man, a former Royal Navy man, I should say, by the name of Thomas Oliver who owes us money. Father calls this Oliver fellow a sailor. Sailor is not the word I would use. Apparently, this Oliver owes debts along the coast, and probably everywhere else he's plundered from, but he is more useful than costly, so Father pays Oliver's obligations with only a few sneering remarks.

Father looked through the window, the diamond panes casting iridescent shadows on the floor whilst the sun struggled to break through this latest winter storm. There was such sharpness in the air that even before the fire I shivered. Suddenly, Father's helping-girl scuttered to the frying pan spitting butter everywhere. She stirred the contents of the pan and the room filled with the scent of browning onions. She added salted cod and chopped parsnips and stirred some more. I pressed my spectacles against my nose, hungry suddenly as the sweet smoke wafted in my direction. The girl wiped her hands on her apron, then turned to me, half a peek, and I wondered what held her attention.

Father nodded at the girl. "Prudence, how fares your youngest sister, Providence?"

Prudence shrugged. "Providence is afeared of the Devil."

"Aren't we all?" Father leaned back in his chair and sipped the tea Prudence placed before him. "I presume your sister has been listening to the sermons of the illustrious Reverend Mr. Parris?"

"The Devil is here in Salem, Mr. Wentworth. Haven't you heard?" Prudence peered round the corner and shivered. "The Devil may be in this house right now."

"The Devil in Salem? Possibly. In this house? Nonsense. You needn't fear anything or anyone here, Prudence." Father winked at me. "I am not the Devil. My son is most certainly not the Devil, so you needn't sneak glances his way. We have no supernatural affiliations. My son is a mere merchant's assistant."

"A mere merchant's assistant?" I laughed. "I'm *your* assistant, Father."

"Precisely. You are not one to fear. There are wars with the French and the Indians in Maine where settlers are murdered in their homes. There are battles here in Salem, Villager against Villager, who squabble over land or do not care for the Reverend Mr. Parris. Parris is waging war against whatever ails his girls. But here in this house we wage war against no one."

"Exceptin' the tide, Mr. Wentworth," Prudence said. "You and your ships are warrin' against the tide."

Father slapped his hand on the table. He looked pleased with the girl. "Too true, Prudence. You are an observant girl, at that."

She curtsied as she refilled Father's teacup. "Thank ye, Mr. Wentworth."

After the salted cod with onions and parsnips was served with bread and ale, after the plates were cleared, Prudence left for her own home where she would meet with her sisters Providence and our helping-girl Patience. Twas then Father leaned toward the hearth, his balding head nearly too close to the flames and I was afeared the gray hairs at the back of his skull would catch fire. He looked at me in his usual manner, as though he would search out any secrets, not that I could hide my thoughts from him even if I tried. Then, as if he could read my mind, he said, "So tell me, James, what is it about Salem that sets your very being on edge? The only time you do not look as though you are grating sand between your teeth is when you are with Elizabeth."

"I'm not certain I understand it myself, Father. I'm not comfortable here. I would say we should have settled elsewhere, only this is where I found Lizzie."

"That's right, Son. Elizabeth was here, so naturally you would end up where she was. Tis destiny that you two are together." He blew into his teacup, it still steamed, and he took a long sip. "I did not realize you were so upset at our joining the Town Church as full members, James. You should have said so."

"I did not want to cause problems with your business associates, Father. At that moment, I did not mind so much, but now I find I'm a member of a Church I do not believe in."

"You still prefer the Anglican ways? There's an Anglican Church in Boston. I shall not tell if you go there when you wish."

"Tis not the Church itself," I said. "Most people believe in a Hailstone and Hellfire God. A God watching angrily over an Earth populated with heedless sinners. That part of their doctrine does not surprise me. But I do not understand their belief in Predestination. How can our fate be determined before we are born by a God who takes vile pleasure in withholding love from His creatures?"

"The Puritan God is an offended God, and an offended God believes in His righteousness and His judgments before He believes in His people. Or at least that is what they want you to believe."

"But the Puritans came here seventy years ago seeking salvation from persecution."

"Aye, but after the starving years they prospered."

"The starving years?"

"Aye, Son. You have been spared the back-grinding labor of we ordinary men. The Puritans, for whatever you think of their beliefs, chopped down trees with naught but small axes until their hands were blistered and raw. They built the homes they lived in. They ate whatever they could find, which during those first winters was little enough. Those who survived prospered. After they prospered, others such as us, who do not share their beliefs, followed to see what successes we might discover for ourselves. Some came believing they were promised God, some came believing they were promised Gold, and some came believing they were promised the chance for a better life. We cannot allow others to determine our fate. We must keep our eye on our goal."

"Which is?"

"You know the story, James. I was born to a poor family. I had humble beginnings. But I learned of the need for English goods such as textiles, metalware, and hardware on this side of the Atlantic. Then I recognized the English need for tobacco, sugar, and cotton, so I worked, and I saved, and then I supplied whatever I could wherever I could. London is a gateway to the rest of the world, so I set up shop and watched my business grow. After your mother died I decided I would be better off on this side of the Atlantic. Here we can see where our wits might take us." Father poked the flames to life and leaned toward their warmth. "Tis no surprise I found my fortune as a merchant. The sea is in our blood. My father was a sailor, as was his father before him, and his before him."

I slapped both hands on the back of Father's chair, I laughed so hard. "You did not look as though the sea was in your blood when we stepped off the ship from England. I thought you were going to trample the captain himself in your haste to be on steady land. You were looking rather mawkish, and, if I recall, I had to catch you to keep you from hitting the dock face first."

"No one could wait to get off that creaking woodpile, James. And you were an odd shade of green yourself. Never was there a more perfect Hell on Earth than being trapped in the confines of that dark, narrow ship in the middle of the ocean with no way off and no way out whilst the waves slapped your innards round for suet. Besides, I did not want to leave myself to the fate my father suffered. As a merchant and a shipbuilder, I can still follow previous generations of Wentworth men onto the high seas but I need not travel across the water so often myself." Father placed a steady hand on my shoulder. "You shall be a different kind of Wentworth, Son. An educated man. And tis a fine thing. But I felt it my destiny to follow the path of my father, even if I hardly remember him."

"Tis true, then? Your father died at sea?"

Father's eyes narrowed. "He went to sea when I was a lad and never returned." His shoulders slumped as though heavy with the memory. "Twas odd, though. Others from his voyage said he returned with them. They said he was with them the whole time. And yet."

"And yet?"

"He never came home. My mother was certain he must have fallen overboard when the others were not looking, but with the ship's watch, with all the men everywhere, that never sounded likely to me."

"What do you think happened?"

"I could not say. But I have spent my whole life wondering. One day I finally accepted that I shall never see him again." He shook his head. "Some ailment or accident stopped him from coming home. I do not believe twas something he chose. Something took him away from his family, something beyond his control. To this day I believe he would have come home if he could have."

"I'm certain of it, Father."

"And now Massachusetts is home. We are blessed with the

opportunity and blessed that you have found Elizabeth. I think of her as my own daughter, you know."

"I know, Father," I said.

I could see he was tired and wanted an early night. That was well by me. Now, as I sit before the window, staring into the gusts of trembling wind pushing the oak tree as though it would slam the branches to the ground, I'm reminded to be thankful for what I have received here in the Massachusetts Bay Colony—Lizzie.

EVERYTHING CHANGED WHEN I MET LIZZIE. WHEN I FIRST NOTICED her I pressed my spectacles against my nose to be certain I saw clearly. Surely, I must have been imagining this dark-haired Angelic beauty. Twas more than the wisps of chocolate-colored curls slipping out from under her white cap, more than her full lips the color of ripe cherries, more than her peach-like complexion. Twas more than the wide, inquisitive chocolate-colored eyes. Her external beauty is merely a physical manifestation of her internal beauty, and that is the woman I was, and still am, eager to know.

Twas merely chance that I was at that house in the Village that autumn day, but that is how Fate works, is it not? Sometimes when we do not mean for anything to happen, everything happens. Ned Rood, the head carpenter for Father's ships, has family in the Village down the field from the Joneses, who were newly arrived from England and settling into their leased farm. Rood invited Father to the meal his wife planned to welcome the Joneses to Massachusetts. Father, always a congenial man, was more than happy to take up the invitation and he brought me along.

Silas Jones is a farmer who had fallen on hard times in England, so much so that he decided to try his luck in New England. Twice widowed, Silas has a son from his first marriage who had already trained as a surveyor and settled in New York. He brought both of his daughters from his second marriage with him across the ocean.

Ned Rood informed Father that the Joneses had been headed to Connecticut where those of their Quaker faith are more welcome. Then Silas met someone aboard ship who knew of a farm for let in Salem. Though the rocky ground here is not so conducive to growing things, Silas was convinced into settling in Massachusetts.

I watched the eldest daughter, Elizabeth, as she brushed an escaped dark curl from her mouth whilst caring for her younger sister, Mary Grace, with such tenderness. We were popping corn, shuffling the long shaker over the fire, listening to the pop! as the kernels burst into tender fluffs that we put into a bowl, smothered in butter and salt, and ate by the fistful. Watching Lizzie, seeing her contentment in such a simple thing—making popcorn with Mary—brought me joy unlike any I have ever known.

At that moment I knew I wanted to marry Elizabeth Jones. I wanted that kind of joy in my life. Though we were strangers, I knew I would love her, if I did not love her already. This marriage had to be for love since she was a farmer's daughter and would bring nothing of financial value or social status to our union. But I am one of the lucky ones. Father did not press me to make a more profitable arrangement, as I might have done had I married a more privileged daughter. Father allowed me to follow my heart, which is so rarely done, but then he is a rare man.

And I do love her. Though I am still learning her, learning her ways, I love her. Tis not logic that tells me so. Tis instinct. In the most secret chamber in my heart, I knew that if Lizzie was half the woman she appeared to be then she would be a miracle. And she is —a miracle. The more I learn of Elizabeth Wentworth, the more I know Fortune smiles upon me.

31 JANUARY 1691, MONDAY

The branches of the tree outside reach like decrepit fingers for the frozen ground. Not one person has passed for more than two hours. I know we are not the only inhabitants in Salem Town, but it feels as though we are. On my way home from Father's I studied the one-room structures with thatched roofs and precariously leaning chimneys and windows with oiled paper and no glass. The red barn with the shingled roof, where the blacksmith lives and works, pokes out, a ray of color in the bleak landscape. The wooden boxes people here call houses are brown, the trees are brown, the sea looks brown, and the ground, though frozen, is brown.

And again I wonder—where is everyone in this New World? Perhaps some have been scared away whilst the Pox still rages. People worry about the Invisible World? The Pox is Invisible too, waiting like wickedness to grab you by the throat and throttle you until you die. People in Salem, Town and Village, traipse about on the tips of their toes, silently, as though the Pox will not find them if it cannot hear them. If we are lucky, it shall pass over us the way God passed His plague over the Israelites. Many here, especially in the Village, would paint blood over their doorways if they were not afeared of being fined by the Church for doing so.

My hand shudders as I think of the Clarksons. Though they were our closest neighbors we did not see them often and only knew they had been struck by illness after Mr. Boxley mentioned it to Father. Overnight, it seemed, the family became feverish, with aching and vomiting, and once the pustules came they were not long for this world. Despite my protestations, Lizzie tended them. She would not let them suffer alone. Thank the Lord, Lizzie is untouched. The whole episode, from beginning to end, was less than one week. I pray tis not soon repeated.

Meanwhile, the fear of Indians remains. I heard tell that the Indians can sneak up on you as silently as the Pox itself and capture you unawares. There was violence as a result of King Philip's War, another of the constant battles between settlers and natives. Maine is all but uninhabitable now, and many have fled here to Massachusetts for sanctuary. As if that is not enough, arguments between Town and Village still rage. Mary told us so. My sister-in-law is precocious for a ten-year-old. Silas left Mary here so he could go about his business in the Town undisturbed. Of course, Lizzie loves any time she has with her young sister. Mary is a good helper to Lizzie, and Lizzie dotes on the girl.

"Pa says the Village is desperate to break away from the Town," Mary said. She looked at me whilst she mended the white coif in her hand. "What do you think, Brother? Will the Town Selectmen allow it?"

I stifled a laugh, thinking twas not much different speaking with my young sister-in-law than with the men by the docks. I kept my voice serious. "I believe negotiations are underway about who owes what to whom and how much. My father believes tis the Village that will owe the Town."

"Pa says the Town will lose the Villagers' tax money since the Villagers wish to keep everything for themselves," Mary said.

"And what is your opinion on the matter, Mary Grace?" Lizzie asked, her voice serious as well. "Do you think the Town should let the Village go?"

Mary's eyes grew narrow as she considered. "It seems a foolish move for the Village to break away from the Town, the Town being so much more prosperous than the Village. But Pa says the Villagers are insistent. The Villagers believe themselves more God-fearing than the people in the Town. Reverend Parris says the Townspeople are only concerned about profits, not God, and they care more about the cut of their clothing or the jewels they wear." The gold of Lizzie's wedding ring caught a flash of firelight, leaving an amber glow on the table. Mary shrugged. "I did not mean either of you. I know you are both good in the grace of God."

"So I hope." Lizzie made bread the New England way, with cornmeal, corn flour, cranberries, crushed seeds, and sugar. She stirred the ingredients whilst adding one spoonful of boiling water at a time. She gestured to Mary, who put aside her mending to break the dough into rounds. Lizzie dropped the rounds one by one into a pot of boiling water. "Take them out with the tongs as soon as they start to float, Mary."

Mary nodded. "Have you heard about Betty Parris, Lizzie, have you?" Lizzie pointed to the boiling water where the doughy patties floated to the top and Mary turned back to her task. Her voice lost none of its excitement. "They say she has been touched by Black Magick, by the very Devil himself! In Church on Sundays Reverend Parris has been saying the Devil is in Salem! Reverend Parris says we are not being good, and God is not happy with us, which puts us in even more danger of being overtaken by Evil." Mary leaned toward Lizzie. "Reverend Parris says the Devil has come! Do you think we should be afeared, Lizzie? Of the Devil?"

"Ha!" Silas stood in the hall rubbing a weathered hand against his chin. I had not heard him come in. "Mary Grace, if I've told you once I've told you a hundred times, be done with that nonsense. No more repeating what Reverend Parris says."

"Are you saying Reverend Parris doesn't know what he's

talking about?" Mary looked aghast. "He's a Reverend, Pa. He knows all about God and the Devil."

Silas sighed. "Mary, you know perfectly well we're Quakers."

"But we do not sit with Friends here," Mary said. "Here we listen to Reverend Parris."

"Well." Silas stared hard at his youngest daughter. "Here in Massachusetts they never took much of a liking to Quakers. We go to Parris' Church because…"

"Tis easier to do what others are doing, Mary," I said. "Tis why my father and I joined the Town Church."

"We do our duty to their Church and they leave us alone," Silas said.

Silas told Mary to gather her things. He nodded at Lizzie, formally shook my hand, which I told him he needn't do, we are family now, so he shook my hand again. Lizzie plucked the rounds from the water, dropped them into a basket, and sent her father and Mary home with plenty.

I took a round with my fingertips since twas still hot and bit into the crusty dough. Then I realized. "Has Patience gone so soon? Tis early yet."

"Patience has returned home. Her youngest sister is ill."

"Still? I remember the other sister saying so some weeks back. What is her name? I can never remember."

"The eldest sister is Prudence. But Providence, the youngest, is worse and their mother has a weak chest and cannot tend the girl."

I heard thunder crack in the distance, the threat of a nor'easter. The window over the table let in whispers of storm light.

I reached for Lizzie but she pulled away, laughing. She stirred a pottage of pease then dropped bacon, celery, endive, and spinach into the broth. She tasted, shrugged, added sorrel and mint, then took a plate of chopped leeks and added butter. She knocked everything into the skillet, which she placed over the fire, shaking it so the butter would not burn. Satisfied that everything was well cooked, she plated two large helpings and set them on the table. I poured ale into our mugs and we sat together.

"Mary did make me curious," Lizzie said. "Is there more news about the negotiations between Town and Village?"

"Father is frustrated. The Villagers do not want to compromise. Those in the Town do not want to compromise. I cannot see how any of it will be settled."

"The people on the Farms face many challenges, James. They're on their own in a way we aren't here in the Town. They want to make decisions about how they use their money. That doesn't seem unreasonable."

"Yet they still want the Town to pay for some of their upkeep."

"Tis important to the Villagers that they decide how they live. The Church is the cornerstone of their lives and they want the right to run it as they think best. Tis why the first settlers came to Massachusetts."

I finished my pottage in two more spoonfuls, then scooped the remaining onions and celery onto my bread. "How did you learn to repress your opinions in a way that did not attract the ire of the Puritans when you lived in the Village?" I asked. "As Silas said, you are Quakers, after all."

"We kept our prayers to ourselves, as I do here. As for my opinions, I don't recall being asked my opinions when I lived in England. What woman is asked for her opinions?"

I grasped Lizzie's hand. "I hope Mistress Wentworth knows that in this house, in my ears, her opinions are most welcome." Lizzie smiled. "In fact, her opinions are necessary for my welfare as well as my sanity. And you may pray however you feel is right, Lizzie. You need not hide your beliefs from me."

Lizzie turned her eyes to the rug beneath her feet. "I know we have only been married this short time, Husband, but I thank God for you every night in my prayers. I have seen women with their husbands, Goody Good and others, and I see how they suffer because of the bad nature of the men they married. How fortunate

I am to have married such a wonderful man who is also easy to look at." She blushed as she squeezed my fingers. Twas inviting, the look of heat upon her cheeks.

"And I, who have seen men with their scolding wives, thank God for you as well. I do not know what I did to win your hand, Lizzie, but I promise I shall spend every moment for the rest of my life doing everything I can to deserve it. And you are the one who is easy to look at."

I wanted to say more, as I felt Lizzie did, but we were both shy again. Lizzie took our emptied plates to the washing pot, dipped the plates in water, and scrubbed them with a cloth.

Grasping for something to talk about, I said, "I do not think I could live in the Village. The Villagers would not have me anyway. They believe the prosperity we have here in the Town threatens their Godly virtue."

"You do not share their Godly virtue?"

I sighed. Tis hard to explain, even to Lizzie. "I do not believe in an angry God," I said. "I do not believe in a vengeful God who punishes all sins great and small. I do not believe sleeping in Church is a sin that should be punished by whipping, and I do not believe that every time someone falls ill tis the handiwork of the Devil. I'm not sure I believe in the Devil."

"Nay?"

"We do not need Satan to cause us suffering. We need only the selfishness of human nature to create Hell on Earth. We all struggle between Good and Evil, but tis our own choices that bring about consequences, not the decisions of Invisible Beings. I know the Puritans believe that the Devil selects the weakest amongst us to carry out his wrongdoings. But who judges what is the Devil's work and what is human nature at its worst? What is caused by mercenary supernatural forces, and what is caused by self-serving people?"

"So what kind of God do you believe in then?" Lizzie's dark eyes sparkled in the orange-blue glow of the hearth flames.

"I believe in a God who says let he who is without sin cast the first stone. A God of Salvation. A God of Lovingkindness. A God of Mercy. A compassionate God. A God of turn the other cheek and helping the ill and the poor and a God of forgiving others when they know not what they do."

"That is the God I believe in too." Lizzie leaned toward me. I'm certain we bonded at that moment. "Did you know there were many in the Village who told me not to marry you?"

"That cannot be true. I did not know anyone on the Farms before I met you."

"The Putnams spread the gossip. They said that you and Father are wealthy merchants who live in the heathen-filled Town. And you both dress well, in the finest fashions from London and Paris, and Father wears jewels on every finger and employs servants by the dozens."

"Which part of that is true except that Father and I live in the Town?"

"Tis not what is true, Husband. Tis what they believe. They believe you have gone to the Devil." She leaned toward me, her cherry-like lips pressing together, begging to be kissed.

"I'm glad you chose not to take their advice."

"The Putnams may have their influence in the Village, but I wasn't afeared you had gone to the Devil. I looked into your eyes and saw your soul in your deep blue gaze."

"Beware," I said. "I may go to the Devil still."

"Then I will go too."

"And what would the Devil want with you? Satan has no use for Angels."

Lizzie's dark eyes widened. "Do you believe you can tell whether people are Angels or Devils by looking at them?"

"Let us hope so." I sighed, saying, "I do not recall having so many issues at home."

"This isn't home?"

I pulled Lizzie close to me. She did not pull away.

"Wherever you are is home, Lizzie. I told myself I should no longer refer to England as home, though I do not seem to be making good work of it."

Lizzie leaned toward me. "Tell me about London. What is it like?"

I closed my eyes as I remembered. "One of my earliest memories is peering into the depths of the River Thames. I remember watching Father oversee the shipbuilding that is still such an important part of his business."

"Where in London did you live?"

"I grew up in the West End. We lived amongst Earls and Dukes. Father paid to be connected to the water supply and we had water from a reservoir pumped into the house through lead pipes. What I would not give to have that here."

"You had water piped directly into your house?" Lizzie leaned back into her chair. "I've never heard of such a thing."

"'Tis not so uncommon there. And transportation is easier in London, as well, since the roads are better. Sometimes my parents and I traveled by boat along the Thames. Sometimes we were driven round in our carriage. Our home was opulent by London standards, comfortable and warm."

"What did it look like?"

I described the home where I grew up whilst Lizzie listened, enraptured by every detail. The exterior was designed in the classic Greek style, the interior decorated in carved mahogany and inlaid with mother of pearl. Father's desk was lacquered in bright blue, and a tall clock with loud chimes stood near the front entrance. Our chairs were padded and comfortable. Mostly, Lizzie wanted to hear about the grand parties and musical entertainments. I told her how Mother changed her gown for every possible occasion. Mother looked so fine the other women always wanted to know who made her fur-trimmed velvet gowns, her scarves, her hoods, her hats.

"I cannot believe Father began life as a sailor's son," Lizzie said.

"Aye. But he has a good head for business, and he has an engaging personality, and he married well. Fortunately, my parents made each other happy. For all her refined tastes, my mother was a good woman. She was a kind mother, and she remained devoted to Father and me until her death. Sometimes..." I shook my head, thinking I should not continue.

"Sometimes?"

"I wish Mother were here. Father would not live alone, and Mother would have the chance to know you. She would have loved you dearly, I know."

"I'm a farmer's daughter."

"Father was a sailor's son, and she loved him. Nay, my mother saw people for who they were, and she would see you for what you are—a treasure. She would see you as her daughter, as Father does. Father was going to build a grand country house for our family, but after Mother died he lost the heart for it. That is when he determined to come here and bring me with him, though it took me away from university."

Lizzie sat silently, nodding, taking it in. Finally, she asked, "What is it like at university? I cannot believe I have a husband who has been to Cambridge."

"I'm fortunate to have a father who would send me to study."

"Do you miss it very much?"

"Aye. I do."

"What do you remember most?"

"I remember my first day when I was handed the instruction book from Duport with his advice about dressing soberly, making honest friends, and being attentive to prayers. Duport believed in proper behavior, no football, no gossiping or picking your nose— at least where others might see you."

Lizzie laughed. "Did the instruction book really say that?"

"Oh, aye. We were told to avoid London at all costs, except for the bookbinder's shop, of course. I laughed aloud when I read that, being London-born myself. I'm certain Duport would have thought I was heading into Sodom and Gomorrah whenever I went home. That etiquette book was written five-and-twenty years before I stepped foot in Cambridge, and tis still passed down from tutors to pupils across the university."

"Would you like to return to Cambridge? To resume your studies?"

"Aye," I said. "I would."

"Then you will. One day."

"Would you go with me? I shall not leave without you." I grasped her hand again. I could not stop touching her. "I shall never leave you ever, Lizzie."

"I promise you the same, Husband. Though we've been married but a short time, I know my place is with you."

"How do you know?"

"My heart tells me so."

I leaned forward and kissed her lips. "That is all I needed to hear," I said.

1 FEBRUARY 1691, TUESDAY

*T*he first day of February in the Year of Our Lord Sixteen Hundred and Ninety-One is bleak, the sky gray-black, much like London after the Great Fire. I was four years old when the flames torched the city. I recall bits and pieces in the tangles of my childish memories. Father told me afterward the Fire began at the house of baker Thomas Farynor, who lived and worked on Pudding Lane. One forgotten spark, one untended cinder, and all of London was aflame. The inferno jumped joyously from house to house and shop to shop as though it hadn't a care in the world except to spread itself as far and wide as wood and nature would allow. For two days the City remained in flames. I remember the charred air, the spitting crackles, the screams. People feared burning to death, yet they stopped to stare as though the violence made prisoners of them. Accusations spread as fast as the fire. Foreigners set the fires, some said. The Dutch and the French, believed to be untrustworthy at the best of times, were lynched on the streets. Finally, the Tower garrison created firebreaks and the Great Fire ended as quickly as it began.

Though no such fires abound in Salem, Town or Village, tempers are on the verge of flaring. People avoid eye contact. Some from whom I might normally receive a *Good morrow*, a *Good e'en*, or a tip of the hat rush past as though they did not see me. This must be what London felt like before the first flames sparked to life in the bakeshop five and twenty years ago. Somehow, everyone knew the destruction ahead.

On my way home from Father's I stopped near the edge of the Commons and watched the sun drop. I shivered, the air knife-slicing raw, my fists clutched within my coat sleeves, my frozen fingers unable to straighten. A blast of wind off the bay cut me between the eyes, and a moment later it snowed, pure white and icy sharp, setting a white blanket as far as I could see. A cowherd pressed his charges onto the pasture and I wondered what the kine would eat with the world frozen over. Icicles dangled from trees, from thatched roofs on the clapboard houses, from gentlemen's hats as they clutched their cold-weather coats closer. I walked home as quickly as my frozen toes would allow.

Inside, I kissed Lizzie's cheek and heard a clank near the cauldron. Patience knocked some pans together, making more noise than she needed to, perhaps to alert me to her presence.

"How is your sister, Patience?" I asked. "And your mother? I hope they are both better."

"Still poorly, sir. I could spare a few hours to come to help the Mistress with some chores, but I'm needed back at home today, sir, if you'll allow it."

Lizzie looked at me, her dark eyes intent as she waited. "Of course you can go, Patience," I said.

"I told her she didn't need to come at all," Lizzie said. "If her family needs her at home then that's where she should be."

"Do you need me to take you home?" I asked. "Tis growing late."

"Oh no, Mr. Wentworth. Prudence has arranged for our ride to the Village."

"You've been a great help to me today, Patience," Lizzie said. "Please, gather your things and go. You needn't come back until your mother and sister are well."

Patience looked as though she might cry. "Thank you, Mistress, but I must come."

Lizzie looked at me. Without words, I understood her. "We shall pay your wages, Patience," I said.

Patience covered her eyes with her hands. After she settled herself, she said, "You're too kind, Mr. Wentworth, but I should work for what you give me. Prudence says we don't take charity."

"Consider it payment for future work then," Lizzie said. "You should be home."

"I want to be there, Mistress. I want to help them. But I'm afeared." She leaned toward Lizzie and whispered. "I may have caused their illnesses."

"Nonsense." Lizzie led Patience to sit down. "How could you have caused their illnesses?"

"I've been sinful."

Lizzie held the girl's hand. "You're such a dear, sweet girl, Patience Connor. I cannot imagine anything you might have done that would cause the Lord to bring wrath upon your family."

"Reverend Parris says when we are sinful the Lord makes us suffer. And we're sufferin' like we've been struck down by the Devil, Mistress."

"But what have you done?" Lizzie asked.

"I haven't been mindin' Reverend Parris' sermons, Mistress."

"Who does?"

A sharp glance from Lizzie and I kept my opinions to myself.

"Tis normal for our thoughts to wander from time to time," Lizzie said. "The Lord knows your heart. He knows tis human folly that your mind wanders now and again."

"But Reverend Parris says..."

Lizzie shook her head. "I know what Reverend Parris says, and he is a learned man well-versed in the ways of God. But no human can truly understand Our Lord. He is too great, too vast for our mere mortal senses to fully comprehend. As for the Devil..."

"The Devil is here in Salem, Mistress. Reverend Parris says so. Prudence says so. Everyone says so. And tis not merely that my mind wanders. Tis what I'm thinkin' on that makes me sinful. There's a young man, Noah."

"The Andrews' son?" Lizzie asked.

"Aye, Mistress. And I can't stop thinkin' on him. He's so handsome and as strong as you like. He's moved full barrels, just lifted them onto his shoulder and walked as though he carried feathers." Patience remembered herself and blushed. "Prudence says there's no way he'll ever want a homely, foolish girl like me when there are others far better for him. Tis not as if I have anything to offer."

"I had little enough to offer my husband at our marriage," Lizzie said.

"I think you're one of the lucky ones, Mistress."

"That as may be." Lizzie straightened the girl's coif over her hair. "You are in no way homely or foolish, Patience. You shouldn't listen to your sister when she says such things."

Patience left smiling, which made Lizzie smile, which made me happy. With Patience gone, I warmed my hands by the fire. Without Lizzie in my arms, I was reminded of the cold.

Lizzie hummed to herself whilst she set the pot on the hook in the hearth. Twas a hymnal I knew but could not place.

"What was Father about this day?" Lizzie asked.

"After our morning's business he spent the rest of the day with the other Town Selectmen to determine the seating arrangements for the Meeting House. One must sit where one can be seen, you know."

"Did they decide the Village's petition for separation?" She removed the kettle and spooned in some tea leaves.

"According to Father, the Selectmen were too busy haggling over who was important enough to deserve a pew and who was nothing enough to languish unheeded. Philip English prefers the Anglican Church, as I do, but he is a successful merchant, as Father is, so he has received a pew, as we have."

Lizzie placed a cup of tea before me and another cup in front of herself. "Have you heard about Betty?"

"Betty who?"

"Reverend Parris' daughter." Lizzie shook her head as though I had forgotten her name.

I sipped my tea and remembered the long-faced minister. "I try to think of Reverend Parris as little as possible. He has a daughter?"

"Really, Husband, you must take your head out of the clouds and pay attention to what is happening round you. Aye, Reverend Parris has a daughter, Betty, and a niece, Abigail. Mary spoke of them yesterday. You and I spoke of them not long ago. His daughter and niece are ill and I said I would like to check on them?" I shrugged and Lizzie shook a wooden spoon in my direction. "Anyway, I heard from Mistress Boxley, who heard from her seamstress, that Reverend Parris hasn't enough firewood to warm his house. The parish isn't paying his salary and they're not bringing him the firewood he says they promised him when he became the parish minister."

"Father says Parris haggled his way into that contract with benefits few on the Farms wanted to give him."

"Whether the Villagers agree with the terms or not, Reverend Parris is their minister and he's owed a living."

"Most of the Villagers are behind on their taxes," I said. "There may be no money to pay his salary with."

"Who isn't behind on their taxes these days? Pa says the taxes are crushing him. If things do not change, if the taxes don't ease, he'll hardly have anything left. He's already talking of leaving the Village to try again. In Connecticut, perhaps."

"You needn't worry for your family," I said. "Silas and Mary shall always be cared for. Father says he wants to build Silas and Mary a fine house here in the Town. They would want for nothing. Would he come, do you think?"

"You know Pa."

I nodded. I know very well where Lizzie's stubbornness comes from. I paused to sip my tea. "As for Reverend Parris, I'm not certain he did not bring his current difficulties on himself. Everything I hear of him says he is preaching sermons of an angry Devil and sinful Villagers, scaring the people nearly to their deaths."

"Most ministers do scare their parishioners," Lizzie said. "Tis how they keep their churches full and the people in line."

"Parris is filled with a particular kind of vile," I said. "Who is he to cast damnation upon the souls of the Salemites because they do not give him the deference he believes he deserves? Quakers do not believe in the need for ministers, do they?"

"Nay," Lizzie said. "We don't believe we need intercession to speak to God. I can speak directly to Him on my own. Still, whatever the Puritans' beliefs, no family should freeze in their own home in this weather, especially not with two sickly children. Both Betty and the Reverend's niece are still ill. Surely, we cannot allow the girls to suffer."

I tugged at the dark curl slipping out from under Lizzie's cap. She seemed startled by the gesture, not in a frightened way, but in a way that said she is still getting used to me.

"Are Parris' girls still so very ill?"

"They are ill enough that we should bring them some of our firewood. We are blessed, you and I, Husband. We want for nothing."

"Thanks to Father. He is the successful one in the family." I meant to keep the edge from my voice but failed.

"Now you are being a dutiful son. Soon you'll find your own path. But you're right, we owe our abundance to our earthly Father, and also to our Heavenly Father who blesses us in each other. Since we have this abundance, we must share it. Tis a good thing, to share with others who are in need. Our Lord commands it of us. You don't mind, Husband, do you?"

"Whatever I think of Parris, his daughter and niece should not suffer for it. But what ails them so?"

"Mistress Boxley says the same as Mary—the doctors don't know what is causing the illness. Dr. Griggs says they've been touched by Evil. Mistress Boxley's seamstress lives in the Village and says the girls contort in unnatural ways."

"Very well," I said. "We can bring them whatever you think they need. I have time to go to the Village next week."

"Nay," Lizzie said. "I want to bring them the firewood as soon as possible. The girls shouldn't suffer any longer."

"Bring Patience," I said. "I do not want you going alone. Parris is…" I was not sure how to finish that thought. Not that it matters. Nothing I said would change Lizzie's mind. She decided she shall go, so she shall go.

"I'm not afeared of the Reverend Mr. Parris," Lizzie said. "I'm only bringing some firewood to warm his house, after all." Lizzie brushed some hair from my face with a gentle touch. "I've only now realized. You're exactly what the Venus glass foretold." I shook my head since the term meant nothing to me. "You don't know about the Venus glass? Tis how some try to foretell the future. Sometimes young girls try to divine who their husband will be."

"Girls do not do that," I said.

"How little you know." Lizzie laughed. "The process is simple enough. You drop an egg white into a beer glass full of water and watch what shapes appear."

"And that shows your husband? The shape of egg whites?" I tried to imagine what that might look like. "How precise are these eggs? Do they show faces or just outlines? And, of course, you participated in no such superstitious nonsense, Mistress Wentworth."

"I may have seen the shape of a book."

41

"Well then." I hesitated, then put out my hand. Lizzie took it and squeezed my fingers. Emboldened by her touch, I pulled her close and she leaned toward me. "This fortune telling must work since I'm indeed most happy in a book. That is when I'm not busy being happy with my wife." I kissed her, deeply, and she was not startled. She opened her mouth, waiting, wanting more.

2 FEBRUARY 1691, WEDNESDAY

*F*ather and I meant to make decisions about what purchases must be made and what goods must be shipped and where. We have time to decide since it seems as though it shall be a miserable winter forever. Entire roads have washed away. Houses have crumbled. People have drowned. Lizzie meant to go to the Village this day, but since we have no boat she would have had to float there. Although she did not want to delay, she knew she would have to call on the Parrises another time.

Before daybreak Father sent word that I should stay home. He made a pretense of the soggy weather, but I think he meant to keep me away from Thomas Oliver. Whatever Oliver does, however he does it, he does it with Father's knowledge, and his blessing. I'm not certain of Oliver's business, which is how Father prefers it. I know Oliver gets us what we need. Living here I see how Parliament's laws can seem unfair. England requires payment for goods in coins, which are hard to get hold of. Oliver smuggles in the currency, silver and gold plundered from ships in the Indian Ocean, which Father uses to purchase whatever he needs. Tis Father's way of avoiding the Navigation Acts. If we do business legally, sugar, ginger, rum, cotton, and wool should only be shipped to England, which allows England to dictate how much we are paid for our troubles. Through Oliver, Father can purchase East Indian goods for less and sell his wares where he can command higher prices. I understand Father's willingness to do business with Oliver, I do, but there is something about the man, his beefy stature, his convenient smile, his too-ready laugh, I do not like.

I did not waste much time worrying about Thomas Oliver and I began the morn leisurely enough. I would have been content to lie in bed, sleeping and dreaming and keeping Lizzie close, but she would have none of it. After she decided the sun was high enough and I too much a sluggard, she tugged the quilts away and pulled me by the arm.

"James Wentworth, you are the most slothful man yet born! Tis time to awaken."

I clasped Lizzie's hand and pulled her back into bed. She pretended to struggle, but I think she enjoyed the game. She threw her arms round my neck and pointed her chin up, ready to be kissed. After obliging, gladly, I pulled myself from the warmth of the covers. I broke my fast with a bowl of samp with bread and butter and coffee whilst Lizzie went about her tasks. First, she chopped the herrings, onions, currants, and raisins and slid them into a pie to bake. Now she scrubs the floor in the Great Room, humming to herself as she presses the horsehair brush to and fro. I see from her smile that she is satisfied. I do my best not to gaze lustfully as she kneels on all fours but I am not making good work of it.

THIS AFTERNOON WE HAD A MESSAGE FROM SILAS SAYING MARY HAS taken ill. Lizzie is worried, but not overly so. After she visited Widow Miller with a basketful of Indian bannocks and two quilts, and after she finished her work for the day, she made a rag doll for

Mary. Lizzie stitched the canvas into a rough body shape, then stuffed it with cotton. She stitched a round head, stuffed that with cotton, and stitched eyes, a nose, and a mouth. Finally, she stitched on black hair.

"It looks like the one I had when I was Mary's age," she said.

"Tis time for Mary to have a doll of her own?"

"She had one but lost it in the crossing. I thought this might help her feel better."

"You do not believe her illness to be the Pox, do you?"

Lizzie fiddled with the doll's stringy hair. "Pa didn't mention any fever or rash, did he?" I shook my head. "Then I shouldn't think so. Hopefully tis a quick illness that will soon be gone." She stitched together a printed linen dress with yellow flowers. "I hope Mary will find some joy in it." Lizzie put the doll aside. "I'll bring it to her as soon as the roads are passable. And I still want to bring the Parrises some firewood. Tomorrow, if possible."

"Would you like a lesson?" I asked.

"Aye," Lizzie said. "Thank you."

I took the Bible from the shelf in the Great Room and opened to a random page, John 8:7. "Let he who is without sin cast the first stone," I said.

"Indeed."

Lizzie has progressed well in her reading. And quickly too. I believe our nightly lessons help bond us more quickly than we might have otherwise since our readings prompt long discussions where we learn much about each other. After we read the rest of the passage together, I did the impossible: I cajoled my wife into reading aloud on her own.

"No one has such a lovely voice as you," I said.

Lizzie laughed. "You think your sweet tongue will persuade me to read alone? When you are such a learned man?" She turned away, her cheeks flushed.

"But you know how I love listening to you speak. Tis like hearing a serenata by Alessandro Stradella."

"Who?"

I reached for our favorite volume of poetry. "Tis time, Lizzie. Read to me."

Lizzie turned the book in her hands, over and over. Finally, she nodded. She tentatively opened the book. "What would you like to hear?"

"You know."

Lizzie's smile rivals the brightest sunshine. She opened the page, exhaled, and read, haltingly, with pauses, some from a struggle to sound out or recall the words, some from embarrassment that she read alone. After the first two lines, her voice grew in confidence.

If ever two were one, then surely we.
If ever man were loved by wife, then thee.
If ever wife was happy in a man,
Compare with me, ye women, if you can.
I prize thy love more than whole mines of gold,
Or all the riches that the East doth hold.
My love is such that rivers cannot quench,
Nor ought but love from thee give recompense.
Thy love is such I can no way repay;
The heavens reward thee manifold, I pray.
Then while we live, in love let's so persever,
That when we live no more, we may live ever.

Lizzie closed the book. "Tis true, you know."

"What is?" I asked.

"This poem, *To My Dear and Loving Husband.* Tis as though everything I feel for you has been written here, by this woman, a magistrate's wife I'll never meet. You are..." Lizzie blushed, hot along her jaw. I touched her cheek and lifted her head so I could see into her eyes. "If ever man were loved by wife, then thee. That is how..."

"Tis all right, Lizzie. You can tell me anything."

"That is how I feel about you. You are my dear and loving husband, James Wentworth."

I knelt before Lizzie, pressing her hand to my lips.

"I knew the moment I saw you over the supper table that you were the one for me. I cannot imagine waking up every morning for the rest of my life without looking into your beautiful eyes. I cannot imagine walking through this world without knowing that you were here waiting for me. I cannot imagine having the strength to breathe without you. You are my dear and loving wife, Elizabeth Wentworth. And I love you. I shall never leave you. Ever."

I swept my wife into my arms and carried her away.

3 FEBRUARY 1691, THURSDAY

*T*hese are the events of the day as related by Lizzie, which she repeated to me as soon as she arrived home. Lizzie is a keen observer and not much escapes notice of her attentive eyes.

The rains have stopped and the floods have dried enough to make the roads passable so Lizzie decided to bring firewood to the Parrises. I helped Lizzie and Patience load the smaller of our two wagons with the chopped wood. Since she was headed to the Village anyway, Lizzie thought to bring some firewood and candles to her father and Mary. Patience hitched Bethuda to the wagon, and together they drove along the Ipswich Road, past the chandler, the wheelwright, the cobbler, and the inn.

When they arrived near the Farms, Lizzie stopped at the parsonage since twas first on her way. Lizzie settled Bethuda near some wet grass outside. The horse doesn't seem to mind the cold, used as she is to frigid winds, and the bay mare munched to her heart's content. Patience gathered some firewood in her arms and followed Lizzie to the parsonage door. I have seen the Village parsonage and tis a respectable two-story dwelling about fifty feet long by twenty feet wide.

Lizzie knocked at the door but no one came. She stood, listening, and since she heard voices inside she peered through the window. Twas smaller inside than Lizzie expected, smaller than our house, certainly. The front room was dark with the lack of firelight but there, in the corner farthest from the window, was one small bed containing one small girl, and there, in another corner, was another small bed containing a slightly larger girl. Lizzie saw Reverend Parris standing between the two beds, his head turned upward, whilst his wife sat near the bed of the smaller girl, wiping the girl's brow with a cloth. Nine-year-old Betty Parris' head flopped to the side, her arms still, so much so that Lizzie was afeared she was too late. In the other bed was 11-year-old Abigail Williams, Parris' niece. Parris turned toward the window, saw Lizzie's concerned face, and he nodded at a dark-skinned woman to open the door.

As soon as Lizzie stepped inside she shivered, but not from cold, she thought. "Good day, Reverend Parris," she said.

Parris condescended a nod in her direction. "Mistress Wentworth." As he turned he noticed the chopped blocks of wood in Patience's arms. "The Lord has blessed us with firewood this day."

Lizzie knows Reverend Parris to be a determined man, powerful in his beliefs and firm in his actions. But something in him has changed. Perhaps tis his arguments with the Villagers. Knaves and cheaters, Parris calls them, and they call him worse. Lizzie remained near the door, searching for some understanding of the scowling man. His strong features are etched into a permanent mask of cantankerous impatience, his brow pressing down and his chin pressing up as though his face means to disappear altogether. He turned a smirk onto Lizzie, but his gaze softened when Patience shifted the weight of the wood from one hip to the other.

I have not taken much notice of the Reverend's wife, but Lizzie describes her as frail. Twas an interesting scene, Lizzie said. Both Reverend and Mistress Parris hovered over their nine-year-old daughter's bed so that Lizzie could see only strands of sweat-soaked hair near the top of the quilts and a hand as translucent as ice. The dark-skinned woman swept between the beds, stopping now and again to peer anxiously at Betty.

Across the room, also covered by several quilts but with no worried faces hovering over her, was Abigail Williams. Whether the Parrises had already given Abigail their attention and were turned now to their daughter, or whether they did not care as much how Abigail fared, Lizzie did not know. She saw the sand-brown hair, also sweat-soaked, and the translucent skin, and Lizzie felt a motherly urge to tend the girl. Mistress Parris approached Lizzie with a bowed head and prayerful hands.

"Blessings on you, Mistress Wentworth," Elizabeth Parris said. She looked toward her daughter.

Parris' hair fluttered as he shook his head. "Christ hath placed His church in this world, as in a sea, and suffereth many storms and tempests to threaten its shipwreck whilst in the meantime He Himself seems to be fast asleep." In that moment, Lizzie sympathized with the man Father calls the opposite of King Midas since everything Parris touches turns to shite. Parris is not an accomplished man. He did not finish his studies at Harvard College. He did not make a success of the family sugar plantation in Barbados. He did not succeed as a merchant. When he returned to the clergy the only parish that would have him was Salem Village, a hamlet of farmers, cantankerous farmers at that. Other reverends had been run out of the Village parish before him, so Parris must have known what he was taking on. At that moment, with his daughter and niece laying ill, perhaps even dying, Lizzie understood why Parris might think God had turned His back on his family.

In two long strides, Parris stood near his niece's bed as though deciding what to do with the girl. A quick movement near the cauldron brought Parris' attention to the dark-skinned woman.

"Tituba!" Parris' voice boomed. "Take the wood! Light a fire so we can have some warmth in this house. Have you such thick hide you cannot feel the cold?"

Tituba did as she was bid. After she set the firewood aside, she lit the fire in the usual way, sweeping the cold ashes into the center of the hearth, laying the kindling and a triangle of logs over the ashes, then touching the flame of a lit reed round the kindling. With some encouragement, the flames blossomed and Lizzie stepped toward the warmth. Parris took two more long strides, this time toward the fire where he stared into the licking blaze.

Mistress Parris gestured toward the growing heat. "Look, Betty. Mistress Wentworth has brought us wood. Would you like to sit by the fire?" Betty showed no sign of understanding.

Lizzie stood near Abigail, still alone, her body limp and her eyes dark against her pale complexion. At first, the girl stared at the white winter sunlight streaking through the window. Then she gazed through Lizzie as though Lizzie was not there. Lizzie's urge to tend Abigail dissipated under the strength of the girl's glare. Whilst the Parrises tried to spark some life in their daughter, Lizzie backed toward the door.

"I'm sorry to see your girls so ill," Lizzie said. "Please let us know if there's anything else we can do."

"You're very kind, Mistress Wentworth," said Mistress Parris. "We do miss seeing you about the Village. How is your husband?"

Parris scoffed. "The merchant? He is busy working for Profit, not the Promised Land. He is worried about Gold, not God."

Lizzie thinks Parris is strict with his flock since he hands out public punishments for minor infractions and nonconformists are beaten into submission. But Lizzie says Mistress Parris has always been kind to her. From the day the Joneses arrived in Massachusetts, Mistress Parris offered Lizzie what helpful tips she could about how to make a life on the Farms. The Parrises have been here but two years themselves.

Mistress Parris' lips pulled thin as she turned her eyes to the floor. "Tis good to see you, Mistress Wentworth. We appreciate the firewood more than you know."

Tituba opened the door. As Lizzie walked past the threshold the ailing girls barked like dogs. Lizzie stepped back inside, unsure what to do. Mistress Parris wiped tears from her cheeks with an unsteady hand, but a glare from her husband dried her eyes.

"I'll return with more firewood soon," Lizzie said. "I hope to find the girls well when I return." She looked again at Abigail. The girl's eyes were closed now, her body prostrate once again. Then, as if pulled upright by a puppet master's string, she jerked into a sitting position and began mumbling. What the girl said, Lizzie could not tell, but the straight back of Reverend Parris, and the worried mouths of Mistress Parris and Tituba, said enough. When Betty sat up in the same puppet-like manner, also mumbling, Parris stood stone-still between the two beds, looking from his daughter to his niece to his daughter again, his face blank.

Lizzie could not get the sight of the girls, first prostrate, then flailing, then prostrate again, out of her mind. As Lizzie and Patience climbed into the wagon, Lizzie saw Parris watching her through the window. Lizzie nodded at him, then steered Bethuda toward Silas' farm. Once there, Silas and Patience loaded the rest of the firewood into the shed. Tis a simple home, with three rooms, one long table for meals, a short round table for work, a chest, and three bedsteads covered with quilts. I was charmed by its simple comfort when Father accompanied me when I called on Lizzie. Twas the first time I realized that home was determined more by the people inside than any objects that might decorate the shelves.

When Lizzie walked in Mary was in bed. The girl looked pale and listless, though she perked up when Lizzie gave her the doll. Mary played with it, pretending to give it tea. Lizzie was happy to drink Invisible tea if it brought her sister from her weakness. Finally, Mary asked Lizzie if she had seen the Parrises' girls when she brought them firewood.

"Aye," Lizzie said. "I just came from there."

"How do they look?"

"They look tired."

"People go to see them, you know."

"What do you mean, see them?"

"Doctors, reverends, magistrates, other Villagers. They go to watch the afflicted girls tremble and groan. I haven't been to see them yet. Will you take me?"

"The afflicted girls?" Lizzie sighed. "I think they need rest more than they need spectators." Lizzie pulled the quilts closer to Mary's chin. "When you're feeling better I'll bring you to stay with James and me in Town. You'd like that, wouldn't you?"

"Oh, aye! Maybe on our way you'll take me to the Parrises. I want to see the afflicted girls too." She leaned toward Lizzie. "In Church, Reverend Parris talks about the Devil and how he's invading Salem. We can never be too careful since the Devil is all round us, ready to prompt us to do ill. We're such weak creatures, Lizzie, and the Devil knows it. We're sinners after all."

"Good heavens, Mary. How about instead of wanting to stare at those ill girls we pray for them?" Lizzie and Mary clasped hands and said a prayer for the girls to be well again. Lizzie kissed Mary's cheek and bid her father goodbye.

Patience drove home. The sky hung overhead like a dark woolen blanket, and the brisk wind whisked their exposed faces. Bethuda chose her footing carefully, aware of the deep puddles that, if stepped in, could send the horse, the wagon, and the women in it toppling. Lizzie stared into the distance, her thoughts consumed with Mary. Patience, never talkative at the best of times, was also lost in her thoughts. As they trotted toward the Town, Lizzie noticed a house, hidden though it was behind bushes and trees. Lizzie squinted at the slanted one-room structure. As many times as she had passed between Town and Village she never noticed it before. It must have been built in a hurry since the wooden slats look as though they might crumble at any moment.

Then Lizzie noticed three women with reddish hair falling from their coifs, their wool petticoats tied behind them as they bent over the waterlogged plants near their door. In a single movement, the three women turned toward Lizzie. They did not speak. They gave no signal. As though they sensed her presence, as though they were three heads controlled by one mind, they turned. And stared. Of course, as Lizzie told me, they likely heard the horse struggling through the mud. But Lizzie felt a strangeness in the way they moved, simultaneously, as though the snakes on Medusa's head turned toward someone enticing. Lizzie felt pinpricks along her skin, not from the weather, but from the stares of six eyes. The women walked toward Lizzie.

"Perhaps we should move Bethuda faster, Patience." Lizzie could not take her eyes off the three women, who must be sisters, Lizzie thought, since they were so similar in appearance.

But twas too late to flee. The women were upon them. They were small for grown folks. They had the wizened eyes of the elderly, but their faces were plump and fresh-seeming. One sister, the tallest of the three, stepped before the others. She peered at Lizzie through squinting eyes. "Tis you."

"Good day." Lizzie nodded in the woman's direction.

"This is a good day. Tomorrow we shall see." The woman gestured to the two women beside her. "This is Malka." The shortest woman curtseyed. "This is Mazel." The middle woman curtseyed. "I am Miriam." The sisters turned toward the parsonage. "You come from the Reverend's." Twas not a question.

"Aye," said Lizzie. She gestured toward the women's garden. "Your plants look well tended even during these cold, wet months."

"You never know which medicinals you'll need," said Miriam. "We must be prepared for all occasions." She squinted at Lizzie as though she sought some clue, though what clue that might be, Lizzie could not guess. "You live down Salem way." Again, twas not a question.

"The Town. With my husband."

"Yet you are from the Village." Still, twas not a question.

Lizzie tried to recognize the woman, any of the women, but she could not recall them at all. "My father and sister live on the Farms."

Miriam turned a blank expression onto Malka and Mazel. The two women stared blankly in return. Without another word, Miriam, Malka, and Mazel grabbed each other's hands, and Lizzie's hands as well. The sisters closed their eyes, still as the grave, their grip on Lizzie tight. Lizzie tried to tug herself free but the women would not let go. When they began to shudder and whisper nonsense syllables, Lizzie's heart beat faster than the rain that began soaking them through. The harder Lizzie tugged the tighter the sisters' grip became. Finally, when the rainstorm stopped, they released her.

"You go back down Salem way," Miriam said. "For now, dear girl. For now."

I sat spellbound as Lizzie told her tale, forgetting our meal of game bird and preserved pears as it grew cold on the table before me. Lizzie's hand shook as she brought a bite of boiled leeks to her mouth, and she glanced round as though afeared the three women would jump out from behind the wall.

"It sounds like a fairy story," I said, "like a tale to settle children for their bed."

"And yet that was not the strangest part."

"There is something stranger than what you have already said?"

"As we drove away from the sisters' house, Patience kept looking at me. She pressed her body away from me, as though she were afeared of me. Finally, she said, *Who were you talking to just now, Mistress?* Surely, she must be joking, I thought." I made Lizzie some flip and the sugary rum and beer settled her nerves some. She placed the poker into the hearth flames, then plunged the hot-red pole into her mug to warm the drink. "I told Patience I was speaking to the women near the house, of course, and Patience said, *What women near the house, Mistress?*"

"Are you trying to tell me Patience did not see the women? How can that be? She must have been playing a joke."

"Have you ever heard Patience joke about anything?" I had to admit I had not. "And then Reverend Parris' girls. When they began flailing I thought they looked much as Lazarus must have after Christ raised him from the dead. How does someone lie incoherent one moment and then flail and bark the next?"

"Parris shall find the best doctors to tend them."

"But the doctors don't know what ails the girls. And I don't know what is wrong with Mary."

"Did she seem so very ill?" I asked.

"Nay, at least I don't think so. But she cannot stop talking about Reverend Parris' girls."

I took Lizzie's fingers from her mug and held them tight in my own. I kissed her hand until she exhaled. "Let us forget about strange sisters or odd illnesses," I said.

Lizzie put her hand over mine and nodded.

10 FEBRUARY 1691, THURSDAY

Father and I went to the Village this morn since twas their turn to host Thursday Lecture. Father talked me into the journey. He had a burning curiosity about Parris in the pulpit, especially after hearing Lizzie's story. Father has seen Parris during various sojourns into the Village, whether to visit the Joneses or the Nurses. Lizzie is forever thankful to Goody Nurse, along with Mistress Parris, for helping her family adjust to this new life. I know Lizzie looks upon Goody Nurse in a maternal way. Lizzie wanted to come with Father and me to see her friend but she has not been well for some days now and vomits back everything she eats.

Whilst I hitched Euripides to the wagon, Father pointed his chin toward the window where Lizzie waved goodbye. He raised his eyebrows and grinned, and I knew his meaning well enough. But I'm not willing to hope. Yet. Lizzie will let me know when there is someone to hope for.

I waved goodbye to Lizzie and Father and I left for the Village. Tis a long journey, up the Ipswich Road, past the North River, past Read's Hill, past Hadlock's Bridge, to the Meeting House Road where the Villagers congregate. Outside the Meeting House, I tugged Euripides' reins and the wagon jolted to a stop. Euripides snorted but was otherwise unconcerned. Some of the farmers' lips pulled tight when they saw us, heathens as we are. Others tipped their hats or bowed, knowing Father is a Selectman, a powerful man in the Town, or at least a wealthy one.

The Meeting House in the Village is not unlike our Meeting House in the Town. Both buildings are squat boxes under a steep-pitched roof topped with a turret. There are three doors, south, east, and west. The door on the south wall is for Parris and his family, allowing the Reverend to pass unmolested to the north wall where the pulpit sits. Father and I followed the men through the east door whilst the women entered from the west. Inside tis as plain as the outside with naught but rows of benches, the deacon's bench front and center before the pulpit. Those who do not have pews stand in the galleries. I sighed at the drabness of the room, for adornment of any kind is disrespectful to God, so the Puritans say. Whenever I must endure such difficulties as a Puritan sermon I think about the ornate cathedrals of home, the spires, the stained glass, the fan vaulting. Listening to the Angelic voices of the choir in an Anglican Church is as close as I have come to feeling God's presence in my life. In music, I hear Him. *But where is God here* I wondered as I glanced round the Meeting House.

Silas Jones nodded at Father and me from where he stood behind the pews. He looks as though he is permanently bent forward and I'm afeared his back is paining him again. I must remember to tell Lizzie so she can make a poultice to soothe his muscles.

I spotted Mary seated amongst the women and I breathed a sigh of relief to see that she was well enough to attend. I recognized several of the men, including Ezekiel Cheever, Jacob Fuller, William Hobbs, Francis and Samuel Nurse, John Felton, Francis Peabody, the Doctor William Grigg, too many Putnams to name, and Giles Corey. There are others I know by face but not by name.

On the women's side I saw my wife's beloved friend, Rebecca Nurse, wife of Francis and mother of Samuel. The Nurses normally attend Church in the Town, as we do, but they had come, as Father and I had, for Lecture. Near Rebecca were Susannah Sheldon, Martha Corey, wife of Giles, Sarah Phillips, Elizabeth Hubbard, Sarah Houlton, and more Putnams. Whispers filled both sides of the aisle, men leaning toward men, women leaning toward women, everyone murmuring behind cupped hands. Then came the cryptic looks to see who might be eavesdropping.

Father watched the scene with his arms crossed over his chest. His keen eyes rested on two girls seated near the front kicking their feet against the pew before them. A stern-looking woman, who may have been their mother, shushed them and they settled.

When Samuel Parris appeared, strutting toward his pulpit like a King toward his Throne, the whispering stopped. Reverend Parris stared straight ahead as he clutched his Bible to his heart. His strides were long and his wife, daughter, and niece struggled to keep his pace. Parris climbed the six stairs, stood behind his lectern, and scanned every face before him as though searching for someone who had been naughty. With his long nose and dark hair falling on either side of his face like masts on a sailboat, he looks like an etching I once saw of the Devil. Perhaps a looking glass would show him the Satan he seeks.

Behind the pulpit, Parris grew larger. The pure whiteness of his neck ruffle stood in contrast to the stark black of his coat. He closed his eyes and exhaled. Then his face scrunched as though he were made of clay and a child pressed his features together. As he squinted at the congregation, the very room held its breath, waiting.

Father leaned close to my ear. "You would think he were about to perform for the King with all this posing."

Giles Corey shot a menacing glare Father's way, though tis a glare we are accustomed to seeing. Corey has become Silas' friend, and though the elderly farmer is often gruff in his demeanor, he has moments of kindness. The deacon with the cane, ready to smack people awake or to prompt deeper reflection, took a step our way. Father turned toward Parris with respectful expectation.

When Parris first spoke his voice was soft, like a snake bite, Father said afterward. You may not feel the teeth sink into you, but later, when tis too late, you realize you have been infected with venom.

"Brethren, I do not have much to trouble you with now, but I have hardly any wood to burn. I want to leave the matter to your serious and Godly consideration. Tis my dearest wish that Captain Putnam and the two Deacons should go and make a rate for me, as your Minister, and take care of the supplies necessary to retain me." His pointed chin nearly reached the floor, so long twas in his disapproval. "The Church must be more mindful of me." He pointed an equally long finger toward the men's side. He scanned the empty rows farthest from the pulpit. "I do not like to warn you at these meetings, Brethren, about the importance of attending Church. I pray you will regularly attend. And again I must point out that my salary has not been paid. The Devil must be loosed in Salem to allow for such treachery. We must take care, Brethren. We must not allow Satan and his minions to rule our lives."

We stood whilst Parris read a psalm. Then his voice bounced off the walls.

"I pray that you will all take care that I am not destitute for wood." He shook his head as though he could not believe he was being ignored. Some who had come from the Town, including Father, whispered amongst themselves. The tittering drew glares from Villagers who thought this display only proved that those from the Town are heathens. When Parris spoke again, everyone sat straighter. The Reverend nodded at the air.

"Tis altogether undeniable, Brethren, that our Great and Blessed God, for wise and holy ends hath suffered many persons, in several families, of this little Village, to be egregiously tortured in body and deeply tempted, endangering their souls." Parishioners leaned forward. "We know these amazing feats to be done by Witchcraft." An audible gasp and Parris smirked. "Tis also known that when these calamities began in my family, the affliction went on for several weeks before Witchcraft was suspected." Parishioners shouted their agreement. "Nay, it never came forth to any considerable light, until diabolical means were used in the making of a cake by my Indian man, who had his direction from our sister Mary Sibley. Now there are Witches amongst us, and much mischief hath followed." Suddenly, everyone wanted to know about the mischief. After a long silence, Parris roared, beating the lectern with his fists. "The Devil hath been raised amongst us! His rage is vehement! Listen to me! Only the Lord knows when the Devil shall be silenced!"

"The Reverend knows how to run his lines to great effect," I whispered. Father nodded.

Parris shook his fist toward the onlookers. "Tis sad that our own Sister Sibley should be instrumental to our distress. Tis a great grief to myself and our Godly neighbors. Nevertheless, I truly hope that our Sister doth truly fear the Lord! Do you fear the Lord, Sister Sibley?"

"Aye!" the parishioners shouted. A woman sobbed, and I guessed the heaving form near the front was Sister Sibley.

"I'm satisfied that what she did, she did under the influence of ignorant, terrible persons. We are in duty-bound, brothers and sisters, to protest against such actions. We cannot go to the Devil for help against the Devil! We must be Godly people who bear witness to such diabolical devices! We cannot fall victim to vile Satan! In this Church of Christ we are bound to protect ourselves against it!"

Cheers rebounded, growing louder until I was tempted to put my hands over my ears. I followed Silas' gaze and saw Mary staring at Parris, transfixed, as though the Reverend were Moses standing atop the mountain, Commandments in hand.

"Brethren! If this be your mind that we are bearing witness against Satan, manifest it by uplifting your hands!"

Every hand in the Meeting House was raised except a few. Father and I did not contribute to the display.

"Have you sinned, Sister Sibley? Have your neighbors? Who amongst you have consorted with the Devil? The Devil is loosed in Salem and we must bring our Village back to Godly good!"

Parris wiped his brow with his handkerchief as the parishioners roared, then climbed down from the pulpit. Everyone stood as Reverend Parris crossed the room. Outside the Meeting House he was an ordinary man again. He was drawn into conversation by a Villager I am not familiar with, but he kept turning his eyes in my direction. I thought he was not looking at me specifically, but at those of us from the Town huddled in conversation. Parris' voice boomed toward us as though he still stood in the pulpit.

"Tis a shame our friends from the Town do not stay true to Our Lord. Perhaps tis those from the Town who have allowed Satan into our midst."

Father, never one to back down from a challenge, turned toward the Reverend. "In what ways does the Town not stay true to Our Lord?"

"By allowing anyone to become a member of the Congregation. It should never be easy to become a member of Our Lord's Church. Only the Chosen should have that privilege." Parris stared in our direction. "I've heard that some in the Town are truly Anglican, hardly a step removed from the heresies of the Catholic Church."

"My son and I attend Church in the Town," Father replied, "and here in the Village. We did not go with the Half-Way Covenant. We are full members of the Church. We made our public declarations."

"But you accept the Half-Way Covenant," a farmer said.

"I am content with any belief that allows more people to know God," Father said.

Another Villager said, "Even those who refuse to make a public proclamation about their conversion to God's Way?"

"The Half-Way Covenant allows those adults who have been baptized but have not made public declarations to become full and participating members of the Church. We all live in the light of the Lord, surely." Father tapped his temple with his forefinger. "I have heard about the new Charter Reverend Mather and Governor Phips have brought from England."

"What about the new Charter?" asked Parris.

"The Charter affirms our land titles," said the Villager. "That's all I need to know of it."

"But the new Charter also guarantees liberty of religion, does it not?" Father asked. "Except, of course, for Roman Catholics, infidels that they are."

Parris' eyes blazed. "Anyone who does not follow the One True Church is an infidel in God's eyes! You," Parris pointed at Father, "and you," he pointed at me, "and your popish ideas!" He looked fit to explode. "Heathens should not be baptized! They are not worthy!"

Father beamed. He enjoys a good argument in a way I do not. "Who determines who is worthy? I read the Bible. I study Scripture. But I dare not assume that I understand the Lord's heart. Surely, the Lord is the only one who can truly judge who is worthy." Father nodded in my direction. "My son, the Cambridge scholar." He grinned at Parris. "You went to Harvard, I believe?" The Reverend did not answer and the murmuring from the onlookers grew louder. Father whispered to me, "He cannot reply because he did not finish his studies."

"Neither did I," I said.

"But you will, James. Parris will never be any more than what he is now, a disliked Reverend in a difficult Village. You have the rest of your life to look forward to."

A raw-boned blast of wind shook everyone standing outside the Meeting House as Reverend Parris left without another word.

Again, his wife, daughter, and niece trailed behind. I did not notice anything odd in the girls and hoped that any illnesses had passed.

Martha Corey joined her husband, then took one step closer to Father. "You're a brave man, indeed, Mr. Wentworth, speakin' to the Reverend as you did just then. And what you say has truth. As you may well know, I'm a Gospel Woman, I am, and even I cannot know the fullness of Our Lord's Goodness. Tis not for us to judge. Only God can do that."

Giles Corey scoffed. "Gospel Woman my arse."

Goody Corey winked at Father in a conspiratorial way. "All this quarrelin' is because of Evil sprung upon us from our Evilin' ways." She leaned even closer and Father took a step back. "The Reverend's girls, they need to learn. You play with fire, you'll get burnt."

"How are the girls playing with fire?" I asked.

"I don't know for nothin', young sir, but I'm sure twas them as doing somethin' they shouldn't."

Giles Corey called to his wife, muttering at her for disturbing important men such as Father with her nonsense. Goody Corey curtsied before scurrying toward her husband as fast as her short legs would carry her.

Outside, Father and I rubbed our hands together trying to spark some warmth, of which there had been none inside. Father watched the Villagers as they left. "There can be no Devil here, Son. Tis far too cold for the hot-weather likes of him."

Silas and Mary found us outside. Father has always taken kindly to Lizzie's sister, my sister having died so young and Father feeling the want of daughters. He leaned down to Mary and smiled.

"You should be at home now, Mary Grace. Tis cold and you just out of your sick bed."

Silas nodded. "We should be on our way."

Mary shook her head. "But…"

"You know tis a daughter's duty to be obedient to her father," Silas said.

Mary looked sullen though she brightened quickly. "Did you hear Reverend Parris speak of the Devil, did you, Brother? The Reverend said we cannot go to the Devil for help against the Devil, and we must be Godly people who bear witness to such diabolical devices." She stopped before Silas' wagon, her dark eyes so wide they took up half her face. She reached before her as though grasping for someone. "We cannot fall victim to vile Satan!"

"All right, child, that's quite enough of that." Silas picked Mary up at the waist and dropped her into the front of the wagon, rather hard, I thought.

"You needn't worry about such things, Mary," I said. "Lizzie told me she wants you to stay with us as soon as you are well enough. That means I expect you to go straight to bed and rest so you can come soon."

"I'll be good, Brother. I'll not fall victim to vile Satan!"

Father and I watched Silas steer his horse away. As I grasped Euripides' reins I saw Rebecca Nurse. She curtsied toward Father and me.

"Tis always good to see you, Goody Nurse," I said.

"We've missed you at Sunday services in the Town," Father added.

"My old bones have been creakin', Mr. Wentworth, but I'm better yet. I haven't seen your wife, young Mr. Wentworth. Is she well? I've been prayin' you'll receive a blessin' from the Lord in good time."

"Thank you, Goody Nurse," I said. "Mistress Wentworth and I pray for the same." I spoke loudly since Rebecca's hearing is failing her.

"That blessing may well be upon us," Father said, "though my son is not yet ready to face the truth."

Goody Nurse clapped her hands as if in prayer. "Nonsense!

Children are the Lord's greatest blessin'. When the time comes, you'll be ready for whatever the Lord sends your way, as will I, as will all His children. Tell your dear Mistress I missed seeing her this day."

I nodded toward the old matron and tugged on Euripides' reins, steering the wagon toward the Ipswich Road and home.

AFTER SUPPER, LIZZIE AND I SAT BEFORE THE HEARTH INTO THE LATE hours, Lizzie mending a tear in one of her skirts whilst I reread *The Ingenious Nobleman Don Quixote of La Mancha*. I can relate to Alonso Quixano, who reads so many romances he believes he has become a romantic hero whilst he roams round the countryside as a knight in search of adventure. As Don Quixote, he means to live a chivalrous life. With his squire, Sancho Panza, Quixote prefers to live in his imagination—where damsels in distress must be saved and windmills are giants to be battled. Others believe Quixote is mad. His brain has dried up due to all his reading, they say, and he is unable to separate reality from fiction. Tis a trait I'm afeared I share. How many times has someone told me to lift my eyes from books to see the world before me? Even Lizzie, who understands me so well, has told me to pay more attention. But sometimes what we create for ourselves in the privacy of our minds supersedes anything the real world might provide. How much of our lives is determined by Free Will? How much is determined by Fate? Why should Quixote not live as a knight-errant if that is who he wishes to be? And yet, with the book's dark ending where the fantasy falls away, leaving a harsh world, I wonder if Fate has more to say over the outcome of our lives than we give it credit for.

As the nighttime grew colder, Lizzie gathered some quilts and set them over our laps. I put my book away since, at that moment, my reality was perfect and I was in no need of my imagination. In two months, Lizzie and I have settled into that comfortable space where we can be silent together. We held hands beneath the quilts, content simply touching one another. I realized then that I do not need to search the countryside for a romantic adventure. I know now, beyond a shadow of a doubt, that my life is with Lizzie.

25 FEBRUARY 1691, THURSDAY

The sky is stitched together with storms—a soggy nightmare, Father calls it. It rains, rains, rains, and I watch the gray-black clouds thinking I shall never see sunlight again. I expect to see Noah and his animals float past any time now. Fortunately, we are buffered enough by land and brush that we are saved from the worst of it. Others are not so lucky, and families stand dumbstruck whilst their homes drift away like rafts on the sea. Finally, this afternoon the downpours abated and the roads are passable, mainly, which is good since it allowed Silas and Mary to make the jaunt from the Village.

Silas greeted me warmly, and Mary did the same. Father joined us, which made for a happy little family gathered round my warming hearth—chatting and gossiping—whilst Lizzie and Mary cooked the roast filet of beef. They laughed as they chopped the parsley, thyme, and spinach, then basted the beef with lard and butter. Mary set a dish beneath the beef to catch the drippings, to which Lizzie added chopped onion, butter, and vinegar for the gravy. Father brought rum for the occasion and we sat for a meal fit for the King.

Silas was eager to speak of his eldest child, his son Peter, whom I have not yet met. "He's thriving as a surveyor," Silas said.

"Elizabeth told me he was able to buy the business," Father said.

"Aye. When Peter's master died the wife needed money and sold everything to Peter, equipment and all." Silas bit into the beef and nodded. "Think on it. My son a surveyor, my daughter a merchant's wife. And me but a farmer, and a poor one at that."

"You raised fine children," Father said. "Tis no wonder they live fine lives." He smiled at Mary. "This one shall lead a fine life too."

Silas nodded. His shoulders, always drooping from years of lifting and pushing, now looked as though they would fall away. "Elizabeth and Mary Grace have their mother's goodness. Peter, I don't know who he takes after." Silas contented himself with another mouthful of beef.

"As James takes his goodness from his mother," Father said.

"Your son is indeed good to my Elizabeth," Silas said, "and I will always be grateful for it. My boy Peter has patience the length of my finger." He held out his thin index finger to illustrate. "But he is knowledgeable in the ways of the world, so much more than I am."

"Of course, that's not true, Pa," Lizzie said. "How is Peter's wife?"

"Apphia is well enough," answered Silas. "Of course, Peter and Apphia squabble, as always. I'm glad they're not here to be touched by the strangeness in the Village."

"The strangeness?" I asked.

Mary nearly leapt from her chair. A stern look from Lizzie and she settled.

"Lizzie, you know about the afflicted girls. You saw them! We spoke of them!"

Lizzie poured more rum for Silas. "The afflicted girls? Are people still calling them that?"

"Have you seen them since you brought them firewood, Lizzie? Have you?"

"Not yet. I was going to bring them more wood but then I was ill myself."

"I heard that Reverend Parris' girls still act strangely," Silas said.

Mary bounced up and down in her chair. "They've been touched by the Devil! That's what Reverend Parris says. That's what everyone says."

"Who is everyone?" Lizzie asked.

"The doctors, the Putnams, others in the Village, even other Reverends beside Mr. Parris. Many in the Village have seen the girls in such a state, as you have, Lizzie. Oh, I want to see them so much!"

"Parris has been making quite a show of denouncing Satan in his sermons," I said.

Father sipped his rum as he fell into thought. Finally, he said, "Those girls are not touched by the Devil. They're touched by Parris, who may himself be the cause of the Evil in the Village."

Silas nodded. "All Reverend Parris talks on is the Devil, his salary, the Devil, his firewood, and the Devil again."

"I did not realize you do not care for the Reverend Mr. Parris, Silas," Father said. "Are your differences with Parris theological?"

"Aye, in part. In truth, I do not like the man."

Father laughed. "So what is it then that you believe in the Society of Friends? Tis so very different than the pronouncements of Reverend Parris?"

Silas looked at Lizzie. "Let my daughter explain. She speaks so much better than me."

"Don't be silly, Pa. You're more than capable of explaining our beliefs." Lizzie gestured to Mary to help set out another platter of beef. "You've heard me speak of this, James. Friends believe we all have our own unique worth. Everyone should be valued equally, and we oppose anything that may harm or threaten anyone."

"Someone should tell Apphia," Mary said. "Pa said that Apphia threw a knife in Peter's direction and nearly pinned him to the wall!"

Silas nodded. "I told Peter to leave the miserable scold to the Indians."

"Pa!" Lizzie looked as though she could not believe her ears. Silas made no move to take back his words until he said, "Perhaps I need another reminder about what we believe. We have been here awhile."

He held up his cup, which Lizzie filled as she continued. "Friends believe that everyone can have a direct experience of God. We don't need ceremony. Rituals are simply barriers between ourselves and Our Lord." Lizzie gestured at our meal. "God is here, in this delicious food we share. He's here in this fire that keeps us warm." Lizzie took my hand. "God is here in my husband. God is everywhere. We don't need Reverend Parris to tell us how to find God's good favor. We have it already."

"Well said, Elizabeth." Silas drained his cup in one swallow. He finished his beef, and Lizzie placed another slice on his plate. "And I believe you may well be right, Mr. Wentworth. Reverend Mr. Parris may well be the cause of the Evil that's sprouting in Salem."

"I'm John, Silas. We are family, after all."

John Wentworth and Silas Jones, the wealthy merchant and the poor farmer, clinked their mugs and drank heartily of the rum. Fortunately, Father brought two bottles for the occasion.

"How are things on the Farms, Silas, besides the strangeness?" Father asked.

"It continues its troubles. Tis too cold. There's too much poverty and too many going without. Too many villains attacking from within and without. Battles between families over property lines. Battles with the Indians since so many have had to send their sons into the militia."

"Aye," said Father. "I had to pay to keep James out of it."

"I don't agree with most anything the Reverend Mr. Parris says, but maybe he's not wrong about God's dissatisfaction with Salem. Why else would everyone suffer so?"

"God does not make people suffer, Pa," Lizzie said. "Tis people who do this to each other."

"Nay, Lizzie! Tis the work of Satan!" Mary cried.

"Hush." Lizzie fed Mary a piece of beef. "Perhaps Salem is not the best place for you to settle, Pa. There's no land here for you to purchase even after you've saved enough. And we cannot practice our religion without fear of being tied to a wagon and dragged to our deaths."

"The new Charter says there will be freedom for different religions," Father said.

"Aye, but those who think like Reverend Parris aren't going to change their minds because of a piece of paper," Silas said. "Quakers have a reputation for being stubborn people. They say we cause trouble wherever we go since we won't conform. Right here in Massachusetts Quakers have been driven out of the colony, branded, even hanged." Silas lit his pipe and took a long puff, releasing a flat line of smoke that lingered near his face. "Perhaps Elizabeth is right and Mary and I should go elsewhere. Perhaps I should have settled in Connecticut to begin with."

"Of course that can't be right, Pa," Lizzie said. "I wouldn't have met James if we had gone to Connecticut."

"True enough," said Silas. "But Mary here is in need of a Meeting, our kind of Meeting, and such Meetings aren't available here. She needs to sit in silence and listen for the voice of God."

Mary was about to respond but Lizzie spoke quickly. "Are there still refugees from the battles with the French and Indians coming into the Village, Pa?"

Silas' face flushed pink from the rum he enjoyed. "There are whole regions in Maine that are unlivable now. The French and the Indians wiped out entire towns and the refugees are seeking safety here. With so many more mouths to feed, and little enough to begin with, some feel the refugees are a burden."

"We must do what we can to help them," Lizzie said. "They flee through no fault of their own. How should they be expected to live where tis unlivable?"

"I do not disagree, Daughter," Father said, "but the extra mouths have aggravated the existing rivalries between families."

"Parris should be here to guide and lead," I said. "He should help us find common ground so we can live peacefully amongst each other. What other role should a Reverend play in his community? Instead he stirs the pot."

Father nodded. "He does indeed."

Lizzie looked at Mary with such motherly concern. There is an age gap between them of 12 years, and though Lizzie is not old enough to be the girl's mother, Lizzie took their mother's place when their mother died giving birth to Mary. Lizzie turned a compassionate look onto her sister, the look that first captured my attention. I hope Father and Goody Nurse are correct and Lizzie and I are blessed.

"Eat your beef," Lizzie said to Mary. "You're still recovering and need your strength. Especially if you still want to help Pa with the plowing when the season arrives."

"The ground is still frozen," Mary said. "There won't be plowing for months yet."

"Tis what the oxen is for, the plowing, after all," said Silas.

"And where is the soap you promised me all those months ago?" Lizzie asked.

"Mary has been distracted by the claims of Witchery and cannot think of much else these days," Silas said.

"And we know the Witches!" Mary said. "We see them round the Village most days."

Silas shushed the girl and everyone fell silent. We chewed our beef, drank our rum, and listened to the crackling flames in the hearth.

Lizzie exhaled. From the halt in her voice, I thought she did not want to ask the question, though she did. "Who are the Witches, Mary? And how do we know them?"

"Tis Tituba, the Parrises' slave woman. She does magick spells!"

"I saw her when I brought firewood to the Parrises," Lizzie said. "She does nothing of the kind."

"What kind of spells?" I asked.

Lizzie shook her head at me. "Don't encourage her, James."

Silas raised an eyebrow to me. "You allow your wife to speak to you such ways?"

"What way is that?" I asked. When Silas waited for an answer, I replied, "Lizzie may speak however she wishes. This is her home, after all."

Mary did not care for this aside. She waved her hands above her head, bringing everyone's attention back to her. "I don't know what spells, but everyone says how Tituba has been contacted by a Bad Man, maybe even the Devil himself, who has been enticing her and other women from the Village to sign his book."

"What other women?" Father asked.

"Goody Good and Goody Osborn. The Devil promises them fine clothes and riches and all sorts of wonders if they'll follow him. And they send their Shapes to torture people until the victims twist and scream. The afflicted girls suffer such torments!" Mary looked as though she were afflicted herself by the way she emphasized her words with exaggerated facial expressions and twisted limbs.

"Mary." Lizzie's tone was sharp. She placed the sweets on the table and passed Father a huge helping of his much-loved Indian pudding. Lizzie sat next to Mary whilst the girl shoveled a large slice of mince pie into her mouth. "Tituba is no Witch. The other women who are being spoken out against are not Witches. You must find other ways to occupy your time instead of listening to such nonsense. What of your cooking, your cleaning, or your sewing? Surely, you're helping with the household chores. You have responsibilities and you shouldn't shirk them." Lizzie stopped herself with some difficulty. In a softer tone, she said, "Please,

Mary, never mind about Tituba and the others. This will all be over soon."

Father leaned toward Mary. "I do not know how much of it is true, Mary, but it certainly does make for a riveting tale, does it not?"

Mary beamed at Father, then asked for more pie. The room fell silent again.

When I could no longer stand the quiet, I said, "How can people be so foolish?"

Lizzie shook her head. "You speak as someone educated at university, James. But not everyone has a rational brain as you do. Look at all the Witch hunts in England. Tis not more of the same here? For the people in the Village, who brought their beliefs from England, tis their nature to believe in magick, white and black. The Devil isn't a figment of their imagination. He is as real to them as God. We cannot recognize the light if there is no dark in contrast."

"What magick do they believe in?" I asked.

"They have their folk remedies," Lizzie said. "They have their charms and spells, their horseshoes for protection, even if they're hidden to avoid being seen by Church officials so they won't be brought to Court."

"And the Venus glass," I said.

Lizzie laughed. "Aye, there are those who believe in the fortune-telling powers of the Venus glass."

Another raised eyebrow from Silas. "You didn't use that fool Witch's magick, did you, Elizabeth?"

"Twas a long time ago, Pa. But this isn't about magick. If people can believe in God, then they can believe in the Devil. If they can believe in Good, then they can believe in Evil."

"Do Quakers believe in the Devil?" Father asked.

"Oh, aye." Silas stood as though he had a pronouncement to make. "We know of the Devil. The Devil is the Tempter, the Reasoner. Mainly, he is the Enemy. We should be afeared of him. Even you," he pointed his pipe at me, "with your educated brain, even you aren't free from his deceiving influence. Perhaps you're most vulnerable with your ability to rationalize when there is no rational explanation to be had."

"There is little enough that defies a rational explanation," I said. "To believe in the Devil is to believe in things you cannot see."

"We cannot see God, yet we know He exists," Mary said. "Do you not believe God exists though you cannot see Him, Brother?"

Father smiled at the girl. "You may well have a point, young Mary. Aye, we do believe in God even though we cannot see Him." He took a long sip of rum and let the warming liquid settle within him. "As for the Devil? We shall have to see."

Silas reached toward the wall. Lizzie clapped when she saw what he had.

"Pa! Your fiddle! I haven't heard you play since I've been married."

"We must fix that then," Silas said.

Silas played a lively tune, and Lizzie and Mary danced along. Father danced too, and he taught Lizzie and Mary the sailor's hornpipe. He showed them how to pretend to haul in the anchor and climb the ropes. Lizzie talked me into joining them. I cannot say I am a great dancer, but I am happy to do my wife's bidding. The joy on her face was worth any awkwardness on my part.

26 FEBRUARY 1691, FRIDAY

*W*e received troubling news this day. Parris, still intent on uncovering the Devil in the Village, pressured his daughter and his niece, and tis exactly as Mary said—the girls named Tituba as their tormentor, and Tituba confessed to being a Witch. Lizzie paced the length of the Great Room, from the shelves to the window and back as she told me what she knew.

"Tituba said the Devil bid her to serve him, and though she tried to ignore him and send him away, he kept hassling her, trying to get her to sign his book."

"His book?" I glanced at the books on the shelves. "What type of book does the Devil have, do you think? Might I have it here?"

"Tis not funny, James." Lizzie shook her head to emphasize her point. "Tis bad enough the girls named Tituba as tormenting them. There have been whispers about Tituba's connection to Witchcraft for as long as I've lived here and probably longer than that."

Lizzie looked through the window and watched the ice flurries float like wings to the ground. She shivered though the fire was hot. "When I called on the Parrises Tituba looked at the girls with such concern. She kept stopping to watch them, especially Betty, to see how they fared. I cannot believe she would hurt them."

"So you do not think this Tituba is a Witch?"

Lizzie shrugged. "She has her own ways, but that doesn't make her Evil." Lizzie wiped her hands on her apron and stared at the onions on the table as though perhaps they knew some secret. "I could see how little Parris regarded her."

"I know you would dislike Parris for even having Tituba," I said.

"And her husband, John Indian. He has them both. The Reverend cannot see the immorality of owning human beings."

"Is that a Quaker belief, that there should not be slavery?"

"Must one be a Quaker to not believe in slavery? No, James, I don't believe in slavery. But when I was at the Parrises' I saw how the Reverend might blame Tituba for anything, even this odd illness. And Ann Putnam is quick to blame the world for her troubles."

"What has Ann Putnam to do with anything?"

"She's afflicted now as well. And she is someone who would point the finger at Tituba." Lizzie dropped a slice of butter into the pan crackling in the hearth, then took up a knife to chop turnips.

"Tituba is a slave," I said, "and has no rights of her own."

Lizzie shook the knife in my direction. "You have concerns about the slave woman, do you?"

"Lizzie, I do not trade for slaves. Father does not trade for slaves. He exports rum and other goods."

"But the rum he sends is traded for slaves, so is that not taking part in the slave trade?"

"What people do with the rum is not our concern." Father has said that to me on so many occasions his words fell from my lips without a second thought.

Lizzie slid the chopped onions into the pan. The butter popped and sizzled, and she pushed the onions from side to side as they browned over the blazing fire. "And what they do to Tituba is not our concern? Or Goody Good or Goody Osborn? The afflicted say they are being attacked by the Shapes of these women."

"What does that mean, attacked by the Shapes?"

"My dear and loving husband, really you are too much in your head and not enough in the world. I mean Parris' girls and Ann Putnam are claiming that Tituba has bewitched them with the Devil's magick, and Goody Good and Goody Osborn's Specters have attacked them. The afflicted say the Spirits of these women leave their bodies and torment them. Goody Good, Goody Osborn, and Tituba have been arrested and taken to Nathaniel Ingersoll's."

I know the place and may admit to stopping at Ingersoll's tavern for a drink of ale and an onion pie on occasion. The licensed ordinary is in Ingersoll's house, one of the few public buildings near the Farms, so it makes sense that the women were brought there.

Lizzie's lips were tight, her glance down and away. I took the knife from her hand. I pulled her close and she stepped into my embrace, her head against my chest, my head on top of hers. I love the feel of her hair when it falls loose and soft round her shoulders. I brushed a dark curl from her face and kissed her forehead.

"Do not worry for them, my love," I said. "Tis nonsense. It shall end soon."

"But tis hard sometimes, seeing how easily people turn against each other. I saw it well enough in England and hoped to be free of it here. I want to live a peaceful life. I want to live content with you. And Mary..."

"What about Mary?"

"She's poorly again. Goody Nurse is tending her, but I should go. I'm nearly a mother to Mary after all."

"Of course you must go." I kissed Lizzie's forehead and she relaxed into me. She looked at me with such tenderness. Her hands touched her abdomen over her apron and she smiled. Despite the threatening skies outside, my home was lit by Lizzie's sunlight glow. "I want to know that all is well in my world, James. Especially now, knowing there will soon be another Wentworth running through these rooms."

I lifted Lizzie high toward the peak of the gables and spun her round and round. My whole body thrilled at the sound of her laughter. Even now, as I write this, I, who make sense of the world through words, cannot find a way to express my jubilation.

Our Blessing is coming. Hallelujah.

29 FEBRUARY 1691, MONDAY

One matter in which I do agree with the Puritans is that we are called to discover our destinies. If one is called to be a farmer, then one must be a farmer. If one is called to be a minister, then the same. One may be called to be a cooper, a miller, a tanner, a furrier, or a surveyor. Tis up to us to discover our calling. Knowledge whispers to us if we are willing to listen. One might be called to the merchant trade, as Father was. What am I called to? I know I am called to be Lizzie's husband. I know I am called to be our child's father. I know I am most comfortable at home with Lizzie by my side, reading, writing, and thinking. I know I long to return to Cambridge. Other than that, I still struggle to discover precisely where I belong.

One place I do not belong is inside a Puritan Church. I'm struggling with mandatory Church attendance these days. Father and I attend Sunday sermons and Thursday Lectures as we should—most of the time, at least. Selectmen, Father amongst them, vote and make decisions for the Church, and by extension, the people. Everything about our daily lives is determined by the Selectmen, the ministers, and the Town leaders. Father does not attend the meetings often enough to have much influence, but he has yet to give up his place. He is frustrated, as I am, that people are brought in for minor infractions such as the cut of their clothing. Clothing is important enough in Massachusetts that the Court must have its say. Slashes in the sleeves are not allowed though they are the fashion in England. Women have been fined for not having skirts that drag along the ground and sleeves that do not reach their wrists. Father and I can wear gold and silver threading because of our social rank. Lizzie wears her gold wedding ring, as I do, and she wears gold threading in her finer clothing. As my wife, she is now free to wear lace, girdles, even hatbands since her new station allows for it. After we married, I bought her new silk gowns with lace and ribbons. I bought her silk scarves of delicate colors like sky blue and soft green. She could not take her eyes off her gifts. She said she had never seen such beautiful things. She nearly refused to take them, asking what she would do with such treasures, but I convinced her that they are hers and nothing is too good for her. Finally, she relented. When others saw her dressed in her finery, they turned up their noses but said nothing. Lizzie is strong enough to pay them no mind.

My thoughts have been wandering aimlessly like this all day, even when I was at Father's attempting to complete my work. I listened to the heavy rains splattering the ground and pummeling the windows, which did not help my concentration. From the forceful cries of the storm outside, I was afeared Father's house would wash away as others have. I wanted to rush home to see that Lizzie was all right, but I looked round, saw not even a leak in Father's roof, so I decided that our house, which is every bit as sturdy, was still as it should be. Again, I struggled to focus on the maths, but then Thomas Oliver appeared. I tried to ignore the man's droning but, short of sticking my fingers into my ears, could not.

"There's four of them now," Oliver said. "Elizabeth Hubbard claims to be poked and prodded by demons as well."

Father held a bottle over Oliver's empty cup. He nodded as he poured the wine. "Aye, we know."

Oliver looked as though he would say more but the privateer finished his wine instead. Holding up his empty cup, he said, "Now what is it precisely that you need me to do, Mr. Wentworth?"

Father refilled Oliver's cup, then looked at me from under hooded eyelids. "I believe we are done for the day, Son. I shall see you tomorrow."

I was more than happy to take my leave. I nodded at Father and Oliver, grabbed my coat from the peg near the door, and left as quickly as I could without tripping over myself. I walked home with a head heavy with questions.

Twas pure dark then and I was slow with my steps. I was so consumed by my thoughts I did not see the tall man in the black cloak standing before me and I walked straight into him. I wore my spectacles so that was not an excuse. I was not paying attention, walking with my pie in the sky, as Lizzie likes to say. The man leaned toward me—we were about equal height—and he squinted his almond-shaped eyes as though studying me. His eyes were blacker than the stormy night sky though his complexion looked pale under the moonlight. He had silver streaks in his red-brown hair, and his long face was contorted by a smirk of either annoyance or amusement—I could not say which. Still, I had stepped on the man's toes, and I felt ridiculous for bumping into him when he was standing right before me.

"Excuse me," I said. "I was preoccupied."

"Did you say excuse me?" The man spoke like someone from a northern English port town. "No one says excuse me anymore. All you young human people running round from here to there and back again without the slightest concern for what's happening right before your nose."

"I'm afeared I've done exactly that, sir. I do apologize."

The long-faced man laughed. "He apologizes! What a polite human person I've found for myself." He leaned closer and whispered. "I've always had a fondness for polite young men. My son was a polite young man. He took after me, you know."

I thought to tell the man that red wine stained his face, but there was something acrid about the smell of him and I stepped away.

"I have no doubt," I said.

Something in the man's manner made me eager to get home. I squinted through my spectacles, trying to see him more clearly. I thought I recognized him from somewhere, but I could not recall where that might have been. By the time I turned round he was gone. That fast—like a snap of the fingers—and he vanished as though he had never been there. I looked into the shadows brought on by the overhanging trees and the slim light of the moon. I decided I must have been hallucinating, the man had never been there, he was simply a figment of my overactive imagination. I shook the jitters off, dismissing my dangling nerves as nonsense. I exhaled when I saw Lizzie through the window.

After I removed my hat and coat I told Lizzie there was one more afflicted now. I did not tell her about the disappearing man since one preternatural problem per day is enough.

"What if Tituba has been practicing magick as they say?" I asked. "What if she has been casting spells and what if something went wrong? What if she caused some black magick illness she never intended?" I hushed my voice as visions of the disappearing long-faced man with the silver-streaked red-brown hair flickered behind my eyes. "What if the Devil is involved after all?"

Lizzie removed her coif and shook out her dark curls. "I thought you didn't believe in the Devil, James."

"I do not. But what if?"

"What if this roof comes crashing down on our heads? What if there's a storm that washes everything away and we must sink or swim? What if there truly be Witches? We cannot live a life of what ifs. We can only live with what we have before us now, this day." She took my hands and rubbed them between her own. I did not realize how cold I was until Lizzie shared her warmth with me. "What we have is rather wonderful. I love our life together and I would not trade you for all the devils in the world."

I laughed. "Thank you. I think."

I placed my hand on Lizzie's abdomen, feeling the barest of bulges beneath her apron. Even that bulge is only visible to me since I know her body better than I know anything else in this world. I kissed her, deeply, and I knew I would agree to anything she said, this day and always.

1 MARCH 1691, TUESDAY

*T*homas Oliver stayed at Father's last night. Father would not send Oliver to the tavern, insisting the privateer would be more comfortable in his home, which no doubt he was. I arrived at Father's to be let in by the helping-girl. She led me to the table where Father and Oliver sat, huddled close in deep conversation. Not wishing to intrude, I stood back, admiring the ornate iron grate near the hearth whilst the sweet, warm scent of baking cornbread wafted through the hall. The helping-girl stood there, hands on her hips, the corners of her coif fallen forward so her face was hidden. Then she turned to me and smiled. Twas only a glance, after all, and she continued cooking as though she did not recall I was there.

"The ships are arriving from Africa at the beginning of next month," Thomas Oliver said.

"They shan't stop here on my account," Father said. "I do not want to see them."

"Well," Oliver said, "the main port for such trade is Boston. I don't imagine they'll have reason to dock in Salem." Oliver held his hands toward the fire. Inside Father's is warm, but chills blow through the wind-lashed diamond panes. "Will you have enough fish and lumber to sell to the West Indies?"

Father nodded. "My fishermen and lumbermen are doing their jobs well despite the difficult weather."

"Good." Oliver leaned back in his chair and ran his hands through his unruly dark hair falling loose at the queue. "From there I can get you the molasses you need. You have a distillery?"

"Surely, you have seen our warehouses near the wharf? Wentworth and Son. The distillery is up and running as it has been these months past. Have you not tasted our product often enough?"

"Oh, aye," said Oliver, "though I wouldn't mind trying it again. Just to be certain of the quality, you know."

Father laughed. "Then taste it again you shall. Prudence?" The helping-girl turned toward Father. "Bring me one of the bottles of rum from the cellar. Make that two." Prudence reappeared carrying two dark bottles. Father took the bottles from her hands, grabbed two silver mugs from the shelf near the hearth, and poured some of the dark liquid for Oliver and me. "We have yeast and water. We have copper stills. What we need is the molasses, which I am assured by Mr. Boxley that you can provide."

Oliver smiled, first at me, then at Father. He watched Prudence as she bent forward to rake some life into the flames. Father cleared his throat and Oliver turned his attention to the bottles of rum. "Don't worry about me, Mr. Wentworth. If tis molasses you need, then tis molasses you will have. There's more than enough if you know where to look for it." He drained his rum and sighed. "I must say, Mr. Wentworth, you certainly have a superior product. Where did you learn to make such rum?"

Father grabbed a third mug and poured himself some of the amber liquid. He breathed in the sweet fumes before taking a long sip. "You can learn how to do anything if you set your mind to it."

Oliver held out his mug, which Father was only too pleased to refill. "Rum was adopted as the official drink of the Royal Navy near forty years ago," the privateer said.

Father looked at Oliver as though making a decision. "You know much about the Royal Navy."

"You know I do, Mr. Wentworth." Oliver gulped the rest of his rum, then excused himself, saying he had to be on his way to find men to sail his ship. Father saw him to the door, and once they were outside they whispered between themselves again. When Father returned inside, I asked, "So tis true? Thomas Oliver deserted the Royal Navy?"

"Oliver knows his way round such ships because he manned one himself."

"I know you are a businessman, Father, and I respect that about you. I owe my home, even my life with my wife to your success. But is it possible that profit is not the most important thing in the world?"

"Of course tis possible, James. I would say tis true. Look at it this way—we're performing a service. People need rum, and we provide it."

"People *need* rum?"

"They certainly like it well enough." Father stretched his arms toward the peak of the gable above our heads, then rested his feet on the hob. He pulled aside another chair and gestured for me to sit. "This rum venture is a challenge for me, James. I had my try at buying and selling coffee and tea. With Oliver I'm able to make the connections to ensure that we always have access to the molasses I need to ferment the rum. Now here's a new game for me, to see if I'm any good at it. So far, it has worked well. Our revenue is strong. We're making a greater profit here in Massachusetts than I ever dreamed possible. I shall be able to retire to the English countryside whilst you return to your studies. You, your wife, and my grandchildren shall want for nothing. Do you know what it means to someone such as I, who worked the docks until my fingers bled? There were so many times, James, so many times I wanted to give up, thinking that was all I was ever going to be—some other man's drudge. Yet something inside me would not let me stop, so I kept going, working every job I could find, scrimping and saving every farthing, determined to make a life for myself that I truly wanted to live." Father gestured to his fineries—his imported furniture, the blue and white Delftware lining his shelves, his William and Mary side tables, the embroidered tapestries on his walls, the blood-colored damask curtains. "And I succeeded, and I married well, and for love, and I have a beautiful son, who also married for love, and now I have this last challenge before me."

"Last challenge? You are not ill, Father, are you?"

Father patted my hand as he did when I was a boy. "Oh, no, Son. I did not mean to alarm you. I only meant I'm getting older now and soon my days of new challenges shall be past. This is my last great adventure and I mean to see it through."

I paced to the window, needing to vent the pinching rush of air flowing from my arms to my legs. "I understand what you are saying, Father, I do. As I said, I'm grateful to you, for everything you have done for me, for Lizzie, for our child. You have been more than a father to me. You have been a friend."

"But...?"

"But the people, Father."

"What people, James?"

"The people who are shipped here. Tis not merely the rum. I'm fine with the rum. Tis what others do with the rum that concerns me."

Father sighed. "You have been talking to Elizabeth."

"Of course I have been talking to Lizzie. She is my wife, after all. But I did not need Lizzie to tell me that what happens to the people is wrong. I heard you tell Oliver that you do not want to see the ships arriving here from Africa, I'm guessing tis because you do not want to see the misery of the people. But not seeing them does not mean they are not there. It only means you are choosing to turn a blind eye."

Twas Father's turn to pace. He was about to respond when the iron knocker banged against his door. Outside was Patience, our helping-girl, crying, panting, and wringing her apron as though twisting water away. "Mr. Wentworth, both Mr. Wentworths, sirs, tis very important Young Mr. Wentworth come straight away." She turned on her toes, ready to spring into the night.

"What is it, Patience?" I asked.

"Mistress Wentworth had word from the Farms, sir, from her father. Her sister is ill, very ill, and you must come straight away, sir, straight away!"

Without another word, I grabbed my hat and coat and followed Patience home where Lizzie waited. By the time I arrived twas already dark and there was little light in the sky to show us the way to the Village. Though twas hard, Lizzie and I decided to leave for Silas' at first light. Lizzie and I fell to our knees and clasped hands, Lizzie leading the prayer asking God to keep Mary well and watch over her through the night.

2 MARCH 1691, WEDNESDAY

*T*is nearly midnight. Lizzie and I arrived home but an hour ago. Such a day it has been. Lizzie is in a state of nervous worry, and she shudders even in her sleep. She blames herself for Mary's worsening condition and it pains me because I know tis not Lizzie's fault. I was there at Silas' whilst she tended the girl. I have never seen such care as Lizzie gave to Mary. Lizzie kept a cool, wet rag on Mary's feverish forehead, fed her whatever broth she would swallow, covered her with more quilts, and kept the fire hot. Lizzie spoke soothingly, sitting on the bed beside her sister, telling stories from England.

"Do you recall the one about the two sisters?" Lizzie asked as she swept dark, matted hair from Mary's eyes. Mary shook her head. "Well," Lizzie said, "once there were two sisters who were so alike no one could tell them apart."

"Like us," Mary said. "We look alike, like mother and daughter though we're sisters. Everyone says so."

"So we do. These sisters looked alike but were not alike. One was nice, the other wasn't. Now these girls, their father had no work so they thought they would go into service to help. *I shall go first to see what I can do*, the younger, cheerful sister said. She said goodbye and left, only she couldn't find a place. She went farther and farther from home but still found nothing. One day, she passed a home where bread was baking. She heard the loaves call out to her *Little girl! Help us please! We have been baking for seven years and no one has come for us. Take us out or we shall burn!"*

Mary sat up straight, hanging onto Lizzie's every word. Lizzie spoke like a master storyteller, which she was, having told stories to Mary the girl's whole life. Lizzie even used different voices for different characters.

"She was a kind person, this girl," Lizzie said, "so she rescued the loaves and went on her way, saying *You shall feel better now.* Then she came to a cow mooing beside an empty pail. The cow said *Little girl, milk me! I have been waiting for seven years, but no one has milked me!* Again, the girl stopped, milked the cow into the pail, and left saying *You shall feel better now.* Next, the girl came upon an apple tree so filled with fruit the branches fell to the ground. The apple tree said *Little girl, please shake my branches. The fruit is so heavy I can't stand straight!* Again, the girl stopped, shook the branches, and again she left, saying *You shall feel better now.*

The girl continued on her way until she came to the house of an old Witch woman. This Witch woman wanted a helping-girl and promised good wages. The girl agreed to work for the Witch. The Witch told the girl she had to clean the house, sweep the floor, and keep the fire hot and bright. But the Witch gave the girl a warning. The girl must never look up the chimney for any reason. *If you do*, the Witch woman said, *something will fall upon you, and you shall come to a bad end.*

"The girl swept, and dusted, and made up the fire, but she never was paid. The girl decided to go home since she did not like working for the Witch because the Witch ate foods the girl couldn't stand to look upon. But the girl couldn't leave without her earnings, so she stayed working for the Witch and never let on that she disliked her job. One day, whilst sweeping the hearth, she forgot the warning and looked up. Imagine her surprise when a bag of gold fell into her arms!"

"What happened next?" I asked.

Lizzie laughed. "I will tell you." She leaned toward Mary and me and whispered. "Since the Witch was not at home, the girl thought it was the perfect time to leave. The girl had only gone a short way when she heard the Witch on her broomstick flying after her. The girl ran to the apple tree she had helped with its fruit. *Apple tree!* the girl cried. *Hide me so the Witch can't find me. If she finds me she'll eat me and bury my bones under her garden.* The tree replied, *Of course I shall help you, little girl. You helped me when I needed it, so I will help you.*

"The apple tree did as it promised and hid the girl within its branches. The Witch flew past and cried *Oh tree of mine! Have you seen my naughty little maid with a willy willy wag and a great big bag who stole my money—all that I had?* And the tree answered *No, mother dear. Not for seven year!* So the Witch flew on and the girl got down, thanked the tree, and started for home again. As the girl drew near to the cow near the pail, she heard the Witch coming again, so she ran to the cow.

"*Cow, please hide me so the Witch can't find me. If she does she'll pick my bones and bury me under the garden stones!* The cow answered *Certainly I shall. Didn't you milk me and make me comfortable? Hide yourself behind me and you'll be quite safe.* The Witch flew by, calling *Cow of mine! Have you seen my naughty little maid with a willy willy wag and a great big bag who stole my money—all that I had?* The cow said politely *No, mother dear. Not for seven year!*

"The old Witch flew in the wrong direction again, and again the girl started home. But as the girl got to where the oven stood, she heard the Witch woman come again. The girl cried *Oven! Hide me so the Witch can't find me.* And the oven said *I'm afeared there is no room for you, as another batch of bread is baking. But there is the baker. Ask him.* The girl asked the baker, and he said *Of course I shall. You saved my last batch from being burnt; so run into the bakehouse, you shall be quite safe there, and I shall settle the Witch for you.* The girl hid in the bakehouse as the Witch called angrily *Oh man of mine! Have you seen my naughty little maid with a willy willy wag and a great big bag, who's stole my money—all I had?* The baker replied *Look in the oven. She may be there.* The Witch peered into the oven yet no one was there. *Creep in and look in the farthest corner,* said the baker. The Witch crept in, and bam!" Lizzie slapped her hands together, jolting Mary and me from our trance.

"What happened next, Lizzie?" Mary cried. "What happened?"

Lizzie winked. "Well! The baker shut the door in the Witch woman's face, and the Witch roasted! When she came out with the bread she was all crisp and brown and had to go home and put poultices all over herself! But the kind little girl got home with her bag of money. When her mean sister heard about her good luck, the mean sister wanted her own bag of money. She traveled the same roads, passed the same farms, but she wouldn't help anyone. Not the oven. Not the cow. And not the apple tree. The mean sister found the Witch's house and got a job as a helping-girl, but the Witch now was wary of any helping-girls and she watched the second sister constantly. One day the Witch left the house, and the second sister looked up the chimney and held out her arms when the bag of gold fell. The sister ran away as fast as her legs would take her. Soon enough, she heard the Witch on her broomstick behind her. As her sister had before her, the mean sister asked the apple tree for help, but the apple tree said it had too many apples. When the Witch asked the apple tree where the girl had gone, the apple tree pointed a branch in the girl's direction."

"Ohhhh." Mary's dark eyes grew wide. "Did the Witch find the girl, Lizzie? Did she?"

"She did. She caught the girl, took her money back, gave the girl a thrashing, and sent the girl home in disgrace."

"Did the Witch make the girl sign the book, Lizzie?"

"What book would that be, Mary?"

"Everyone knows about the book, Lizzie. Tis the Devil's book!

The Witches say the Devil makes them sign his book. Maybe the Witch wanted the girls to sign the book and the girls wouldn't do it. That's why she went after them. I bet she would have possessed the girls soon enough. She would have made them say strange things and pressed their bodies in odd ways."

"Mary." Lizzie's concern for her sister left a crease between her brows. "Weren't you listening? The story is a lesson about the importance of being kind to others. The first sister was nice and obliging to all she met, so they helped her when she needed it. The second sister was mean and helped no one, so she received no help in return."

Mary sat up, her back so straight twas as though a rod had been forced through her spine. "Am I afflicted too, Lizzie? I've heard him, Lizzie. I've heard Reverend Parris' sermons where he speaks of the Devil and his Evildoings in Salem." Mary pulled the quilts over her head. "Is he here now, Lizzie? Is the Devil here now?"

Mary slunk back and her head hit the wall with a thud. Lizzie lifted Mary and helped the girl lie down. Lizzie pulled the quilts closer round Mary's shoulders and touched her hand to Mary's forehead. "You feel feverish, Mary." Lizzie pressed a cool cloth against Mary's cheek, wiping away beads of sweat from the white-pale face. Lizzie looked through the window at the wet day. "Tis too bad the snow has melted. I could have used some to cool Mary's fever."

"I'm sure she shall be well soon," I said.

Lizzie did not look convinced. She kissed Mary's temple. "Rest now, Mary. You'll feel better soon."

Lizzie closed the curtain round Mary's bed, giving the girl some privacy. Lizzie ladled some broth into a trencher and brought it to Mary, but she was already asleep. Though twas cold, Lizzie and I went outside so we could speak without disturbing Mary. Lizzie's shoulders slumped and her head drooped.

"Did I do wrong, James? I shouldn't have told her that tale, I can see that now. But I told her that story so many times when we were in England. She loves that story."

"You did not do wrong, Lizzie. You saw how happy Mary was whilst you told it." I reached for Lizzie's hand and she reached for mine.

"But that's all Mary has been speaking of lately, the accused Witches. I should have thought." Lizzie slapped her hand against her forehead. "How could I have been so foolish!"

She shivered, and I took her into my arms, both to settle and to warm her. I rested my chin on her head and we stayed there, close, until we heard the clopping of horse hooves. We pulled apart, reluctantly.

"Tis not your fault, my love," I said. "Mary saw meaning in the story that is not there."

"But to tell her a story about Witches?"

Silas' cart stopped beside us. Father and two Villagers I'm not familiar with alighted whilst Silas climbed down after them. The two Villagers, both men, tipped their hat in Father's direction, nodded at Silas, then glanced at Lizzie before walking away. Father smiled at me, but his eyes, always small, were narrow slits. Silas went inside and Lizzie followed him. Father gestured for me to join him across the road.

"There are whisperings in the Village," Father said.

"There are always whisperings in the Village," I said.

"Aye, but this time it concerns Mary. Some believe she is afflicted as well."

"Rubbish! Who says such things?"

"The Putnams have been saying so."

"Tis always the Putnams." Tis no coincidence the name sounds like spittle. "Mary has a fever. It happens. Lizzie is taking excellent care of her."

"Of course she is, Son. I do not need convincing. Do you believe Mary has the Pox?"

"Lizzie does not think so. She tended the Clarksons when they were ill with it and what Mary has does not seem the same."

"There are few who can be so near the Pox and not become ill as well."

"What are you saying?" I asked.

"Nothing against Elizabeth, James. You know that. But I do wonder if Elizabeth is graced by God."

"She is an Angel on Earth, Father. But Mary has no rashes or pustules so tis not likely the Pox. The girl is confused, but who would not be confused listening to Parris' scare-mongering sermons and the nonsense about afflicted girls and the Devil and whatnot? Mary was afeared the Devil was in her room before, but then she settled. She fell asleep, rather suddenly."

Father stared at the flat, soggy farmland rolling toward the horizon. "What was Elizabeth speaking of when she said she had been telling Mary stories of Witches?" I looked at Father. How had he known? As though he read my mind, Father said, "I heard her speak of it as Silas drew near."

"She told Mary the story about the nice, helpful sister who is rescued from the Witch and the mean sister who is not. After Lizzie told her the story, Mary started thinking of the Witch accusations. Lizzie is angry with herself for telling Mary the story."

"No harm was meant by it. Tis a good story. I enjoyed that one myself in my day."

Through the window I saw Silas puffing on his pipe as he rested before the hearth. After another puff he rubbed a well-worked hand over his eyes. Twas the look of a man overcome with weariness. Lizzie set a mug beside him, but Silas did not seem to notice. Father nodded toward the window.

"I should talk to him," Father said. I knew I should go back inside too, but I was annoyed by the thought that Mary's name should be associated with the nonsense in any way. I turned to the sound of crunching rocks and saw three women who had to be sisters nearing the Joneses' door.

All three struck me as small for grown women. The tallest curtsied in my direction, though there was a sense of defiance in her action, as though she did it grudgingly out of social courtesy. "Good day," she said. Her sisters—they must be sisters—followed her lead. I nodded in their direction. When none of the women said anything more, I asked, "Is there something I can help you with?"

"Nay," the tallest sister said, "but there is something we can do for you." She handed me a muslin bag that smelled of spices and herbs. "Give these to your goodwife. Have her boil the herbs and give them to the girl to drink. If the girl can be helped, these will help her."

"Are you Witches?" I asked.

The eldest sister, the only one of the three who seemed to speak, laughed loudly, her head swaying on her neck like an apple bobbing from a nearby tree. "If we were, we wouldn't tell you, now, would we? They are not taking too kindly to Witches nowadays. Or any days, for that matter." The woman nodded at me, and her sisters, if they be sisters indeed, nodded as well. They turned in unison and wandered back the way they came. I watched, wondered at the curiosity of them, then went inside.

Lizzie kept her mind occupied and her hands busy with household chores that needed doing. It had been Lizzie's job to wash, dye, card, spin, and weave the wool, though Mary and a hired girl took over such tasks after Lizzie and I married. For now, Mary's wheel and loom sit unheeded near the window closest to her bed, and the hired girl was nowhere to be seen. Lizzie had already sanded the floor and the pewter and she had polished the hearthstone. When I walked in with the herbs Lizzie was scrubbing the linen as though venting every fear she had. I pulled Lizzie away from her work, handed her the muslin bag, and told her what the sister-woman said.

Lizzie peered at Mary, sound asleep in her bed, and sighed. "They sound like the women I saw coming home from the Village that day." She studied the herbs in her hands. She smelled them and nodded as though agreeing with the ingredients.

We remained silent as Silas wandered outside. Lizzie watched him through the window as he grabbed handfuls of weeds overtaking his onion patch. She shook her head. "I don't know, James. Those women are…" I understood her meaning. The women are so odd there is no sensible way to describe them.

I picked up the Bible I found on the table and kept myself occupied reading Psalms whilst Lizzie tended to Mary some more. Finally, I persuaded Lizzie to come home. She needs rest and I was afeared she would not get any at Silas' since I'm certain she would have sat up all night watching Mary. After we arrived home she let me care for her. I unfastened her laces and stays, folded her into a blanket warmed near the hearth, and helped her into bed. I brought her a cup of flip and sat with her as she drank it. After she stretched out on the bed I rubbed her back, from her neck down the length of her spine, until she slept. Then I came here to my desk to write it all down since my mind is too full and I cannot yet follow Lizzie into the world of dreams.

4 MARCH 1691, FRIDAY

*A*musements, Father calls them.

He arrived early this morn as the slivery winter sun streaked like disconnected diamonds on the Great Room floor. Tis still thundering these March days as water like arrow-darts pierces the ground. Tis as though God sees the wickedness here and bangs His fists and sheds sharp tears in His knowledge. Father knew the accused would be examined this day by the magistrates—for public spectacle, he said. I did not want to go. I did not want to see. Perhaps tis some foreboding brought on by the dismal weather. When I expressed my concerns, Father shrugged.

"One could say you were conjuring visions of the future with all these worries of what shall come of it," Father said. "The examination is in Town, Son. We are in the middle of Nowhere during these wet, windy months. Tis not London, after all. What other diversions have we?"

"Diversions?" I searched near the bed for my spectacles until Lizzie handed them to me. I set them on my nose and looked at Father, seeing him clearly for the first time since he arrived. "Roman arena games were diversions."

"No one will be eaten by lions this day," Father said.

"Are you certain?"

Father sat in the chair nearest the window and scanned the bleak outdoors. The rain stopped, the ground a trail of ankle-deep mud. Despite the weather, Father was certain the Town would be filled past capacity with curiosity seekers. He wanted to leave early to get a good view.

"I know those in charge of the examinations, James, as do you. Hathorne and Corwin are merchants, as are we."

"They asked you to run for a Council seat," I said. "You should have. Then you might have a place amongst them and you could dismiss this nonsense straight away."

"I'm still too new to these shores. I have made my way to Selectman of our Town Church, but to many I am still unchartered territory. I must be certain I shall have the full backing of those in charge before I can expect to be elected to any kind of governing office."

"But why else did we go through the charade of joining the Church except for you to have the backing of those in charge? You help settle matters for the Church. What other sacrifices might we be expected to make for their tight-fisted, smite-filled God?"

"Are you saying the Anglican God has no smite in him?" Father could not hide his amusement.

"Everyone has smite," I said. "The difference is what we choose to do with it."

"I'm confident in the magistrates, James. They shall see these matters as nonsense and dismiss the cases as they should be dismissed."

"Even though they have been failures in everything else they have done? What of their military commands meant to bring peace with the French and the Indians? There are still battles with the French and the Indians as far as I can tell. What of that ridiculous display where that pirate and his followers were granted their freedom because they are friends with a few of these so-called leaders?"

"Whatever mistakes they have made in the past they shall make up for now, I assure you."

"Then what spectacle are we going to see?" I asked.

"I want to see the afflicted put in their rightful place, at the bottom of a dung heap." Father put such an odd emphasis on the word *afflicted* I wanted to laugh until I saw Lizzie's face. She said nothing, but there was something in the tilt of her head that made me pause. She brought hot cups of tea for Father and me, then refilled the kettle with water.

"Would you like to come, Elizabeth?" Father asked. "The day may provide some entertainment, of which we are rather short here in Massachusetts."

"Nay, thank you, Father. I have much to do here, I think."

"As you wish."

"Will Patience be back today?" I asked.

"I do not think she'll be back today," Lizzie said. "The roads are still hard to travel with the weather so arduous. Besides, her sister Providence is ill again. Prudence is rather poorly now as well."

Father slapped his hand onto his knee, which cracked loudly. "Prudence! I wouldn't mind having that girl tied to a post and whipped."

"Father!" Lizzie's wide eyes betrayed her shock.

"I speak in jest, Daughter, but the girl has tried my patience— no offense to your girl. Prudence has been claiming illness for two days now. Heaven knows what is wrong with her."

"Perhaps she has been poked by the Invisible World," I said.

Father shook his head. "Let us see the nonsense end this day, James." Once again thunder boomed and rain drenched the already desolate landscape, matching my waterlogged mood.

I had dressed in my shirt, breeches, and woolen socks before Father arrived. With him intent on seeing the examinations, and his equal intent that I should accompany him, I pulled on my jerkin, doublet, and shoes. I added my overcoat and wide-brimmed hat, the best I could do to keep the whims of the weather from soaking me through. As Father and I were about to leave, Lizzie held her hand out to me. I grasped her warm fingers and joined her near the hearth.

"Are you certain you do not wish to come?" I asked.

Lizzie shook her head. "I don't want to go. I don't want you to go, either. Tis hard enough for the accused women without everyone looking on. They have been called out though they have hurt no one. The fewer there to witness it, the better. The more tis ignored, the faster it will end and be forgotten, as it should be."

"If only that were true." Father walked to the door, his hand outstretched, ready to press it open. "We are going to support the women, Daughter. Goody Good and Goody Osborne may not be the most endearing women in the Village, but everyone knows they are no harm. I want to be there when they are vindicated."

Lizzie opened her mouth but no words came.

"What, Lizzie?" I asked.

"What do you think caused Reverend Parris' girls to bark and moan when I was there?"

"They were play-acting." Father spat the words.

"But why? No one outside of the family was there but me."

"Precisely," Father said. "You were there. What were they doing before you arrived?"

"I could not say."

"You could not say or you do not know? They are not one and the same, my dear."

Lizzie stared at the gray splotches of desolate sun on the wall. "I do not know."

"You see? Play acting. Tis time this is all exposed as the childish games they are."

Lizzie nodded, but I could tell by her pulled expression she was not convinced.

As I write tis growing late. Whatever sparse sunlight there was this day is gone. I'm surrounded by darkness, the only light from a single candle on my desk and the dwindling fire. Lizzie, exhausted by worries about Mary and her own illness brought on by our future joy, has retired. Yet again I'm distraught by sleeplessness. I cannot possibly write everything I saw at the examination. Twas too much. Too much was said, too many fingers pointed, too many girls writhed and screamed and barked for me to recall it in exacting detail. Reverend Parris took notes, so the events have been documented for everyone to read. And yet, despite my yawns, despite my drooping eyes and the late hour, I'm compelled to write this out. I shall not be able to rest until I do. Tis gnawing my bones as though I too have been infected with Black Magick. I must do something to clear these strange sights from my mind or else I shall go over them and over them until I have fits and see Shapes. I shall write for no other reason than to purge the images from my mind.

When we arrived at the Town House I was reminded that tis yet one more boring, boxy building. Benches and chairs lined the walls but twas so full inside everyone remained standing. At the far end was the long table where the magistrates sat, Hathorne in the center. Some of the Town Selectment sat nearby, though Father stayed by my side, declining his spot with the others. Father and I squeezed in amongst the crowd, lingering close to the door in case we had to leave. Whenever we are engulfed by crowds, Father, who still has nightmares of the skin-searing flames from the Great Fire, prefers to stand where we can escape quickly if need be. Hathorne banged the table and the room silenced.

Goody Good was brought out first. She stood before us in her tatty clothing, her tea-stained coif tipped to the side as though she had one too many sips of something. People pushed forward for a better view and I thought I could not breathe, we were all too close. The pock-faced constable led Goody Good toward the front to face the magistrates. The clerk read the charges of Witchcraft against her, and then we watched as Hathorne scrutinized Goody

Good, a poor woman with a dubious husband, an infant, and a small daughter, Dorcas. Everyone knows that Goody Good smokes a pipe and walks door to door begging alms. She may not be a model Puritan woman, and she argues when she feels herself ill-used, but that does not make one a Witch so far as I know. Finally, Hathorne said, "Sarah Good, what Evil Spirit have you familiarity with?"

"None," Goody Good answered.

"Have you made no contract with the Devil?"

"Nay."

Hathorne gestured toward the afflicted. "Why do you hurt these children?"

What children? I did not see any children. From the moment I walked into the room I sought out the afflicted—Abigail Williams, 11 years of age, and Betty Parris, aged nine. Aye, I reckon they are children. But there was also Ann Putnam the younger and Elizabeth Hubbard, the latter two hardly girls at ages 20 and 17, respectively. Sitting quietly, they seemed harmless enough, ordinary young women watching, listening, whispering to each other, catching the eye of someone seated behind them.

"I do not hurt them," Goody Good said. "I scorn it."

"Who do you employ to do it?" Hathorne asked.

"I employ nobody."

"What creature do you employ then?"

"Nay creature, but I am falsely accused."

"And what happened when you visited the Reverend Parris' home, Goody Good? Did you mutter curses?"

Goody Good shrugged. "I did not mutter curses, but I thanked him for what he gave my child."

"Young Betty Parris and Abigail Williams were hurt by you shortly after you left. How did they come to be so tormented?"

"What do I know?" Goody Good shook her fist in frustration. "You bring others here for Witchcraft yet you charge me with it."

Hathorne's eyes grew small. "Who was it then?"

And that is when I knew what it felt like to be caught inside Dante's Inferno. The afflicted screamed at Goody Good, rolling their eyes, writhing like demons climbing toward some descending darkness. Every neck in the room strained over the heads of those in front, watching, fascinated. The room fell silent as everyone held their breaths. Father stood with his back against the wall, his arms crossed over his chest, his lips pulled into a line of disbelief. Sarah Good appeared entirely unconcerned with the afflicted.

"I do not know," Goody Good said. "It must have been someone you brought here with you."

Hathorne grinned. "We brought you here."

"You brought in two more as well."

"Who was it that tormented the children?"

"Twas Osborn."

The afflicted stopped screaming and folded their hands neatly in their laps. When Hathorne turned toward them, Ann Putnam said both Osborn and Good were hurting them there in the court-room. How, if the accused stand here and the afflicted sit there? Osborn and Good employed their Shapes to do it, Ann Putnam said.

"So one need not stand over a person to commit violence?" I whispered. "How convenient. One would think one must be at least within arm's reach to pinch and prod someone."

Standing opposite Father and me were the three sister-women squinting at the afflicted. The sisters looked as I remembered them, dressed as other Village women in simple garments, their reddish hair covered by tea-stained coifs. I shuddered, thinking how they arrived at Silas' to give us the herbs for Mary when no one had gone to them for help. Then I remembered what they said to Lizzie. As though she read my thoughts, the tallest sister grinned at me as she had when she handed me the herbs. Fascinated by the sisters, I paid little attention to the rest of the examination. I lost all interest when it became clear that Goody Good had no chance to redeem herself. Hathorne had decided that she was touched by the Devil and that was all he needed to know. The sisters' eyes moved from Hathorne to the woman under question to the afflicted, from one to the other and back again as though they watched sport. The accused said what she could to try to save herself whilst Hathorne twisted her words any which way. Through it all, the afflicted wailed and writhed. Twas like being at theater in London watching actors pull faces on the stage. I turned back to the sisters but they were gone.

I had heard enough. I moved quietly toward the door, careful not to step on anyone though twas hard since everyone was pressed together. I needn't have worried since the onlookers paid me little heed. Outside, I walked round to where the sisters had been standing and found the area empty. I looked toward the road in the distance and no one was there. The women had vanished. I thought for a moment to yell at the magistrates *I have found the women you're seeking. They are three sisters who shrink with age and have red-blue hair and show up unexpectedly with herbs they claim will heal the sick.* But I said nothing. I do not know for certain that they are Witches, and I would not want to accuse innocent people. They should not suffer arrest for being mindful of what goes on round them. I went back inside and found my place against the wall near Father. Sarah Osborn was brought in next for questioning and twas much the same. No matter how she tried to defend herself, Hathorne twisted her words until she could no longer say she did not hurt the girls since someone must have.

When Parris' slave, Tituba, was brought out, she admitted to everything Hathorne put before her. She sent her Shape to hurt Parris' girls after she was threatened by a man. She was threatened by Goody Good and Goody Osborn. She was bidden by a black dog to serve him, and she was told by a tall, white-haired man in black to sign her name to the Devil's book. The man hounded her, offering her pretty things like a yellow bird whilst mean red cats nipped at her ankles. The four afflicted shrieked as though someone punctured them with pitchforks.

Tituba, bent forward, perspiring, could say no more. "I am blind now," she said. "I cannot see." She groped before her, her hands outstretched like a sightless woman struggling to find her way. "Goody Good and Goody Osborn hurt me."

Hathorne nodded. He had what he wanted. He and Corwin sent Tituba and Goody Osborn to the Salem jail to await trial whilst Goody Good was sent to the jail in Ipswich with her infant. Goody Good's young daughter, Dorcas, was sent to live with the dubious husband. Father and I heard whispers that Dorcas, all of four years old, has been pressing the junior Ann Putnam to sign the Devil's book. That Witchcraft is a deadly offense was not spoken of but the knowledge hung round the women's heads like nooses. Father was so certain the accusations would be laid to rest this day, but twas not to be. Spectral evidence is allowed and the afflicted are believed when they say the Shapes of the accused are pinching them from across the room. Even the most trusted of Puritan ministers, Cotton Mather amongst them, questioned the use of the Invisible as a means of prosecuting Witches. But Hathorne and Corwin are convinced that everything the afflicted say is true.

Father and I left in silence. What was there to say? When I arrived home Lizzie pressed me for details, but I did not know how to explain everything I saw. Even reading what I have written here seems wrong, like I am lying, like I am making this up to tell a story like *Don Quixote* or *The Pilgrim's Progress*. So far, all I have said to Lizzie is the women were being held for further questioning, which is not a lie, quite.

"What else must they be questioned about?" Lizzie asked.

I shrugged, nodded, and shook my head. Twas no response, I know, and Lizzie shall not accept it as an answer for long. She shall find out, one way or another, and it might as well be from me that she learns what has happened and not from gossip or hearsay. But I shall worry about that another day. Now, I must sleep.

10 MARCH 1691, THURSDAY

*W*here is the springtime? The sun? The warmth? At home, in England, March can be warm and sunny or cold and even snowy. In like a lion, out like a lamb. But we are still in the clutches of the lion's great claws here in the Massachusetts Bay with sharp, biting rains and frigid winds. I wonder if the weather is merely an external manifestation of our inner turmoils.

Father cannot get enough of it, listening to Parris spew his venom about the Devil as though the minister were personal friends with the Fiend, as though the minister himself were responsible for unleashing the Evil fate of his daughter, his niece, and the others who are now afflicted. I have told Father I shall no longer accompany him to watch the examinations. I fear I am becoming paranoid, searching everywhere, particularly at night. In the darkness, when there is naught but distant stars and silver strands of moonlight, I feel myself trailed by the Man so many swear is upon the Village, spreading his turbulence amongst guilty and innocent alike. At Lecture today, with our minister Noyes presiding, I saw the three sisters again. Noyes is generally an affable fellow, but his sermons have become robust in their anger toward the Devil and his minions. Again, I was more interested in the sister-women. With their squinting eyes and their arms crossed over their chests they appeared petulant as Noyes brooded aloud about how Salem is consumed by the Devil. Parris continued along the same theme.

"When I say Salem has been overtaken by the Devil," Parris said, "I mean any wicked Angel or Spirit. Sometimes Satan refers to the prince or head of the Evil spirits, or fallen Angels. Sometimes it means vile and wicked persons, the worst of such, who for their villainy and impiety, do most resemble devils and wicked spirits. Like Judas Iscariot, these people are not devils by nature, but devils in their likeness and operation." Parris reminded his listeners that Christ's Church "consists of good and bad, as a garden that has weeds as well as flowers, not only true saints but hypocrites who give lip service to Christ but prefer earthly goals above Him and above His ordinances."

Residents of the Town grimaced as they left, nodding towards those from the Village, discreet in their whispers. Villagers pointed in the direction of those from the Town. Townspeople told stories about how many in the Village—men, women, even young girls and boys—were bitten and slapped by beasts of the Invisible World, Evildoers in the Shapes of neighbors and friends. Farmers, as they climbed into their wagons, claimed they had been abused by Goody Good's Shape or Goody Osborne's Specter. My ears hurt from listening to it all. I had work to do with the ledgers, but Father saw I could not possibly calculate numbers after the Lecture so he sent me home.

As I opened the door I heard girlish giggles. Mary was there, and Silas as well. Lizzie was laughing with Mary, ladling some broth into a bowl. Mary accepted the broth Lizzie fed her, taking large bites of an Indian bannock between spoonfuls. Silas sat before the fire, puffing on his pipe, staring into the flames.

Lizzie smiled when she saw me. "Look, James. Mary is well."

I sat beside Mary and accepted a bowl of broth from Lizzie. "You look well, Mary. Are you feeling better?"

"I am." Mary spun round as if to demonstrate her point. Lizzie tried to feed Mary more broth, but the girl shook her head. "Nay, nay, Lizzie. I want to play with my doll." Mary pulled the rag doll Lizzie made from the waistband of her skirt.

"Have you named her?" I asked.

"Her name is Jezebel," Mary answered.

"Mary." Lizzie could not hide her concern. "Do you think that is the most appropriate name for your doll? Do you even know who Jezebel was?"

"She was a queen," Mary said. "From the Book of Kings."

Silas puffed his pipe, the room filling with white-gray smoke rings that combined with smoke from the hearth to make my eyes sting. "She was indeed a queen, Mary. She told her husband, King Ahab, to abandon worship of the Lord, Our God, and worship false prophets. Jezebel wanted the prophets of the Lord, Our God, to be executed."

"She also ordered the death of a law-abiding landowner whose land her husband coveted, if I remember correctly," I said.

"What happened to her?" Mary looked bright-eyed, as she had when Lizzie told her the story of the two sisters. Lizzie noticed this as well and she became concerned. I saw it in the attentive way she watched Mary.

"Jezebel was thrown from a high window and wild dogs consumed her flesh." Silas tapped his pipe onto the table and set it aside. "Is that what you want for your doll?" Mary shook her head, and Silas nodded. "Perhaps you ought best to find another name, Mary. We don't want her confused with someone who disobeyed God."

Mary held the rag doll close. "I'll think of a new name, Pa." Mary brought the doll to my desk, where she whispered to her inanimate friend. Perhaps they sought a new name together.

"I'm glad she is feeling better," I said to Lizzie.

"I think the fact that Pa hasn't been bringing her to hear Parris has helped." Lizzie spoke softly, not wishing Mary to overhear.

"I believe you are right," I said. "After everything I heard this day, I'm certain we would all do better if we did not have to hear the Reverend Mr. Parris preach."

"Mistress Putnam stopped by the farm this morn," Silas said, to no one in particular.

"Mistress Ann Putnam?" Lizzie asked. Silas nodded. He was nonchalant in his manner, and I would not have found anything odd in his statement except for the confused way Lizzie looked at him. "What did she want?"

"She asked after you, Elizabeth. She wanted to know how you were enjoying your new life in the Town. She noticed you at Lecture last week in your embroidered cape and your gold threading and wanted to know how you fancy being Mistress Wentworth, wife of a well-to-do merchant."

"Twas a present from me," I said. "I'm allowed to give my wife gifts. What does Mistress Putnam care about such things?"

"She only mentioned it in passing," Silas said. "I don't think she meant anything by it. And you know how those people are." By those people, I assumed Silas referred to the Puritans. "They do like their things unadorned."

"Our Lizzie's cape isn't so very fancy," Mary said. The girl had been paying more attention than we thought. "Mistress Boxley wore gold and silver threading in her cape at Lecture, and her dress had slashes in the sleeves. Four of them. And she wears rubies round her neck and sapphires round her fingers! Lizzie is very plain by comparison."

"Material things aren't important, Mary," Lizzie said. "They are nice, certainly, but they don't matter, not really. What is important is that we love our God and our Family as well as those less fortunate. Helping others is far more important than how many things we own that sparkle."

"Don't be silly, Lizzie," Mary said. "Of course nice things

matter. How else could the Devil entice the Witches if they didn't care for luxurious clothing and shiny jewels? The Witches covet the finest things, and Satan agrees to furnish them as long as they do his bidding. Isn't that right, Jezebel?"

Mary held the doll close to her ear as though listening for an answer. Lizzie said nothing. She watched Mary play with the rag doll and sighed.

14 MARCH 1691, MONDAY

The night grows darker whilst the drooping sun falls plum, pink, and gold behind the low-tide bay. I have been sitting here, quill in hand, ink dripping onto the blotter, for an hour or more. I feel like a blotter myself. Tis as though every thought I have ever had has been left somewhere, out there, in the stable with the horses, perhaps. Lizzie putters round the house lighting candles so I can see well enough to write by, though I accomplish little. Ideas will not straighten themselves out in my head no matter how hard I twist and tug. Tis as though I have never known any words ever.

As I write this nonsense Lizzie chats to me about how she cannot get over the honey sweet smell from the beeswax candles, she being used to the foul smell of tallow in the rushlights. She thinks, she says as she settles with her long-hooked needles to knit a jumper for me, that she shall bring more candles to Silas and Mary since she is certain they must have used up their portion by now. Unfortunately, Mary is poorly again and Lizzie wants to give her sister every comfort. Lizzie asks if I mind the expense. Of course, I do not. I would never begrudge Lizzie anything she asked, least of all some candles for her father and ill sister. There is no expense I would spare to bring Lizzie even the smallest happiness.

She continues to speak, and I'm being a bad husband since I'm not paying attention to her words—I'm simply enjoying the sound of her. I love the sweet melody of her voice. Her words send me spiraling into a sing-song lull of joy. I hear the harmony in her undertone and I lose all sense of time and place, elevated to where only comfort exists. Lizzie smiles at me, aware that I'm not listening. She knows me so well.

Then, for a reason I cannot name, I worry that perhaps Mary has been bewitched by the Man after all. Villagers insist that they have been touched by Magick, the Devil spreading his Evil in Salem through those gullible enough to believe in his enticements. If they are servants, Satan promises they will work no more. If they are poor, he promises fripperies. If they are in want of a husband, he keeps their beds warm. I glance round in my need to know that no one is close enough to read what I write or eavesdrop on my thoughts, which is foolishness, I know. But then I think that the Man, in his Invisible Form, could be in this very room. Again, I think of the sister-women, and I think of the herbs they handed me. I wonder who they are—

Lizzie interrupts me and I must write down what she says. She has been looking over my shoulder to see what I'm writing (she can read almost everything on her own now) and she said, "I gave Mary Grace the herbs the sister-women left for her. I was so desperate, James. Mary was so poorly and I didn't know what else to do. I boiled the herbs into tea and gave it to Mary to drink like the woman said. She drank it all and said it tasted sour. After she finished it she slept, and when she awoke she said she felt better. She looked better too."

"Aye, my love. I saw myself she was better."

"Then why is she ill again?"

I held my hands out to Lizzie and she slid her arms round my neck and leaned forward so that our foreheads touched. I patted my lap, and she sat, her arms still locked round me.

"I do not know," I said, "but whatever causes Mary's illness, tis not your fault, Lizzie. You are doing all you can for her."

"Perhaps I did wrong to give her the herbs."

"What if you did right? What if the herbs made her better?"

"But she's ill again."

"Then we shall make her well again."

Lizzie sits here still, her head against my chest. With the rhythmic rise and fall of her chest, I think she has dozed off. In a moment, I shall carry her to bed so she can rest more easily.

I write this with my chin resting atop her head with one arm round her and the other stretched at an odd angle to draw these words. I wonder if I should tell her what I have heard about Goody Nurse. I'm afeared it will hurt Lizzie somewhere deep if she knows her friend is being called out.

Father does not seem concerned. We spoke of it at the warehouse this morn. "Tis only because her name was suggested to Abigail Williams," he said. "She seems highly suggestible, the Reverend's niece. Someone says a name to her, and suddenly that person afflicts her."

"Goody Nurse has been so ill of late," I said. "Lizzie told me that Goody Nurse hardly leaves her hearth these days. Who would think to mention her in connection with this?" I walked toward the barrels lined against the wall. Half of the barrels were filled with rum and ready to be rolled onto my father's ship and sold across the sea whilst the other half were filled with Barbados molasses ready to be stored in the next warehouse where tis fermented in hot water with sugar and yeast, then cooled and siphoned to make more rum. For a moment, as I stood there hearing the squawking seagulls and the shouting sailors, the sickly sweet fumes from the molasses overcame my senses. I was befuddled and imagined Lizzie and me stowing away on one of Father's ships bound for England. We could hide amongst the barrels,

Lizzie and I, and then we would be home. But tis a long journey across a cruel ocean, and in my right mind I cannot think that now is a good time for such travels.

To distract myself, I asked, "Tis only Abigail Williams who speaks against Goody Nurse?"

Father shook his head. "Ann Putnam junior, as well, I hear. But I believe tis the Williams girl who is most to be feared. There is a rumor that the Reverend Mr. Lawson paid a visit to the Parrises this morn. Lawson said Abigail ran about the room, her arms spread like wings, shouting *Whish! Whish!* as though she would take flight. Abigail claimed that the Shape of Rebecca Nurse was beside her. She said Goody Nurse demanded that she sign the Devil's book. Abigail stared at Nurse's Shape and yelled *I won't take it!*"

What happens here is hardly new, I know. Such accusations happened in England and across Europe. Thirty years ago in Connecticut parents believed their daughter was possessed by a woman named Goody Ayres. Four people met their deaths, convicted as Witches. Fifteen years before that, also in Connecticut, a suspected Witch, Alice Young, was sent to the gallows. To the Puritans, if tis not in the Bible, it does not exist. If tis in the Bible, then tis God-given truth. And the Bible does enjoy its Witches. Father reminded me of the line from Exodus, "Thou shalt not suffer a Witch to live." He also told me of Leviticus, "A man or woman that hath a familiar Spirit, or that is a Wizard, shall surely be put to death." When stringent people run the land, those who do not conform become outsiders, or worse, dangerous. Anyone considered a threat to the established way of life is suspect. Beyond this is a simple fact: people believe in Witches. They believe in Magick. Most importantly, they believe in the Devil. Perhaps I should too.

Lizzie stirs. I brush her silken curls from her cheek, and she settles back into sleep. I was about to lift her from the chair when I saw a shadow outside. I saw some movement but decided twas merely a reflection of the candlelight. Then I recognized him, the man I saw lurking before, the long-faced one with the wicked smile and the wisps of gray in his red-brown hair. I wonder if there is something sinister in the way he pulls his black cloak close to his chin, something avaricious in the way he pulls his hat to his nose so his face is all but hidden. Again, I wonder: is *that* the Man everyone is searching for? If he is, should I tell everyone I have found him? And then my rational mind kicks in and I think the same as I did with the sister-women. The man does not seem sinister, quite. He is curious, perhaps, as though he knows me, or wants to know me, which in itself is not a hanging offense.

Lizzie is awake. She stands, stretches her arms toward the gables, accentuating the curves beneath her shift. She walks from the Great Room into our bedroom, shaking her dark curls loose round her shoulders. I think it must be time to drop this pretense of writing great thoughts, as though a merchant's son should have anything of importance to say. Tis a far more enjoyable prospect to help Lizzie's flimsy shift float freely to the floor.

.

18 MARCH 1691, FRIDAY

*I*s there a God, I wonder? Is there someone high above us, looking down, deciding if we go to Heaven or Hell? Is there some Intelligent Being? Some Thing, bigger than we could ever understand, mere humans that we are? For all my book learning, I do not know. Where does belief come from? Do we have belief because there truly is a God and we struggle to make sense of Him? Is belief merely passed down, one generation to the next, because our ancestors decided there must be some Supernatural reason for Life and Death and everything in between?

Locke describes the human mind as a blank slate which is filled with ideas through experience. He questions how we come to understand ourselves through religion. Locke does not believe in innate knowledge since no knowledge is accepted by all human beings. Therefore, our knowledge of God must have been learned. Whatever some claim to know about Him, no matter how firmly they are convinced, there are others with their own ideas.

I cannot say for certain *Aye, there is a God*, just as I cannot say *Nay, there is nothing up there but sky*. Lizzie believes in a benevolent Almighty. I'm not yet convinced. I want to be, but there is too much I do not know, too much I cannot see. Is this a God of Love whose Light shines in every human being? Or is this a God of hailstones and Hellfire? Is the God of Peace the same God who allows people to be tied to a wagon and dragged to their deaths because they believe differently? Or the same God who allows human beings to be branded and sold like cattle? And who allows the afflicted to make claims against friends and neighbors, saying their Invisible Shapes do violence in the night? Who allows sweet, young girls to die for no reason at all?

Rereading my words, I see that these are disconnected thoughts brought on by my morose mood. But the death of a loved one can do that to you.

Two nights ago the brass knocker banged against the door in angry thuds. Lizzie and I were asleep and we jolted upright at the thunderous sound. I made my way to the Great Room, careful not to trip over a chair or anything else since I had not put on my spectacles. Outside was Goodman Henderson, a farmer from the Village, his fist in the air, ready to pound until he had our attention.

"Mr. Wentworth," Henderson said, panting from his effort. "You and your wife must come to the Village. Right now you must come."

"Is it my father-in-law?" I asked.

"Tis Mary." Lizzie stood behind me, drawing her shawl close round her shoulders. "It must be Mary."

Henderson's cloak flapped in the quickness of his movement. "How did you know?"

"I don't know." Lizzie spoke as though she had left her voice elsewhere. "Is she dead?"

"Nay," said the farmer. "But we don't know how much longer she has. She grew poorly so quickly that there weren't much we could do."

Lizzie and I dressed and grabbed our cloaks. Henderson helped me hitch Euripides to the wagon, and Lizzie and I were off. It felt like forever, getting to the Village from the Town. Lizzie was silent during the ride. I tried to pull her out of herself, to talk to her, but she looked as though she needed to be left to her thoughts. She jumped from the still-moving wagon when we pulled in front of Silas' house. She tripped in her haste, but she grabbed hold of Euripides. The horse did not appear to mind Lizzie holding onto his neck. She was inside before I was out of the wagon.

Candles flickered in Silas' hall and the room glowed soft. An older woman leaned over Mary, and when she lifted her head I saw twas Rebecca Nurse tending the girl. Goodman Henderson looked in, saw Mary unconscious, then backed out the door, making his excuses. When I offered to pay him for his trouble he waved his hand with a halting movement that made me think he was offended.

"Goodman Jones is my neighbor," Henderson said. "We do such things for neighbors in the Village." And then he was gone.

"You didn't need to come," Lizzie said to Goody Nurse. "I know you're unwell yourself these days. Please, I beg you, go home and rest."

"I've been restin', my dear. I've been puttin' these old feet up afore the hearth. When I heard your little one was poorly, I had to see what I could do."

Mary groaned, and Lizzie knelt next to her sister, stroking the girl's cheeks. Mary looked to be sleeping, but twas a fitful sleep, full of twists and turns and grimaces. She looked like the writhing afflicted I saw at the examinations. Lizzie called Mary's name but the girl did not respond. Lizzie shook her sister's shoulders. "Mary! Mary!" But Mary did not answer.

I stood helplessly by whilst Goody Nurse bathed Mary's forehead with a wet rag. Lizzie sat on the bed beside her sister, holding Mary's hand. Silas lingered in the background, oddly detached, as though he watched an ill stranger. He stood at the far end of the room, glancing toward his daughter occasionally to see if anything had changed. He puffed his pipe, long inhalations, releasing smoke rings that evaporated as soon as they hit the air. I could not blame him for his disconnection. We must find some way to handle things that distress us. Smoking is as good a way as any.

I walked outside to watch the sun break as a thin, white line. I heard voices in the distance and walked toward the farmland behind Silas' house. Two men I was not acquainted with were watching me. I moved toward them.

"Excuse me," I said. "Can I help you?"

They tittered, something about wanting to see how Goodman Jones' daughter was, and then they meandered away, glancing back in my direction, their heads close, speaking amongst themselves as they disappeared round the bend. I wished I had extrasensory hearing so I could know what they said. I sighed, thinking there was no end to people's curiosity. By the time I was back inside Goody Nurse had gone, her husband having collected her. Through the open door I saw them driving deeper into the Village.

I sat near Lizzie but she did not notice me. She did not leave Mary's side for hours. Finally, when the day was bright, I said, "Why don't you go for a walk, my love, or at least have a lie-down?"

I took Lizzie into my arms and held her close. My shoulder was wet with her tears. After her weeping subsided, she pulled away. "I think you're right, James. I'll go for a walk."

"Shall I accompany you?"

She glanced back at Mary, too still for comfort. "Nay. I need air is all. Besides, I need you to stay with Mary. I'd feel better knowing you were watching her."

I wanted to stay with Lizzie, but I was pleased that she trusted me with her most precious possession—her sister. Lizzie opened the door, looked again at Mary, managed a weak smile, then disappeared outside. I stood by the open door and watched her walk round the field. Silas was already outside directing the two oxen as they dragged the plow behind them. I went back inside and pulled the rickety chair, with one leg shorter than the others, closer to

Mary. I looked into the girl's face and worried. On the one hand, she appeared to be sleeping, her eyes closed, her head turned to the side, but she was so pale and her breath was shallow. Once I feared she stopped breathing but then her chest moved again. I got up carefully, not wishing the chair to creak, and pulled the book I brought from my cloak pocket.

I grabbed the first book I set my hand on—*Paradise Lost*. As I flipped the pages, I realized I could not have brought up a more inappropriate story. Milton wrote of the Devil and Adam and Eve. The Devil, after his banishment, and with his way with words, creates a legion of followers and determines to destroy the Garden of Eden. Even Milton thought the Devil could cajole others to his bidding. The three-day battle between devils and Angels results in the corruption of Adam and Eve. The Devil rejoices in his victory. Many believe he enjoys such a victory in Salem. I closed the book, I could not force myself to keep reading and watched Mary in her lugubrious sleep.

I must have dozed off. I was startled awake by Lizzie rushing into the room. She stood before the door as though keeping it closed with her body, slight though she is even with child. Her eyes were wide. She turned her head as though listening for something. I stretched my hand toward her.

"What is it, Lizzie?"

"I think I've been followed."

"Who has followed you?"

She shook her head, then laughed. "Twas the strangest thing. Do you remember when the three sisters came here with the herbs for Mary? After I gave Mary the tea she became better, so I thought perhaps they could help me with more of the same, or perhaps they had some different medicinals they might give me. I walked to their house, the one I saw with Patience when I visited the Parrises, and I told the sisters Mary was ill again. The tallest sister asked me about her symptoms, I told her, and she gave me the herbs. She told me the same thing she told you, that I should boil the herbs in water and serve the tea to Mary. As I was leaving, I saw Goodman Henderson staring at me. I told him I was seeking medicine for my sister, and he asked from whom. I pointed to the house and told him from the sisters who live there, or at least I think they are sisters. Goodman Henderson stared through me as though I were mad. His mouth opened like an O whilst he hopped from foot to foot. Then I showed him the muslin bag." Lizzie's shoulders slumped as she placed the herbs on the table before me. "I've never seen anyone move so fast. He was down the road before I could say more. Then I felt as though I were being watched all the way back here."

It had been drizzling, and though she was not soaked through, Lizzie was wet enough, and cold. I added more fuel to the fire and prompted her to sit in the chair closest to the hearth. She stared into the flames.

"What do you think it means?" she asked. "You've seen the sisters. I've seen them. No one else sees them."

"Of course they see them," I said. "Or perhaps they are Witches after all."

"Perhaps we're the ones who are afflicted." Lizzie tried to laugh but the sound caught in her throat. Mary groaned and Lizzie looked in her direction. "Or Mary."

Mary thrashed in her bed, arms and legs flailing as though she were beating someone away. "Nay! Nay!" Mary cried. "I won't do it! I won't!"

Silas came inside as Mary cried out. He stood near the wall, still not willing to get too close to his youngest daughter. "What is going on here?" he asked.

"Perhaps you should send for the doctor," I said.

"I sent for him before you came," Silas said. "He's not come yet. Goody Nurse said he had an emergency at the other end of the Village."

"There are other doctors," I said.

"Doctor Griggs is the best," Silas said. "Everyone says so."

Lizzie added water and the herbs into a kettle and set it over the fire to boil. She gave the concoction time to brew, then poured some into a mug and brought it to Mary's lips.

"Here, Mary," she said. "This will help you feel better. Just as it did last time."

Mary swallowed a few drops before falling back into a death-like sleep. Lizzie pulled her sister into her arms, rocking the girl as she shall soon rock our child. As sunlight burst full upon the day, people from the Farms stopped by to see how Mary fared. They cast sidelong glances at Lizzie, and at me, whispered polite words to Silas, and said prayers over Mary. Someone, a farmer I'm not familiar with, asked Silas if he wanted to send for Reverend Parris. Silas shook his head.

"Not yet," he said.

The herbs did nothing. We sat unmoving, without speaking, barely breathing, sorrow hanging over us like the dull gray sky. Then, as the sun disappeared and all was dark, Mary died. Twas tranquil, which is all we can hope for in the end. Mary looked as though she slept peacefully, with a content smile on her lips. Lizzie held her sister close to her heart and would not let go. A guttural sob, like an injured animal's cry, escaped Lizzie's lips and she crumpled over the small form that had been her sister, in many ways her daughter. An anguished storm passed over my Angel's delicate features and I did not know how to help her.

We sat with the body for a long while. Then Silas said he wanted to be alone with his little girl for the last time on this Earth. Lizzie asked him if he was sure he wanted to be left alone, but he said he was sure. He sent us home, and though Lizzie was reluctant to leave, I took her away. We arrived back a short time ago. I held Lizzie whilst she wept herself to sleep. Now, she is resting.

Dear God, if You do exist, if You are there, I beg You. Let our beloved Mary rest in peace.

21 MARCH 1691, MONDAY

We buried Mary this day. Ashes to ashes. Dust to dust. To the clay of the Earth we shall all return. Perhaps tis to some purpose, but I cannot say right now what that purpose might be.

Twas hard, too hard. Some say we should not become attached to small children since they die so often, but I cannot see how you do not attach your heart to your own. We love our small ones no matter how little time they have on Earth. We cannot help it. They are closest to God, after all, but newly come from Heaven. And twas heartening to see many from the Village, even some from the Town, come to pay their respects. When people asked how she died, we had no answer. I'm not sure it matters. Mary is not here anymore. What else is there to know? Lizzie aches and that is my main concern. Father told me of grumbling amongst some Villagers, he did not say who, complaining of a bewitched girl buried alongside God-fearing people. The mere thought of such slander infuriates me. Who are they to say Mary was bewitched? They did not know her at all. But that seems to be all Salemites are about nowadays. Very well. Let them say their bit over there and leave mine to me.

"Tis planting season," Silas said at the gravesite. Twas as though the fact of Mary's death had not hit him. I nodded, not knowing how else to reply. Silas said he needed to get home. He needed to finish plowing his field.

"Doesn't the soil have to dry first?" Father asked. "I do not know how anything can dry in this wet weather."

Silas shrugged. "The rocks need to be loosened and readied for seeding. The ground needs to be harrowed."

"I shall hire help for you, Silas," Father said. "You need to rest now."

Silas nodded but said nothing.

Father, Silas, and I stood over the freshly covered grave shivering under a soggy sky whispering windy secrets in our ears. I wished the sun would break through somehow, a sign from the Almighty that He understood our sorrow, but there was only drizzle. Perhaps those were God's tears at the loss of a much-loved life. I kept my eye on Lizzie, who stood stone-still over the land where Mary lay as though she hardly understood what she saw.

After the service Lizzie and I brought Silas here so he would not be alone. Father came to help Silas get settled. Silas is not keen on the idea of staying in the Town. He says he must return to his farm soon, many tasks need tending, but meanwhile he sits as though he does not know what else to do. I told him that he is welcome to stay as long as he wishes. But Silas says nay, he must return to the Village, and we do not argue with him. The poor man looks lethargic, as though he hardly has strength enough to lift his pipe to his lips. There are moments when I think the life has been expelled from him and he has become inanimate. He stares into a cupful of rum but does not drink. Who can blame him? His little girl is gone.

Lizzie suffers the opposite of Silas. She is consumed by a furious need to keep moving. She cooks the suet and polishes the silver and sows the seeds for our pumpkin patch. Busy, Lizzie says. She must keep busy. Patience came to help however she could, but no matter how much I begged Lizzie to allow Patience to stay, Lizzie was determined that the girl should leave. Lizzie asked me to pay Patience's regular wages, which I did, and Patience was on her way. Tis as though Lizzie thinks that if she stops, for even a moment, Mary's loss will overwhelm her and she shall float out to the ocean where she shall remain drowned by misery forever.

Tis hard, this helplessness. I want to do something to take Lizzie's pain away. I would take her agony, her torments, her wounds all upon myself if I could. Yet no matter how much I love her, I cannot take the burden of losing her sister onto my shoulders. What can you do when someone you love dies? Mary's cheerful voice and her childish laughter are gone forever. We shall never see her play with her doll, watch her make soap, or hear her sing a favorite hymn again. We can see her and hear her in our hearts, certainly. But when Lizzie wants to speak to Mary, she shall not be there. When Silas wants to laugh at his young daughter for wanting to help plow the fields despite her small size, he cannot, except in memory. I shall miss the child too. She was shy of me when I first went round to the Joneses' to court Lizzie. Mary would not speak to me at all before the wedding, and even after it took some time of prying responses from her, mainly through bribery with sticks of licorice root. When she realized I did not mean to bite her, and I enjoyed a good laugh myself, she warmed to me and soon enough called me Brother. I shall miss the dear girl.

I am afeared of bringing up Mary's odd illness to Lizzie. I cannot help but think how obsessed Mary was with Parris' sermons. I cannot help but wonder if Parris' odious words had something to do with Mary's death. Of course, I shall never know for certain, but I wonder.

·   ·   ·

FATHER MANAGED TO PULL SILAS FROM HIS SHELL WHEN HE returned this eve. Father is good at such things. He could be in a roomful of people and notice the one shy person. Father always sits beside that person, tells stories, makes jokes, and soon the person is as forthcoming as the chattiest man in the room. With several cups of rum and some broth in his belly, Silas opened up to Father in a way he had not since before Mary's passing. They spoke of farming, of which Father knows little, and they spoke of the barrels of rum Father is storing in our warehouse. And then, when the house grew quiet, Father brought up a new topic of conversation.

"I was not able to attend the meeting this day..." Father paused, though we knew why he had not attended. He was watching Mary being buried with the rest of us. "There was a team of Village representatives at the Town meeting."

"Did they cut the Village loose, then?" I asked.

"Not as the Villagers wished," Father said. "The Villagers are exempt from supporting the Town ministers as long as they pay other expenses they share in common with the Town."

Father kept talking, I think, for the same reason Lizzie kept moving—in an unsuccessful attempt to keep the sorrow away.

"There was a new Witchcraft examination this day," Father said. "This one had to be moved to the Meeting House since so many wanted to watch. They say fields on the Farms are going untended whilst so many are preoccupied by the proceedings. They say there are more than ten afflicted now. Constable Herrick has Martha Corey in custody at Ingersoll's."

Lizzie dropped a platter and a crash! filled the room. "Goody Corey? What has she done?"

Father retrieved the platter for Lizzie. "Besides being a cantankerous old scold? Nothing, I'm sure. She had some sort of salve when they searched her house, which they are saying is a magick potion, made personally by the Devil, no doubt. Whilst she was being examined, Goody Corey asked to go to prayer and that put everyone in a distemper."

"Why was that a problem?" I asked. "That should be exactly what the Puritans would want from her, to pray."

"You know how tis here," Father said. "Women cannot speak for themselves. Their menfolk must speak for them. And several people visited Goody Nurse as well. They said they were there to check on her."

"More like they were there to catch her out," I said.

"The visitors tried to get her to admit to Witchcraft. Goody Nurse told them she was surprised that she had been called out. She prayed for Parris' girls, though why she would pray for them when they're speaking against her is beyond me."

Lizzie dropped into the closest chair, her head in her hands. I shook my head at Father, who understood my meaning. He approached Lizzie, tentatively.

"My dearest Daughter," Father said. "Forgive me. I did not think."

Lizzie looked at me. "Did you know that Rebecca has been called out?" I nodded. "Oh, James..."

When Lizzie shuddered, I took her into my arms, hoping the closeness would comfort her. Silas filled his mug with rum and turned away. Father muttered apologies and backed toward the door. When he was gone, Silas disappeared into the room behind the hearth and shut the door. Twas a long time before Lizzie's trembles subsided.

"What is happening, James?" Her hand went to the bump where our babe grows.

"I do not know, my love. But now tis time for you to rest." I carried her to our bed, helped her undress, and sat with my arms round her until she slept, which has become our habit of late. I'm happy to hold her close as long as she wants, whenever she wants. I do not know how much I help her, truly, but when we are close together I feel as though I'm doing what I can for her.

Tis hard, but life continues. That is what our child represents, is it not? The circle of life. Ends and beginnings. Sorrows and joys. Moments and memories. In the end, what else do we have? We must cherish the experiences that create those remembrances, the bad and the good, since those are the moments that make a life, even if we do not realize it at the time.

22 MARCH 1691, TUESDAY

I drove Silas back to the Village. He appeared too lethargic to move his arms, but when we broke our fast this morn he insisted that he needed to return to his farm. Lizzie and I tried to persuade him to stay with us, but he was determined. Before I left him at his house, I told him again that he could live in the Town and Father will make certain that he has everything he needs. But Silas stood firm.

"I'm not comfortable in the Town. I don't belong there."

"You belong with your family, and we are in the Town. I know Lizzie would like very much for you to stay with us."

"Thank you, but nay."

He hesitated near the wagon, perhaps wondering at the emptiness inside. He nodded at me, then shuffled away. He stopped, reaching his hand toward the blood-ochre door bright against the dark wood slats. Finally, he shut himself inside. I stopped at Ingersoll's for some refreshment, thinking about the prisoners held there. The white building with the red brick chimney and a pale blue door looks like other structures here—simple, square, symmetrical. I could not shake the thought of Ingersoll's role in the unfolding drama. I finished my ale as quickly as I could and returned to the wagon. I grabbed Euripides' reins and the horse hopped from foot to foot anticipating a "Walk on!"

There's a lot of nothing between Village and Town. Farms populate the area, along with rivers, rocks, and more nothing. Euripides knows the way home and needed no guidance from me, so my thoughts wandered to Lizzie. The loss of Mary weighs heavily on her. I still cannot think of something I can do to help alleviate her misery. I have to accept that the loss of Mary is a wound that will never fully heal and there may be nothing I can do to help Lizzie through this sadness. To distract myself, I thought of Cambridge and King's College, punting on the River Cam, drifting and dreaming whilst rounding the water's serpentine bend. I thought of the Chapel, similar to other churches in England, the stained glass windows, the high arch of the ceiling, the hush of reverence inside. I thought of hours spent hunched over books in the Library, reading everything I could get my hands on as fast as my eyes could skim the words, desperate to absorb the knowledge as though for sustenance. I thought of long hours sitting aside the riverbank engaged in lively debates about literature, philosophy, and religion with friends. When it began to drizzle I pulled my coat closer to my ears and my hat closer to my nose. Euripides paid me little heed as he looked straight before him, his long head swinging from side to side, shaking his wet mane as though tis no mind, tis only a little water, after all.

I should have gone straight home after I arrived in the Town. I should have rushed to get back to Lizzie. Instead, I stopped by Father's. He has already told me to take as much time away from our business as I need, but perhaps Lizzie is onto something. Perhaps keeping busy is the best tonic of all.

I settled Euripides into a corner of Father's stable. I fed the horse some hay, gave him clean water to drink, and set some blankets over his back to keep him warm. He nickered to himself and looked content. I let myself into Father's and found myself greeted by his helping-girl. She took my soggy coat and hat and led me near the hearth where Father sat with Thomas Oliver. They stood when they saw me. Oliver said something about being sorry for my loss, to which I replied with a polite "Thank you."

"You're back from taking Silas home then," Father said. I nodded. Father gestured to the chair beside him, the one closest to the fire, and I accepted the place gratefully. I leaned toward the warmth hoping to unfreeze my brain. The helping-girl placed a cup of hot coffee before me, which I looked at but did not drink.

"Tis as though the Town feels smaller, suddenly, as though we are under the same scrutiny as the Village," Father said to Oliver.

I turned my attention from the coffee to Father. "What do you mean?"

"Reverend Parris' daughter, Betty, has come to Town to live with Stephen Sewell."

"Do we know Stephen Sewell?" I asked.

Father shook his head whilst Thomas Oliver laughed. "Aye, James," Father said. "We know him. The man is a fellow merchant. We speak to him frequently."

"You speak to him frequently," I said. "I stand there and watch." I was sharp with Father when I did not mean to be. Tis only now, as I write this, I realize why the pointed words. I had been thinking of Cambridge, my studies, my College, my Chapel, my Library, and my friends. At that moment I was frustrated that I was in Salem when I wanted to be punting down the River Cam.

Father, always my friend, looked at me with compassion. "Sewell is a relative of the Reverend Mr. Parris and he has taken the girl into his home in an attempt to keep her away from the goings-on in the Village."

"I paid a visit to Sewell," Thomas Oliver said. "I said I had business with him, but really I wanted to see the girl. I did not see her there, but I did get a glimpse at the Meeting House."

"What did you find?" Father asked.

"She appeared normal enough, like any nine-year-old. She was curious and looking at the people who were looking at her."

"Did she speak out during the sermon and give the Reverend Mr. Noyes her opinion about what he should read from Scripture as the other afflicted have done?" Father asked.

"She didn't. She sat quietly whilst Noyes spoke. I saw nothing that made me think there was anything special about her. But everyone wants to see her, observe her actions, hear her speak in hopes of puzzling out how and why this child particularly has been touched by the Devil."

"Why do you suppose she plays such games?" Father asked. "People she calls out are jailed whilst they await their examinations. Why does this girl make a spectacle of herself?"

Oliver shrugged. "It could be foul play. Or she could truly be touched by the Devil. The afflicted must have been affected by Evil somehow."

"Do you believe in the Devil?" Father asked the privateer.

"How else do you explain the Evil in the world?"

Father gave Oliver his full attention whilst his slanted eyes grew smaller. "The girls have been influenced, not affected."

"Influenced by whom?" Oliver asked.

"By Samuel Parris. I'm not the only one who thinks so."

Oliver knocked back whatever was in his mug, rum, I guessed from the over-sweet fumes, and sighed. "I cannot say for certain, but tis rumored that Betty Parris is no better in the Town than she was in the Village. She has such seizures living with the Sewalls. She nearly died after one such attack. She says the Devil promised her riches beyond her wildest dreams."

"Who cares for those who have been arrested?" Father asked.

Memories of Mary flooded me and I thought twas time to return home. Even my silent presence must be at least some comfort to Lizzie. I asked Father's helping-girl to fetch my coat and hat. She watched me with her hands on her hips, looking remarkably like Patience, her sister. But where Patience has kindness, yes, patience, in her demeanor, the girl in Father's house appears to have a smirking cunning. She does what she is told well enough, but she leads me to think she does so grudgingly. I took my leave and Father followed me outside where it had stopped raining. A pink-yellow sun painted the sky.

"Are you all right, Son?" Father's concern was everywhere on his face.

"I'm as well as I can be right now."

He clasped a firm hand on my shoulder. "You know I'm here if you or Elizabeth need anything at all."

"I know, Father."

Since I arrived home Lizzie and I have been quiet with one another. She goes about her day as normally as she can. Though tis growing late she works, baking bread for Silas, scrubbing dishes, sweeping sand from the floor. I asked if she might send for Patience tomorrow, and she said she would not.

"I must keep moving, James. I must."

I persuaded her to sit whilst she ate some samp. I pulled her feet onto my lap and she leaned her head against her chair. Finally, she dozed off. I have retreated here so I can leave her to some much-needed rest.

23 MARCH 1691, WEDNESDAY

J am in a dark mood this night. Where is the progress I have seen in my lifetime? Where is the sense of looking forward? Salem has become a place of pointing voices and barking fingers. We versus you. We accuse you and you accuse we, and in the background, snarling loudest of all, is the Reverend Mr. Parris. His thunderous voice booms, his finger largest of all, pointing to Hell. I can only shake my head in wonder. What has happened to our capacity for Reason, I wonder? Perhaps we never had Reason to begin with.

I did not begin the day in such a dark mood. I was all right when I awoke this morn and saw the sunlight. Finally, beginning wisps of Spring color the landscape. The blooming buds burst in reds, golds, and blues amongst the bright green grass, still wet from the frequent rains. My cow friends down the road chew the long stalks gladly. This morn, for a moment, the world looked bright.

I had to leave my warm hearthside, and Lizzie, when Father summoned me to visit the shipyard with him as he makes plans to send his rum on *The Elizabeth*. To my unpracticed eyes the ship looks ready for her maiden voyage. As we stood on the wharf the new canvas sails and knotted ropes flapped in the brisk breeze whilst the stark odor of turpentine filled our noses. Father and I stood near the stern and he ran his hand over the freshly dried paint. "Tis good work, Son," he said. He looked toward the crow's nest and smiled. "Perhaps I should have followed my father onto the sea after all."

"And spent your life an odd shade of green," I said.

Father laughed. "Too true. And if I had followed that path I would not have met your mother, and we would not have been blessed with you, and I would have been a lesser man indeed. Nay, you are right. Things work out as they should in the end."

"Do you believe that, Father?"

"Aye, James. I do."

We walked the gangplank and stepped onboard for the first time. As we walked toward the bow we stopped near the stairs leading down to the hold where the goods shall be stored during the voyage. Father followed the captain he hired for *The Elizabeth*, an affable fellow by the name of Trenton, and Captain Trenton gave us a tour of the upper deck. Father asked for a moment alone with the captain and they headed down into the belly of the ship. I stayed above where the wind tossed my hat from my head whilst the angry waves rocked the ship and knocked me off my feet. In truth, I was happy to stay where I was. I do not care to be entrapped in closed spaces, and whatever sailor's legs previous generations of Wentworth men have had, I did not inherit them. I had quite enough of seafaring on our journey to Massachusetts, and though I long to return to England, at that moment, standing on the deck of *The Elizabeth*, I recalled that indeed I had been the same shade of green as Father upon arriving on steady land. I would have to endure such agonies again for the return trip, that is, if Lizzie and I decide to go home, and we may well just. Father had news for me as we meandered from the bay. He also had an offer. Twas not one I had expected.

Father's news was about Rebecca Nurse. He heard it from one of the shipbuilders with family in the Village. When I arrived home I stood outside with a heavy heart, watching Lizzie through the window, wondering how I would tell her. She bears up after the loss of Mary though I see her wipe her tears away with the back of her hand. Does she think I mind her grief over her sister? I know how her heart breaks, and it pained me to give her more bad news. Still, I had to tell her. As I write this, Lizzie sits before the hearth, shivering, though I know tis not the damp weather but the frigidity of loss. She stares into the flames—I was going to write like a conjuror, but with all that is going on now I am afeared to even write the words in case some unfriendly person peers over my shoulder, meaning to make accomplices of the Wentworths.

When I walked inside Lizzie was stirring a pottage in the cauldron. Again, I wondered how to say the words. They should come out like any others and yet I opened my mouth and nothing came. When Lizzie saw me she smiled. Twas the first genuine smile I had seen from her since Mary died, which tugged at my heart even more since I knew that what I had to say would wipe that fleeting joy away. I sighed from the effort of it. Lizzie helped me remove my cloak and she hung it on the peg near the door. The babe grows quickly, and already her back aches. She put her fists into her lower back and stretched like a cat. When she finished chopping the carrots and celery she dropped them into the frying pan. I could not stay away from her any longer. I put my arms round her and held her to me, pressing her head to my chest. Her smile became uncertain.

"What ails you?" she asked.

"They have arrested Rebecca."

"Our Rebecca?"

"Aye. They have arrested her as a Witch. Edward and Jonathan Putnam appeared before Hathorne and Corwin to make a formal complaint against her for tormenting the Ann Putnams and

Abigail Williams. They have also made a complaint against Dorcas Good."

"Sarah Good's daughter? The girl is but four years old." In Lizzie's face I saw every confusion, every panic, every fear. I saw the pain from Mary's death reawakened in a visceral way. Lizzie closed her eyes and exhaled loudly. Finally, she said, "Of course Rebecca is no Witch. Someone must speak for her. They must know she is no Witch."

"They should know, but they do not. She has been accused so she has been arrested."

"Who would accuse her? Who would accuse her of such a crime?"

"We know who accused her. The afflicted girls."

Lizzie seemed to struggle for words as much as I was. I wanted to offer her comfort, but all I could think to say was, "I'm certain she shall be cleared at her trial. All the evidence shall come out then."

Lizzie's voice grew in anger. "The false evidence from those horrid girls." Lizzie turned back to the hearth, venting her frustrations on the pottage, stirring faster and faster, pausing to wipe a tear from her cheek. I was at a loss for what to say. My need to safeguard Lizzie and our child rose again. I felt like a hunter, a lion in the wild protecting his pride.

I thought of Father's unexpected offer and said the first words that came to mind. "I think we should return to England." Lizzie stopped stirring to watch me. "Father says he shall send us home on *The Elizabeth* and give us money enough to get settled and assist me in starting a business there. Or, if we go to Cambridge, he shall assist us whilst I continue at university."

Lizzie wiped her hands on the closest rag she could grab. "I thought you were happy here."

"I was. I am. But I do not understand what is happening. I do not understand how someone like Rebecca can be arrested. I do not know the facts from all the cases, and I do not know that all the people accused are innocent. I'm questioning my own beliefs about whether or not the Devil exists. Perhaps there are such things as Specters and other unnatural beings. I realize now I know nothing of the supernatural world. But I know that some of the accused are innocent, and as long as innocent people may be condemned then Salem is not a safe place to live."

I could see that Lizzie thought of our babe by the way her hands fluttered to her middle. "It would depend on when we could catch the next crossing. I don't want to give birth on the ship. Those ships are horrid enough. They are overcrowded and the food is barely edible and the air is foul. There's so much death. I saw two newborns and so many others die on my voyage here."

Aye, I thought. It would be taking a risk. But I cannot tell which risk is greater—the voyage to England or remaining in Salem where every day new people are accused and taken away with nothing but Spectral evidence against them. Lizzie stroked my forehead and I leaned into her. I meant to be a comfort to her, yet she comforted me.

"Let us wait until the babe is a few months old and we know she's healthy," she said. "If things are still difficult then, we'll leave."

I kissed her berry-like lips and exhaled fully for the first time since Father's news. Together Lizzie and I shall find a way through whatever this is.

I had forgotten that Lizzie had given in to my proddings and asked Patience to return this day. Patience, who, unlike her sister, comes and goes so silently that she disappears into shadows. I did not realize she was there until she giggled like a four-year-old when my lips touched Lizzie's. When I looked for the girl, she was gone. Suddenly, Lizzie's words struck through my haze.

"She?" I said.

"Aye. I feel tis a girl so I think of her as she. We'll call her Grace. Though I'm certain you wish for a son."

I think of Lizzie's loss, her sweet, smiling, open-hearted Mary, and I think of naming our child, a daughter, for that sweet, smiling, open-hearted girl. Right now I am happy, not at the loss of my dearest sister-in-law, but at the dawning of new life and new hope.

"I wish for a healthy child who shall not have to live in fear," I said.

Lizzie stroked my brow again, and together we spoke of the day when we might return to England. For now, I shall concentrate on my wife, our child, and the beautiful life we have together.

24 MARCH 1691, THURSDAY

J attended Rebecca Nurse's pre-trial examination this day. Tis a sight never to be witnessed again in my life-time, my child's lifetime, nor any lifetime after that. Father remains fascinated by the happenings in the Village, and though I would rather bury my head in the sand and pretend all is well, I was once again persuaded to accompany him to the proceedings. In truth, I did not go entirely because of Father's wishes. I went for Lizzie, who begged me to see for myself. Lizzie wanted to go, and she would have gone, but for the first time since our marriage I put my foot down and forbid her. There is too much randomness to the accusations. I do not want anyone to see Lizzie anywhere near the accusers or the accused. I do not want her associated with anyone naming or named. Aye, tis selfish, especially since Goody Nurse has been such a friend to Lizzie. But my job is to protect my family, and to protect both Lizzie and our babe I must keep them as far from others as I can. Lizzie has suffered enough loss. She bristled at my assertion of authority as the head of our family, but after some persuasion she agreed to stay home. Before Father and

I left, Lizzie asked me to tell Rebecca that we are praying for her and keeping her close in our hearts.

"I shall try, my love," I said. "I do not think I can get close enough since Rebecca is being held as a prisoner. But I shall try."

I kissed Lizzie's soft lips, grabbed my cloak, and joined Father outside. With Euripides leading the way we bumped and jostled along the muddy road, determined to witness the events whilst remaining unseen in the background.

Twas quiet when Father and I arrived. The grave nature of the day weighed on me, and instead of watching the people settle themselves I studied the barrenness of the building. Soon enough the pews were filled with interested onlookers. Latecomers packed themselves in. Those who could not press inside remained outdoors.

When I settled my mind to it I sought out the afflicted. They sat calmly, silently, ignoring the hundreds of eyes fixed on them. Then John Hathorne appeared. I thought of the man I knew, Father's business associate, a fellow merchant who helped Father find his way amongst the Salem ports. He is fiftyish, Hathorne, with sagging jowls and sad eyes, though his finely tailored clothes give his drooping features a sense of authority. Since his notoriety as a result of these hearings he looks as though he has expanded somehow. He carries his back straighter, his head higher.

"Hathorne thinks the world finally sees him for the influential man he has been all along," Father whispered. "It only took the extraordinary circumstances of these trials for the rest of us to realize how important he truly is."

Hathorne was accompanied by three assistants. Along with Corwin, they made five imposing figures seated like royalty. Parris was in his usual place near the front, quill in hand, ready to record the events. I blame the Reverend for the sickness that strikes this place. I blame the Reverend for the whisperings and the finger-pointing. I blame the Reverend for the grotesque spectacles. But since no one has asked my opinion on such matters, I limit my discussion of them to these pages.

Suddenly, heavy irons scraped the floor, the crunching reverberating round the room, and everyone turned. Rebecca Nurse, elderly, sickly, frail, was bound like a common criminal, chained and dragged forward by the pock-faced Constable like a murderer bound for Newgate. Everyone silenced as Rebecca stopped near the magistrates to hear the charges against her. Her illness showed in the deepened creases in her face and neck, and she tilted her head since her hearing still fails her and she could not understand what was said.

The afflicted poked each other when Rebecca appeared. In the blink of an eye, Hell unleashed its fury. Such shrieks, such howls, such wails I have never heard before. Twas as if the Devil himself held the afflicted in his hands, slapped them, scratched them, and dragged them away. The afflicted grimaced at Rebecca and screamed. The spectators leaned forward as though waiting on every sound or movement and expectation sparked the air. Twas as though a lightning bolt struck the place. Even Father held his breath as he waited to see what would happen.

Hathorne glared across the room, a King scanning his loyal subjects. He asked the child Abigail Williams to explain her accusations.

"Just this morning she accosted me," Abigail said. "She's tormenting me."

"Who is tormenting you, Abigail?" Hathorne asked.

Abigail pointed at Rebecca. Observers turned disgusted looks in the old woman's direction. Hathorne called the room to order, and then several men from the Village came forward as witnesses. Each claimed to have seen Rebecca engaged in some form of Witchery.

"I saw her Specter try to strangle someone," said one farmer. Onlookers nodded in agreement.

Another man said, "I know her Specter bedded several men

from the Village." Father laughed aloud at the thought of elderly, sickly Goody Nurse giving herself to men. Father received some disgruntled looks from those nearest us.

Next, an old farmer said, "I saw her turn into a bird the color of the sky during a storm."

When Hathorne asked the next man what he had witnessed concerning Rebecca, the man said, "What is that you say? Her Specter is putting her fingers into my ears and I cannot hear you."

I wished some Specter would put fingers into my ears. I could not stand hearing how Hathorne pummeled Rebecca with his words, browbeating her into a confession that she had been consorting with the Devil. And poor Rebecca, ailing and unable to hear hardly a word of anything said to her, did her best to defend herself. But Hathorne would not let her. Rebecca is an easy victim, after all.

Others called as witnesses claimed that Rebecca had accosted them too. Spectral evidence was all they had against her. The Chief Justice, William Stoughton, found ways to justify Spectral evidence. If you look for something hard enough, you shall find it. If you say someone's Shape left their body and attacked you, how does the accused deny that? You can be at home, in the comfort of your bed, sound asleep, and if someone says twas not your physical form but your Specter that attacked them, how do you answer? By admitting Spectral evidence, the magistrates say there is no difference between a person and the idea of that person. The only evidence is offered by the hysterical cries of those who claim to be injured. If someone says Lizzie—not her physical being but her Shape—was responsible for the black magick that killed her sister, how might Lizzie respond? Nay, I must stop myself. I cannot think this way. But my argument remains. If the accused can poke, punch, bite, stab, blind, or deafen someone without being anywhere near the person who is hurt, then there are problems here beyond anything Parris, Hathorne, or Corwin can fix with harsh words and hard prison terms.

By the end of her examination, all Rebecca could say was she thought the writhing girls were possessed and she could not help it if the Devil appeared in her Shape. Twas enough of a confession for Hathorne to order her held for trial. Dorcas Good, but four years old, suffered a similar fate.

Whilst the observers meandered away, I saw them yet again, the sister-women. They stood silently, their arms listless by their sides, their bodies still, their eyes following Hathorne as he marched out. Why have they not been named, I wondered? They are exactly the kind the afflicted like to accuse—those who are different, those who do not conform. Rebecca should have been safe. She is God-fearing. She regularly attends the Town Church. She does good works. She is charitable. Certainly, she may have lost her temper now and again when others allowed their animals to trespass on her land, but she is a human being, is she not? The fact that she is not always saintly does not mean she consorts with the Devil. I must be paranoid, unnerved by everything, including the Weird Sisters, who appear out of the air as though they come directly from Shakespeare's play.

On the ride home Father and I jolted along in silence. My thoughts blurred and my brain throbbed as I realized I must get my family out of Salem, I must. A stricken panic settled at the base of my skull as a tightening in my bones. Since I have been home I have been struggling to rationalize my fear away. I must believe the afflicted will be called out for their folly. Rationality will overcome confusion in the end. And yet...

I do not know what to do. I go back and forth, thinking that Lizzie and I should remain in Salem until after our babe is born. With my next breath I'm ready to leap from my skin with the knowledge that we must flee for England now, yesterday, because we must free ourselves from the madness here. Lizzie and I will have to make a decision one way or the other soon.

25 MARCH 1692, FRIDAY

The new year arrives clear and cold. Tis the end of March, and despite the budding greens the winter weather still nips our toes like hungry dogs. We—Lizzie, Father, and Silas—quietly saw in the Year of Our Lord Sixteen Hundred and Ninety-Two. We kept our celebration to ourselves lest others should hear us, wonder what we are up to, and report us to the Court for making merry. Heaven forbid such a thing.

Tis hard, the lack of celebrations here. Puritans do not like holidays, so holidays we do not have. In England I did not feel the narrowness so much. I used to think of myself as a man who believed in live and let live. I live my life over here, you live yours over there, and as long as you do not interfere with my world I shall not interfere with yours. But that is not the way of it here. We cannot celebrate Yuletide since the day offends Puritan Beliefs. Tis no longer outlawed as it was in former years when anyone caught celebrating the Season (even with an innocuous act like singing a carol) was fined five shillings. Increase Mather made it clear that Christmas is celebrated on the twenty-fifth of December, not because tis Christ's birthdate but because Saturnalia was kept in Rome and he says the Catholics combined a heathen holiday with a holy Christian one. Besides, he says, there is no Biblical basis for Christmas. Since it says nothing in the Bible about celebrating Christ's birth then we should not celebrate it. Easter, Whitsunday, and Mayday are more a product of Satan than Christ, or so our Puritan neighbors say.

There is little enough here to celebrate. Commencement Day, when students graduate from Harvard College, is a rare holiday on the Puritan calendar. On Election Day everyone elects their local representatives. On Training Day the local militia completes their training exercises—a necessity with the constant battles between the French, Indians, and settlers. Thanksgiving, a day of prayer and feasting, is occasionally celebrated. The Sabbath is a holiday, as tis throughout England, and all work ceases except for Church services. Sitting through long Puritan sermons is work enough. With such a lack of entertainments I miss England more. I miss decorating our home with holly, ivy, and mistletoe. Yuletide in London is such a festive occasion. As a boy, I helped cousins and friends gather greens into a kissing bush. I remember laughing as girls tripped over their skirts when the boys tried to kiss them. Drummers drummed, pipers piped, and costumed carolers sang, the gaieties lasting until Twelfth Night. Though December is the bleakest, coldest month, for those few weeks, despite the dark midwinter, all is well with the world. This year, as last, I did not get my Yuletide celebration, though now I have Lizzie who shines brighter than any bonfire.

I wanted to bring in the New Year the English way by giving gifts and passing goodwill from rich to poor. But here, at the edge of the shore, we had a quiet day to ourselves where we shared aloud our gratitude for what we have, which is quite a lot and certainly more than most. We are thankful for Mary. We are thankful for my mother and Lizzie's mother. We are thankful for our friend Rebecca. Father asked Our God, the Merciful Lord, the

God of Lovingkindness, to make 1692 a fine new beginning. We prayed for the release of the innocents and for the madness to end.

I could not help but see Lizzie's concerned glances toward Silas. She watched him, then turned away as though she did not want him to notice that she paid him any especial attention. Tis true Silas has grown colder, more bitter since Mary's passing. Before Silas' arrival this morn, Lizzie shared her thoughts with me.

"He feels as though he gave Mary his all," Lizzie said. "He worked his fingers to the bone to provide for her. He prayed through silence and contemplation. And still, she died."

"Tis hardly his fault," I said. "What else could he have done?"

"That's what I've said to him. But he doesn't hear me." Lizzie sat on the edge of our bed as she tied her shawl round her shoulders. Since twas only family coming she wore her usual calico, nothing as fancy as some of her newer clothing, but tis what she feels most comfortable in and what she wears round the house. I tied her coif into place and she laced my stays.

"Tis too bad your brother could not come to help tend your father in his grief," I said.

"True, he is my brother, yet I hardly know him. It wasn't convenient for him to come to Salem after Mary died, so he didn't come." Lizzie exhaled. She helped me shrug into my coat, the jewel-blue one she loves so much, and she tied my cravat. "Pa has become a shell of a man, and I don't know how to help him. I tried again to persuade him to live with us but he says he must not leave the farm." Lizzie reached toward me and I pulled her close and held her tight, as if for sustenance. She squeezed me with equal strength. I rested my cheek on top of her coif-covered hair, the linen soft against my face. "My father can be stubborn."

"So can mine," I said.

When Silas arrived he looked stubborn indeed, nearly angry, as he greeted Father. Father wore Silas down with mugfuls of rum. Silas even smiled during our meal. Lizzie boiled an ox tongue, mixing it with beef suet, currants, raisins, and preserved apples and seasoning everything with nutmeg, lemon peel, and sugar. She pressed the filling between two slices of puff pastry, and when the pastry was browned and the house smelled deliciously sweet, she decorated the pie with candied lemons. Lizzie passed plates of pie and cornbread all round.

"This New Year we honor our dear Mary," Father said. "May she rest eternally in Our Lord's embrace."

We raised our mugs and drank to Mary. But the gesture only seemed to make Silas more melancholy.

Silas looked at the food Lizzie served. "Minced tongue was Mary's favorite."

"I made it in memory of her," Lizzie said.

Silas squeezed his eyelids together.

"She's watching us," Lizzie said. "I know she is."

"I believed that once," Silas said.

"Have you lost faith?" Father asked.

Silas stared into the dancing fire as twas whipped by the wind slipping down the chimney, back and forth, higher and lower as though caught in a storm. He glanced toward the door, the windows, up toward the attic, back toward the Great Room. His eyes were wide as though he expected a Specter to appear, arms outstretched, mouth ghoulish, finger-pointing.

"There's no one here but us, Pa," Lizzie said. "You can speak freely."

Silas sighed. "For all my life I believed in the Almighty God the Father and I believed in His Son. I joined the Church here for the same reasons you did, John—to make my life easier in Salem. I had nothing against their beliefs. Good luck to them. The Puritans have their ways, I thought, and I have mine. I didn't see why one should hinder the other."

"Let he who is without sin cast the first stone," Father said.

Silas sighed. "I knew they believed in the Devil, as we believe in the Devil. But I didn't know Satan had made a home for himself here. Now I wonder. Is the Devil always able to lure the most vulnerable, the most susceptible to do his bidding?"

"People in England believe the Devil has plenty of friends as well," Father said.

"He's quite the busy one," I said, "always recruiting."

Silas ate a bite of pie. He washed it down with rum, thought a moment, then said, "Forgive me for rattling on. I've been thinking much about Mary with the New Year. I know how she loved the celebrations in England. She would have loved this day, with this pie, with her sister, her new brother, and her second father. I know some have whispered about Mary's illness. I know some think she was bewitched. Perhaps she was afflicted. Peter thinks so. I certainly don't know."

"Pa." Lizzie sat beside Silas. "Of course Mary wasn't afflicted. She became ill, as many have before her, and many will still. God took her, too soon for us, but we cannot know His intentions."

"God?" said Silas. "Or Satan? Peter says Mary was enticed to enter the darkness. Maybe the Devil offered her beautiful gowns and jewels."

"What has Peter to do with it?" Lizzie asked.

"Peter sent me a letter," Silas said. "He has opinions about what has happened."

"I'm sure he does." Lizzie served Silas another slice of pie. "Peter met Mary perhaps twice in her life. If he knew her, he would know that Mary never cared for such things as gowns or jewels."

"All women care for such things. Tis not why you married him?" Silas gestured toward me with his thumb. "Tis why women are so susceptible to Evil influences. That's what Peter says. And what were those herbs you gave Mary in that tea? Who gave those to you?"

"The sisters living down the road from you," Lizzie said. "At least I think they're sisters. They're healers."

"How do you know they're not Witches? How do you know

they don't have malevolent intent? We do not know these women. I've heard you speak of them before, but I have yet to see them. Do they not go to Church? Why would they stay away, that is, unless the Devil won't let them attend worship in the presence of God-fearing people?" He took his pipe from his coat pocket and filled it with tobacco from the pouch Lizzie handed him. He tapped the pipe until the tobacco settled and lit it. He nodded at his thoughts as the first puffs of smoke filled the air.

"I trust those women because they haven't given me any reason to think they aren't trustworthy," Lizzie said. "They aren't the ones to fear. The Ann Putnams, the Abigail Williams, they are the ones we should be concerned about. They accuse others freely without concern for how the accused are affected by their words."

"The Devil's power corrupts children," Silas said. "With your babe coming, you should know that children are Evil from birth. I should have raised Mary with a stricter hand, but I felt sorry for the girl, losing her mother the day she was born. Why, I'd say Satan could have corrupted our Mary quite easily." Silas set down his pipe and crossed his arms over his chest. As though the Almighty passed judgment on our conversation, the clear, cold day fell black and thunder cracked, drenching the Town around us.

Father took quick steps round the Great Room. He wagged his finger as though telling off Betty Parris herself. I was afeared he would walk to the house where the girl stays, drag her outside the Meeting House, lock her in the stocks, and throw rocks at her head.

Then, as though to emphasize his point, Silas said, "They've arrested a dog for consorting with the Devil. Even animals aren't safe from recruitment."

Father looked as though he wanted to laugh but Silas' firm features said he was not fooling. Father opened the door and stared in the direction of the shore, his hands on his hips. He looked as though he were making a decision of vital importance. "Tis a new year," he said. "The New Year always brings good cheer.

So let us be of good cheer. Let us remember our thanks for everyone we love, and let us look forward to the great fortune that 1692 will bring us all." Father smiled at Lizzie. "Despite our terrible losses we have much to be thankful for. We have a new life coming, my first grandchild. A new member of the family is always a blessing." He raised his mug toward Lizzie. "'Tis a grand thing."

We pressed our mugs together and sipped some warming flip, hoping to carry that sweetness into 1692.

1 APRIL 1692, FRIDAY

*L*izzie is busy making candles. Tis not easy work, but she says she enjoys it, especially since she is making batches for Silas and Mistress Thompson, who lost her newborn but two days ago. Now Lizzie stirs the boiling juice of the berries she and I gathered with beeswax. Twas a joy being outside this morn with thin streams of goldenrod sunbeams illuminating our path and only birds and trees for company. Lizzie pointed with child-like glee whenever an iridescent hummingbird poked its delicate beak into new-blooming buds. She listened to the warbler's sing-song melody and when she sang along the bird squawked away. She giggled like a young girl, and my heart was glad to see her so relaxed and joyful for the first time since Mary's death. We meandered along hand in hand, stealing shy glances at one another, her blush red-hot along her jaw. I had thoughts of removing her cap, and other things as well, whilst laying her down beside the stream. As tempted as I was, there was too much of a possibility of being seen since that part of the forest is well-traveled and I do not want to cause Lizzie the embarrassment of being brought before the Court for indecency though we are married and what business is it of anyone's anyway? Instead, I was content with the simple pleasure of being out on a sunny new spring day with my beautiful wife. Lizzie found the berries she needed and we made a game of it, racing each other to see who filled their basket first. With her smaller, faster hands she had her basket full before I covered the bottom of mine. The stickles on the vine kept pinching my fingers.

"You see," Lizzie said. She took my hand and pulled it close to her face, kissing away a drop of blood. "Your hands are softer than mine, James. You have never had to work with your hands a day in your life."

"Is that a bad thing?" I asked.

"Not at all. Your gifts lie elsewhere. You are a great thinker and writer. You will return to university and then you will spend your days teaching and writing as you should."

"I'm not so sure about that, Lizzie. I wonder if I have worked at maths too long and now my knowledge of words eludes me. I sit down to write and stare at the blank page for hours. When I'm working with Father I feel as though I'm wasting my time balancing ledgers and writing invoices when that is not what I feel called to do. But when I have time to write my brain is as blank as a new slate. Tis as though I'm being pulled in two directions—one here in Salem where we have made a comfortable home for ourselves. The other in England, where I can return to my studies." I sat on an overturned log and helped Lizzie sit beside me. She pressed her head into my arm. "Have you thought more about Father's offer?"

"Do you mean have I changed my mind?"

"Aye."

"You want to leave now." Twas not a question.

Lizzie shivered and tugged her shawl closer to her neck. I put my arm round her shoulders. Though tis the first of April the air still nips and twas cold under the shade of the trees.

"I do not know what I want, Lizzie. Nay, that is not true. I know what I want. I want you. Wherever I am, however I am, if you are there, then that is home. If you are here, then here is home. If you are in England, then England is home."

"But I think you would like a home where you can be your own man."

I kissed the tip of Lizzie's nose. "How did I find such a perceptive wife?"

"You were lucky." Lizzie laughed. "I want what you want, James. I want to return to England. I want you to be happy."

"What about your happiness?"

"My happiness is with you. I'll be happy wherever as long as we're together. I think, if you listen to your heart, you know that England calls to you. Cambridge shouts your name. We should do it. Let's go home to England. But I still think we should wait until after the babe is born, after she's a few months old when she's better able to handle the voyage."

"You still believe the babe is a she?"

"I don't believe it. I know it."

"I shall never doubt you, Mistress Wentworth."

Lizzie and I returned home, Lizzie ready to make candles, me to stare at empty pages that mock my lack of imagination. As I write this, Lizzie boils the berries and beeswax then skims the thickness from the top. She walks the candle rods back and forth from the kettle to the line on the wall. She dips the wicks into the wax, hangs them to cool, then dips them again and again until a candle forms. The heat from the dipping flushes Lizzie's cheeks pink, but she washes her face with a wet cloth and continues about her work as though tis no matter. Perhaps I should take a lesson from her. Perhaps I should be more practical with my time.

THE HOUSE RATTLED UNDER THE HARSH THUDS FROM THE BRASS knocker against our door. Outside was Mistress Boxley.

Mistress Boxley comes round from time to time, mostly to cast her glance over our Delftware and silverware. She comments on the same carved English furniture and the same tapestries. She makes admiring remarks on whatever new items of clothing she has noticed Lizzie wearing, the bows and ribbons, the jewel-toned dresses fashioned by elite couturiers in Boston. Of course, Lizzie is often found round the house in her calico, and of course Mistress Boxley makes a point of how lovely Lizzie looks though she "did not make an effort at all this day." Fortunately for the woman, Lizzie has more patience than I do.

After the matron had her usual say about our possessions, Lizzie invited her to stay for tea. The woman sets my teeth on edge, but Lizzie is kindhearted, and besides, she does not know anyone in the Town except for Father and me. Perhaps Lizzie enjoys the company. Other women of our social status do not call on Lizzie. People know her as a farmer's daughter from the Village, which is all they need to know to make their pronouncements on how she married above her station and therefore does not require the condescension of their notice. Lizzie does not seem to mind. She says she is content with her life with me and our future child and I believe her.

To my chagrin, Mistress Boxley agreed to grace us with her presence and remained for tea, saying she could stay a bit before she was needed at a meeting for the Town Society matrons. She enjoyed an entire platter of candied fruits and nuts, a whole pitcher of sweet apple cider, and a potful of hot tea before the gossip began. She is one of those people I call a watcher. Her large pale-blue eyes glance everywhere at once under hooded lids, and even when you speak to her she does not look at you. Instead, she follows the gaze of everyone nearby as though she cannot take another breath without knowing who watches her in return. The woman is no beauty, certainly. Her round face is creviced with pockmarks she tries to hide under layers of powder. I'm surprised she has not been brought before the Court for impropriety, but her husband is a wealthy man and the wealthy are not scrutinized like the poor. She dresses well, flaunting her husband's success, and she is always seen in her finest silks and brocades, her shawls embroidered with gold and silver, her fingers flashing with rubies and sapphires. But even her finely stitched clothing and flashing jewels are no match for Lizzie's pure, unadorned beauty. So many fail to realize that tis not what is on the outside that makes one beautiful. Tis what is on the inside. Lizzie's heart is as big as the sky, and no amount of money can purchase that kind of beauty.

When Mistress Boxley ate her fill she slunk toward the hearth where Lizzie brewed more tea. The matron noticed the drying candles hanging from the rods and she smiled at Lizzie as though they shared a secret.

"Your helping-girl is making candles, I see."

"I made them myself," Lizzie said. "I enjoy the work. I prefer to be useful."

"Useful! You are so quaint, Mistress Wentworth. It must be because you are a farmer's daughter. No proper Society woman would be caught dead doing something as common as making candles."

"But doesn't everyone need candles?" Lizzie asked. "Why not spend your time doing things that bring comfort to your family?"

"Really, Mistress Wentworth, we must rid you of those silly notions. You are a merchant's wife. You should act according to your station. Now," Mistress Boxley drank a mugful of apple cider in one swallow, "you must let me tell you about Rebecca Nurse." Mistress Boxley leaned toward Lizzie as though conspiring with her but she spoke loudly enough for me to hear from my desk. "She's been arrested, you know."

"Aye." Lizzie poured fresh cups of tea for our guest and herself, then set two bowls, one with cream and one with sugar, on the table. Mistress Boxley helped herself to most of the cream and all the sugar. "My husband and his father were at the examination."

"Really?" Mistress Boxley turned her watching eyes onto me. "What did he see?"

Lizzie related bits of what I had told her about the examination, bits that anyone who was there could have said. Mistress Boxley nodded as though she knew it all already, which most likely she did.

"What did your husband think of it?"

Lizzie hesitated. Her open face closed before my eyes and I could see her growing distrust. "He does not know what to think," was all Lizzie offered.

"And you were not there?" Mistress Boxley leaned toward Lizzie, her round face bright with expectation despite the heavy layers of powder that left her complexion an odd shade of egg yolk.

"Nay." Lizzie hesitated, and the matron noticed. Mistress Boxley leaned even closer, and Lizzie leaned so far back that her chair creaked. "I was not well."

"Oh! Well, if you are not well, Mistress Wentworth, then you must be home resting and not sitting through those long, boring examinations." She ate another handful of candied berries. "What ailed you?"

"Tis nothing." Lizzie waved her hand in firm dismissal of any problem.

Round another mouthful of candied walnuts, Mistress Boxley said, "Have you heard about Mistress Whitby?"

"I haven't," Lizzie said. The name sounded familiar, but I could not remember whether or not I knew the woman. Then I did recall her, unfortunately. She is tall and rather manly in appearance and voice. She barks Commandments at passers-by as though she has authority over heavenly matters. She does not, to my knowledge, but then I am no religious scholar. "Ladies and gentlemen!" she shouts outside the Town Meeting House. "Ladies and gentlemen! Ladies and gentlemen! Here are our Commandments! You must listen to me! Those who do not listen to me will suffer the wrath of God!" Not one person listens to her as they hurry past in their haste to be too far to hear. She should not be allowed to speak such ways since the Puritans believe women need a man to speak for them, but she is wealthy and, again, concessions are made for the wealthy. When no one listens to her, or when she feels she has been slighted in the least, she runs to Reverend Noyes with her complaints.

"Here's a tale for you!" Mistress Boxley wiped her hands on a linen napkin and winked at Lizzie. "Mistress Whitby is married a second time, did you know? She found her husband, the one she has now, Whitby, whilst she was still married to her first husband. Her first husband was a wealthy landowner in Connecticut, and she was but a scullery maid in his employ. She caught his attention, we both know how she did that, and he married her. Then she met her second husband, a groom in her husband's stables, and they fled together to Salem to escape the old man's wrath."

"I heard she inherited her first husband's wealth," I said. "How could that be?" Lizzie smiled at me. I should not have intruded, but my curiosity got the best of me. Mistress Boxley was only too happy to have another listener.

"The first husband never changed his will. When he died, Mistress Whitby inherited everything."

"No wonder she struts about as though she owns the Town," I said.

Mistress Boxley whispered to Lizzie and I had to strain to hear. "Mistress Whitby is afflicted." When Lizzie shook her head, not understanding, the matron said, "She's been tortured by Sarah Good and Rebecca Nurse. Mr. Whitby made a formal complaint against them this morn."

"What the bloody hell kind of lunacy is this?" I said.

I must have offended Mistress Boxley since twas as if a curtain closed over her eyes. The openness with which she had just shared stories with Lizzie was replaced by a cold formality.

"I should remind you, Mr. Wentworth, that Mistress Whitby is a respected member of Salem Society. She is indeed afflicted. She showed me the bite marks on her arm put there by Rebecca Nurse."

"Are you certain it wasn't a dog bite?" I asked.

"They were definitely human teeth."

I could not hide my exasperation. "When did this biting supposedly happen?"

"Two nights past," said Mistress Boxley.

"Rebecca Nurse has been imprisoned for some time now. She could not have bitten your friend two nights ago."

"Twas her Shape, Mr. Wentworth. Know you nothing of Shapes?"

"Obviously, Mistress Boxley, I do not. Shapes are figments of our imaginations, after all. Tis as though whatever strangeness we conjure in our heads is real if we can convince others of its truth. We are lunging at windmills and no one sees it."

"There are no windmills in Salem, Mr. Wentworth." She smiled as she considered. "Whatever strangeness you conjure? Hmm." Mistress Boxley stood like a queen at a pageant. I expected her to wave at us. "I thank you for a lovely afternoon, Mistress Wentworth. We must do it again soon."

Lizzie showed her out. When our guest was gone Lizzie joined me by my desk. She pressed her hands into my shoulders and rubbed my annoyance away. She kneaded my neck and my back. She kissed my cheek. I exhaled and leaned into her warmth.

"I'm sorry, Lizzie," I said. "I should not have spoken to her like that. She irritates me so, she and her friend Mistress Whatsit."

"Mistress Whitby," Lizzie said. "And you needn't apologize. I don't much care for them either. I didn't mind her comments about my dresses and our furniture, but now I don't know. How could she speak to me so of Mistress Whitby calling out Rebecca? She knows Rebecca is my friend."

"Tis exactly why she does it, I'm afeared. She is one of those people who likes to stir the pot. She sees you here, happy, content, and unconcerned about what others say or do, and she knows she does not have what you have. She is one of those people who always compares herself to others so tis unlikely she shall ever be satisfied. People like that make themselves feel bigger by trying to make others look smaller. Perhaps you best stay away from her, Lizzie."

Lizzie nodded. "I was thinking as much myself. After all, if she speaks so freely about others to me, I'm certain she speaks as easily about me to others. I'll excuse myself from our afternoon teas as discretely as possible. I'll tell her I have too many tasks to attend to. She already thinks I'm odd for doing my own chores." She walked to the end of the hall and examined the candles still drying on the line. She reached out to touch one and pressed the hardening wax between her fingers.

"How are the candles coming?" I asked.

"They should be dry soon depending on how wet the weather stays. After the candles set I'll bring some to Mistress Thompson and then we can bring some to Pa."

"Of course, Lizzie. Whatever you need." I put down my quill and set aside any pretense of writing. "Come back here. I miss your hands on my shoulders. I only feel at peace when you are near. I cannot stand to be without you."

"You have me, James. I'm right here."

"Aye, my love. But there is not here. You are not close enough." I held my arms out to her. "Here is where you belong."

Lizzie slid her arms round my neck. "My dear and loving husband," she said. "Where else on Earth would I be?"

4 APRIL 1692, MONDAY

I have never been prone to nightmares. I have never given credence to the Invisible World despite those who believe in magick, spells, and Specters. I have never been one to see Shadows in the corners, and I have never heard Whisperings in the night. I have never been suspicious of Unseen Forces which others dread with mortal fear. I have accepted life, and everything in it, the way I have found it—natural causes and all. Father says tis my book learning that prompts me to think such ways, but what else is knowledge for but to question and challenge?

Despite my belief in Reason, or perhaps because of it, I again broached the subject with Lizzie of our leaving for England. Father repeated his offer this morn, saying he would give Lizzie and me passage on one of his ships, we need only say when. I want to leave as soon as possible, but Lizzie refuses to be turned out of our home by fear.

She put down the pitcher of water she carried and stretched her back. The vomiting has lessened as the babe grows but she tires so easily. She rubbed her weary eyes with her hand. "There's something we must learn from this, James. When we have learned our lesson, all will be well again."

"It must be one bloody hell of a lesson," I said. Lizzie shook her head at me but said nothing.

Now I wonder—am I afeared of goblins after all? I should not listen to the whisperings, I know. But I know what they say, and I know how they say it, and I hear them, over and over in my mind, the pettiness, the sharpness. I can feel their malcontent in the scrape of their words. Mary's Shape walks the Earth, such people say, searching. Searching for what, I wonder? No one says, though I feel the answer is implied: "Why, she searches for Witches, of course. The girl's Specter recruits for Satan as we speak." The Devil works in mysterious ways, they say. Massachusetts is but a dull, tedious place, barely civilized. Of all the places in the world, the Devil worries about provincial Massachusetts? Hasn't he somewhere more interesting to ply his trade?

Lizzie sits near the fire, her shawl falling round her shoulders as she stitches a quilt for the babe, a content smile on her sweet lips. She does not look concerned by loitering Specters. She does not sneak glances in the corners seeking Shadows or other ill omens. She speaks aloud sometimes, to Mary or to the babe she carries, but that is not a bad thing. Lizzie wants to feel her sister close. She feels the babe, whom she calls Grace, growing inside her, and tis natural she should speak so to our daughter. Sometimes I look over my shoulder, through our windows, to see if anyone watches. Can a passer-by see her talking to the air? I think not. How could a random stranger, even a known neighbor, see that Lizzie is not speaking to me?

Lizzie's shawl falls nearly to the floor now and she is bare in the flimsy shift that reveals her curves made rounder. She smiles still, a contentment men will never know since they do not birth the children. Tis as though she has a secret with the babe growing inside her, and even I, with my closeness to them both, shall never know the truth of what they share. But I do not begrudge them a bit of it. They are my family, Lizzie and the child. I take comfort knowing that this babe will be one of the most fortunate children ever born with Elizabeth Wentworth as her mother. Lizzie has the right amount of strength, courage, kindness, and compassion. She has the kind of deep, soul-filling love that will help this child, and any future children, girls and boys, become strong, courageous, compassionate souls of their own.

I'm on a see-saw as I swing between the high of contentment, as though all is right in the world, and the low of concern, a bundle of exposed nerves and jittering fears. I must come clean about what is truly on my mind. I cannot escape it, no matter how much I write about my beautiful wife and our joy over our unborn child.

This morn I was getting ready to leave for Father's, wondering whether to take my cloak since, though the April weather is warmer, tis still shivery at times. Seeing my indecision, Lizzie handed me my cloak.

"Tis better to be warm than sorry." She slid the cloak over my shoulders. I took her hands, pulled her to me, and wrapped my cloak round both of us.

"I would prefer saying here, wrapped up in you," I said.

"We will still be here when you come home." She patted the bulge under her apron, more visible now but still faint, perhaps, to others. "We can warm each other then."

I opened the door to see Father. He nodded at me, at Lizzie, and he smiled at the growing bump. Without a word, he removed his cloak and hung it on a peg near the door. Lizzie gestured to the chair nearest the fire.

"Father," I said. "I apologize for being late. I was on my way to you now."

"Nonsense," Father said. He sipped the steaming coffee Lizzie placed before him. "You are not late at all. But I wanted to see you here, privately." He pressed his coffee aside and walked toward the hearth. He leaned toward the large cauldron and sniffed the sattoot of turkey boiling in lard. He nodded in appreciation, then looked at the ladder that led to the attic. "There is no one else here?"

"Nay," Lizzie said. "Patience has gone to the McGowerns' to see if they have any lard for sale."

"Good. I wanted to be away from my girl as well. I fear she may be worst of all." Father sat again. He leaned his forehead against the cool wood of the table, then clasped his hands to his bald head. Lizzie sat beside him and patted his shoulder in a soothing way that comforted me even if it did not seem to have much effect on Father.

Finally, I said, "Father, you are worrying me. Is something wrong? Is someone hurt?"

"Nay, James. Nothing like that." But the way he would not make eye contact with Lizzie or me made me think something was wrong indeed.

"Has someone else been arrested?" I asked. Father turned away. I never should have asked. In truth, I did not want to know. I did not want Lizzie to know either.

Father turned toward the diamond panes revealing the burgeoning Spring outside. The thin rays of sunlight spilling through the glass left him green. "Tis Elizabeth Proctor. Abigail Williams says Goody Proctor's Specter tortured her. The Proctors' helping-girl, Mary Warren, believes she's been afflicted by Goody Proctor as well. And that is not all." Father stared at the pointed gables overhead as though waiting for inspiration. "Sarah Cloyse, Rebecca Nurse's sister, is accused. Goody Cloyse spoke out in defense of Rebecca and now she rots in jail for it." Lizzie grabbed the back of Father's chair as though to keep herself upright. I stood beside her, ready to help. Father took Lizzie's hand. "This will all blow over soon, Daughter."

"I believe that, Father," Lizzie said. "I believe our Heavenly Father looks out for us. But I do hope tis His will that this ends sooner rather than later."

"How will this end?" I asked. "Things grow worse, not better.

More people speak out, and more are accused. These...these..." I could not think of a word for the afflicted. What do you call them? What can you say? They have the protection of the highest-ranking men in the Village, in the Town, in all of Massachusetts. They blow their accusations down on helpless others faster than storms charging in over the bay. "I wonder..."

"Aye?" Father looked me in the eyes for the first time since he arrived.

"The illustrious Reverend Parris has not been paid three quarters in a row. Tis his daughter and niece who were first afflicted. What does he think of this madness that infects Salem through his own family?"

"He believes he has been shown the Light," Father said. "He believes he is helping the Village by weeding out the infected ones."

I scoffed. "I do not give a rat's arse about what the man believes. Parris sits there taking notes during the examinations, a right proper Daniel in judgment on the unfortunates who are called out. He is so busy puffing his cheeks and crinkling his nose I do not know how his hand moves fast enough to keep up with everything everyone says." Father paced to the door, opened it, and looked outside as the sunlight struggled to bring some brightness to the day. "And now this with the Proctors? Lizzie has known the Proctors since she arrived in the Village. I know Goodman Proctor well enough to know he has no problem speaking his mind. How could he let them take his wife away?"

"What could he do?" Father closed the door, but the crooked oak seemed to hold a strange fascination over him and he watched it through the window. "I heard Mary Warren received a thrashing when she returned to the Proctors' after playing her part in the accusations. Goodman Proctor said there was no way Mary Warren was hurt by Goody Proctor. Apparently, Proctor informed Mary Warren that if she hurt herself during one of her spells—if she ran into fire or fell into water—he would not stop her. One neighbor saw Proctor chasing the girl through the fields with hot tongs."

I laughed. I'm not sure why, twas not the appropriate response, except that it was a humorous sight to consider—Proctor, who must be in his 60s now, chasing a screaming young woman round his farm with nothing but a red-hot pincher between them. Then I recalled the reason why he chased her—his expectant wife, his Elizabeth, has been called out with false accusations. I glanced at my own expectant Elizabeth and shuddered.

Father helped himself to some hot water off the hob and made himself some tea. Lizzie stood to help him but he waved her back into her chair.

"When did this happen?" Lizzie asked.

"Twas last week when Mercy Lewis and Abigail Williams claimed that Goody Proctor's Shape tormented them. This morn John Walcott and Nathaniel Ingersoll filed a complaint against her."

"Even helping-girls cannot be trusted now," I said. "Perhaps we ought to dismiss Patience. You have always said you prefer doing things yourself, Lizzie. Perhaps tis time."

Lizzie leaned toward me. "Is it fair to deprive her of her livelihood when she's done nothing wrong?"

I rested my chin atop Lizzie's uncovered curls. "I have nothing against the girl, Lizzie, truly. She seems a good soul. But with everything happening, I do not know who to trust. And whilst I have nothing but pleasant words for Patience, her sister is…"

"Aye?"

"I do not know, Lizzie. She is forward. She says what she thinks."

"You've told me that you like it when I say what I think."

"Aye," I said, "of course I do. But that is between us, husband and wife. Father's helping-girl is…" I still could not think of how to describe her. "Father does not trust her, and I trust his opinion."

"Is that true?" Lizzie asked. Father nodded. "Then why don't you dismiss her, Father?"

"I shall when the time is right. Prudence Connor is another matter entirely from Patience. Besides, Daughter, have you not heard that Prudence is in want of a husband—your husband?"

Lizzie's eyes sparkled. "Should I be worried, James? Are you in want of a new wife?"

"I? What?" My cheeks flushed with the heat of embarrassment. "Nay! I mean, Father said he thought she might be interested in me, but I told him I did not need another wife, not now, not ever. I'm more than happy with the wife I have now, Lizzie, I assure you."

"You needn't worry about Prudence Connor," Father said, nodding at Lizzie. He could not hide his amusement. "She's a vain, silly girl, and I shall not allow her to make away with James."

Lizzie stepped closer to me, standing on her toes so she could see into my eyes. "Are you sure you won't tire of me?"

"How shall I ever tire of you, Elizabeth Wentworth? Who else understands me as well as you do? There is no one else in the world for me but you. I shall never leave you ever."

"And I promise you the same," Lizzie said.

I kissed her lips until Father cleared his throat, reminding us he was there.

10 APRIL 1692, SUNDAY

We should have gone to listen to the sermons this day, but neither Lizzie nor I had the heart for it. If they notice we were not there (as I'm sure someone shall) I shall say twas Lizzie's condition that kept us away. If we have to pay the fine for not attending, then I shall pay the fine. I have paid it many times before.

My mind is too full to sit through a day-long sermon. I saw a list of the accused and there are so many of them. I've reread the names so often I can recite them from memory. Even when I do not want to know who they are, the names poke me, tug me, stir at my conscience. Lizzie sits by my side repairing my blue stockings, humming an English tune. At first, I could not name it and it frustrated me. Now I laugh as I recall the lyrics:

If music be the food of love,
Sing on till I am fill'd with joy;
For then my list'ning soul you move
To pleasures that can never cloy.
Your eyes, your mien, your tongue declare
That you are music ev'rywhere.

Pleasures invade both eye and ear,
So fierce the transports are, they wound,
And all my senses feasted are,
Tho yet the treat is only sound,
Sure I must perish by your charms,
Unless you save me in your arms.

I smile at Lizzie and she smiles at me. Surely, I shall perish from her charms. I know no comfort that is not her arms. She is right, we are fortunate here in our comfortable home, with every object, ordinary or luxurious, we need. I have leisure time at my disposal, and I have money for such things as pens, ink, and paper. I have time to write, or at least to try to write. And then I am reminded, again, though I do not wish to be, of the long list of accused. Tis an odd thing, the mind. Whatever tis I wish to think about least, that is the only thing I can think about.

I know I shall do whatever is necessary to protect Lizzie and our unborn child from the madness. If I'm not here to protect them, who shall? Some of the women who are called out suffer because they have no man—no father, husband, son, uncle, brother, or even cousin—to speak on their behalf. They are tossed aside like hog slop, left to rot.

"I shan't allow that to happen to Lizzie," I said to the gables above my head. "I must protect her."

I climbed down to the basement, grabbed my musket, headed back to the Great Room, and pulled a chair close to the door. This is what I can do, I thought. I can stop anyone—human, Specter, or otherwise—from invading my home. This house—with its two gables, its spacious rooms, its attic and its basement—is our sanctuary, Lizzie and mine and soon our babe's. Tis where we cocoon ourselves from the world and everyone in it. If the Shapes invade here, I thought, we are doomed.

I had to stop writing for a moment. I do not know what prompted those inane thoughts and foolish actions. I had no spirits to drink. There is none of Father's rum about. With my sleep-deprived thoughts, it seemed perfectly rational to stop an Invisible Being from overtaking my home with a gun. Lizzie saw me there, a soldier on patrol, and she spoke soothing words to me. I was so caught up in my crazed thoughts I did not hear her at first. I did not want to eat. I wanted nothing to drink. I had to keep the intruders away.

Lizzie pressed the nozzle of the musket aside. "James." She knelt by my side. "You know you won't use that."

"How do you know? We may be accosted by…"

"Aye? By?" She slipped a strand of my hair behind my ear and kissed my temple. "Were you going to shoot a Specter? Where might the bullet land, do you think? Will it hover in the air? Or will it fall through to the ground?" She tugged at the gun, and with some reluctance I released my grip. She leaned it against the wall. "My love, tis not even loaded. You haven't loaded it since Father gave it to you. Do you even know how to shoot it?"

"I should learn." I gestured at the books on the shelves. "Those will do us no good if we are accosted in the night. I should learn how to properly protect you and the babe."

"Would you really shoot someone?"

I did not think she was trying to catch me out. She was simply sharing what she knew to be true. I'm her bookish husband who does not always know how to handle the world. And then I realized—I am Don Quixote after all. I say I ride into battle and strike at giants, but in reality I strike at monsters of my imaginings. But what if the monster does truly come one night? Would I know what to do?

Of course, Lizzie is right. Despite occasional daydreams to the contrary, I am not a violent man. I have never even raised a fist at another. If the moment came when I had to protect my wife and child or lose them, then aye, I believe I could do whatever violence was required. To save my family, there is nothing I shall not do— even taking the life of another pales in comparison to losing Lizzie forever. But sitting in the corner with naught but an empty barrel on my knee, waiting for who knows what to appear, was not helping. That much I knew.

Lizzie bent over and coughed as though she would vomit.

"What do you need, my love?" I asked. "I thought the sickness had passed."

"Some days are better than others. Right now I need to rest." She made her way back to bed. "I'll sleep awhile and then I'll be well again."

"But Lizzie." I wanted to do something to help her feel better.

Lizzie shook her head. "Truly, James, tis normal. Let me rest and later we'll talk about how you were going to shoot your empty gun at something that wasn't there."

I tucked her into bed with the quilts close to her shoulders and rubbed her back until she slept. When she was resting I wandered back into the hall and stoked the fire. It has been chilly despite the more frequent sunshine. Back in the Great Room, I stared at the chair by the door. Again, I thought to grab the gun, compelled to guard my wife as the names haunted me.

Abigail Barker
Mary Barker
Bridget Bishop
Sarah Bishop
Mary Black
Mary Bradbury
Hannah Bromage
Sarah Buckley
Elizabeth Cary
Sarah Churchill
Mary Clarke
Rachel Clinton
Sarah Cloyce
Sarah Cole
Elizabeth Colson
Giles Corey

Martha Corey
Deliverance Dane
Mary De Rich
Ann Dolliver
Lydia Dustin
Daniell Eames
Rebecca Eames
Mary Easty
Martha Emerson
Joseph Emons
Phillip English
Thomas Farrer
Edward Farrington
Abigail Faulkner, Sr
Dorothy Faulkner
Elizabeth Fosdick
Ann Foster
Nicholas Frost
Eunice Fry
Dorcas Good
Sarah Good
Mary Green
Elizabeth Hart
Margaret Hawkes
Sarah Hawkes
Dorcas Hoar
Abigail Hobbs
Deliverance Hobbs
William Hobbs
Elizabeth Howe
Elizabeth Hubbard
Mary Ireson
John Jackson, Sr
John Jackson, Jr

Margaret Jacobs
Rebecca Jacobs
Rebecca Johnson
Stephen Johnson
Jane Lilly
Mary Marston
Susannah Martin
Sarah Morey
Rebecca Nurse
Sarah Osborne
Mary Osgood
Alice Parker
Mary Parker
Susannah Post
Elizabeth Proctor
John Proctor
Sarah Proctor
Sarah Rice
Susannah Roots
Henry Salter
Susanna Sheldon
Abigail Somes
Martha Sparks
Mary Taylor
Tituba
Mercy Wardwell
Samuel Wardwell
Sarah Wardwell
Sarah Wilds

With so many accused, the pre-trial examinations continue. Husbands turn against wives, as when Giles Corey called out Martha, and then he was called out in his turn. Neighbors speak against neighbors. In a provincial land like Salem, few people are strangers. Either they are related by marriage or they are cousins or distant cousins, or they heard of someone from someone from someone. Perhaps they heard good things about these people, but more often than not tis the bad that sticks in the brain. Whenever we hear conflicting stories about someone, tis always the story that paints the person in a negative light that we remember. If we hear rumors about someone, whether or not that gossip is true, then that is what we believe. If we hear that Goody Crenwell beats her husband over the head with a fire poker, then we believe Goody Crenwell beats her husband whether she does or not. When we hear negativity about others, we want to suck the marrow from those bad feelings. We want to ingest it into ourselves. Ha! we say, I knew years ago that Goody Crenwell beat her husband. You can see the anger in her eyes. And we all agree. Tis a human illness, to want to believe the worst in others so we appear superior.

But why is that true? Why do we choose to believe the worst and not the best? Perhaps such negative thoughts about others allow us to forget what we do not like about ourselves. When we point a finger at others—look at how bad a husband he is; look at what a terrible mother she is—we deflect attention from our own shortcomings. These days, when so many look for reasons to make accusations, tis not so hard to pull names out of their arses. Everyone has a store of people they do not like—for various reasons. Goody Whatsit cut me on the street. Goodman Whoever let his horses graze on my land. That little girl took something, however trivial twas, but twas ours and she took it. Some of these families—the Putnams, the Nurses, and others—have been riding each other for generations. Now they have a weapon, a deadly weapon at that, and they cast that weapon far and wide until others beyond the scope of their blood feuds are caught. Again, I thought of my musket. I even thought I might load it this time. When the toe-tapping restlessness grew to be too much I had to do something besides sit. I checked on Lizzie, who was breathing deeply in sound sleep, then grabbed my coat and left.

Outside in the hazy sunlight fresh-blooming grass crunched beneath my boots. I hitched Euripides to the wagon and drove to the Village. I had no intention for where I was going. Finally, I decided to see Silas. I thought Lizzie would appreciate the gesture. She has been worried about him living on his own, and I was happy to check on him and perhaps try once again to persuade him to move to the Town. Silas saw me through the window and came outside as I tied Euripides to a tree. Puffing on his pipe, Silas blew the smoke away from my face. After exchanging pleasantries about how things were on the farm now that sowing season was in full swing, he clasped me by the shoulder and brought me inside.

Silas gestured to a chair and handed me a mug of apple cider. He puffed smoke rings into the air and we watched them dissipate near the window. Finally, he said, "I know you're worried about me being here on my own, the both of you, but you needn't be. I do get lonely from time to time. I can admit it, and it costs me nothing to do so. I've been used to having my daughters about. Peter has been gone since he was a boy, so his absence isn't felt." He gestured at everything in the bare room—the simple chairs and tables of various woods, the bed where Mary slept, the blankets cleared away. "Don't get me wrong. I'm appreciative that Elizabeth wants me near. But I need to be here."

"Near Mary."

"She's buried in the Village after all." After some silence, Silas said, "You're missing England, aren't you?"

"How did you know?"

"Elizabeth told me. Tis nothing to be ashamed of. I used to wonder if I made the right decision coming here." He winked at me. "But I know for certain my daughter wouldn't have made as fine a match there, now, would she?"

"Lizzie has given me my life, Silas. It frightens me to think who I would have been without her. I'd be half a man, I think, a shell of a person. My heart would have no reason to beat. I would have no reason to wake up in the morning. My life would be empty. Where would I be if Lizzie weren't there to keep me going? As for England, there's not much to be done about it. Lizzie and I are here for now."

"You still want to return to Cambridge?"

"Aye."

"Well." Silas puffed away the last of his pipe. "I'm an old farmer, and no one asked my opinion, but I'd say you've earned the right to do what you please. You've helped to get John set up here in Massachusetts. I'd say tis your turn." Silas squinted at me with that inquisitive glare only a father-in-law can turn on you. He raised his mug in my direction. We drank Lizzie's health, and Silas grew somber again. "The weather has warmed. You could leave for England soon if you wanted."

"Lizzie fears for the child."

"Aye, well. The passage isn't pretty, is it?"

"Tis not. Perhaps we can go after the child is born." I spoke more to myself than Silas. I finished my ale. "Would you come, Silas? If we returned to England? I know it would make Lizzie so happy. You would always have a home with us whether we settle in London or Cambridge."

Silas held the pipe close to his lips before remembering he puffed it out. "Before Mary died," he said, "I would have said no. Mary loved it in Massachusetts. She loved the curiosity of it, the differences in the way people act, the differences in religion, and the excitement of a new adventure. Now?" He gestured once again at our simple surroundings. "I reckon these things, this farm, well, it wouldn't have the same meaning if my family weren't near."

"You would leave Mary buried in the Village to return to England? You won't leave her to live with us in the Town."

Silas laughed. "That doesn't make much sense, I reckon. I'm a farmer and I don't belong in the Town with fancy folks such as yourself. But England is home for me as much as you. I think, if I said a prayer to Mary, if I told her I was going home with you and

Elizabeth, I think she'd be all right with it. I'd be a failure, but I'd be home."

"You would not be a failure for returning to England," I said.

"And neither would you."

Silas brought me outside. Pointing at the flat fields with his thumb, he told me that now that the land is drying he plows and seeds nearly every hour of daylight. I offered to help, but he laughed at me.

"There's no way John Wentworth's son is working my field."

"My back is as strong as the next man's," I said.

Silas studied me from the top of my head to the bottom of my boots. That must be how horses feel when they are being appraised. "You may be stronger yet for you're so much taller."

"Then let me help." I grabbed the plow lying on the rocky ground but Silas snatched it away and pressed me toward Euripides. Reluctantly, I walked toward my horse.

Silas tugged on my arm and I turned to him. "Promise me you'll protect our Elizabeth. She's a woman and women can be weak. The Devil is real, you know." He dropped his voice and I strained to hear. "I cannot save Elizabeth from Satan if we're under his domain here. Tis about saving Elizabeth's soul. Women are more susceptible to Satan's Evil influence. But I know I can trust you to watch out for my daughter." Before I could respond, Silas said, "Good day to you, James. God bless you." He walked toward his field without looking back. I wanted to yell out to him that Lizzie shall never be touched by Evil, but then I remembered that, just this morn, I sat near my door with an unloaded musket over my knee.

I tugged Euripides' reins and steered him toward the road. Twas growing late when I headed home. The light in the sky faded and I wondered if I would be back before twas too dark to see.

Twas not too dark for me to see the Weird Sisters in the middle of the road. They stood, a circle of three, holding hands, their uncovered reddish hair flowing down their backs. Their eyes were closed whilst their lips pressed into slits. I looked back and saw Silas in the distance hitching his plow to his oxen. He was fixed on his task and did not seem to notice the women. I left Euripides to snicker at me, I'm certain he was perplexed as to why I left him in the middle of the road, and I walked toward the sisters, stepping as quietly as I could though I was certain they could hear the twigs snapping beneath my boots. Who are these women, I wondered? Why do they appear as if out of the air? They huddled close and chanted words with the cadence of an old-time melody. What language did they speak? Greek? Latin? Hebrew? I stood a few paces away, afeared to come too near. The women stopped as though frozen. It took a moment, I'm not always good with names, but then I remembered Lizzie telling me: Malka, Mazel, and Miriam. Staring at the three sisters, I wondered if they were indeed in league with the Devil.

As the word Devil flashed through my mind, the tallest sister, the one called Miriam, laughed. I see you, she seemed to say. And I know you see me.

I opened my mouth to speak. I had so many questions. But all I could say was, "Did you mean to help Mary with your herbs? She died, you know."

"Aye," Miriam said. "We know. And we're sorry for it. Truly. She was a good girl."

"She was," I said. The others nodded. Do they do everything in unison, I wondered? "There are those who believe Mary was bewitched."

The women laughed, again in unison.

"Stuff and nonsense!" said Miriam. "We tried to cure her. The first time, the girl believed our herbs would help and they did. The second time, she believed she was beyond help so they didn't. Our herbs only cure when people believe they can be cured. Yet you believe she was bewitched! Can you people not tell when someone is trying to help or trying to hurt? Tis why you cannot find your way out of your arseholes." The other two cackled, a sad attempt at a laugh, I thought. "Perhaps one day you shall know a good thing when you see it."

The women turned back into a circle and raised their arms toward Heaven.

"Wait!" I called. "Tell me—are you sisters?"

They were gone, quick as you like. The wind picked up, howling its strength inland from the bay. The brisk air stung my eyes and I covered my face with my arm to protect myself from the whips of cold. Twas such a strong current I would not have been surprised to find myself blown back to Town, Odysseus in the temper of the storm. Then the wind vanished. No matter where I looked there were no traces of the sister-women, not a footstep, not a bent blade of grass.

There has been such talk about Witches and Wizards and Devils nowadays I think I see them everywhere. I decided that when I arrived home I would grab my musket again and take my watch near the door. But what would I shoot at, the darkness? A falling leaf? In that moment I understood how people might call out others as Witches. Again, it crossed my mind to make a complaint against them. But what would I say? The women have not afflicted me or anyone else as far as I know. And again, I think, what if they are what they seem to be? Healers trying to heal? And if I do not believe in the Devil then how can I believe he recruits for his army of dark angels?

Standing in the middle of the road, surrounded by no one, I climbed onto the wagon, tugged on Euripides' reins, and headed home. Twas well dark when I arrived. I thought, with some satisfaction, that I had in fact traveled my own Odyssey, encountered my own strange beings, and found my way into the arms of my own Penelope, waiting for me.

28 APRIL 1692, THURSDAY

ather and I attended Lecture in the Village. Lizzie, still ill on a morn, stayed behind, though Silas was there. He would not sit with us, though. He says he is too humble a farmer, though Father and I insist otherwise. On and on Parris droned, mocking those who would not see what he commanded them to see. False and Untrue Prophets, he called them. Only by turning our true faith unto God can we overcome the dangers the Devil has sent upon we sinners of Salem. Parris urged us to shake off our spiritual and moral apathy. With a voice of thunder, Parris said we are watching the dawn of End Times.

"These are dangerous days." Parris pummeled his fist to the lectern whilst his face flashed fury. I thought the lectern would shatter and Parris would disappear where no one would see him again. Not that I would mind. "Before us we have the final reckoning. The Lord Almighty shall strike us down for our sins! We have disobeyed! We have allowed Witchcraft into our midst! We have been wicked, and now we are damned!" The man next to me shook in his seat, his arms and legs twitching. One woman stifled a scream.

After Lecture Father and I mingled outside with the round-headed Mr. Boxley and the lean-faced Mr. Stevens, both of whom spoke of the Reverend Mr. Parris as though he had important things to say. Their minds had been easily swayed in Parris' favor, I thought. Father, needing to change the subject, lured Mr. Boxley into a discussion about readying the ships that would soon disembark with their cargos. I nodded when appropriate but otherwise did not care. A woman stopped near us, polite in that simpering way the wealthy have. I sighed with some irritation when I recognized the woman as Mistress Boxley, her face, as always, heavily powdered in a failed attempt to hide the pockmarks. She glanced furtively round, seeing who paid her mind. She must always know who else is there so she knows she is the better of them. I bowed in her general direction and her head tipped so I could see her pearl-lined coif and the iridescent pearls dangling near her high collar. From the short walk from the women's door to where everyone congregated outside whilst the wealthier waited for their servants to pull round their carriages, she heaved for breath.

"Mr. Wentworth the younger!" she called. Her tone was cloying but I did not care enough to wonder why. I wanted to get home to Lizzie. Then Mistress Boxley said, "And where is Mistress Wentworth? Not here again? She missed Church in the Town last week, did she not?"

"My wife is not well. I'm certain she shall attend services soon."

I looked for Father—he is much better at escaping unwanted social advances than me—but he was still engaged in a hearty conversation with Mr. Boxley. I tried to make eye contact with Father, a silent plea for help, but he was not paying attention so I was on my own. I turned to Mistress Boxley, hoping she would remain silent whilst waiting for her husband. I had no such luck. I searched for Mistress Whitby since her puckered features would provide me with a welcome escape. Certainly, Mistress Boxley would prefer the company of her esteemed friend. Again, I had no such luck.

Mistress Boxley smiled demurely at me. "I do miss seeing your wife, Mr. Wentworth. She is always so lovely in that embroidered brown cloak." She waited as though expecting me to reply. When I did not, she added, "And that ruby ring she wears. How lovely."

"Twas a wedding present from me," I said.

"Lovely. Lovely. She is so fortunate, your wife. To marry the son of a wealthy merchant when so many young women far more suitable to your station were available? How on earth did Mistress Wentworth manage that? Twas as though she put a spell on you. Especially since you are your father's sole heir, is that not so? He has no other sons?"

"He has no other living children," I said.

"My point precisely. If something were to happen to you then your excellent wife would inherit everything, would she not?"

"If our child is a son then he shall inherit."

"And if tis not a boy?"

"Excuse me," I said, "but what business is that of yours?"

"None at all, Mr. Wentworth. I was merely curious. Ah." Mistress Whitby appeared, dour as always. "Please do allow me to pay my respects to Mistress Whitby." I nodded, and Mistress Whitby and Mistress Boxley left with their heads close together. They glanced in my direction one too many times for my comfort.

I could not shake the feel of their prying eyes pecking holes into my skull. My blood flamed like hot spots under my skin and the faint breeze ruffling the spring-green leaves was not enough to settle me. I had to get away so I climbed into Father's carriage, the awkward-looking one with two smaller wheels in front and two larger wheels behind. I believe Father collects carriages the way others collect dust. Twas the French carriage modeled after the Baroque fashion with scarlet-colored scrollwork along the door. Father has his fancies, after all. I pulled out my copy of *Don Quixote* whilst I waited. I cannot get the story from my mind.

Father, Boxley, and Stevens continued their conversation. Finally, Father said he would meet them at the dock. The merchants nodded in my direction and I returned the gesture with as much good nature as I could muster. Father and I traveled the barren road from Village to Town chatting of nothing in particular. At the dock seagulls squawked and workmen hammered, sawed, and swore enough to prompt the Reverend Mr. Parris to pray harder for Salem's salvation. Father stopped his carriage only feet from where the *Rachel*, every inch as steady as Mother, sat. The ship was long, lean, and hearty, bobbing with the tide, the sails flapping in the snappy breeze whilst men carried barrels of rum and textiles to the hold below.

"Shall you still travel aboard the *Rachel* as its supercargo?" I asked.

"Not this time," Father said.

"I thought you wanted to see your expensive bounties reach their destinations."

"I did think to represent the safekeeping of our wares this time round, but I'm not sure I should go now."

"Perhaps next time," I said.

"Aye," Father said. "Next time."

Mr. Boxley and Mr. Stevens had already arrived and they shuffled toward us from the sea. "Wentworth and Son!" Boxley cried. "We almost did not come to meet you. I had forgotten there shall be another pre-trial examination. The Reverend Mr. Parris himself shall record the events."

"And Hathorne, Corwin, and the others shall make pronouncements," I said.

"They are most certainly enjoying themselves," Father said.

"Reverend Parris knows of which he speaks," Mr. Stevens said. "He understands the people of Salem. He knows what is best." Twas perhaps the third time I heard the man speak. With his raspy voice, I understood why he said so little. Father looked at him but said nothing. "Did you know Reverend Parris' family used to prosecute Quakers?" Mr. Stevens turned to me with a smirk. Tis hard to tell sometimes when his expression changes since his features are frozen into a perpetual grimace. "Hathorne's father was an enemy to the Quakers as well. He had Quaker women whipped. The son takes after the father, only in this case tis the Witches who are punished."

"The suspected Witches," I said.

"The suspected Witches?" Stevens stepped toward me. "Have you not heard? They send their Shapes to torture people in the night. They must be removed from polite society."

I turned toward the wharf where there was much coming and going, cargo loaded, cargo hauled away, sails lowered, sails hoisted. Loudest of all were the fish women shouting their wares. When Mr. Richards appeared I was grateful since I no longer felt obliged to respond to Mr. Stevens.

"Speaking of Hathorne, were ye?" Mr. Richards asked. "Hathorne's father was a wealthy man. Owned much of the farmland in the Village, he did." He nodded as though Hathorne himself were there, staring down upon some poor accused woman. "He had my job, keeping books for the merchants."

"Cooking the books?" Father laughed at his joke. "The elder Mr. Hathorne bought land, then a ship, then a crew, then a mansion."

Mr. Richards nodded. "With wealth came self-importance, and with self-importance came judging appointments."

"Those appointments come with great responsibility," Father said. "And what of Corwin? Do you know anything of Corwin?"

"You know him perfectly well, Wentworth," said Mr. Boxley. "You've done business enough with him."

"I thought I knew him. I cannot say I know anyone for certain anymore. It does not take much for people to become turgid toward one another."

"I reckon I know the same as anyone," Mr. Richards said. "He too comes from a family that dislikes Quakers."

"What can anyone possibly have against Quakers!" As the words left my mouth I knew I spoke out of turn.

As always, Father came to my rescue. "The Quakers believe that everyone is loved and guided by God. They believe that everyone has a direct relationship with God. What is so terrible about that?" He squinted into the endless rise and ebb of the tide as though expecting Poseidon himself to swim in on the waves. "And where is that dastardly Thomas Oliver? He said he would be here with news about that shipment of molasses I have been waiting for."

I wish I were a braver man. I wish I dared to do as Prometheus and give humans the power of fire, the light of civilization, despite knowing I would be tortured daily until Heracles saved me—however long that might be. I am no Titan but a mere mortal and there are times, many times, when my courage falters. Still, I wanted to stand at the rocky edge of the shore and shout to the world, "The accused are not Witches! My wife is a Quaker!" But I said nothing. I kept my head down and waited for Father to finish his chat. I wondered if I could leave Father alone in Salem after all. How can I leave him to the whims of these unpredictable folks?

Finally, we left the merchants by the sea. After our short journey, Father stopped his carriage and we sat for some time staring at this house, the dark wood slats, the two pointed gables, the diamond-paned casement windows, and the green door. I glanced round, checking that no one was within hearing distance. I saw no one but Father and me and the oak tree leaning like a crooked old man.

"Really, Father," I said as I climbed down from the carriage and walked toward the door. "One of these days you'll say something that shall get you into trouble."

"One of these days, Son. But not yet."

"What else do you know of Corwin besides the fact that he dislikes Quakers? You know him better than I do."

"You never have been much of a social butterfly."

"I do not need to be social. I have my books, and I have Lizzie."

Father laughed. "Aye, James, you do have Elizabeth, forever and always, I believe. As for Corwin, I know he went with Hathorne to discover the reason why Boston wasn't sending more men to fight the Indians. I know Corwin married well, above his station, some might say."

"It happens." Mistress Boxley's words rattled like seashells in my skull.

"I'm concerned that Corwin has not handled cases of the magnitude of these Witch examinations before," Father said. "He has handled petty crimes like public drunkenness and theft. He serves on the Witch examinations only because Saltonstall resigned."

I stopped walking. "Why resigned?"

"Spectral evidence. Saltonstall objects to the use of Spectral evidence, but Hathorne is in favor of it so tis still being used."

I saw Lizzie through the window chopping the veg for our evening meal. Father removed his hat and held his face up to the sunlight and the ocean spray. He followed me inside and Lizzie greeted us both with apple cider cold from the cellar. She looked better when I arrived home, her cheeks blushing the color of sweet williams. Father pulled a chair aside and gestured for her to sit.

"What are people speaking of these days?" Lizzie said. "Or need I ask?"

"James and I were just discussing the fact that Hathorne shall continue to allow Spectral evidence at the examinations."

"So they will allow nothing to be used as proof of a crime?"

"They are, indeed, Daughter. The Devil is strong enough to send his minion's Spirits to hurt others in body and lead their souls astray. The afflicted claim to have marks on their bodies where they have been hurt by Specters."

"What do you think the marks are from?" I asked.

"Honestly, Son, I do not know. Hathorne and Corwin are not trained lawyers, or doctors for that matter. They are men, merchants like us, who are respected in the community. They believe that Salem is infected by the Devil. And they believe that the marks on the bodies of the afflicted were put there by Specters."

"Do they truly believe that?" I asked.

"I think they are doing the best they can with what they know. Still, some do not believe in Spectral evidence. Despite Hathorne's decision, they may yet rule it out."

"Ha!" I paced from the window to the hearth. "With Cotton Mather on the side of Spectral evidence there is little chance of that. He has quoted Reverend Hale's idea that Spectral evidence may be suitable when necessary. I'm certain in Hale's eyes a war against the Devil would be one instance where such evidence is necessary."

"They should give it up," Father said. "Admit what it is—a silly game that got out of hand."

"The afflicted are easy to believe," Lizzie said. "When I saw Betty and Abigail thrashing about I didn't know what to think."

"So we put them on the stage," Father said. "We let them play-act. For all the world's a stage."

"But they are already on the stage," I said. "A bigger stage than any in London."

Lizzie rested her weight against the table and pressed into her lower back with her fists. "What is the one thing these girls have now that they didn't have before?" When neither Father nor I answered, Lizzie said, "They have attention. You may not realize, being men as you are, but women are much ignored in this world. We're to be seen and not heard, perhaps even more so here in Massachusetts than in England. We're not to speak unless spoken to. Boys are honored children. They carry on the family name, after all. When they're older they support their families, or at least they're expected to. Girls are a burden to be clothed and fed until they're old enough to marry."

"Silas never thought of you like that," I said. "He promised your mother he would never force you to marry."

"I was one of the lucky ones, James. I found you. Mary, had she lived, would have hopefully been fortunate in her husband as well. But look at the women round you, Town or Village, and tell me you envy their lives. Everything about them—from the moment they are born until the moment they die—is decided for them by whatever man is in their lives. That man may be a father, a brother, a husband, a son, or even a son-in-law who feels no love for her. Imagine having your life decided by someone who considers you a burden, someone who doesn't care whether you live or die?"

Father nodded. "You are right, Daughter. There are neglected women everywhere."

"Sarah Good is only one such woman who suffers," Lizzie said. "There are women whose husbands abandoned them. Women whose husband drank away their earnings. Women whose husbands beat them. Goody Good begged door to door for enough for her children to eat. Now she and the others are accused because the afflicted have everyone's attention. People are paying them mind."

"Why doesn't someone stop the afflicted from making such accusations?" Father asked. "Haven't they done enough harm?"

"Some have tried, Father," Lizzie said, "and they have failed."

We fell silent. I certainly did not know what to say.

"Ah well. Tis a puzzle for another time." Father grasped Lizzie's hand. "You, my dear, need rest."

He excused himself, and Lizzie and I were alone. Twas dark then, the sun all but gone behind the edge of the sky, the bay barely visible but for a ripple here and there in the moonlight. Lizzie lit candles and poked the fire higher and hotter. She pulled her needlework from the basket and showed me her work—clothing for the babe. She is sewing a long-sleeved gown as well as an ivory linen biggin with ribbons. I nodded at the little cap, content at the thought of the three of us together, living our lives, fulfilled in one another, whether it be here or in England. I wondered again if I could leave Father alone in this strange land with these strange people and their strange customs. I cannot make a decision, and I do not like that I am constantly swinging back and forth, a clock pendulum, remain, leave, remain, leave, again and again, until I hardly know which end is up. Again, I broached the subject to gauge Lizzie's reaction.

"Silas said he would return to England with us," I said. "Tis odd. He shall not come to live with us in the Town yet he said he would return to England because tis home."

"England will always be our home," Lizzie said.

"Do you truly want to return, Lizzie? To England?"

Lizzie held the biggin close to her heart. Her full-lipped smile took my breath away. "Tis just as I've said, James. Wherever you are is home to me. You must know that. Have you decided again to return to England?"

I grasped a book from the shelf for want of something to do with my hands. I flipped the pages, set the book down, picked it up again, then flipped the pages some more. "I do not know what I want."

"Aye, you do."

I closed my eyes. What did I truly want, for myself, for Lizzie, for our growing family? I saw my University, my College, my River, my friends, my books. "I want to return to England," I said. "I see us there, Lizzie. I see us with our child…"

"Our daughter."

"Aye, our daughter, in Cambridge, joyous in one another."

"That sounds right, my love. I know you aren't content here. I see it in the way you hold yourself so stiffly round everyone but Father and me. I hear it in your clipped tone of voice when you speak to others when tis not your way to speak so. I feel it in the troubled air surrounding you." Lizzie took my hand and held it to her heart. "If going home to England means so much to you, then we should go."

"Truly?"

"Gladly. And we'll take Pa and we'll settle him well and make him as happy as he can be." Lizzie picked up her sewing and worked the babe's cap. She watched me over the top of her bobbing needles. As has become her habit, she read my mind. "You would be all right leaving Father here? Can we not persuade him to come as well?"

"He is happy now in a way he has not been since Mother died. He has found his place here, importing molasses and exporting rum, making himself a greater fortune in the process." Lizzie's eyes watered. "What is it, my love?"

"The thought of Father here by himself makes me sad. I don't want him to be lonely."

"Father is never lonely. He is far more sociable than me. He shall always have a table where he can dine in company." I spoke to convince myself as much as Lizzie.

Lizzie shook her head. "I can still hardly believe he named a ship for me."

"I can think of no one more beautiful to name a ship for."

I grabbed Lizzie's hand and kissed her fingers. She dropped the cap into the basket and leaned toward me. I kissed her lips and kissed her lips again. So tis what the great songs are about, I thought. Tis why the poets write about love. For this feeling alone.

"Read to me, James," Lizzie said.

"You're reading well enough now. You should read to me."

"But I love the sound of your voice. I don't know if tis because you're educated, or the tone of it, but it soothes me. Won't you read to me?"

Always one to do my wife's bidding, I nodded. "What would you like to hear?"

"You already know."

I reached for the slim brown volume. Amongst all the books we have, Lizzie always wants to hear Anne Bradstreet. I opened to a random page, the one with the poem "A Letter to her Husband, absent upon Publick employment." I read:

My head, my heart, mine Eyes, my life, nay more,
My joy, my Magazine of earthly store,

If two be one, as surely thou and I,
How stayest thou there, whilst I at Ipswich lye?
So many steps, head from the heart to sever
If but a neck, soon should we be together:
I like the earth this season, mourn in black,
My Sun is gone so far in's Zodiack,
Whom whilst I joy'd, nor storms, nor frosts I felt,
His warmth such frigid colds did cause to melt...

Lizzie and I finished the poem together.

"You are my head, my heart, mine eyes, my life, and more," I said.

Lizzie leaned her head against my shoulder. "And you are mine."

3 MAY 1692, TUESDAY

Sunday's sermon sits like bricks on my brain. I cannot get Parris from my mind, his long hair curling round his face, though there is nothing youthful in his hardened gaze. I wonder how his mind works, how he makes connections from one to the next. Is he a logical man? I cannot say. Tis true he has not received his salary for some time, and anyone working without payment has reason enough to be bitter. His lack of payment stems from the fact that the people of the Village are not in connection with themselves. Half the Villagers want this, half the Villagers want that. Some Farmers squabble for this. Some Farmers squabble for that. Parris, though I may not like what he says or how he says it, suffers for it. Since he continues without his salary, since he does not get what he wants, he remains steadfast in his proclamations that the Devil has overtaken Salem. He is hardly the first in New England, the first anywhere for that matter, to follow such logic.

Every day more people are persuaded by Parris, parroting his words. Perhaps they have always believed ill of their friends and neighbors but now tis appropriate to say so aloud. Witchcraft accusations are nothing new. People have been accused of Witch-craft for centuries. But tis the first time I have witnessed it myself, and I see how Parris infects many with his browbeating words. These are people who feel neglected, forgotten, swept aside with the horse dung. Then here comes Parris with his booming voice, his hardened gaze, and he speaks for them. And since he speaks for them, they decide he must be right in everything he says. Who else understands them so well? If Parris says the Devil has overtaken Salem, then the Devil has overtaken Salem. If Parris says the Devil must be flushed from Salem like putrefaction from a wound, then Satan must be vanquished.

I reckon twas something Parris said in his sermon that caught my attention particularly. He addressed the congregation with the text from 1 Corinthians 10:21: "Ye cannot drink the cup of the Lord and the cup of the Devil. Ye cannot be partakers of the Lord's Table and the Table of the Devil." Oh, aye, Parris is a good one for choosing tasty bites for his followers to swallow. He knows the right passage for the right moment. Yet, conveniently, he left out the next passage: "Are we trying to arouse the Lord's jealousy? Are we stronger than he? I have the right to do anything, you say—but not everything is beneficial. I have the right to do anything—but not everything is constructive."

Father, who attended the sermon as well, leaned forward as he listened. I whispered the missing line, and Father, who knows the Bible far better than I, said, "There is yet one more line Parris forgets: *No one should seek their own good, but the good of others.*" I could hear the hmph! under his breath. "And pray tell, which of these Witchcraft examinations are for the good of others?"

A farmer turned a rude squint onto us and Father and I fell silent, listening whilst Parris berated the congregation for attempting to drink from both the cup of the Lord and the cup of the Devil. As Parris raged, Abigail Williams, Ann Putnam Junior, and Mercy Lewis flailed and jabbered. The magistrates were sought out and brought to the Village. With the presence of those in authority, several of the afflicted complained against the widow Bethia Carter, her daughter Bethia junior, the widow Ann Sears from Woburn, and Sarah Dustin from Reading. These women, simply going about their lives, were dragged to the Meeting House. George Burroughs, himself a former minister of the Village, had his examination as well. Burroughs was arrested four days prior, though few took his accusation seriously since it came from his former congregation to whom he owed money. Despite my misgivings, I followed Father to Burroughs' examination. As Burroughs was wheeled past, his hands bound, his head down, spectators jeered.

"He's a minister," I said. "Are not even ministers safe?"

"But Burroughs isn't ordained, is he?" said the wheelwright beside me. "And he don't take communion, do he?"

Burroughs' examination was something new so the crowds trebled in size. Everyone wanted to see the former minister accused of Witchcraft. Hathorne and Corwin called for extra hands, and William Stoughton and Samuel Sewall joined them. Parris sat at the front, his frown etching deep lines round his mouth whilst he took notes. At first, the magistrates spoke to Burroughs in private, but when Burroughs was brought into the Meeting House the afflicted screamed.

Hathorne, in the role of Judge, pummeled Burroughs by twisting his words. Burroughs admitted that none of his children but one were baptized. He moved to Maine, but he did not know of any Witches or Ghosts there, only toads. Was he cruel to his wives, Hathorne demanded?

"Ha!" Father said. "If cruelty to wives were proof of Witchcraft, half the men in the Village are Wizards. Many men throughout the World, for that matter."

Burroughs would not be beaten down by Hathorne's verbal taunts, and the former minister insisted that he had not been cruel to any of his wives. Whatever was or was not admitted to, the magistrates heard enough to order Burroughs held for trial. The women from outside Salem were brought in. They were called Bitch Witches, accused of signing their names to the Devil's book, sending their Specters to torment people, using black coins as bribes to entice innocent others to touch the book. The women's Shapes were crying for vengeance, the afflicted said, grinding their teeth, blinding their victims. One afflicted cried that she could not see since one Specter covered her eyes. Another afflicted screamed because a Specter poked her. A man next to me nodded, saying, "I knew that one was a Bitch Witch. I knew it all along." And those poor women were held for trial as well.

Then something happened, something perhaps even the afflicted did not expect. Someone confessed to Witchcraft. The woman from Woburn was asked if she was a Witch, and she, like Tituba before her, said aye. The woman agreed with whatever the afflicted accused her of. Aye, she put her fingers in their ears. Aye, she signed her name in the Devil's book. Aye, she consorted with the Devil. Aye aye aye. When asked if she repented of her Evil ways —aye. And she was reprieved.

Lizzie did not see the examinations. She spent time with Silas instead. I tried to explain what I had seen, but I could not. All my learning had been wiped from my brain as though I spilled ink over every word I ever knew. For Lizzie, the hardest part was understanding the woman from Woburn.

"Why would she confess if she is no Witch?" Lizzie asked.

"Now she is free," I said. "She is no longer under suspicion. As far as Hathorne is concerned, she has repented so now she is back with God. She is no longer a threat to the people. Wouldn't you do the same if it meant you could be free?"

Lizzie scrubbed Silas' table as though venting her agitation. "They must know she's only saying what she thinks they want to hear."

"The magistrates, the people for that matter, do not believe the accused when they say they are not conspiring with the Devil.

Perhaps this woman is onto something. Perhaps confessing is the way out."

Silas said nothing. He puffed on his pipe, the smoke swirling above his gray head in ringlets. Lizzie stared into the red-orange flames shooting upward from the hearth as though they would whip the tipping chimney back into place. She shrugged at her own thoughts. Finally, she said, "I could never lie like that. People would think I was Evil. God would think I disobeyed."

"No one could think you are Evil," I said. "And God, if He be all you believe, knows the truth of your heart better than anyone, better than me, even, and I know you best of all."

Lizzie nodded but she did not look convinced. I could see she was tired. Twas time to return home.

19 MAY 1692, THURSDAY

*A*s with any Election Day, here or in England, nothing changes. People on this side of the Atlantic particularly enjoy their elections. As soon as one ends, another begins. And yet everything stays the same.

Election Day was unusually warm for a May day. Father and I visited the dock where the *Elizabeth* receives her final coats of paint in preparation for her maiden voyage. We chose not to go to hear the election numbers as they were called. The results were predictable—the same, and the same, and the same. We knew who would win, who would always win. Danforth is again Deputy Governor. Sewall, Hathorne, and Corwin remain amongst the 18 assistants. Sir William Phips—shepherd boy, shipwright, captain, pirate, major general, becomes the first appointed Governor of Massachusetts Bay due to his charter from the very King himself. Those of us unhappy with the direction of the Witchcraft examinations are let down. The same, and the same, and the same.

This Sunday past we attended Church in the Village. Since Lizzie's absences from the sermons have been noted she did her due diligence and appeared before the Puritan God. Her own God, a quiet, thoughtful God, does not need sacrificial lambs to be led to the slaughter as the Puritan God demands. I shall do what I must to quell the questioning of the likes of Mistress Boxley, and if that means parading Lizzie before the busybodies then that is what shall happen.

When Lizzie appeared at the Meeting House the women crowded round her, admiring her finely tailored skirts and her gold wedding ring as they have many times before. She is always patient with everyone, Lizzie. She answered questions about her illness without letting on the true cause since we keep our blessing amongst only family for now. Even so, a few of the matrons nodded at Lizzie with the solemnity of understanding. Lizzie accepted the kind words for Mary, and she did not appear to notice if others glanced at her over their shoulders with pinched mouths and whispering eyes.

"Well," Father said after the services as we headed toward home. "They have seen you now, Elizabeth. They have seen that you are well. Let that nonsense be done with."

Lizzie watched the rural scenery, the trees and the grass, the edges and the ridges, the rocky ground and the rivers, but said nothing. Father steered his carriage down the well-worn road and there they were yet again, the Weird Sisters. As they had the last time I saw them, they chanted their strange gibberish and raised their hands toward the white-cloud sky. From the affrighted look on Lizzie's face, I thought she felt the same as me—perhaps these women were beckoning Satan after all. Father, however, kept his eyes straight ahead. He spoke to Poppers and Gertrude, his brown mares, about the sturdy blue sky in Salem. Lizzie and I did not speak of what we saw. We exchanged a glance that said all.

WHEN I AWOKE THIS MORN I FELT A GRASPING HAND REACH FOR MY neck, as though it would strangle the very breath from me. In my mind's eye I saw the sister-women summoning the long-faced man

I've seen before, the one with wisps of gray in his red-brown hair. I saw the man turn his cackling, blood-dripping grin in my direction. Twas that strange state where you are conscious but not quite awake, and behind my closed eyelids I saw Goodman Ackrood, dead this year past, walking round as though naught was amiss, all was well, and tis every night when the dead walk amongst us. Finally, with some struggle, I opened my eyes and saw myself safe in my bed with Lizzie beside me. I woke Lizzie and told her my dream. She took my hands between hers and ran her fingers through my hair, pressing some ever-stubborn strands behind my ear. I held onto her, thinking she would keep me anchored to the Earth—this woman, with this smile, with these eyes, with this soul. This woman, who is my reason for living.

After I settled some, she said, "Tis your imagination that's got away with you, James. You've had a bad dream. That's all." She fluffed the pillows and gestured for me to lie down. "Go back to sleep. Father said he didn't need you this day so you can stay in bed as long as you like. Sleep, my love."

"How can I sleep when we cannot escape? I am afeared we are trapped here, Lizzie. I think we are caged."

"In Massachusetts?"

"Aye."

Lizzie gestured at our bedroom, the damask wall coverings, the finely carved furnishings, the wall-length wardrobe. "Tis no cage, James. Tis our beautiful home. No one can touch us here."

"Are you certain?"

"There are no chanting sisters or dead men nearby. Tis only me and I'll never encage you."

I kissed her lips. She tastes like strawberries. "Lizzie, you encaged me from the moment I first saw you."

Lizzie stroked my cheek. "Which is as it should be since you did the same to me."

My heart still pounded as though it would break free from my chest and fly away. I stretched back in bed, though I did not sleep again and watched the sunrise. Later, after I dressed and broke my fast with beef, bread, and milk, Father arrived to say that some of the jailed Witches were being transported to Boston that very moment.

"Why?" Lizzie asked.

"Because the Salem Jail is bursting past capacity. There is no room for everyone. Meanwhile, more complaints are made. Mercy Lewis and Mary Warren are always in the middle of such things, are they not? They are the first to cackle and moan during examinations. They are first to accuse."

"Are these newly named women arrested?" Lizzie asked.

Father shook his head. "Not as of yet. Hathorne and Corwin are too busy taking depositions against Bridget Bishop."

"She was one of the first arrested," I said.

"Aye. But they have not bothered with her until now. She was not important enough, I reckon."

Lizzie held a mug of cider toward Father. "You look as though you could use it, Father."

"Aye, Daughter. Thank you. In fact, I could use something stronger."

"We may have some rum in the cellar," I said.

"Then I shall take some. I shall take the strongest of whatever you have right now."

Lizzie went down to the cellar and returned with a bottle of rum, the white Wentworth and Son label an eyesore against the dark glass. Sometimes I have to remind myself that I am the son, which is why I still struggle with the decision to leave Father in Salem.

Father filled his mug with the golden brown liquid. He sipped the top layer so it would not spill onto the lace tablecloth. "Now," he said, "they shackle the accused in prison. At first, when those called out against were arrested, the afflicted claimed to feel better. But now the afflicted say that even from jail the accused Witches violate them so they chain the accused to the wall."

"They are shackling the women in jail because the afflicted say the Shapes hurt them?" I said. "They believe pinning down the body will stop someone's Spirit from leaving? I thought they believed someone's Specter could do ill will no matter what the physical body did. They must make up their minds. They cannot have it both ways."

"Are you still trying to make sense of this, Son?" Father laughed with a stage actor's depth.

After Father left restless energy poked my legs, so much so I went for a walk across Town. At the tavern, I overheard two men saying how Attorney General Newton wrote a report stating that someone's social status did not save them from being accused, not this time, even though such status has saved others in the past. As more are accused, suspected Witches now occupy all ranks, including the most respected members of Town or Village Society.

By the time I headed home twas well dark. The night was bright, the light of a full moon filtering through water-filled clouds whilst the ground rattled under knocks of thunder. It had not started raining yet, but I felt damp in the air and knew I had to get home before the storm broke. The gloomy night sky reminded me of my nightmare and my skin prickled and my breath came in stilted bursts. The hair on the back of my neck stood on end. My mouth went dry and humidity lingered as sweat beneath my shirt. Twas a quiet night, no one else was about, but still I played the owl, twisting my neck in unnatural ways, turning in every direction at once. Footsteps slapped behind me. Twas our neighbor, Mr. Russert.

"Young Mr. Wentworth!" Mr. Russert cried. He wiped his brow with his handkerchief. "Thank the Lord tis only you. I was afeared when I heard footsteps and could not see in the dark. I've heard tell there have been bodies found with bite marks on their necks."

"Are there wolves about?" I asked.

He leaned toward me and whispered. "Tis marks from human teeth!"

"What rubbish."

"Oh, no, young sir. They are indeed marks made by humans for no animal—wolf, dog, or otherwise—has such teeth."

"You have seen such things?"

"Oh, aye. And the people who are bitten have their blood drained dry until they shrivel like prunes. No one sees them in the sunshine, that is, if they are ever seen again."

I laughed. "You tell such tales, Mr. Russert."

"They are no tales, Mr. Wentworth. These walking corpses are white-skinned and black-eyed, and there is blood everywhere about them—on their mouths, on their hands, on their clothing. They walk about dazed, wandering, looking for their families, slaughtering people or animals for blood to drink—"

I had to stop writing. There was such a thud outside the window my hand stuttered. Perhaps twas the remembrance of my conversation with Mr. Russert. Perhaps twas some other Invisible terror. Whatever twas, I had to look. I pulled aside the draperies and then, as he was in my dream, I saw him—the tall, long-faced man with the silver streaks in his red-brown hair. He saw me too. He tipped his long-brimmed hat toward me, bowed, and vanished faster than I could snap my fingers.

I must be losing my mind. Perhaps I am afflicted after all.

1 JUNE 1692, WEDNESDAY

*Y*esterday Father was at the end of his rope after he learned what has been going on along the coast. He could not contain his wrath for those involved.

"Who knew French privateers could wreak such havoc!" He did not intend his tone for me, I knew, so I continued to work the maths, listening to him rant whilst I did my best to balance the ledger. The numbers came out correctly a third of the time, incorrectly a third of the time, and I had no idea, right or wrong, the rest of the time. At least, I thought, we have not yet gone bankrupt. "Those Frenchmen captured a coasting vessel and two fishing shallops!"

"What has been done about it?" I asked.

"They say the Council has ordered the *William and Mary* to be refitted to return to active duty alongside the *Nonsuch*."

"Is that not the ship on which Governor Phips arrived?"

"Tis. But apparently, it has no sailors."

"Not one?"

Father shook his head. "When the ship docked the captain gave the men leave and they disappeared. Vanished, never to be seen again. Now the captain sends press gangs across Boston for local volunteers."

"Is volunteers the right word to describe men who have been forced into service?" I asked.

"I do not care what they call them, James. But the Governor must get this situation under control or else our ships will suffer. How can we get in and out of harbor if we are going to be accosted by any oaf who chooses to challenge us?"

This day was no better. Father arrived in the early morn looking as though he swallowed a stinking egg. He had a greenish pallor and his breath came short and fast. When Lizzie saw him she helped him sit in her chair. He would not speak, odd for him on any day, but especially since he had so much to say yesterday. Lizzie asked him if he wanted some ale, which he did. She brought his drink in one of the silver cups he gave us as a wedding present.

"What news, Father?" I asked. "What do you know that you do not wish to say?"

"They have ordered a court of Oyer and Terminer. It begins this day."

"What does that mean?" Lizzie asked.

Father looked at me. "My son, the Cambridge scholar. What does Oyer and Terminer mean?"

"Oyer and Terminer," I said. "From the Latin for to hear and determine."

"Hear and determine?" Lizzie looked from me to Father. Father nodded at me. I had to be the one to tell her.

"It means they are putting the accused Witches on trial. If they are found guilty…"

Lizzie paled. Her hands went to the bump where our babe grows. "'Tis the same as England. If they're found guilty, they will be put to death."

I wanted to say something comforting, but my brain was oddly devoid of words. Father explained that the Court of Oyer and

Terminer will sit in Salem Town and arrangements are being made for the prisoners to be brought forward for their court dates.

"And they shan't be quick about it either," Father said. "These trials will be tedious for the magistrates. There are so many accused, so many trials to be carried out."

"I am not at all concerned about the magistrates," I said.

But Father was right. There are so many accused now. Rebecca has yet to have her trial. Tituba still languishes in prison, as does Sarah Good, her infant now dead. Good's accused young daughter, Dorcas, remains alone in the Boston prison. Tis said the girl no longer speaks. Rebecca's Shape has once again been on the rampage, they say, threatening death to an assortment of Putnams.

"It seems," Father said, "the Putnams play an especial role in this."

He looked exhausted. He grasped Lizzie's hand, bringing it to his lips. He held onto Lizzie a moment longer, then stood, steadying himself. He did not look well. He lingered by the door, setting his hat atop his head. Lizzie's beautiful face, like the mirror I know it is, reflected my agitation.

"I must be on my leave," Father said. "The first trial will begin soon and I must be there."

"Father." Lizzie led him from the door. "Why not stay here with us? Or take James to the docks. I'm sure there must be something that needs your attention. Jamie is here to help you with anything you need, as always."

"Aye," Father said. "There is much to be done, Daughter. And yet I cannot pull myself away from the trials. I must see what happens with my own eyes. I must know for myself since I do not trust anyone to tell me."

"You are not the only one who cannot tear themselves away," I said. "Half the dock workers are not on the docks, and you would be hard-pressed to find anyone on the streets of Town or Village. Madness has infected everyone, afflicted, accused, or onlooker. Everyone must be close to it, like moths to a flame."

"The flames of Hell," Father said.

"Aye," I said, "which is why Lizzie is right. You should stay away. Let others clean up the mess."

"But you do not understand, James." Father ground his feet into the floor with such force I expected to see a groove where he stood. "The madness is too far gone already. It will continue radiating out, like the Plague or some other sickness, until not one family in all of Massachusetts remains untouched. If we do not know what is happening, if we do not know who is afflicted and who is accused, then we may become vulnerable."

"Vulnerable to what?" I asked.

"My brilliant son. All that education and you are still so naïve about human nature. Who amongst the accused has done anything to draw such attention to themselves? If anyone has drawn undue attention tis the afflicted. But instead of making them pay for their folly they are paraded about like Angels come to save the sinners. Everything they say and everything they do is honored. And the flesh and blood human beings who are accused are treated worse than Satan himself would be if one day his horns appear in Salem."

Father gripped me now as well as Lizzie. He is not a tall man or physically strong, but his fingers clamped round my wrist with such severity I flinched. "We are none of us safe, James. To think we are whilst everyone else is gripped in such insanity makes us as irrational as the afflicted."

I stared at Father as though I had never seen this man before. His scowl etched deeper lines into his forehead and I realized he has not laughed but once for weeks at a time. He seems a different man from the one I have known all my life. Lizzie must have seen it too since she brought him a soothing cup of tea and led him back to the table. Father sat, cradling the warm cup between his hands, sipping after the boiling liquid cooled. We stayed silent for some time.

Father finished his tea, thanked Lizzie, then stood. He returned to the door. "You need not come if you do not wish, James, but I must go. I must see."

"I shall come, Father. I do not want you going alone."

I slipped my hat onto my head and Lizzie held my coat whilst I slid my arms through. She straightened my cravat and kissed my cheek. When she pulled away I saw the same crease between her brows I had seen on Father.

Father and I walked to the trial. When we arrived we were stopped by Mr. Grimshaw, who was only too eager to inform us that at ten o'clock in the morn a jury of nine women and the surgeon John Barton appeared at the jail to search the bodies of the accused, including Bridget Bishop, Sarah Good, Elizabeth Proctor, and Rebecca for Witch Marks. What precisely Witch Marks look like, no one can say.

As the first Court of Oyer and Terminer convened, the crowd pressed into the room. Chief Justice William Stoughton presided, along with Samuel Sewall, John Hathorne, Jonathan Corwin, and one other whose name escapes me. Reverend Noyes delivered the opening prayer, Parris sat near the proceedings to take notes, and the trials began. All went according to procedures set during the examinations. Hathorne verbally accosted the witnesses as he twisted their words until it sounded as if the accused admitted their guilt. Poor Bridget Bishop. From the start, the woman did not have a chance to defend herself. For years people have connected Goody Bishop with Witchcraft, and this morn every one of her accusers was vindicated. Hathorne prodded Goody Bishop with his words until she did not know herself what was what. In the end, she was convicted. She would die, as accused Witches before her have died, by hanging.

At the end of Goody Bishop's trial Father's head slumped forward. He sighed loudly enough to get the attention of the men nearest us. After a moment, he said, "Let us go, James. I have seen enough. I thought Hathorne and Corwin would be fair. I am sad to see I have been proven wrong time and time again. Especially now, with so much at risk."

As we passed through the door Father and I overheard two men talking about the second examination for Witch Marks. Excrescences of the flesh discovered in the morn were no longer there. Upon further inspection, only a bit of dry skin remained. Furthermore, Goody Martin's breasts, full and firm earlier, were now, according to the report, lank and pendant.

Father laughed for the first time in days. "My life was much less meaningful before I knew that Goody Martin's breasts lost their fullness this day," he said.

9 JUNE 1692, THURSDAY

The trials continue. The same, and the same, and the same. People cannot get enough of them. I want to tell the spectators, some of whom have come from far away, to go to London to see real theater. Though this is as real as it gets, I reckon. Poor Goody Bishop will learn as much soon enough.

Father and I returned to work this day. He has finally seen enough and we are back to business. I took one ledger, he another, and together we added, subtracted, multiplied, and divided, calculating percentages and other necessities until we knew our income and expenditures, who we owe and who owes us. Father laughed at the creases between my brows as I concentrated on the numbers dancing circles before my eyes.

"Really, James. For a scholar, you're so easily puzzled by maths."

"You know how I feel about numbers. They're annoying, particularly when they do not come out correctly."

"Do not underestimate numbers, Son. They determine much of our lives, for better or worse."

I was about to say for worse when Father's helping-girl

appeared near the hearth. She stirred a pottage, adding spices and then tasting to see if it suited her. I breathed in the mouth-watering scent of frying onions.

She grinned. "Hungry, are you?"

"Aye," I said.

"Doesn't that wife of yours feed you?"

"That wife of yours?" Father's eyes narrowed until all I saw were silvery eyelashes. "Don't you have anything else to do, Prudence?" There was a sternness to his tone that made me sit up straighter, though Prudence did not appear concerned.

"Aye, Mr. Wentworth. And I'm doing it."

Father watched Prudence go out to the garden. "Petulant girl. I have half a mind to send her on her way once and for all."

"Now what has she done?" I asked.

"Do you not hear the cheek of her?"

"Aye, Father, I hear it, but I've heard it before. She's a silly girl who does not know better."

"Doesn't she?"

"Words from silly girls do not matter to me."

Father crossed his arms over his chest as he studied me. "Do you not realize her intentions for speaking against Elizabeth as she does? As I have told you before, that girl, as you call her, speaks in a doting way of you when you are not here. She speaks as though she has every right to say such things to me."

"Aye, Father, we have had this conversation before. Why is it different now?"

"Tis different because now she speaks against Elizabeth. Prudence says how much better care she could take of you than that farmer's daughter you took for a wife."

Outside, Prudence knelt beside the green batches of basil, foxglove, and hyssop, adding handfuls to the basket dangling from her wrist. Prudence may be near Lizzie's age, but she is rather childish looking, or perhaps childish acting is more like it. She pouts frequently, the picture of insolence. As though she felt me watching her, she turned to me. Her eyes focused on mine and she smiled. I have seen that smile from her before. She stood, and her own hands had their way with her, stroking the length of her body as though they were a lover's hands. All I could think of was how she reminded me of a blueberry with her indigo blue kirtle, her sky-blue linen partlet, her tea-stained linen apron tight round her ample waist, her woolen oversleeves pinned near her elbows. She noticed Father watching her and returned to work.

"Might you require assistance, Prudence?" Father called through the open door. His stage actor's voice crackled with amusement.

Prudence shook her head and her braid flew out from under the tight wrappings of her coif, Medusa's hair as one long snake. She leaned over the crop of anise, pulled a bundle, and dropped it into the basket. She brought the basket inside, set it on the table, and grabbed a wooden spoon to stir the baked beans and browned onions into the pease pudding simmering in the Dutch oven.

"Well?" Father shook his head at the girl. The purple veins at his temples looked ready to burst.

"I'm cooking your supper is all, Mr. Wentworth," Prudence said.

Father stood, nearly knocking his chair over in the suddenness of his movement. "Come, James," he said.

I followed him outside where another maidservant stooped over the tomatoes. Father shooed the girl away and paced from one end of the garden to the other.

"Does it not bother you that you have an admirer?"

"You already know the answer, Father. I do not care."

"But now I find that I do care, Son. Very much. Prudence's brazenness concerns me."

"You cannot possibly think I would be unfaithful to Lizzie."

"No, of course I do not. But that girl," he jerked his elbow in the direction of the kitchen where Prudence worked, "is trying my patience."

"You speak foolishness, Father. You know quite well I love no one but Lizzie."

"Aye. But does Prudence know that?"

"I have done nothing to encourage her."

"So I know. But now I think you must discourage her. She has been even more in a delirium lately."

"What kind of delirium?"

"She struts round as if she owns the place."

"Are you sure tis no exaggeration, Father?"

"Tis no exaggeration, and I have heard her speak of no other man the way she speaks of you. She speaks not only of your hair and eyes, James. She speaks of your strong hands and broad shoulders. She speaks of your care for Patience and your concern for Providence and their mother when they were ill. And then she speaks ill of Elizabeth, how her hair and eyes are black like the Devil's, how she heals with Witch's herbs, how she put a spell on you because how else could a farmer's daughter win such a husband."

I laughed but Father did not so much as smile. "Perhaps Lizzie has cast a spell on me," I said. "I have been struck by the magick of her smile, entranced by the depth of her beauty, ensconced in the warmth of her heart. One look across a crowded table was all it took for her to entrap me forever."

A thud echoed near the hearth and Prudence watched me through the window, again with that knowing smile, staring at me the way men sometimes leer at women. Then, as though she did not know me, she turned away. The last of the evening sun reflected dull prisms on the polished wood floor, and Prudence disappeared into light and shadows. A vision of full lips that taste of strawberries and dark, wondering eyes flashed in my mind, and my arms felt empty. Tis the way I always feel when I am long away from Lizzie. Tis as though an essential part of my self, my heart, is gone.

I nodded toward Prudence as she chopped herbs and dropped them into the frying pan. "Should I be worried about her?"

"I thought not, but now I wonder. There is such mischief nowadays with people accused of all such."

I forced myself to exhale whilst I saw visions of myself pleading, cajoling, begging this Prudence to turn her eyes to another man, one who wishes to know her better. I imagined myself falling to my knees, holding out my hands as though in prayer, and still she did not care. I imagined her thinking I was being coy, playing it cold when really I was wildly in love with her. Father must have gleaned my thoughts because he slapped my shoulder, his head thrown back in a manly guffaw.

"Prudence isn't the first victim of those blue eyes," he said, "and she shan't be the last."

"Can you not let her go?"

"I thought you were not concerned, Son?"

"I was not, but now I am."

Father turned from the window, lost in his thoughts. Finally, he said, "She may be brazen but she is good at her work. I reckon she will find other employment soon enough. Perhaps I might ask if someone is in need of house-help."

The sky darkened all at once, the sunlight gone, a finger-wagging storm blowing in over the bay despite the warm June day. I could not stand to be there any longer. I was aching with missing Lizzie, whom I had not seen since dawn.

Father opened the door for me. When I stepped outside I saw him, the long-faced man with silver threads in his red-brown hair. He winked at me as though we were intimate friends, and then he stared at Father as though he recognized him. Father did not seem to see him and he has certainly never mentioned the man before. The long-faced man pulled his floppy hat over his large eyes and then he was gone. I wanted to yell, point him out, but he was already too far away.

Father clucked his tongue. "Prudence does keep looking at you. And in a rather inappropriate manner. I gather we could haul her before the Court and have her whipped for provocative behavior."

Heat spots flushed Father's cheeks. He stormed into the house, and though I wanted to get home to Lizzie I followed him.

Father spoke more gruffly than I have ever heard him. "This nonsense must stop, Prudence. My son is married. He does not welcome your attention. More to the point, you are annoying me." Father stopped within an inch of her. He grew taller in his agitation and he towered over the short-statured Prudence. "Tis time you be gone, girl. Find a husband of your own. You can only aspire to be half the woman my daughter-in-law is, and that is on your better days, which are fewer and farther between."

Prudence's face remained empty, as though her features were a blank page. If Father expected her to explode in distress or anger, he was disappointed. She untied her apron and grabbed her cloak from the hook near the door. She opened the door, stepped outside, then stopped. She turned a scowl onto Father.

"I think you may be Witched yourself, Mr. Wentworth. Surely you know Goody Bishop will be executed tomorrow, hanged at the gallows. She's a spawn of Satan, she is. The Devil is holdin' court in Salem. We don't know who all may be infected by Evil."

Prudence winked at me, a blatant, lascivious ogle. Father slammed the door in her face, panting from the exertion of his anger. His attitude changed as fast as a storm-filled wind as he went from aggravation to laughter. He smiled as he turned to me. But instead of relief, I felt the chill of deadly fingers scratching icy trails down my spine.

Father sat near the hearth staring into the blackness of the swinging cauldron. His anger had returned and his fists clutched into balls beneath his chin. He looked at me, shrugged, and said nothing.

. . .

AFTER I ARRIVED HOME I COULD NOT SHAKE THE SIGHT OF Prudence Connor winking at me. I paced from the Great Room to the hall and back again. I climbed up to the attic and found nothing there to occupy me, so I climbed down into the cellar. I grabbed a bottle of rum and returned to the hall. I did not bother with a cup. Lizzie took the half-empty bottle from my hands.

"I'll make some chamomile tea," she said. "To soothe you."

"I do not think chamomile tea will help me now." I took Lizzie's hands and pulled her toward me. The scene at Father's gnawed at me from the inside out, so I told the one person in the world I trust more than anyone. Lizzie listened to my tale of Prudence.

"She was likely trying to scare Father," Lizzie said. "She must have been embarrassed, being caught out trying to ensnare you for herself and losing her position for it." Lizzie pressed her lips near me and I kissed them, gladly. "And you maintain that you aren't interested in Prudence Connor in any way?"

I slid my arms round Lizzie's waist and clutched her so close twas as though we were not two people but one. "To think that there is any woman who could ever capture my heart and my body as you have, Elizabeth Wentworth, is blasphemy. How can you not know by now that you have complete possession of my beating heart and my eternal soul?"

Lizzie pressed her cheek into my shoulder. "I was jesting, but I'm glad to hear it."

"As if you did not know."

"Tis nice to hear it sometimes still."

With reluctance, I pulled myself away, not for need of being separate from Lizzie but because my stomach rumbled with hunger. Lizzie placed some brown bread on a plate and scooped some baked beans on top. Though she had eaten already, she sat with me whilst I finished my meal. I noticed a sheet of parchment unfolded on the table.

"From Peter," Lizzie said to my unasked question.

"Are he and his wife still coming to visit us? I hoped seeing them at Silas' last week was enough of a visit with them."

"You did not like them," Lizzie said.

"Nay, and I do not believe they cared much for me, so we are even. Are they coming?"

"From their letter they seem undecided about whether or not they should come. Peter says he must return to New York and his business as soon as he can. And it sounds as if Apphia may not wish to come."

"I know why Apphia does not want to come," I said. "Your sister-in-law is jealous of you."

"Jealous of me? But why?"

"Look at you, my love. Where else on earth is there such Angelic beauty? She is no beauty, your brother's wife. She is haggard, with blackened teeth, and dark rings beneath her eyes. She is unlucky in love with your brother. I saw it myself. They argue constantly and find no happiness together. She brought her problems to their union—her two unruly, spoiled children—and he brought his problems, an angry, violent temper. She sees us happy together, happier than anyone has a right to be, and she has plenty to be jealous about."

"Of course we should be happy," Lizzie said. "Our Lord does not want us to be unhappy."

"Nay? Have you listened to Parris' sermons? Or Noyes' sermons? Or anyone else's sermons in Massachusetts? They think everything in this life is about biding your time until you get to Heaven."

"Apphia believes this life is about suffering."

"And suffer she does, married to your brother." Lizzie frowned. "I'm sorry, Lizzie. I do not mean to speak ill of your brother. I have had an odd day, I'm afeared."

"Nay," Lizzie said. "You speak true, James. Peter was difficult even as a child. My mother, when she was alive, spoiled him so. He grew to manhood believing he should have everything he wants when he wants it. He's always been angry, pampered, insincere. I cannot blame Apphia for being unhappy with him. But I cannot believe she is jealous, certainly not of me."

I could not help but laugh. I pressed Lizzie's head to my chest, kissed the top of her hair, and pulled her onto my lap. We spent the next hour gazing into each other's eyes.

10 JUNE 1692, FRIDAY

The night wanes whilst the horizon fades into pink and shadow. Again, I struggle, quill in hand, and the words, and the words, and the words escape me. When I cannot work with what I know, when I am dumb, what becomes of me? When words no longer make sense, who am I?

Perhaps I should stop here. I hardly know what I write. I watch my hand move as though it belongs to someone else, and I am as surprised as anyone at what appears on the page. I am beyond numb. Beyond thinking. Beyond expression. Perhaps I am as engulfed by the madness as anyone. I do not know what else to call it but madness. The finger-pointing, the accusations, the leers, the cheers when things go badly for others. The onlookers who cannot turn away are compelled to see how it turns out for the unfortunates whilst they remain unscathed. For now, tis the death of one woman we must contemplate. I cannot say how many more shall follow.

The signs of brutality remain, there, on the tree. As if the tree knew it would take a life, it hunched forward in supplication, or duty. The markings of the murder were etched into the heaviest branch as though the bark had been sliced by a butcher's knife. The rope fell here. The branch was that far from the ground there. It looked, I thought, like a game I played when I was a boy when my parents and I visited the country house of family friends. The other boys and I threw a rope round a large tree and tied it tightly into a sailor's knot as Father taught me. My playmates and I tugged heavily on the rope to make certain it would hold our weights, and then we would swing to the other side of the lake, or as far as we could manage before we fell into the rippling cold water. We were silly boys and thought the game the best part of summer. We would fetch each other from the water, dry each other off as best we could, and then we would laugh about who would make it all the way across next time.

But this was no game. The rope tied round the heaviest branch was not meant to swing this woman to safety but to her death. What is she guilty of besides being in the wrong place at the wrong time? Bridget Bishop made herself obvious in a society that values silence. Now she has paid the ultimate price.

I had been on my way home to Lizzie. I met Father early, before daybreak. He had some concerns about a shipment of rum due to go out soon and he had to make the unpleasant decision to delay. We heard the clomps of horses' hooves and the rumbles of heavy wheels and we knew—twas the wagon rolling away from the prison. A common pasture at the edge of the Town was chosen for the site, close enough yet not so close and those who wished to watch the execution could. Father glanced at me but I shook my head. Nay, I screamed in the silence of my mind. I do not want to see. Father nodded his agreement. He did not want to see either. But then, as though yanked by the Devil's string, we left the safety of Father's house to watch the wagon pass. Like the Pied Piper of Hamelin, the wagon drew onlookers toward it. People left their homes, their work, and their families to follow the trail. Unlike the Pied Piper, twas not beautiful music that drew the crowd but a death rattle. Father and I, pulled as if by magick, followed as well.

Down Prison Lane we went, on the road toward Boston, through the hills, along the stream and the salt marsh.

I should have left. My heart screamed in my ears—Go! Go! Leave now before tis too late! Once I see this, I shall never forget it. But Father and I continued with the crowd, caught up in the rolling tide of people. Then the wagon and everyone round it stopped. The Hanging Tree grew from the clefts in the rock, its trunk the width of 20 men pressed together, the branches that of the heftiest wood you can imagine. Bridget Bishop looked to be the calmest one there. She stood straight whilst onlookers shouted hateful words at her. You would think she was the Devil in the flesh come to take all of Salem into her realm the way they screamed. A heavy rope hung loosely round her neck, the long strip that would be fastened to the tree trailing on the ground. Goody Bishop's hands were fastened behind her, her petticoats tied to prevent them from getting in the way. I glanced toward the scaffold and saw the hangman, the black mask covering his features, and I felt ill. I was not personally acquainted with Bridget Bishop though Lizzie was. When Lizzie lived in the Village she had given food and quilts to Goody Bishop. Goody Bishop was a troubled woman, but Lizzie, with a heart as big as the sky, did what she could to help. Now, because Goody Bishop had angered many, no one spoke for her and she stood at the base of the tree ready to meet her Maker. Goody Bishop had her say, protesting all the way. She is innocent, she said. We must see that. But no one listened. The woman was blindfolded, hooded, and left standing on the ladder until the ladder was no longer there. The mob gasped. Father gasped. I turned away. I imagined I was home with Lizzie instead of there by the Hanging Tree. I imagined I held Lizzie in my arms as she relaxed into me. I heard Lizzie sigh with contentment, my favorite sound in the world next to her laughter. And then, as quickly as I imagined myself at home, I imagined Lizzie on that ladder, her arms behind her back, her legs swinging as the ladder fell away.

"Nay!" I yelled. Father pressed his hand between my shoulders. "Come, James. Tis time for home."

I followed him as I had when I was a child, without asking questions, without wondering where we were going. As we left I whispered a silent prayer for the soul of that poor woman.

And there they were, the Weird Sisters, behind the crowd, watching Goody Bishop hanging lifeless from the tree. Whilst their faces remained impassive their hands danced about in circles round their heads. Father and everyone else walked past unawares, or at least it seemed that way to me. In that moment, though, I had other matters to concern myself with so I pressed thoughts of the sisters away. Another time, I thought to myself. I shall worry about the strange women another time.

I have often wondered why people are drawn to watch tragedies unfold. I suffer from it the same as anyone, I reckon. I did not want to be at the execution, but I was. Tis as if I were drawn by an Invisible line pulling me by the hand toward the one place I did not want to be. I heard that citizens of the Village were ordered to attend so they could witness the punishment that would be theirs if they dared to side with Satan. As citizens of the Town, we were not under such strict orders that I was aware of, yet I, and many others, went anyway. I nodded at Father when we neared his house. Twas the only goodbye I could manage. I had every intention of going home to Lizzie. I still felt nauseous after that unwanted vision of Lizzie with the hanging rope round her neck and I wanted to kiss her lips, tell her I love her, feel the kicks of our growing babe. But I felt leaded down, as though my boots were dead weight. I stopped near the Commons, watching, waiting, for what I could not say. Finally, when the sharp pain of being away from Lizzie became too much, I went home. I found some comfort in the warmth of Lizzie's embrace. I did not tell her where I had been. But even if she did not know exactly what was wrong, she knew I was upset by something. She knows me so well.

"Tis all right, Jamie." Her lips were close to my ear and her words tickled. "You're all right now. You're home."

I pulled her closer, closer, trying to meld her to me. We are already one, after all. In our hearts, we are one and the same, JamesandLizzie, two halves made whole. If we were intertwined, I thought, then no one could tear us apart. I did not mean to start trembling. I must stay strong, I reminded myself. I must be a comfort to Lizzie. I exhaled and steadied my voice.

"I love you, Lizzie. I cannot bear to be without you. I shall never leave you ever."

"And I promise you the same."

At that moment, I knew twas true. We shall never be without each other again. Lizzie tightened her arms round my waist, and I thought she wanted the same as I did, to become inseparable. And we are. Forever. What God hath joined together, let no man put asunder.

29 JUNE 1692, WEDNESDAY

There is naught to do at Father's since our ships are stuck in harbor. They cannot come and they cannot leave. Tis all down to the French and Indian forces that marched upon the garrison in Wells in Maine. Whilst those on the inside wished to surrender, the captain, a man by the name of Converse, would have none of it. He threatened to execute anyone caught leaving the fort. After harried gunshots and a fair share of obscenities, the French and Indian attackers disappeared into the night, slaughtering whatever men and cattle they encountered.

Many are on edge since Major Appleton has been ordered to detach part of the Essex regiment to relieve the depleted Wells garrison. Younger men fit to serve are called up. The wealthier amongst us, Father included, have once again paid whatever they must to keep their sons out of harm's way. Perhaps for the first time, I'm genuinely grateful for Father's wealth. The things he buys with his money—bigger houses, imported furnishings and tapestries, fancy carriages, fine wines—do not matter so much to me. But that he would spend his money keeping me away from these skirmishes means more than all the gold in the world. Father has hired a substitute to serve in my place. I do not pray often, or well, but I have been praying in earnest. I pray for the man, his name unknown to me, who shall put himself in harm's way in my stead. Lizzie often reminds me to be grateful for everything I have, big and small. And I am, even more so these days. I have heard that when it comes time you shall shoot even if tis against your natural inclination. After all, if you do not shoot them then they shall shoot you—that is, unless they spear you with their bayonet first. Most likely, I would die shortly into my first battle. Some men make natural soldiers. I do not happen to be one of them.

Even so, the possibility of military service is not our main concern now. After the Wells attacks, French ships continued to wreak havoc up and down the coast. Without warning, Governor Phips placed an embargo on all ships in the Massachusetts harbors. Whilst the French recklessly roam the seas no one is allowed to sail anywhere. Father was furious. He ranted and raved at the very air, waving his arms as though he were about to fly away. Finally, Father realized that Governor Phips does not care what John Geoffrey Wentworth thinks of the embargo. Father stopped the red-fisted talk and got back to work, engaging in private conversations with Thomas Oliver. I'm not privy to what is said between them.

"The less you know, James, the better," Father said.

In truth, I'm not entirely sorry about the embargo. Tis becoming hard, sitting at Father's, day after day, the heaviness of boredom weighing me down until I feel as though I'm shackled to the floor. My very soul feels heavy. I sit at my desk knowing I should be concentrating on the numbers, but after a few minutes I cannot think my way through the most simple calculations. Instead of adding or subtracting, I stare out the window an hour at a time. Then I have to force myself to balance the ledgers, just one more line.

I have become a clock watcher in a way I never have been before. Father has a beautiful scroll-carved clock taller than me on the wall opposite my desk. The clock, designed by Thomas Wentworth (no relation, to my knowledge), has a silver Roman chapter ring enclosing an engraved center. On the hour, the weight escapes, the count wheel strikes, and the bell sounds. The hours chime brightly enough. Tis the minutes that drag. I smile daily at my idiocy as I look at the clock, see tis ten minutes past the hour, I look again, tis 12 minutes past the hour. A third time, tis quarter past. I do this every minute of every hour I find myself attempting to calculate income and outgo. Such days feel like punishments for a crime I did not commit. I do not know how much longer I can keep up the pretense of being a merchant's assistant, even my beloved Father's. Then Lizzie reminds me, again with all patience, that I should be grateful for Father's extraordinary business sense. I am, and always have been, the proudest son in the world. Tis only that I do not feel his business ventures are for me any longer.

My frustration stems from my tipping back and forth between remaining in Salem and leaving for England. Lizzie has asked me several times about what my heart tells me. Of course, Lizzie is always first in my heart. But when I think of where I want to settle with Lizzie and our growing family, I know England is home. I have come to this realization several times now, yet I have not dared to make the declaration aloud to Father. Aye, he made the offer to send Lizzie and me home, yet I still waver. I must be brave. I must tell him, once and for all. Aye, Father, Lizzie and I and our babe are going home. And we hope you shall join us.

I'm unable to make a final decision because I suffer the same as others, I reckon. I doubt myself. I doubt my ability to support my family. Father has offered to pay our way, but I feel, as a man of thirty, that I should have something of my own now. Father's generosity allowed me to marry Lizzie. Father's generosity bought and furnished one of the largest houses in Salem Town for us. I know Father's generosity shall continue providing for my family and me. But I believe tis time. Tis time for me to break away, to rely on myself, to trust in myself. I can do so now because of

Lizzie. Her love for me, her belief in me show me something I have never seen in myself. I have always been John Wentworth's son. To Lizzie, I am James, her James. In Lizzie's eyes I am strong. In Lizzie's eyes I am able. And if such a remarkable woman sees me so, perhaps there may be some truth in it. I shall make Lizzie proud.

I see it so clearly now. Tis as if the sun has broken through the storm-filled sky and angelic rays of light have cleared away the fog that clouded my thoughts. Aye, we must go home. Of course, I have decided to leave and now we cannot because of the embargo. But all embargoes end and the ships shall sail again. I'll tell Father once and for all that Lizzie and I are leaving. I have made up my mind to take my family home where I shall be free, where we shall be free, where we can be free together.

Perhaps twas Goody Nurse's trial this day that prompted me to make a decision. Was it just days ago when I determined to keep away from the spectacles whilst others simmered in the stew of their own madness? Perhaps twas also another argument with Lizzie that prompted me to realize that we must get away. I know husbands and wives quarrel. I saw my parents do so, not often, but on occasion. Many in the Town and the Village know which husbands argue with which wives and vice versa. Lizzie and I never disagree except over whether or not she should attend the trials. This morn Lizzie wanted to see Rebecca's trial and I said nay. Lizzie looked as though I slapped her face, which I certainly had not.

"I could not go last time, either," Lizzie said. "Are you forbidding me from going this time as well?"

"Aye," I said. "I'm sorry, my love, but once again I cannot have you anywhere near the madness. What if…?"

Lizzie sat with a thud. Her hands went to the bump where our babe grows. "Again, the what ifs. Rebecca is still my friend, and I still want to be there for her."

I knelt next to Lizzie and pulled her hands into mine. Though tis a hot summer, her hands were cold and I rubbed them, kissing her fingers for added warmth. "Please, Lizzie, you must listen to me. You haven't seen the spectacles as I have. People are accused for no reason except their names were suggested by someone with malevolent intent. People languish in prison because someone claims their Shape did violence. Please," my voice cracked under the strain, "listen to me this time as well. Do not go."

"I cannot stay in the house until I die."

"Perhaps until we leave for England?"

"James…"

For a moment I thought to tell her of my vision, that when I saw Bridget Bishop hanging from the Tree I saw her dangling lifeless. But I could not find the words. Instead, I said, "Aye, Lizzie, I would keep you locked in here with the shutters down and the draperies drawn if I could. Instead, I'm asking you to stay away from the trials and anyone connected with them."

"That's most of the Village and the Town."

"I know. But this madness shall pass, and I want you here beside me when it does so we can return to England together." Lizzie looked at me quizzically but I offered no more. She turned away. I kissed her cheek, her lips, her belly where our babe grows. Finally, I said, "You have done what you can for Rebecca. We all have. Father, Silas, you, I, and countless others, we have signed our names to affidavits stating that everything we know about Rebecca is exemplary. Rebecca's family has been working ceaselessly on her behalf, gathering evidence in her favor. There is nothing more you can do."

"I want her to see a friendly face."

"My love, from where she'll be standing, I doubt she'll see anything friendly this day."

"I'm not afeared, James."

"I know, my love. I wish I had half your courage. Stay here, Lizzie. Please."

She did not protest further. She did not look convinced, but she conceded. My sweet, beautiful Lizzie. I married a stubborn farmer's daughter who does not take kindly to being told what to do. Tis one of the many reasons I love her so. But I had to risk her frustration to keep her safe. Lizzie is not ripe for the plucking by someone with ill will. Lizzie stayed home and I went alone. Father had enough on his mind with the embargo so he did not accompany me.

I do not know why I was surprised to find that Rebecca's trial was much the same spectacle as her pre-trial examination. I had some hope as the day began that Reason would find its way in Salem, but twas not meant to be. A jeering crowd yelled slurs and other abominations at the old woman. The afflicted shook and jerked and moaned, pointing at Rebecca, claiming she had committed all acts of violence. And Rebecca, with her poor hearing, had to lean toward her accusers in an attempt to make sense of their words, which she could not do no matter how hard she strained. At one point Rebecca slumped forward, perhaps from the weight of the lies spat so easily in her face. She misheard a lot of the questions directed at her, and Hathorne had an easy time twisting her words to his intentions. When Rebecca called Goody Hobbs "one of us" Hathorne made a meal of her.

I gasped aloud when I noticed one of the afflicted sitting front and center—Prudence Connor. Prudence was not wearing a coif, her sandy brown hair left uncovered like a young girl's. She was as riveting a performer as any of them, screaming, convulsing, writhing. Father said that she disappeared after he released her from service. No one had seen her and no one had heard from her. When Lizzie questioned Patience, who still works in our home, Patience averted her eyes and mumbled something Lizzie did not understand. Patience would keep her sister's secrets. I could not see Prudence's face from where I sat, but I imagined her features exaggerated like a Greek actor's mask with wide eyes and a mouth a circle of horror. Suddenly, as though she felt my presence,

Prudence turned to me. She smiled, that same suggestive smile. Then she turned away.

Two men sitting next to me leaned toward each other in a whispered conversation.

"Did you hear Guv'nor Phips is none too pleased about that Boston Baptist minister, Milborne his name is. Milborne has published pamphlets against the use of Spectral evidence in the trials." The man rubbed his long face with a calloused hand.

"Aye," said the second man, an average-looking fellow with heavy brows that jumped round his forehead as he spoke. "If he don't believe in Invisible evidence he ought to come and see for himself. She's," he nodded toward Rebecca, "deservin' of all she gets, she is. She and her husband hired a substitute to serve in the militia to keep her son safe at home whilst my boy Bill's out there fightin'. We don't know whether he's alive or dead."

The men turned wrinkled eyes onto me and I sensed the disgust wafting from them. I held the gaze of the average-looking man for a moment then turned away. They must have known that Father has done the same for me.

I watched the travesty unfold and thought to speak out on Rebecca's behalf. Again, my fear overtook me and I remained mute. To speak out would draw the afflicted's eyes my way, which might lead them to Lizzie. After all, Prudence had no problem speaking against Lizzie to Father's face. A glacial wind blew through the Town House and I shivered. Then I realized twas not the wind at all but my fears that covered me in gooseflesh. I wanted to be brave, but my courage, whatever I had of it, abandoned me. I wanted to silence everyone, the afflicted, the magistrates, the crowd, and make them understand. Rebecca Nurse is no Witch! How can you not see that? I took one step forward, but even that was too hard and my feet became leaden balls. I felt as though I were deep underwater, as though I had been tossed into the sea and now I was drowning. No matter how hard I struggled, I could not break my fetters. Down,

down, down I went until I was so deep the sky, the land, and the air were lost to me forever. So I did nothing. I watched those loitering near the afflicted, and one or two of them whispered something. They were giving advice, I was certain of it, prompting the afflicted to scream whenever Rebecca moved as much as a finger. The magistrates sat, their mouths flat, their eyes squints. Whenever one of the afflicted shouted an accusation Parris scribbled furiously.

And then it happened. A miracle. The Nurses had done their due diligence and found enough evidence to convince the jury. Enough documents had been submitted on Rebecca's behalf, enough Church members had spoken out for her. The jury returned with a Not Guilty verdict. I was about to make my way forward to speak to Rebecca, to congratulate the Nurses, the imaginary fetters on my feet suddenly gone. Rebecca could not hear and did not realize what had happened. The magistrates looked surprised, unhappy even, as though they had a personal stake in the conviction. When Rebecca's acquittal was known throughout the room, the afflicted unleashed unholy screams. They began writhing on the floor, kicking and screaming as though beating the Devil off them.

Chief Justice Stoughton had enough. He told the jury they were wrong in their verdict and sent them back to reconsider. The verdict came back Guilty. Rebecca was convicted. Suddenly, the room was silent. The afflicted sat without speaking, looking at each other, the magistrates, the onlookers, wondering, perhaps, who their next victim would be.

I left as fast as I could without drawing attention to myself. I needed to get home to see Lizzie. I wanted to take her into my arms, comfort her, protect her. But then I saw them again, the Weird Sisters. I thought they followed me.

"Do you know those women?" I asked the man beside me. I did not know him, but he looked as though he might be from the Farms. Perhaps he had seen the sisters about.

The man looked where I pointed. "Know who?"

"The three women." I gestured to where they stood. "The sisters over there."

"I see an empty road but not one woman." The man bounded away from me. "If you see three women perhaps you're afflicted as well." He pulled his neckcloth closer to his mouth as though afeared I were contagious somehow. "Perhaps you ought to call the doctor. Or Reverend Parris." He disappeared into the oncoming crowd. Many had come to see Rebecca Nurse convicted and they left looking content whilst heading to the tavern for refreshment.

The thick summer air is ripe for hallucinations, I decided. I headed for home, walking faster and faster, afeared suddenly that a bystander might have overheard my conversation and believed I was indeed afflicted. Then a whish of air brushed past me. The three sister-women walked beside me, matching me stride for stride though they were much smaller than me. The one I had spoken to previously, Miriam, grasped my sleeve and stopped me with such force I tripped over my own feet. She did not seem concerned for her reputation, publicly touching a man. She stood on her toes and leaned toward me, so close I smelled fish and onions on her breath.

"Go!" Miriam yelled. That must have been what Moses sounded like when he commanded the parting of the Sea. Miriam waved her arms toward the bay in a frantic gesture. "Take your Sarah and run! Run from Salem as fast as you can as far as you can. Go! Or else there's but one way to bring you and she together again, and very long it shall take too. You shall miss her for oh so very long." Her voice, no longer forbidding, dropped to a comforting whisper. "You must go, James John Wentworth. Or you shall suffer one long night waiting to return."

"My wife is Elizabeth."

"Now Elizabeth. Later Sarah. She's all the same to you. But you must go. There are too many of them, do you understand? There are too many accusations, too many accusers, too many fights to fight. Do you even know the names of all the accused? The accusations have spread farther than Salem, farther than Massachusetts even. You must go, James. Take your Sarah and go!"

"Who the bloody hell is Sarah?" My frustration boiled like molten lead in my gut. "What are you saying, woman?"

"You don't understand. But you shall. You are who you are, always, no matter what form you take. You love who you love, always, no matter her name. And you shall return. And she shall return. All shall be well again. But it shall feel like forever until it is."

Before I could ask again what gibberish she spoke, the women were gone, disappeared with the wind. I wandered the rest of the way home in a daze. Did I imagine it? Miriam's words made no sense. Go where? Return from where? When? Why? Since I walked through my door I have been wanting to tell Lizzie what the weird woman said. I do not like keeping secrets from her, but I do not know what exactly tis I should say. One of the odd sisters said something I did not understand. What does it matter? Twas enough to tell Lizzie about Rebecca's fate. Lizzie slumped forward when she heard the news. I caught her in my arms and comforted her until her tears subsided.

For now, I shall stay silent about Miriam. I shall tell Lizzie when I understand enough to explain.

4 JULY 1692, MONDAY

This morn I spent time with Father, though there is little enough to do whilst the embargo remains. Father goes daily to the docks to stare at his grounded ships, the *Elizabeth* still waiting for her maiden voyage. I paced with him near the lapping shore, the tips of our boots wet from the low-tide waves. Tis quiet these days since there is not much work to be had, the workers sent home, grumbling as they go. As we stood near the flat blue line of the bay Father told me how Captain Short still rounds up sailors near Boston whether the men are willing or not. Father laughed when he said how Short's conscription gangs are entering the chambers of the legislators fighting against the press gangs, parading the legislators through the streets in their nightclothes, and calling them rude names whilst beating them bloody and leaving them far from their homes.

With little to do for business, I have more time with Lizzie. I have become dependent on her, her easy presence, her lovely smile, her sweet caresses. She is more than life itself to me. She is the air I breathe. I feel as though I'm caught in a stranglehold when she is not near. After visiting with Father, I rushed home. When I arrived, Lizzie was in the garden picking beans and tomatoes. I stopped near the oak tree, satisfied simply watching her. She stumbled as she stood and I lunged forward, ready to help, but she straightened herself easily enough by grasping the tree. She smiled when she saw me, sheepish, as her hand settled on her growing belly, the reason for her awkwardness.

I helped Lizzie inside. She leaned up her face and I kissed her, gladly. She was chopping tomatoes when the door knocker startled us both. Like a punch to the stomach, I remembered that this was another painful day in Salem. Our neighbor, Mr. Miller, was outside. He had come to tell us that Goody Nurse was excommunicated. According to Mr. Miller, a chained Rebecca was dragged into the Meeting House where the unanimous vote banished her from the Church. How could God-fearing people allow a convicted Witch to taint their holy activities? How indeed. Rebecca's only reply was, "You do not know my heart." Lizzie could not stand to hear it. She went inside to stir the stew. As Mr. Miller left, I felt guilty about not going to see the proceedings myself. I could have voted for Rebecca. I should have voted for Rebecca.

As if reading my mind, Lizzie said, "Tis no matter, James. Even if both Father and you had gone to vote on Rebecca's behalf, you would have been the only two to vote in her favor. She would have been excommunicated anyhow. It would have made no difference. You're not responsible."

She looked as though she would cry but she did not. "Rebecca would want us to keep on living, and that's what we must do." Lizzie took the fine china from the shelf and set the pieces on the table.

"What is the occasion, my love?" I asked, brushing a few escaped curls from the nape of her neck. I kissed the warmth of her flesh below her ear. She smiled whilst removing my hands from her hips.

"Peter, Apphia, and my father are coming to dine this night."

She returned to the hearth where a game bird broiled in the Dutch oven. "You remembered, of course."

"Of course," I lied. "But do you feel up to it, with the events of the day?"

Lizzie shrugged. "We knew twas coming. The worst had already happened. Being excommunicated from the Church is pointless in comparison."

"Do you believe being excommunicated is pointless?"

"That," Lizzie gestured toward the door, indicating the madness out there, "is the result of moral blindness. I'm not sure I see the point of any of it."

"I would not say that out loud, my love," I said. "In Salem, Town and Village, the walls have ears."

"The only ears I care about are yours, and I know I can speak freely with you."

"You can tell me anything, Lizzie. You must know that by now."

"Aye, I do. Why do you think I love you so much, James Wentworth? Tis because I know I can trust you with anything. I trust you with my life."

"I shall protect you with my very breath, Lizzie. I shall never leave you ever."

Bursting our bubble of joy was another petulant knock at our door. Outside was Lizzie's brother, Peter, his flopping hat in his hands, the finely tailored black clothing announcing his wealth. Apphia, Peter's wife, stood a half-foot taller than he did. Twas only the second time I had seen either of them, and I still thought they made an interesting sight. Lizzie greeted her brother politely, if with some distance, the way one might meet a stranger whom one has heard much about. Peter acknowledged her with strained manners. Silas came up behind and all three entered in silence.

I listened as Peter and Apphia made small talk with Lizzie. Whilst Apphia spoke the customary compliments about our furniture, our china, and our silverware, she grimaced at her husband when Lizzie turned away. Lizzie saw the secret looks between her brother and his wife but said nothing. She would keep the peace for Silas' sake. Apphia was an odd duck, indeed. She smiled to Lizzie's face, following Lizzie everywhere round the house, listening to every word Lizzie said even when twas not directed to her. Apphia looked at the lines of Lizzie's clothes, measuring Lizzie's green dress to see how it differed from hers or how the sleeves were cut. I imagined Apphia mentally calculating the price of Lizzie's dress versus the price of her own. Apphia then gave our home the most acute attention, rubbing her hand over the book-shelves and the books, then inspecting her hand as though expecting it to explode from the dust that must overrun this house in the middle of provincial Massachusetts.

Peter is lighter than Lizzie, Lizzie inheriting her mother's dark eyes and dark curls, and Peter inheriting his mother's gold-brown eyes and sand-colored hair, or at least that is what Lizzie tells me. When Peter smiles he looks pleasant enough, but when he does not, which is most of the time, there is a foreboding about him that makes him appear imposing for a man only a few years older than I am. Before her family arrived, Lizzie told me that though her brother can be unpleasant, even impatient, Apphia is harder to understand. One moment she is friendly and sister-like, and the next she spits foul words.

I thought, rather unkindly, that Apphia Jones is one of the ugliest people I have seen. When I whispered so to Lizzie whilst she plated our meal, she swatted me with a wooden spoon. Apphia is at least a decade older than Peter and she has the bloated look of someone who has been dead this month past. She has corpse-like bags under her eyes, and I cannot say what color her eyes are since her lids are swollen, as though she drinks a barrel of Father's rum daily. Her black hair fell from her cap in oily strings. Peter is Apphia's second husband. Husband number one was known for living in an alcohol-induced haze and Apphia, practical if nothing else, watched him die before marrying Peter, who was by then respectable and wealthy, even if he was a farmer's son. Apphia had two children from her first husband—a son who followed his father into a drunken delirium and a daughter banished from the Massachusetts Bay Colony for living in sin with a fat barkeep and delivering a fat baby soon afterward.

With the meal ready, Lizzie called everyone to table. She served a hashed game bird with roasted turnips. The bird was browned to perfection with onions, carrots, and fennel, seasoned with thyme, rosemary, and peppercorns. Lizzie outdid herself yet again, serving another feast fit for the King. I dabbed the sides of my mouth with my napkin to stop the juice from staining my shirt.

"Everything is delicious, Lizzie," I said. I would have reached out to her, but Apphia is a Puritan and I did not wish to offend my sister-in-law. Peter puckered his lips as he brought a roasted morsel closer to his nose. He sneered as though he had been served unpreserved meat from two winters ago.

"What is this?" he asked.

"Tis game bird," Lizzie said. "You liked it well enough when we were children."

"I was near grown when you were a child," Peter said. "This is overcooked."

Several rude words came to my mind, arse being the least among them, but Lizzie slipped her hand onto my knee under the table. I grunted in response. I could not guarantee that I would not say something unkind to Peter Jones, no matter how much my beloved silently pleaded with me to hold my tongue.

"If you don't like it I can fix you something else," Lizzie said. She reached for Peter's plate, but Peter shook his head.

"It will do," he said.

Silas had been silent, keeping his eyes down whilst he ate his meal. Lizzie stood near him and reached for his plate. "Tis not to your taste, either, Pa? I can fix you something else."

Silas opened his mouth to speak but his son was too quick.

"There isn't time," Peter said. "Apphia and I must leave now if we're to have Father home before tis too dark."

Lizzie looked out the window. "Tis summer and there are more hours of sunlight yet. You have time before you must leave."

Apphia, who did not seem to have an issue with the doneness of the bird, ate her meal in silence. Whenever Peter spoke, Apphia watched him, closely, perhaps with a twinge of fear until she realized his words were not directed toward her. After she finished eating, Apphia returned to scrutinizing our home.

"Your furniture is not as finely carved as ours," Apphia said.

"I believe our possessions are quite beautiful," Lizzie said.

"You would," said Apphia.

"My generous father-in-law had some of the finest furnishings in London brought here for us. Perhaps our belongings are not as expensive or fashionable as yours, Apphia, but my husband and I prefer to live simply. Tis enough for us. This house is bigger than we need. Even after this one," she patted our babe growing within her, "has a sibling or two this house will still be too big. And a table is a table no matter how many flowers or cherubs are carved into it." Lizzie smiled at me. "Besides, my husband and I will return to England after our daughter is born. A scholar is James. He'll return to university, to Cambridge, soon enough."

Twas the first time Lizzie had told anyone of our plans, and hearing her share our dream aloud made it more real to me. I shall be returning home soon, I thought, to England with my family.

Peter's head snapped toward Lizzie. "How do you know tis a daughter? Did a Witch tell you?"

Lizzie laughed. "What nonsense, Brother. I did not need a Witch to tell me tis a girl. Tis merely something I feel."

"You have grand thoughts for yourself, Sister," Apphia said. "Fortune-telling the gender of your babe. Your husband going to Cambridge. And you a farmer's daughter."

"Aye," Lizzie said. "As your husband is a farmer's son."

"A farmer's son I may be," Peter said, "but I'm a gentleman now. For the life of me, Elizabeth, I cannot understand why you would not want to be a gentleman's wife."

Twas as much as I could take. I stood, towering over the imbecile, ready to grab him by his fashionable collar and knock his fashionable head into the wall. Peter tried to stand as tall as me but since he does not have the height for it he backed down. I would not be surprised if Apphia protected Peter from things that go bump in the night.

"James, please," Lizzie said.

With some struggle, I managed to sit beside Lizzie though the heat still flushed my face.

Lizzie shook her head at me. "Despite this display, my husband is a gentleman. Never has any wife been more fortunate in her mate. James and I have everything we need. We have a solid roof over our heads to protect us from the whims of the weather. We have more food than we can eat, even in winter, and we're blessed to be able to share with our neighbors who are in want. We have cows for milk and butter, and we have chickens for eggs, and we have hogs for curing. My husband works with his father, and tis a prosperous merchant business. And he's so clever, my husband. One day he'll write and teach great things."

"Hmpf." Peter shook his head. "But what is the point of prosperity if you do not use it to live well?"

"What about our home is not well?" Lizzie asked.

"Where are your servants?" Apphia asked. "Why do you do everything yourself?"

"I have help," Lizzie said. "But I like cooking. I like cleaning. I like tending the garden. I have always kept busy, haven't I, Pa?" Silas nodded. Twas the most he had contributed since he arrived. "I had to take over my mother's work after she died. I'm too used to keeping busy to enjoy being idle."

"Idle hands are the Devil's tools," Apphia said.

"I agree," Lizzie said. "My husband and I may live differently than you, but we're quite happy. Possessions are fleeting, after all. I learned that when my mother died. When she was gone twas as if nothing about her life mattered anymore. That she was a farmer's wife, that she lived in a one-room house, that she worked from dawn until dusk. The only thing she had worth anything was love, the love she had for others and the love others had for her. My husband and I have love, more than most people will ever understand, and we know we are blessed in each other."

"You see." Peter nodded toward Silas. "She does not know of which she speaks. Women are too weak to understand anything of importance. Tis no wonder the Devil works his Evildoings through women. Your daughter says her love of her husband is greater than her love of God."

"That's not what I said," Lizzie said.

"Nay?" Apphia smirked at Lizzie. The woman looked, I thought, like a bloated toad. "That is what it sounded like to me." Apphia watched Peter, who nodded consent. "With so many afflicted here, how do we know what you have been up to, Elizabeth?"

I slammed my fist onto the table. "That is enough! I shall not have you speak so to my wife. Be gone from our home, both of you!"

Peter stood and Apphia and Silas followed his lead. "We'll go," Peter said, "but I wonder—how is it that Elizabeth tried to heal Mary with herbs yet our sister died anyway? What is your Familiar, Elizabeth? A bird? You always liked birds." He glanced at the books on the shelves. "You have too many books. The only book we have in our home is the Bible."

"I do not doubt that," I said.

"Are any of those special books?" Apphia asked.

"Special books?" I said. "As a matter of fact, they are. They are books for people who can read. Good night."

Lizzie stood outside whilst her family climbed into Silas' wagon. I remained inside watching through the window. I would not believe they were gone unless I saw them ride away with my own eyes. Silas took the driver's seat, checked that Peter and Apphia were safely seated, then tugged the horses' reins. He looked subdued, Silas, sad even. He did not make eye contact with Lizzie as he steered the horses away, but I must have imagined his coldness. What problem could Silas have with Lizzie? Unless Peter and Apphia have been chirping in his ear like Satan's own birds as they did this night.

Inside, Lizzie handed me a cup near overflowing with rum. She gestured to the chair nearest the hearth, and though the fire burned low, it had been a hot day, I was still comforted by the gentle red-gold glow. Lizzie pressed her fingers into the fleshy part where my neck and shoulders meet. She worked the tight muscles the way she kneaded bread, digging in with her fingers here, smoothing away the tension there. I closed my eyes and exhaled.

"You must be patient with them, James."

"Your brother and his wife come into our home, criticize you, criticize me, criticize Father. They criticize the food you cooked for them. And Silas sat there as though he did not know where he was."

"He is still struggling with Mary's death. I am afeared Pa has grown harder somehow since Mary has gone to God."

"That as may be, but your brother does not seem bothered by the loss."

"Peter hardly knew Mary."

"I do not see why you keep in touch with him."

"Things have been hard, but he is still my brother." Lizzie sighed. "'Tis not his fault, James. He was coddled from the time he was a boy."

"And he has not changed."

"No, he hasn't. Poor Apphia."

"Poor Apphia? She married your brother of her own free will. And she is not such an angel herself, I think."

Lizzie removed her hands from my neck and I felt the loss of her warmth. She leaned her head lower so we were eye to eye.

"James Wentworth, do you truly believe women do anything

from free will?" I stroked her cheek from her temple to her chin and her skin warmed to my touch. I tried to kiss her but she pulled away. "Apphia married Peter because she had to. She was a widow with two young children and Peter was willing to take them on. Do you think she enjoys listening to his rants? Do you not see how she flinches when he speaks, watching him from the corner of her eye to see if he will mock her for what she said? If she's mean to me tis because she's frustrated in her own life. It must be hard for her, knowing what a dear and loving husband I have and then having to go home to bitterness and disdain. And no matter how many problems they have, they are still my family."

"I'm your family," I said. "You are the most important family I have. You always shall be."

Lizzie smiled. "I know, my love. You will always come first in my heart."

At that moment, I understood the meaning of gratitude.

6 JULY 1692, WEDNESDAY

Father and I attended Commencement Day at Harvard College. Tis the closest Massachusetts has to a holiday. Graduates, faculty, families of the graduates, and other notables, including officials and alumni, crowded into the Meeting House in Cambridge. From the tittering and unsteady hops from the men twas apparent that the day's gifts of wine had already been consumed, one gallon per student whilst graduates earned three gallons for their troubles. The effects of the tickling liquid were already on display, and the air ringed with tumultuous shouts, some from the graduates, some from the onlookers, and some from the hucksters come to line their pockets. Proud fathers' eyes brimmed wet with their sons' accomplishments, their young men soon to be ministers, lawyers, teachers. Increase Mather, President of the College, appeared at the front and even the drunkest amongst us silenced. Bewigged, small-eyed, narrow-faced, and sending a blast of icy indifference our way, Mather led a doggerel of Latin exercises. This is what they do at university here, I wondered. These were schoolboy lessons in England. Still, I watched intently as the degrees were conferred, the morning for

Bachelor's degrees, the afternoon for Masters. I'm not certain why I felt drawn to attend Commencement Day. Perhaps twas to torture myself. I'm not up there, I thought bitterly. I'm here, watching others achieve what I have not yet done myself.

I wanted to be happy for the graduates. Lizzie, had she been there, would have told me to search my heart for good wishes for them. I know the sacrifice, from fathers and sons, necessary to complete such studies, even somewhere as provincial as Harvard College. I was a bit envious—a large part of me was envious, actually. I want to be able to say that I have completed my studies. I'm achieving things. I'm making my way in the world. Father, sensing my thoughts, put a comforting hand on my shoulder.

"Your day shall come, James." He gestured with an open hand at the graduates. "You could study here. This is Cambridge, after all."

"The area is called Cambridge, Father. This is Harvard, not Cambridge. Not my Cambridge, anyhow."

"No, Son, tis not your Cambridge." Father sighed. "You should return to your Cambridge. Return to your studies. You know I shall see you to England and help you begin again there." When I protested, still unable to tell him Lizzie and I had already made the decision to leave, he shook his head. "I know you are not surprised by my offer, James. I have made it several times before. Do you tarry because of me? Do not worry for me, Son. I'm a grown man. You need to follow your heart, and your heart is not in Massachusetts. Your purpose in coming here was to find Elizabeth, and now that you have her, take her and your child within her and go." I recalled Miriam grabbing my arm and what she said. Sweat formed on my upper lip and I touched my handkerchief to my face. I had not told Father or Lizzie about Miriam's words to me after Rebecca's trial. I did not know how to tell them she said I should take my Sarah and run. Father's words brought the memory back to me, but I pressed it aside.

Father noticed that I was having an internal dilemma. I hoped he would not ask me what was wrong, and I was thankful when he did not. "You deserve to complete your studies as these men have," he said. "You are brighter than all of them put together. You have more deep thoughts before you get out of bed in the morn than most of these graduates shall have in their lifetimes. No one is wiser than you, my boy, and you should share what you have to say with the world. Who knows? You may well be the next Spinoza."

"I hardly think so." I shivered in my seat as the sweat dripped down my neck.

"You have been more than a dutiful son, James. You are my dearest friend in the world, since the day you were born. But you have served your time. Now you must find your own way."

"But what about the business?" All my fears about leaving Father returned with a hurricane-like ferocity. "Tis Wentworth and Son. As you have always said, where would you be without the Son?"

"I would be far less a man than I am now, that is for certain. You and your mother gave me a purpose, a reason to keep going when life felt too hard. But now you are thirty years old, long past the time when you should have staked your claim in the world. You are not an old man by any means, certainly not to my eyes, which are near eight-and-sixty now. But tis time."

"But what shall you do?" My throat constricted at the thought of leaving Father alone in an inhospitable land of intolerant knaves. Worries cracked like thunder in my brain. Indian wars. Pox. Cries of Witchcraft. Am I to leave Father amongst the illnesses of the body and distresses of the mind everywhere here?

As always, Father understood my thoughts. "There are wars and Witchcraft in England, too, Son. We were lucky enough never to be troubled by any of it. But I shall be fine here. I shall be lonely without you, but I shall be fine. Truth be told, I shan't stay much longer. I'm growing weary of the backhanded compromises. And, aye, I'm tired of the role the rum I export plays in the selling of people. You can tell Elizabeth she has won with her quiet persistence. I can no longer deny my role in it all. I cannot convince anyone else what I believe, but at least I shall no longer play a part." Father shook my arm as though to emphasize his point. "I'm going to finish out the season, assuming our ships ever sail again, and I shall sell the business. Then I shall come home to England and build a country house near the Cotswolds. We shall all live in comfort together."

"Near Oxford?" I shook my head. "I cannot live near Oxford."

"Ha!" Father kicked the pew before him and the man sitting there turned in annoyance. Father tilted his head in apology and the man turned back to the ceremony. "Very well. I shall build the house near Cambridgeshire."

"Aye," I said. "I would like that very much."

"Then tis decided. I shall sell the business after the last of our dealings here are settled. I'm certain Hathorne or Corwin shall want the business, perhaps even the ships."

"Please, promise me, Father, no matter how desperate you are to get out of the business, you shan't sell to the likes of Hathorne or Corwin. Look at what sorrow they have brought down on so many innocents. Remember what they did to Rebecca."

Father nodded as he watched one more man receive his degree. "You are my conscience, James. You always have been. Nay, I shan't sell to Hathorne, Corwin, or any of the other magistrates involved in the trials. Hathorne and Corwin shall have their share of fame after the dust is settled. Their fortunes shall rise without my contributing to them. I shall sell to some worthy soul, assuming I can find one, and then I shall return to England, build our house— near Cambridgeshire—where you can read and write and teach. Lizzie will keep a warm, loving home for you and your children, and I...? Well, I shall find ways to busy my time. Perhaps I shall take up gardening. Perhaps I shall start a farm. I shall bring Silas over as well, and we two old men can tend the fields together."

"It sounds like Heaven," I said.

"Why, I shall send you both home on the *Elizabeth*, and you and Elizabeth shall be treated like the King and Queen during your voyage. I shall follow in the coming Spring after the ice thaws and the sailing is smoother."

I could not stop thinking of Miriam and her odd words. I decided to gently touch on the subject.

"I was told not long ago that I needed to leave here and soon. Some strange woman stopped me as I was walking home and said I should take my Sarah and go."

"Who is Sarah?"

"I hardly know. If the child Lizzie carries is a girl we have agreed to name her Grace."

"The woman must have confused you with someone else."

"Aye." I wanted to tell him how eager Miriam had been, how convincing, but I let the subject drop. "If Lizzie and I leave after the embargo is lifted, can't you come with us?"

"Nay, James. I need to see the business properly disposed of. There is still merchandise to sell and profits to be made."

"We have more than enough, Father."

"Aye, but we cannot let the hard work we have put into Wentworth and Son simply disappear, can we?"

I shook my head. "Of course not."

"So tis settled. You and Lizzie will return to England as soon as the embargo is lifted and I shall follow soon after. We shall be together again before you know it."

I felt someone sit next to me and I turned to see Mr. Boxley. Boxley grabbed Father's arm as though they were the greatest of friends. Father nodded in a gentlemanly way as he pulled his arm from the man's grip.

"Wentworth! What are you doing here? Your boy isn't graduating, is he?"

Father smiled. "My boy, as you call him, is returning to England shortly, so no, he shan't graduate from Harvard. How are you, Boxley?"

"Can't complain, old boy." The man smiled at me. "My wife says she misses Mistress Wentworth and cannot wait to see her again."

"I'm certain my wife would be happy to see her again," I said through clenched teeth.

"Clarissa wonders if Mistress Wentworth is still enjoying her new life."

I was going to reply, but Mr. Boxley recognized another man across the room and excused himself. With Boxley gone, Father looked serious.

"What is it, Father?"

"Perhaps I could sell the business to Boxley. He always seems interested in what we do. We certainly make enough of a profit, and we already have our contacts established."

"Tis better than selling to Hathorne or Corwin. What else troubles you?"

"I'm merely thinking of what Justice, my new helping-girl, said this morn." I waited whilst Father watched a proud father stand to shake his son's hand. "Justice said Prudence Connor is one of the afflicted."

"We already knew that."

"Prudence named Rebecca as one of her tormentors."

"We knew that too."

Father sighed. "Then Justice said that Prudence is going to name some new tormentors. I tried to press Justice into saying who would be called out, but the girl wouldn't say. Then I asked if she, Justice, was amongst the afflicted. *Oh no, sir*, she said. *I have quite enough excitement watchin' is all.*"

I watched one more man walk away with his degree. The graduate, who could not have been more than one-and-twenty, stumbled as he crossed the floor. I guessed he had already imbibed all three gallons of wine. At that moment, I wished to join him in his intoxication.

19 JULY 1692, TUESDAY

*M*y breathing is stilted. My hand shakes. My bone marrow quivers. Lizzie sleeps, but fitfully. She tosses and turns, her delicate features twisted in an unease I cannot soothe away with easy touches and soft words. I want to hold her close, hold her safe, but I do not wish to disturb her. Whatever rest she gets is better than none. We did not mean to be there this day. We did not want to see it. I wanted Lizzie anywhere but there, but there we were anyhow.

We began the day normally enough. Father visited this morn to pass along news of more skirmishes with the French and their Indian allies near Gloucester.

"With this latest raid in Lancaster and Haverhill, and with the farmers killed in the meadows, Phips is adding more men to his rosters. We may need to pay more to keep you," he pointed at me, "out of the militia." Father crossed his arms before his chest as he stared into his empty cup. Lizzie offered to refill it, but Father shook his head. "Thank you, Daughter, but nay. Even rum cannot help me. Did either of you know that Phips had the nerve to make last Thursday a day of Thanksgiving?"

"What is he thankful for?" I asked. "An abundance of young men he can force into military service?"

"Phips invited Boston ship carpenters, his former colleagues, to a feast celebrating God's blessings on his life. He's celebrating his humble origins…" Father stopped speaking, shook his head, and reached toward the rum. Lizzie meant to pour it for him but he waved at her to stay seated and he helped himself. "Most of us try to hide our humble origins. Phips celebrates them."

"Fortunate for him to be so blessed." I did not intend to sound bitter, but I did.

"James." Lizzie took my hand. "We are blessed too. The embargo has been lifted, hasn't it, Father?"

"Aye, Elizabeth. Twas lifted yesterday so our ships can sail once again."

"You don't look happy about it," Lizzie said.

"You know, Daughter, I'm not at all sure that I am. Everything —the business, our contacts, our sales, even our profits—seems pointless suddenly. What am I doing this for? What does it mean? I have enough put by to support us all, and your children, and your children's children, and at least their children after that, if not longer. Why am I trudging through such inane trivialities?"

"What are you proposing?" I asked.

"What we spoke about on Commencement Day. We can leave for home. The ships are freed. We can sail whenever we wish. They are my ships, after all."

"I thought you wanted to sell the business first," I said.

Father sighed. "You are right, James. I was speaking from frustration just now. I cannot let everything we've worked for flounder. I should settle our accounts and sell the business before I leave. I should do at least that much."

"Can someone else not handle that for you, Father?" Lizzie asked.

"Aye, Daughter, someone else could. But these days I'm not sure

I trust anyone enough to leave him with such responsibility over my accounts."

After Father left I realized that Lizzie was uncomfortable. Tis the middle of a humid July, with air so heavy I think I can see it, and she feels the weight of the child like a clenched knot in her back. I knelt beside her and wiped her sweating brow with a wet cloth. She smiled at me and nodded her thanks.

"I think I will walk," Lizzie said. "Sometimes moving helps when the babe feels heavy."

"I shall come with you," I said. I held out my arm and helped Lizzie stand.

"Won't Father need you? With the embargo lifted there must be much to do."

"He did not seem eager to get to work. After all, as he said, he may sell the business, and soon. At least, I hope he does."

I opened the door and helped Lizzie step over the threshold. Twas cooler outside, if only a bit. Inside the humidity mingles with the cooking fire and there are times when I think for certain the Devil would be most comfortable before our hearth. Lizzie and I meandered as we walked. We had no destination. We simply wandered as a means to stretch her legs. Soon enough we headed toward the water. Near the bay, we saw the joiners, the sail makers, the coopers, the painters, the caulkers, and the blacksmiths all about their tasks, their work singing busy tunes above our heads. The hearty calls of the fish women and the ceaseless banging from the carpenters rattled inside my ears. Barrels of timber, fur, cotton, flour, rice, indigo, fish, guns, ammunition, wool, and rum were rolled onto waiting ships. The raised voices and ceaseless clanking made my brain ring, and there was no breeze to be had even by the shore. Lizzie and I turned away, heading inland. We walked on a bit and saw the green, rolling land where Mr. Gambing breeds beautiful Andalusian horses. Two of the horses, tall, fine specimens white as snow with long ears pointed toward the clouds, nickered at us in greeting. Lizzie stopped to pat their necks and offer apples she brought for the walk. Shouts of timbermen and crashing birch trees filled the air. Beyond that is the sawmill where the plentiful trees are sliced into planks for shipment to England. The stark odor of resin, tar, and turpentine overtook the salty smell from the sea, and soon enough we found ourselves on the road toward the Village. Lizzie watched me with questioning eyes.

"Is that what you want, James, truly? For Father to sell the business?"

"Aye, Lizzie. I want to leave the merchant business, the ledgers, the maths, all of it behind. I want to take you and our child home. I want Father to come, and Silas too."

"I don't know if Pa will leave now. Peter has invited him to live in New York. I think Pa is going with Peter."

"Would you be all right with that?" I asked.

"I would prefer Pa to come with us. I worry that Peter won't care for him properly."

"He might. Peter's not a friendly man, but he seems to do well by Apphia and her children. And Silas is Peter's father too. Perhaps there is some family sentiment in your brother after all." We walked on, but the day grew hotter and Lizzie looked as though she were wilting like an unwatered flower. She stumbled over the rocky ground and I caught her in my arms. A Puritan matron puckered her lips in our direction so Lizzie and I pulled away from one another.

"Should we leave now, Lizzie?" I wanted so much to take her hand and draw her to me. I thought of the Puritan woman's grimace so I pushed the impulse aside. The woman could have had us hauled before the Court for public indecency. "What do you want to do, my love? If you're ready to leave now, we shall leave now. But if you're still worried about the babe…"

"Grace."

"Aye, if you're still worried about Grace then we shall wait. But tis summer and the sailing is as smooth as tis possible to be. If we leave now we could be in England in about six weeks." I pressed into Lizzie's side, drawing a bubble round us. "We could arrive in England before Grace is in our arms." I grasped Lizzie's hand, hoping those near us were so intent on their destination that they would not notice. The road we walked grew crowded with others heading in the same direction. I stopped and Lizzie stopped beside me. "Please, Lizzie, I beg you. Say you will come with me. Now. As soon as the *Elizabeth* is ready. Wouldn't you like to sail home on a ship named for you?"

Lizzie's face was as radiant as the sun. "Aye," she said. "I would." We walked on, hand in hand, oblivious to anyone. After some thought, Lizzie said, "Let's go home, James. Tis time you returned to where you belong."

"The only place in this world I belong is with you. I cannot live without you, Lizzie."

"That's good to hear," Lizzie said, "because my place is with you."

The crowd surrounding us grew larger. Lizzie and I stepped quickly to avoid being trampled. Some came from the Town. Others walked from the Village. Everyone converged on the road, marching with intent. Everyone seemed to know where they were headed except Lizzie and me.

"What is it, James? What's happening?"

I shook my head. From the grimaces on some faces and the jubilant expectations on others, I realized where we were headed. I wanted to knock myself on the head. I could not believe I had been such an idiot. I had forgotten the day. I wanted to go back and begin again so Lizzie and I could take a different road. Looming before us, tall, wide, and ugly, with branches hunched like the elderly who knew their time had come, was the Hanging Tree. I shuddered when I remembered my last time there.

"James? What is it?"

"We should go, Lizzie," I said.

Before Lizzie could respond we heard the rumble of the wagon, the wheels creaking under the weight of the women it carried. The ground rattled beneath my feet, shaking me from the inside out. Lizzie saw Rebecca Nurse in rags, looking sickly and scared, and she let out a sob that tore my heart in two.

"We should go," I said again. Lizzie tried to speak but only nodded. Her hand felt clammy in mine. I tried to find a path through the mass of bodies, but the people were pressed together and I could not get Lizzie away without stepping on others. The wagon with the prisoners lurched forward then stopped. In a moment, guards stationed themselves round the women. I saw Rebecca's family nearby, trying to catch their matriarch's eyes so she would know she did not leave this Earth without love. They had done all they could, the Nurses. They gathered letters of commendation, which we all signed. They gathered evidence and tried to discredit the accusers. All to naught. There she was, old, frail, and barely believing where she was or why she was there, with a rope round her neck. This would be the last sight she would see on Earth. And twas all wrong.

Lizzie pressed herself into my side. I did the same to her and discreetly slid my arm round her waist to keep her upright. Lizzie clasped her hands together, closed her eyes, and bowed her head, praying silently for the soul of her friend and the other women. I wanted to be a source of strength for Lizzie. I hope I was at least that. But then I saw the shaking fists that wanted blood. Men and women, some from the Village, some from the Town, who normally went about their lives the best they could, as all of us do, were different. With the hangings so near, they were ready for death. They craved it. I could feel it on them.

"We should go," I said yet again. But Lizzie had changed her mind and she stayed stubbornly in place.

"I must be here for her," Lizzie said.

When the sun was at its hottest, everyone strained to see the five women—Rebecca Nurse, Susanna Martin, Elizabeth How, Sarah Good, and Sarah Wildes—as they were brought forward. It pained me to see them. They were already corpses, too pale for the daytime, dark circles under their eyes, frail as skeletons, their clothing frayed rags clinging with a stitch or two. Twas impossible to tell what they were thinking from their impassive faces. Perhaps they did not want their last acts on Earth to be angry or spiteful. They had one more Judgment before them—the most important of all—and they would want to go to their Heavenly Father with a clear conscience. Perhaps, after months in a frightful dungeon, they saw their impending deaths as a release.

Lizzie stood rigid, her hands landing in fists at her lower back. Again, I said we should go, and again she refused. Twas painful enough to see five innocent women executed. Twas painful to see the crowd waiting impatiently for their deaths. The most painful of all was seeing how Lizzie suffered watching.

"They should confess," I whispered to Lizzie. "They should save themselves. There may yet be time."

Lizzie shook her head. "They won't confess to a crime they didn't commit because they are afeared for the damnation of their souls. They believe there will be no peace for them in the next life if they admit to being demons in this one."

"But if the Lord is as wise as everyone thinks He is, shouldn't He know they are not Demons and forgive them for saving themselves when they are innocent?"

"If the Lord is as wise?" Lizzie shook her head at me. "Are you still having trouble reconciling your faith, Mr. Wentworth?"

I looked into Lizzie's warm, dark eyes, struggling to understand. "Standing here, seeing this, aren't you?"

An old woman, a farmer's wife by the look of her, edged closer to us. Though she stared at the five women near the tree her ear leaned in our direction. I pulled Lizzie away from the elderly eavesdropper toward the back of the crowd.

When we were far enough from the others, Lizzie said, "This is not the work of God, James. Tis the work of those who know not what they do. Isn't that the God you said you believed in? A God of forgive them when they know not what they do?"

Some bystanders turned our way. I leaned toward Lizzie and whispered. "These are not ignorant people in charge of this. They are literate and well educated. They are community leaders, magistrates, town leaders, and others who most definitely know what they do."

"We live in a world run by people, James, and people are fallible."

The crowd grew silent as the five women with the ropes round their necks realized their time had come. Sobbing came from the crowd, from where I could not tell.

Whilst the other four women appeared to be taking their impending deaths with quiet acceptance, Sarah Good would have none of it. After she was led to the Hanging Tree, Reverend Noyes urged her to confess. When she denied the accusations, Noyes said she knew she was a Witch.

"Why not confess?" Noyes asked. "At least you will not die a liar."

"You are a liar," Sarah Good snapped. "I am no more a Witch than you are a Wizard, and if you take away my life God will give you blood to drink."

I could not watch when the rope did its dirty work. Lizzie too watched the feet of those pressing closer to better see the spectacle. Better their feet than their faces, I thought. Their feet do not make accusations.

When the deed was done I whispered, to no one in particular, "Why?"

Lizzie sighed. "When times are hard, even the most conscientious people have a life-preserving instinct. They point at others first so others do not point at them." Lizzie saw Reverend Noyes look toward Rebecca Nurse. Lizzie slumped forward and I caught her in my arms. The same elderly eavesdropper we had escaped moments before made her way back toward us and she watched

Lizzie with eager eyes. I felt a nauseous pit in my stomach but I could not give in. I had to stay strong. For Lizzie.

Rebecca Nurse, elderly, frail, sickly, and barely able to hear what was said, was led toward the tree. Rebecca hobbled forward and I watched her family crumple with the disbelief that after all their hard work this day had come. The crowd cheered at the sight of an old woman off to her death. Suddenly, a face from where the afflicted gathered smiled at me. Twas Prudence Connor. I stared through her as though I did not recognize her and she turned away.

My only concern at that moment was Lizzie. There was nothing more to be done for Rebecca. Suddenly, Lizzie pressed her hand to her mouth as though to keep herself from screaming. But her anguish would not be stifled. "They're hanging her!" Lizzie cried.

Twas too much. I could not allow my expectant wife to witness the horror any longer. I placed my hand on her lower back and took one step beside her.

"Come," I said.

I tried to mask my horror, for Lizzie, for our babe, for Rebecca and the others waiting for their deaths, but Lizzie knows me so well. She nodded, understanding. Finally, we walked home. As we made it some distance away, we heard the death sounds, the slap as Rebecca was pushed, the snap of her neck as she dangled. I was afeared Lizzie would look behind her and see the carnage so I walked where I blocked her view. Would Lizzie turn into a pillar of salt if she glanced back? I did not want to know.

Lizzie could not contain her sorrow any longer and she sobbed. I dabbed away the wetness from her cheeks with my fingers whilst keeping my other hand gently on her lower back, steering her away. Her hand reached for our babe, who bulges clearly now.

"What kind of world are we bringing this child into, Husband?"

I shrugged. Twas no response, I know, but I did not know what to say. As we drew closer to home, Lizzie's face set into grim lines of determination, as though she had made up her mind. "You're right, James. Tis time to go home to England. We should go home and never look back."

I exhaled fully for the first time in weeks. Lizzie and I, and our child, are going home where we shall be free of this madness.

MY BELOVED LIZZIE

Can you see me, Lizzie?

She is out there, Miriam, under the trees, beneath the laughing moon, dancing a dance of devils I have never seen nor wish to see again. Her arms wave and her hips sway lasciviously. I would think she wanted me, but she hardly knows I'm here. I'm an object in her house. Something to step round. But she beckons to someone, some man I reckon, as if she tries to enchant him her way. She laughs, bubbling, delirious. She speaks in tongues and gibberish escapes her lips. I do not know how she spins and spins like a child's toy without falling, falling, like London Bridge during the plague years, yet there she is, upright and joyous. I watch her through the doorway, or what should be a doorway since tis merely a slab of wood I drag before the opening before I fall into my deathly slumber each dawn.

Tis strange looking at her, thinking, well, she is Miriam, an oddity like me in her way. Then I think how unfair tis. Everyone in Salem searched for Witches, and for nearly a year everyone down Salem way was consumed by it. Everything was a conspiracy theory. Everyone believed I was right and you were wrong, and if you disagree with me you are going to Hell. They wanted to find Witches so badly they accused their wives, daughters, aunts, grandmothers, husbands, sons, and brothers, and yet here is Miriam, cackling and baying and shimmying and only me to see her. Part of me wants to drag her back to the Village so they can see, you were not so crazy after all, the Witches you seek exist. But then I think about what I have become and I realize they would take me along with her.

I have asked her, Lizzie. When she comes in from her nightly moonlight dances dressed in flimsy linen that barely covers anything, I ask her if she dances for or with the Devil. She is a perpetually annoying little woman, Miriam. She stands with her shoulders back and her head high and she has the confidence of ten of my kind. Yet she does not answer any of my questions.

I think of you every moment of every night. When I crawl into my makeshift bed on the dirt floor of Miriam's shack, when the light-pink morning breaks the fast of darkness, I have nothing but empty arms and memories of you to lull me. I feel you with me wherever I go, my love.

I'm not so far from our home, only a few miles into the woods, but I'm far enough that I cannot see the Salem shore. I realize now I had grown used to the rocky seaside and the breeze coming off the bay. For so long I thought Salem was too small, too provincial. Now I miss holding you in my arms whilst listening to the whispering sea. I even miss working with Father. Aye, Lizzie, tis true. I even miss doing maths. I would give anything I have, all of Father's fortune, to return to the life we had.

Our house sits sad and empty waiting for you. Tis hard, walking through our green door, thinking how passing that threshold was always the best of my day. Deciding to come to Massachusetts with Father was the best decision I ever made, Lizzie. You were born for me, my love, and I was born for you.

Pray for us, Lizzie.

25 JULY 1692, MONDAY

Father visited early this morn. He joined Lizzie and me and we broke our fast together sharing memories of Rebecca and drinking her eternal salvation. Father told us, in hushed tones, as though the wood beams would betray us, that the bodies of the executed women were buried under the rocky ground near the Hanging Tree. Not content with such an arrangement, the Nurses rowed up the North River, removed Rebecca's body, and brought her home for a proper burial, which is as it should be.

This has been a hard day for more reasons than one. I thought nothing could beat the sadness of Rebecca's death, but now we have more unwelcome news. First, Patience, our helping-girl, left us. Twas unexpected and I, for one, did not know what to make of it. As Patience told us the news, her face swelled from the copious tears she shed.

"What has happened?" Lizzie asked. "How can we help?"

The poor girl could not respond whilst she heaved for breath. When her tears settled enough to speak, all she could stammer was, "Tis illness, Mistress. My family is overcome with illness."

"Your sister Prudence is amongst the afflicted," I said. "Are you afflicted too?" Lizzie shook her head at me but I could not control my brusque tone. The girl burst into a fresh wave of tears and ran from the house.

Lizzie sighed. "Whatever her reason for leaving I hope she's all right."

"That girl's sister is one of those who called out Rebecca," I said.

"I know, James, but whatever Prudence's involvement, that doesn't mean that Patience is involved as well. We have no reason to distrust Patience."

"Her sister is convincing. Someone as soft as Patience may be easily manipulated. Many have been."

Shortly after Patience left, I went to Father's to start settling debts, collecting what is owed us, and finding a buyer for Wentworth and Son. Perhaps I felt a twinge of guilt at the realization that the merchant business Father spent his life building would soon belong to another, though in truth, I felt more relief than guilt. Father and I walked to the port and found the *Elizabeth* strong, tall, and ready to sail. Father asked questions of Captain Trenton, who will sail the ship on her maiden voyage to England with her namesake and me aboard. He is an affable fellow, Trenton, always ready with a laugh. Still, the man has a backbone strong enough to command men safely across the sea and back again. I like Trenton and trust him to see my wife and me to England. He promises us safe passage and I take him at his word. I rest comfortably in the knowledge that Lizzie and I are going home.

Our leaving cannot come soon enough. Whilst I was with Father inspecting the *Elizabeth*, Lizzie drove herself to the Village to see her father. I firmly believe that Silas has lost his mind. Whether he is poisoned by nonsense from Peter and Apphia, or whether he is converted by the nonsense spewed by Parris in the pulpit, or whether he has observed his neighbors' eagerness to accuse, he would not let Lizzie in his house. I cannot believe I'm writing these words, but they are true. Silas no longer trusts Lizzie. When he saw Lizzie outside, he slammed his door open and stormed toward her. Lizzie nearly tripped in her haste to be away from him.

"Twas the first time I've ever been afraid of Pa," Lizzie said when she arrived home.

She was still shaking when she walked through the door. I helped her sit near the open window, hoping some coolness from the bay would waft inside. I removed her coif, brushed her dark curls from her face, and lifted them off her neck. She exhaled and leaned into me, and I pulled her close. I knew my body heat was probably the last thing she wanted near her then, but I needed to hold her whilst she was upset. I had to soothe her however I could.

Finally, she said, "He told me to be gone."

"Silas told you to leave?"

"He called me a Witch. *Witch, be gone!* He told me I sickened his kine. He told me I killed Mary with black magick." Her hand went to her mouth as it had when Rebecca was led toward the tree with the rope round her neck. I pressed Lizzie's head to my chest and held her there for a long time. When her breathing settled, she pulled away. "He didn't mean it. He has suffered so much since Mary passed."

"Sounds like Peter and Apphia have been in his ear," I said. "I'd like to knock some sense into that old man's head. Does he truly believe you of all people killed Mary?"

"He doesn't know what he's saying." Lizzie clutched my hand. "Please, James. Don't go to see him. It would only make things worse. Let him settle down. Let him come to his senses."

"Who in Salem has sense these days?" When Lizzie did not answer, I shrugged. "Fine then. I shan't go to see Silas. The captain of the *Elizabeth* says we can set sail within a fortnight. We should start going through our things, and we ought to pack what we wish to take."

Lizzie held onto the table before her. I thought perhaps the babe was coming early, but she shook it off and stood upright again. "I didn't think it would be that soon. I don't know what to do about Pa."

"We should leave him to Peter and Apphia if that's what he wants."

Lizzie nodded but said nothing for a long while. Finally, with a lightness in her tone I had not heard for some time, she said, "I'm ready for a new adventure, James. Tis time to start our lives in the place we will call home together."

Instead of looking relieved, Lizzie's head drooped and she sighed. I cannot explain how that look cuts to the quick of my soul. The only goal I have, the only goal that means anything to me, is keeping Lizzie safe and happy. But I saw in her downcast eyes that she did not feel happy, and perhaps not even safe. I sat in the chair near the window, pulled Lizzie onto my lap, and rocked her the way I shall rock our babe when tis born. She closed her eyes, nestled into me, and her breathing slowed. I sat there for hours, letting her rest.

"Tis all right, my love," I whispered in her ear. "I'm here, and I shall protect you from every Evil the world throws at us. I shall never leave you ever."

Lizzie smiled as she slept. I'm certain she heard me.

26 JULY 1692, TUESDAY

I had a restless night and could not sleep. I did not wish to wake Lizzie so I left for Father's before daybreak. I closed the door behind me as silently as I could, leaving a note in case she wondered where I was, though she could guess easily enough that I had gone to Father's. Where else might I be? I watched the pink-blue lines of the dawning day as I walked down the road, past the harbor, and round the Commons.

Though twas early when I walked, I saw the widow Mrs. Bentley leaving Father's red ochre door. I laughed to think how Father has more than his share of eyelashes fluttering in his direction. The widow Mrs. Bentley brings him sweetmeats and Indian pudding because she knows how much he likes them. Several mothers of unmarried daughters younger than me bring their daughters to say *Good day* to him after Church services. At eight-and-sixty Father has more energy than most, more energy than I most days. I'm not opposed to the idea that he marry again. I have told him so, but he insists he shall never love another woman the way he loved Mother. I used to think he was foolish for such thoughts. Certainly, he loved Mother, I do not doubt it, but Mother would not want him wasting his life away lost in what was. She would want him to be happy. But now that I have Lizzie I understand plain as day. There is not one woman who could replace Lizzie. She is my all to me. She is my beating heart and my very being. My breath and my life. Without Lizzie my blood would not flow and my lungs would not breathe. When you find your soul mate, that perfect love, the one person who is meant for you and you for her, then anyone else becomes a poor substitute. I shall never love another woman as I love Lizzie. I know this as well as I know the sun rises in the East.

I took the long way round to Father's since I needed time with my thoughts. I knocked when I arrived but no one appeared so I let myself in. Father has a new helping-girl named Justice. Whether she be aptly named remains to be seen. The girl looked surprised to see me. She curtsied in my direction, poured water into the kettle, and set it on the hook in the hearth. She took a biscuit from the silver platter on the table, placed it on a porcelain plate alongside a scoop of marmalade, and set it before me. I bit into the biscuit, twas crumbly and warm, and Justice placed a cup of tea by my side. Disembodied thoughts of the last time I had seen Prudence floated through my mind, but I shook them aside.

I went to my desk, sharpened a quill, readied the ink, and pulled out the latest ledger with the most current accounts. I thought of the date, the 26th of July, and realized twas one of the last times I would do this hated task. I should have been more joyous at the thought that Lizzie and I were leaving soon, but instead I felt an odd disconnection from myself and everything else. I struggled to stay focused. At that moment my main task was to see which accounts might be settled straight away. I glanced over the numbers and felt my eyes spin, but I saw that the business was in good shape and Father should be able to sell out soon enough. He put feelers out to Boxley and the man seems interested, as Father hoped he would be. I worked until I could not force myself to concentrate any longer. Again, I thought of Prudence Connor and my knees quaked with such violence I grasped my desk to keep from slipping to the floor. In some deep part of myself, I must have known. Twas a Premonition, a sense that something Evil waited for me and mine. I steadied myself with the thought that soon the madness in Salem shall be none of our concern.

I stared out the window toward the bay. Then I heard Father say, "Perhaps they should go to Dutch New York first and leave for England from there."

Another male voice said, "Others have escaped to New York. The Dutch are too practical to believe in Witches, after all."

Father pressed the door open and stepped aside for Thomas Oliver to enter. Oliver tucked a loose strand of black hair behind his ear as he walked casually through Father's home, as though hobnobbing with wealthy merchants is a daily occurrence for him, and perhaps tis. Though I cannot say I trust Oliver, he does not concern me as he did when I first met him. Perhaps he is a good man making the best of a bad situation. Whatever he is, however he is, he has Father's trust, which is no small thing.

And then I wondered—who were they discussing? I was hidden from their view by the short wall between the door and the hall so they continued their discussion without realizing I overheard them. No matter who they discussed, I decided it might not be a bad idea. Lizzie and I could go to New York first. Lizzie is ready to leave Massachusetts but she still fears for the babe. If the weather does not cooperate and the voyage across the Atlantic takes too long then she may well give birth on the ship, which does not make her, or me, glad. As much as I'm ready to leave, I shan't risk her life or our babe's any more than childbirth already puts them at risk. Perhaps New York is a good choice for now.

"James?"

Father's voice woke me from my reverie. I stood, nodded at

Thomas Oliver, and tried to shake off the gooseflesh I felt rippling along my arms. I struggled to pay attention to Oliver's words.

"...Babson was searching for his cattle when he found the three churlish sods who have been pestering the garrison in Gloucester. The farmer fired his musket at the men but they simply walked on by."

"The musket must have misfired," Father said.

Oliver shook his head. "Babson checked his musket when he arrived home and twas fine. Now Babson's told everyone they were Specters, the men. The Devil's Specters."

"Are there any other kind?" I asked.

"Indeed." Oliver rubbed his calloused palm through his unkempt hair whilst Justice placed silver cups of rum before each of us. Oliver was the first to enjoy the sweet warmth.

"How goes the Governor's quest for adding sailors to his rosters?" Father asked.

"Sailors?" Oliver spat the word. "You mean prisoners. But he means to do well by those who volunteer. Men who volunteer in one of his vessels will share whatever plunder is captured. Already they got hold of a French flyboat with more brandy and textiles than you'd know what to do with."

"Oh, I'd know what to do with it well enough." Father smiled at the thought. "What has gone on with the General Court? I heard it finally convened."

"It did," Oliver said. I marveled at the privateer. Though he looks like a common enough man, it seems as though there is little he does not know. "Twas the usual."

"The usual?" I said. "Little enough is usual these days."

"Aye," said Oliver, "but they continued as though there are no afflicted, no accusations, no executions. They discussed the illegal selling of ale, the granting of liquor licenses." He finished his rum and held his cup out, which Justice filled. "I reckon with every-thing that's going on with the Specters spectating and the afflicted afflicting, folks need their liquor well enough."

I heard more than my fill. I was not going to get any more work done, and Father did not seem concerned about balancing the ledger at that moment. I excused myself to return to Lizzie and smiled at visions of passing the rest of the day quietly, reading, writing, contemplating life with my beloved wife and our beautiful babe (because what child could Elizabeth Wentworth make but a beautiful one? The girl, as Lizzie is so certain tis, will have beautiful dark curls like her mother, I'm sure of it). I imagined us together in England, in Cambridge, where we shall be free of this nonsense.

As I left Father's house I heard footsteps behind me. Thomas Oliver grabbed my arm in a familiar manner.

"I've heard talk," he said. He looked round to be certain he was not overheard, a common enough gesture these days, but there were only trees swaying in the breeze. "I believe Mistress Wentworth is... she's..."

"She is what, man?"

"She's being discussed. In the Village."

"Discussed? By whom? What do you mean, discussed?"

"I mean, your father told me you're planning on leaving for England. But he and I think perhaps New York is better. And you need to leave now."

So they had been speaking of Lizzie and me.

"You're wrong." Anger sliced my throat and my words were harsher than I intended. "Lizzie harms no one."

"I know that and you know that. But others do not want to accept that."

Father stood beside me. "Tell him, Thomas. He needs to know."

Oliver sighed. "Very well." He thought a moment, studying the flattened green grass beneath his boots. Though the heat was heavy, the sky was beautiful, deep blue speckled with white, billowy clouds. A seagull flew overhead, its squawks breaking the silence.

"The Putnams and others from the Village have visited your father-in-law's house."

"Silas?" I said. Father nodded and took a firm grip on my arm.

"They searched his house and found a doll," said Oliver. "They say tis a poppet."

"Of course that is not right," I said. "Tis only a doll Lizzie made for her sister. Mary was not well and Lizzie hoped it would cheer the girl up. Mary loved that doll."

"There is another problem, Son," Father said. "They say Mary herself was afeared she had been touched by Witchcraft, and they say Lizzie talked to Invisible Familiars outside Silas' door."

"Nay!" I shouted at the wind since only it could understand the intensity of my anger. "Mary was repeating nonsense she heard from Parris! And Miriam and her sisters are healers."

"Her name is Miriam?" Father asked.

"There are three sisters, or at least Lizzie and I believe them to be sisters—Miriam, Malka, and Mazel."

Father exhaled. "All right, James." But I saw in his far-away eyes that he did not believe me.

"They're not Invisible, Father. Lizzie has seen them. I have seen them." Thomas Oliver shrugged. Father looked away. "I tell you I've seen them! They live not far from Silas. How could he say he does not know them? They brought herbs to heal Mary. It worked the first time, but the second time twas too late."

"Aye," Thomas Oliver said. "Twas too late."

My breath came in painful bursts, as if Lizzie's sharp-edged sewing needles poked my chest. Father held onto my arm with one hand and supported me round the waist with the other. For some strange reason, I thought that if I did fall over he was too short to catch me. I prepared myself to hit the ground.

When I calmed enough to speak, I grasped Oliver by the shoulder. "What else do they say, Thomas? You must tell me."

Thomas Oliver looked at Father and Father nodded. To stall for time, perhaps, Oliver untied the black ribbon that held his dark hair from his face, gathered his hair together, and retied the queue. He straightened his coat, fussed with the ruffles at his neck, and sighed.

"I'll tell you all I know. But I have to warn you, sir, it isn't pretty."

Father pointed toward his house. "Perhaps we should return inside. Tis not the type of conversation one wants to have outdoors."

We returned to the table before the hearth and I listened to Thomas Oliver confirm my worst fears. Sweat dripped every-where—along my scalp, down my back, along my sleeves, inside my boots, and a chill shook me to the bone.

Oliver removed his coat, loosened his ruffles, and leaned toward me. "There's a long list of worries circling your wife right now. Some have concerns about her rise in station through her marriage to you. Suddenly, she's seen in fashionable clothing, expensive jewelry, and fine shoes. They say she must have cast a magick spell over you for her, a farmer's daughter, to marry a wealthy merchant's son. Some speak of how she tended to a family that died of Pox and she remained untouched. They say your wife already knew Mary was sick before she even got to the Village. They talk about the Invisible Familiars who gave her the herbs for Mary. Mary herself was convinced she had been bewitched. Your wife told her helping-girl that Reverend Parris doesn't know God's heart and cannot understand His intentions."

"That is completely out of context," I said. "I was there. Lizzie said Parris is a learned man. She said no human could truly know God's heart, which is true, is it not?"

"It does not matter what is true, Son," Father said. "It only matters what people believe."

I dropped my head into my hands. "What else do they say?"

"Your wife tried to divine who her husband would be with a Venus glass."

"How on Earth does anyone know that?" I asked.

Father leaned toward me. "At that dinner we had with Silas and Mary, Son. Remember?"

I sighed. "What else?"

"Both you and your wife have been irregular with your Church attendance, your wife more so."

"I pay the fines when we're asked," I said. "Lizzie was sick with the child."

"Aye, but tis rumored that your wife is a Quaker, which immediately makes her suspect in Puritan eyes. And tis said that her own father accuses her of being a sort of Jezebel, disobeying God as she seeks false prophets."

"Nay! Mary named her doll…"

I gave up trying to explain. I wandered close to the fire and stared into the flames, thinking how in England suspected Witches were burned at the stake. What must it feel like, to have your body burned away from your bones whilst you lived to watch? I shook my head, needing to press such thoughts aside. I was fully sweating then, not one inch of my skin was dry, but the sweating helped me feel as though somehow even the worst thing in the world might be purged clean. The pain of this knowledge shall wash away in time.

"Who says these things?" I asked. "Who has called out my wife?"

"Mistress Boxley, Mistress Putnam, Prudence Connor and her sister Patience, and…"

"And?"

"And your wife's own family. Her father, her brother, and her sister-in-law. Her brother says she's been touched by Satan her whole life."

"Those shitten liars! If any one of them stood here now I would shake them to within an inch of their lives! Mistress Boxley and Mistress Putnam do not surprise me. Prudence Connor does not surprise me. But Patience? After everything Lizzie has done to help her? Lizzie's father and brother? What the bloody hell is wrong with everyone?"

Father put his arm round my neck and leaned his head onto my arm. "I am so sorry, James. I should have seen it coming. I should have known."

Thomas Oliver turned away, giving me a moment to pull myself together. Finally, he said, "Prudence Connor said your wife used Black Magick potions to kill Mary after Mary wouldn't sign the Devil's book. Your father-in-law told everyone about the books in your house and how he sensed all along there was something Evil about your success because how else could someone accumulate such wealth except in collusion with Satan?"

"I'm afeared Silas repeats Peter and Apphia's words," Father said. "I cannot guess why a brother would turn against his sister in such a way."

"It wouldn't be the first time such a thing has happened," Oliver said. "And it won't be the last."

My mind understood what was happening but my soul would not accept it. I stomped my feet into the ground. "Nay," I said. "No one could believe such things about Lizzie. People know she is a good woman, a kind woman, a generous woman."

"People knew that about Rebecca too. Here in Salem we are judged by the company we keep. Elizabeth was close to Rebecca and people know it and judge her for it. Tis not right, Son, but that's how things are." Father's voice was so soft I had to strain to hear. He grabbed me by the arms and turned me toward him.

"You must go now, James. Do as Thomas says. Go to New York. Stay until Elizabeth feels safe sailing to England. But you must go."

I tipped forward but caught myself without Father's help. Then the rage struck me. I screamed rude words at Father when I knew, even as I shouted at them, that I did not mean what I said. Father, ever my friend, took no offense. He wept, not from what I said, but from the circumstances that prompted me to say them.

I ran home, desperate to be with Lizzie, to hold her in my arms, to tell her everything would be all right, I would never leave her ever. But the closer I came, the more I saw ghosts, Specters, shadows, Shapes, everything, all of it. Every supernatural creature I have ever heard of reached toward me with sharp claws and slicing teeth, reading to gnaw me to dust and bones whilst they drove Lizzie away to where I would never see her again. I worked myself into such a frenzy that when I got home I frightened Lizzie, yet I could not bring myself to tell her why. Tomorrow I'll tell her, gently, that Father has arranged passage for us on one of his ships, that we are to stay in New York until she is ready to go to England. Here tis, I'll tell her. Here is our adventure. She shall be none the wiser, and then we shall leave here. Forever.

Lizzie knew I was not myself but she did not question me. She grows heavier with child and tires easily. She retired as soon as the sun went down. Tis just as well. She needs to rest as much as possible for the journey. She shall not be caught up in the madness.

I SAT BY LIZZIE'S SIDE AS SHE SLEPT. I HELD HER HAND AND smoothed her hair. Then my thoughts turned in more sinister directions. I thought of the three sisters, the one called Miriam who speaks to me, smiles at me, laughs at me as though she knows me. She is too forthright by Puritan standards, too knowledgeable about the ways of the world, too bold in her speech. Others in the Village, who have done or said far less, have been called out as Witches. Why does no one call out the sisters? Why have none of the afflicted fainted at the sound of their names? Can Salem indeed be possessed but the wrong people are accused? Are these three women the ones doing the bewitching? I recalled Bridget Bishop hanging from the tree and I was reminded how I turned away when Rebecca was pushed to her slow, strangling death. I was so shaken by my thoughts I was afeared Lizzie would feel my agitation so I went outside in a desperate search for air for my shriveled lungs.

I passed the Boxleys' and saw two men, one on the ground, face up, the second leaning over him. If I had not known better I would have thought they were lovers the way the second man pulled away as though he had been in an embrace with the prostrate form. Though the moon was high, twas dark under the canopy of trees and it took a moment for me to see that the man on the ground was Boxley. I crept forward, I did not want to be heard, and saw Boxley, his eyes open, staring at the stars twinkling overhead as though all were well. There was a bite mark on his neck and blood on his skin. The second man pressed his dark cloak aside and I recognized him, the man with the silvery red-brown hair and the long face. He wiped red from his lips with the back of his hand. Had the man with the wicked grin been drinking Boxley's blood?

The man turned as though he felt my presence. Quick as you like, he stood near me. I must be imagining this, I thought. I felt the exhaustion behind my foggy eyes. I must have been hallucinating the shadow shape drinking Boxley's blood. The moonlight disappeared behind incoming clouds and the night grew darker whilst a summer storm blew in over the bay.

"Aye," the man said.

"Aye?" I responded.

"You're doing the right thing, leaving this. Even dogs aren't safe from the hangman's noose. Salem is no place for a mortal man like you."

"We are all mortal men."

"Are we?" He laughed and stepped closer.

I looked at Boxley, unmoving on the ground. "Is he dead?"

"Oh, aye. His wife has been a naughty girl."

"How did you know?"

"I know everything, young man. You'll learn that soon enough."

He inspected me until I shuddered. His closeness left me cold though twas a heavy summer night. The man's almond-shaped eyes were slits whilst his lips pulled back into a snarl. I looked again at Boxley, felt the fear of God, and ran as fast as I could. I was certain the long-faced man would bring me to the same end he had Boxley.

Once I was back inside I felt better. Again, I thought I must have imagined the whole thing. How can one man kill another by biting his neck? Tis ridiculous, I know. Even as I write this I'm embarrassed by such thoughts. I'm sure twas brought on by my fears for Lizzie. But she shall be safe. We shall leave here, and we shall be together always.

N.D.

I do not know what to say or how to say it my mind is running, where is it running, tis running to Lizzie in the jail and I cannot say what or how or where or why is this happening and what do I do? Dear God, what do I do? Just yesterday I learned they had spoken against her, spoken out against Lizzie, who has never harmed a soul, who helps birds fallen from their nests, who cares for everyone round her as though they are her kin. Who will help us now?

I knelt in the dirt, for hours, hours, the dust and the wind and the storm splashing down on me with the force of fury, making me wet from the inside out but the water on my face was not from the sky. I called for Lizzie, banging the grassy ground with my fists until I bled and the sinew in my flesh flattened with the strength of my anguish. Father pulled me up, brought me inside, sat me down, bandaged my hands, and wiped my face. Now he speaks to me, soothing words, but what do I do? Dear God, what do I do? I have to stay strong, stay strong for Lizzie, but right now I cannot think and I can barely push the pen against the paper as the pain in my hand slices like a knife in my skin, but tis nothing near the pain cracking me in half. My heart is gone, gone in chains to Salem jail, and I'm here with not enough air to breathe. But I must stay strong, stay strong for Lizzie. Father speaks to me but I cannot hear him for the thunder in my lungs.

I watch Father as if I am watching some other family, over there. I recognize the man who gave me life, who has cared for me all of my thirty years, I recognize his hearty voice, soft now. I feel his kind tending of my injured hands and my severed heart. He places a cup of tea beside me, but this is the end, the end of everything, and I shall go mad if I am not already.

He places a gentle hand on my shoulder. "Breathe, James. Slowly. Breathe. I cannot stand it if you become ill this night. We shall fight this, you and I. We shall do whatever we must to rescue Elizabeth. Thomas Oliver shall help us. He has a crafty mind, that one, and he shall know what to do. But we must stay strong, Son. We must see this through together."

I hear his words, understand them even, and I try. I try to stay strong. I close my eyes, breathe in, breathe out, in and out, again, but with my eyes closed I see the pock-faced man wielding his chain toward Lizzie as though twas an extension of him, as though he enjoys taking terrified women away.

"Talk to me, Jamie," Father says. "Please, Son. Say something. Anything. Let me know you are well."

Well? He thinks I can be well? I wonder for a moment at his sanity, but I wonder at mine more. I think of how this happened, how this came to be, that my Lizzie is gone, gone, to where I cannot comfort her, to where I cannot hold her, to where I cannot see her, and I am gone, gone, and I think I shall never be fully here again.

I must go back to the beginning or nothing makes sense.

I arrived home shortly before dark. I had been at Father's, and together with Thomas Oliver we made a plan to get Lizzie to New York over land instead of by sea since we could leave faster that way. Twas better to go, go tomorrow, Father said. I arrived home and told Lizzie our plan, and though she said she was saddened to leave our home so quickly, she was ready to go, go to New York until the babe is born and we were ready to sail for England. We packed our clothing, the objects in our home to be left behind and cared for by Father, either sold or sent to us wherever we settled. Father was on his way to join us for one last meal in this house, the one that will always be home for Lizzie and me. As we discussed our plans to leave on the morrow, Lizzie stirred an Indian pudding since tis Father's favorite.

"It may be some time before we see Father again and I want him to enjoy his last meal with us," she said.

Lizzie did not look afeared at the need for our sudden departure. I did not tell her everything Thomas Oliver said about the accusations, I did not see a need for it, and she looked content. She smiled at me and I went weak at the knees, as I do whenever she smiles. I pulled her into my arms and kissed her lips.

She laughed. "What was that for?"

"Seeing you is the best part of my day, every day. I miss you when I'm gone."

"You were only at Father's."

"Aye. But you were not at Father's and I missed you."

Lizzie's brows came together at a point. "There's something you're not telling me, James John Wentworth."

"It does not matter. All that matters is we are leaving tomorrow, together, and I shall never leave you ever."

"I promise you the same."

I sat at table, again pulled Lizzie close, and again I kissed her. Lizzie blushed, which made her even more beautiful, and I kissed her again. She pulled away first, insisting that the Indian pudding was more important than me.

"I need to keep stirring or the pudding will scald. Indian pudding tastes terrible if the cornmeal or the molasses burn." She tried to stay away from me, but I pulled her closer, and we laughed because tis funny that I cannot let her go.

When I heard the banging I thought twas Father arrived for our meal, but even before I saw the man's face I knew something was wrong. Lizzie knew it too. She stopped, her body tense, her face troubled, her head tilted as she listened. The banging grew louder, fiercer, like the walls would buckle and the gables would crash and the world as we knew it would spin away forever. I was afeared to open the door but I knew I must. When I saw the pock-faced constable I knew twas over and everything would be a struggle and Lizzie would suffer and what was I supposed to do when the man with the chains is there waving them before her, taunting her, the worst scum in the world is at my door with a piece of paper saying my wife is called out as a Witch and what the bloody hell was I to do?

Lizzie cringed in terror. Her hand reached for the bump where our babe waits. And I knew. I knew that no matter how much I loved her this was beyond my control. No matter how many promises I made to keep her safe I could not help her. No matter how many kisses I gave her. No matter no matter.

Father places his hand on my chest. Again, he reminds me, "Breathe, Son. Breathe. There we go. I know tis shredding your very being to pieces, but you must stay strong for Elizabeth." His breath comes in short bursts, and I look at him for the first time since Lizzie is gone and see the sheen in his eyes, the white streaks on his cheeks. I touch my hands to my cheeks and realize I weep too. What else is there to do?

My hand shakes as I write this, but I must write this down or else I shall truly explode. No matter how much I write the scene shall never be far from my consciousness. If I live another hundred years, it shall always be the first thing I see when I arise from my sleep and the last thing I know before drifting into unconsciousness.

What shall I remember? Lizzie slapped her hands over her eyes so she would not see the constable, her mouth open in a circle of fear, her body rigid. She was about to be dragged away to Hell, she knew it as I did. I shall remember a groan, like an animal caught in a trap, a pain-filled cry of agony, and then the realization that the sound came from me. I waited for someone to jump out of the shadows, to say this was a mistake. But no one did.

The constable grimaced at Lizzie as though he wore a skeleton mask.

"Are you a Witch?" he asked.

I laughed. I was ready for the joke. Dear God, please, I begged in the silence of my mind, this has to be a joke. But I knew. No matter no matter. This was no joke. The man had come to take Lizzie away.

"Did you sign a pact with the Devil in your own blood? How long have you been a Witch?" The constable's eyes blazed with haughty fire.

"I am no Witch, sir," Lizzie said. I was proud of her. Her voice was strong, her back was straight, and she held the man's eyes.

"I can assure you," I said, "my wife is no Witch. What proof have you for such groundless accusations against my wife?"

"We know she's a Witch because witnesses have spoken against her." He turned to Lizzie. "Why don't you confess?"

"I am no Witch, sir," Lizzie said again. She backed into me, hoping, I'm certain, that I could protect her. Dear God, why could I not get her away sooner? Just one day sooner? I have been wanting to take Lizzie to England for as long as we have been married, but we are here and not there and now my wife is in Hell. I am in a different kind of Hell but tis Hell all the same.

Whatever turmoil I felt, as though my innards quivered and I would heave everything I had ever eaten, I had to hold myself together. When the pock-faced man showed us the arrest warrant where Lizzie was named, she sobbed. I put my arm round her waist. I would be her rock. I would keep her strong.

"I have a warrant for your arrest, Goody Wentworth, and you must come with me."

"Mistress Wentworth," I said in my most haughty tone, but

what did such distinctions matter then? I tried to stop him from taking Lizzie but the man knew what he was about. He had done this many times before. When Father arrived I ran to him, shaking him, needing his help as I hadn't since I was a boy. And then I remembered. Father is an affluent member of Society, a Selectman of the Church. Surely, he could do something.

"Father, please," I begged, "we have to help Lizzie."

Father watched the constable bind Lizzie in chains. Lizzie looked fluid, as though she melted away. She tried to pat the bump where our babe waits, but the irons were too heavy. I ran to her, and as she reached for me she tripped and I caught her in my arms. The constable jerked her away. My life, he took her away.

Father did what he could. "What business have you with Mistress Wentworth?" he yelled.

"I have a warrant for her," the pock-faced man said.

Father grabbed the paper and read it. He shook his head. There was nothing he could do. I raged at the pock-faced man. I promised Lizzie I would never leave her ever and twas up to me to put an end to this.

"You dare take an innocent woman away on false charges?" I yelled. "Ask her to recite the Lord's Prayer! Ask her to recite the Ten Commandments! You think Witches cannot speak them because the Devil won't allow it. Test her! If you knew the Commandments yourself you would know the ninth—thou shalt not bear false witness!"

The constable grinned. "If you know the Bible so well then you also know 1 Peter 5:8." He waited for my response, but my mind was blank. Father knew.

"Be sober, be vigilant, because your adversary the Devil, as a roaring lion, walketh about, seeking whom he may devour."

"And from Exodus?" asked the constable.

Father slumped forward. "Thou shalt not suffer a Witch to live."

"My wife is no Witch," I said. "She is an innocent woman. Please. Let her go and we shall leave here and never return."

"If she's innocent then it shall come out at her trial," the constable said.

And I knew. No matter how wrong this was, no matter the cowards who falsely call her name, Lizzie suffers. No matter what is true. No matter no matter.

"Here, Son." Father places a bowl of broth before me, but the smell makes me want to vomit and I push it away. "You must eat, James. You must have nourishment. You must stay strong." He wipes his tears away with the back of his hand. "We must stay strong together. Elizabeth needs us now more than ever, and we shall be here for her. You shall be here for her."

Aye, I must stay strong. For Lizzie. She needs me and I need her and I shall stay strong. How I shall ever do that, I cannot say. But it must be done.

Breathe in. Breathe out. In and out and in and out. Right now tis all I can do. Remember to breathe.

15 AUGUST 1692, MONDAY

I must do something with my hands other than strangle the magistrates, the pockfaced constable, or anyone else involved in this unholy cacophony, so I write. I pace, I bang my injured fists into the wall, and I lie on our bed, hugging the quilts where she sleeps hoping for some sense of her. I know she is alive, she is not gone, not in the eternal sense, but she is not here and I cannot stand it. I cannot stand to be in my own skin.

Father has been staying with me. I know he says tis to help me settle everything, to help me prepare so that after we get Lizzie out of that Hellhole we can flee to New York, to England, to Wherever, but I know the truth—he is afeared for me. He is afeared I shall go mad and I may well just. I also know what he will not say. Thomas Oliver whispered to me, before he left on some errand, that Prudence Connor now accuses me of. She has been telling all who will listen, which is nearly everyone, that my Shape has been visiting her in the night, taking advantage of her in her bed. Only in her dreams would I ever approach such a vile creature the way I touch Lizzie. Now that his wife is away, she says, James Wentworth shall play. She cannot understand the love I have for Lizzie. Tis beyond her limited capacity. I know Lizzie would tell me to have compassion for the girl. I want Lizzie to be proud of me so I try to live without malice in my heart. Tis a struggle, but I try.

Meanwhile, Father works every angle to rescue Lizzie. He appeals to the magistrates but they have no more heart for Lizzie than they have for the others. They believe in Spectral evidence. They believe Salem is infected with Witches, Satan's minions, and they believe tis their duty to release us from Evil. Parris would say tis our own fault. We brought this down upon ourselves. We were not reverent enough. We were not obedient enough. But how do you obey a God that allows this?

I know the game by now. I have seen who is condemned to die and who is reprieved, still in prison but reprieved. Some of the accused have started confessing, aye, they are Witches. Those who confess live and those who do not die. I must get to Lizzie. I must see her. I know there are family members that have visited their loved ones in jail. Besides, Father and I must pay for Lizzie's upkeep. That is the way of it. They arrest you and chain you and keep you confined in a dark, damp, putrid dungeon, and you must pay them for the privilege of eating, of having a place to lay your head, of having any little comfort that might bring you a reprieve from the horror. Father and I shall pay them whatever. I shall give them everything I own, everything I have, I shall give my very life to help Lizzie. But I must persuade her to confess. Of course Lizzie is no Witch. She has never caused a moment's difficulty for anyone in her two-and-twenty years, but her confession is the best chance we have to keep her alive. Father said she shall have some reprieve, at least until she gives birth. But our child shall be here before we know it, and then…

WHEN I AWOKE FROM MY HALF-SLEEP I HEARD THOMAS OLIVER IN conversation with Father. They stood away from me, near the shelves in the Great Room. At first, I did not care. If Oliver was not bringing Lizzie home then he has nothing for me. When I felt Father's eyes on me I sat up. I felt so warm. I opened the front door and felt a soothing breeze come in over the bay. I wiped at my cheeks and felt wet on my fingers.

Oliver leaned close to Father and whispered.

"Already?" Father said. "Did they not think to tell us before making such a move?"

"She's a prisoner," Oliver said. "They don't need your permission."

Father dropped his head into his hands. I heard him take a steadying breath.

"Do you have news of Lizzie?" I asked.

"They've moved her to the prison in Boston," Father said.

I grasped Father by the shoulders and shook him until his head bobbed. "We must go," I said. "Now. We must pay her way. She must know we are there for her."

Father and Oliver nodded their agreement. I dressed as quickly as I could, and then Father and I grabbed whatever necessaries we might need for the journey.

"Do not worry, Son," Father said. "We can buy anything we might have forgotten in Boston."

Outside, I hitched Euripides and Aeschylus to the wagon and told our groom we were on our way and did not know when we would return. He is a good man, Collier, and I trust that the horses and other animals will be well tended. Finally, Father and I, accompanied by Oliver, traveled to Boston.

When we arrived the noise of the town grated my ears. I was overcome by the press of people, the horses and wagons blocking the roads, the shouts of the crowds, the stink of feces blown into our faces by the breeze off the Charles River. Oliver knew the way, and he steered us to a public house where we could stay whilst we wait for Lizzie. Tis a basic room with two beds, a table, and the raucous laughter of the tavern patrons below. I want to join them. I want to drink myself into oblivion and forget the pain stabbing my skull, my eyes, my heart. But I know I cannot. Lizzie is just down the road, and knowing she is so close keeps me strong.

16 AUGUST 1692, TUESDAY

J saw Lizzie today. Father bribed the jailkeep, I know not for how much, and the jailkeep's wife looked away as I headed downstairs into the dungeon. The first thing to hit me was the stench—urine, feces, and unwashed, sweltering bodies. The place is a living nightmare. I stopped at the foot of the stairs since all I saw was blackness. Twas so dark inside, and so bright outside, that I could not see my hand before my face.

Then I heard her, my Angel with clipped wings.

"James? Jamie? Tis you?"

Finally, I saw her. Lizzie sat against the wall, her ankles bleeding where the heavy shackles cut into her skin. I meant to stay strong but I could not stifle my sobs. I pulled my Angel into my arms and wept.

"Oh, Lizzie," was all I could say. "Oh, Lizzie…Oh, Lizzie…"

Even then she comforted me.

"I'm all right, James. Will I be home soon?" She pressed her hands to the bump where our babe waits. "Grace. I worry for her."

"You needn't worry, my love. Father and I are doing everything we can to get you out. We have been writing letters to Governor Phips, both the Mathers, the magistrates, and anyone else who might help us. We have been getting signed statements that you have been a faithful member of the Church and many have said you helped them in their times of need."

"Did that help Rebecca?" Lizzie asked.

I could not dwell on that thought then. I had to focus on Lizzie. Though twas dark, I saw a flicker of a smile on her lips. Her eyes looked far away, as though she remembered something that brought her joy. Tis only a fortnight since her arrest but she is already so changed—pale, thin, shivering, blood and pus on her infected ankles where the shackles rub. Yet she is not worried for herself. She worries for our babe inside her, and I wept because I could not help either of them. Lizzie took my hands and pressed them to her middle. I felt a swift kick and sighed with relief. The babe still moves. Grace must be all right.

I wanted to scream but I had to stay strong. For Lizzie. But she understands my most secret thoughts. She knows me so well.

"Put your faith in God," Lizzie said. "We must trust in His grace now."

"God?" I gestured at the darkness, the tittering rats, the floor wet with every disgust, the moaning, praying women chained as Lizzie is chained. "Where is God here?"

"Remember, James. A God of Salvation. A God of Lovingkindness. A God of Mercy. A compassionate God. A God of turn the other cheek and helping the ill and the poor and a God of forgiving others when they know not what they do."

"They know exactly what they do. And I will despise them forever for it." Twas a struggle to calm myself, but I did not want to distress Lizzie any more than she already was. "Are they feeding you?" I asked. "Do you have the bedding we paid for?"

"Aye." Lizzie's voice sounded far away. "And they did more than that for me after you paid them."

"Such as what?" I asked.

Lizzie shook her head. She sounded oh so very tired. "Tis no matter now. You're here. And soon I will be free."

I wanted to say more to her but the jailkeep grabbed me by the arm and dragged me away.

"Lizzie!" I called. "I love you. I shall always love you!"

"You are my dear and loving husband, James. I will love you forever."

And then I was at the top of the stairs and the heavy door slammed in my face and Lizzie was gone. Gone. I stood, unable to move, how could I leave when my life suffered beyond that door? Father's voice brought me back to myself. He haggled with the jailkeep, offering him gold to give Lizzie more blankets, more straw for her bed, better food, better drink. The jailkeep eyed the money greedily and said he would see what he could do. I was ready to argue with the man, hell, I was ready to beat the man raw, but Father led me away, first to the tavern where he pressed a beef pie into my hands and all but poured wine down my throat. Then we went up to our room so I could try to find some rest. Then that damned Oliver showed up with news I did not need to hear.

"You've been formally named," Oliver told me. "Prudence Connor had her brother go to Salem Town to file an affidavit against you."

Father sighed. "What do they say?"

"They say your son is a tall man who wears black and he is in league with the Black Man who bewitches Salem. They say he bewitched Prudence into doing salacious things. They say his golden-haired looks are a gift from the Devil as a means to lure innocent women to Satan's path."

"That is it." Father grabbed me by the shoulders and lifted me upright from the bed. "You must go to New York, James. You cannot dally. Oliver." He looked at the privateer as the man gulped a bottle of wine in two swallows. "You can get my son to New York without being noticed, can you not?"

"I've shipped cargo far bigger than that," Oliver said, poking his thumb in my direction.

I crossed my arms before my chest. "Nay," I said. "I shall not go. I cannot leave Lizzie."

"I shall stay to care for Elizabeth," Father said. "I'm not asking you, James, I'm telling you. You shall go to New York and you shall leave now!"

I laughed in Father's face. "Do you think you can make your grown son do something he does not wish to do? I'm a married man, Father, with a child on the way. I'm the head of my own family, and I shall not leave my wife, not for anything. Do you understand me?" I screamed at Father, venting my frustration, my anger, my sorrow, my fears, everything I had circling like a cyclone within me. Father sank onto the bed beside me.

"Please, James." He sounded as broken as I felt.

"Nay," I said. "I shall not go."

"You'll be no good to anyone if you're arrested," Oliver said.

"If I'm arrested then at least I shall be with Lizzie. I'd rather be beside her in prison than out here doing nothing."

"We are not doing nothing," Oliver said. "Far from that."

Father grabbed the closest bottle of wine, drank the contents, then wiped his lips with his coat sleeve.

"So what do we do?" Father asked. "Our efforts have proved fruitless. We are faring no better than the Nurses. No one is listening. No one cares." Again he asked, "So what do we do?"

"We break her out." Thomas Oliver spoke so matter-of-factly that it took a moment for me to realize what he said.

Father's eyes lit at the thought. "We have spoken of it, James. And others have done it. We can break her out and then you can leave for New York together. Why, you could be there in a matter of days." Father grabbed Oliver's hand. "You can find a way to do it, Thomas?"

Oliver nodded. "Oh, aye. I don't think it will be much of a bother, if you've got the proper funds, that is."

"Whatever expense," Father said. "I shall spare no expense to get my daughter out of there. She belongs here, with James, with her family." Father looked at me. He smiled for the first time since Lizzie has been taken away. "James? What say you?"

"Aye," I said. "Oh, please God, aye."

30 AUGUST 1692, WEDNESDAY

I am dead.

I am certain of it. I am dead. My heart does not beat. I do not breathe. I sit here writing this and I do not know how.

The last thing I remember before waking in the abandoned house was sitting outside the prison where they hold Lizzie. I had taken to sitting there whilst Oliver talked to this fellow over here, bribed that one over there, making plans to rescue Lizzie so we could get her far away from here. I had been reciting "To My Dear and Loving Husband," hoping Lizzie could hear me through the thick wall dividing us:

If ever two were one, then surely we.
If ever man were loved by wife, then thee.
If ever wife was happy in a man,
Compare with me, ye women, if you can.
I prize thy love more than whole mines of gold,
Or all the riches that the East doth hold.
My love is such that rivers cannot quench,
Nor ought but love from thee give recompense.
Thy love is such I can no way repay;

The heavens reward thee manifold, I pray.
Then while we live, in love let's so persever,
That when we live no more, we may live ever.

I prayed that she heard me. I prayed that she knew I was there. I waited for Father and Thomas Oliver to arrive, to say they had done it, they had paid enough, the jailkeep would look the other way, and we could get down to the dungeon, the keys to her fetters in my hand. I would unlock her chains and Lizzie and I would walk out of Hell together. I spoke aloud to Lizzie.

"Stay strong, my love. Just this little while longer. Father and Oliver are on their way. I shall have you out of there this night. We shall escape from here together. I shall have you in my arms again soon, and you shall never suffer again."

The shadow of a man crossed the road. First the man passed to the right, then to the left, then disappeared altogether. When I realized the man was gone my heart stopped. I would have gasped for breath, but I felt nothing. I thought I imagined it, as though I awoke from a dream. Twas as if everything, the world, my body, the ground I sat on, was wiped blank. I watched people passing by with an odd detachment, as though I sat in a void and the world continued as though nothing had changed.

But what did change, I wondered? What happened? An icy prick pinched my heart and I sat in a ball, my knees pulled to my chest, my head down, my back pressed against the prison wall, hoping Lizzie could feel my presence. I had felt her so strongly a moment before but then I struggled to find her. Where had she gone?

The man who disappeared into the shadows stood across the road. When he was close enough I recognized him, the strange man I have been noticing these months past, the one with blood on his lips leaning over Boxley, the long-faced man with the silvery wisps in his red-brown hair. He wore that ridiculous grin, as always. He allowed a man on horseback to pass and then he crossed to me.

"What is that you're saying?" he asked. "You're speaking aloud, to no one, it appears."

"I'm speaking to my wife," I said.

"That beautiful dark-haired girl you're married to? She's in there?" The man nodded toward the jail. I dropped my head into my hands and sobbed before this stranger who seems to appear and disappear at will.

"I can help you," he said. I looked at him, dumb, unable to think. I still could not feel Lizzie. Where was she? I desperately needed help, any help, even help this strange man might offer. I stood, and he smiled. "You'll thank me later."

He led me away from the bustling part of town where people still passed though twas late into the night. He stopped before an abandoned house that looked as though it had been left behind by time, tossed out, alone in the wilderness. My heart raced and my breath came in short bursts. I should have turned away. *Run!* screamed between my ears. But I did not run. Something I did not understand compelled me forward. I followed the man because he said the magick words—he could help Lizzie. But once we were away from everything I worried about what the man wanted. My money? I had but little on me. My life? My life is chained to the wall in the prison.

The man walked into the house and though I wanted to yell for help I followed him. Perhaps he could help Lizzie after all. Twas well dark, with barely enough moonlight to see by, but I could make out enough to know there was nothing inside the house, no furniture, no windows, nothing. My legs rumbled and my head pounded. Then I realized. I made a terrible mistake following him. He turned his wicked grin onto me. His lips were pulled abnormally wide, showing the sharpness of his eyeteeth, not unlike wolves on the attack. I turned to the door. *Run!* But the man was too fast and blocked my only way out.

"As I said, you'll thank me later."

Before I passed into blackness I thought, if I scream, would anyone hear me? We were so far from everything. I felt the man's strong hands, his fingers pressing into me as though my bones would crunch to dust under his strength. I felt his teeth in my neck, breaking my skin, digging into my muscles, the flow of my blood. And then…

I must be hallucinating. What nonsense is this I dreamed? Of course I breathe. Of course my heart beats. I must wake myself and return to the prison so I can rescue Lizzie.

And then we shall be free.

AUTHOR'S NOTES

After *Her Loving Husband's Return* was published, Loving Husband fans from all over the world emailed me or left messages on my blog asking, pretty please, could I continue the Wentworths' story? I was so touched by their desire to see more of James and Elizabeth/Sarah, but I felt that their story had run its course. In time, I realized that I hadn't touched on James and Elizabeth's experience in Salem in 1692 as much as I would have liked to in *Her Dear & Loving Husband*, so this missing piece provided the inspiration for *Down Salem Way*. My original intention was for *Down Salem Way* to be written using the two timelines in the past and the present like the books in the *Loving Husband Trilogy*, but I saw as early as the first draft that the dual timeline didn't quite work for the Wentworths' story during the Salem Witch Trials.

The idea for writing *Down Salem Way* as James' journal came from my rereading of *The Salem Witch Trials: A Day-by-Day Chronicle of a Community Under Siege* by Marilynne K. Roach. Roach's book was instrumental in allowing me to piece together the events of the witch hunts in real time, so to speak. Other books necessary for the writing of *Down Salem Way* were *The Devil in Massachusetts: A Modern Inquiry into the Salem Witch Trials* by Marion L. Starkey; *A Storm of Witchcraft: The Salem Witch Trials and the American Experience* by Emerson W. Baker; *The Devil in the Shape of a Woman: Witchcraft in Colonial New England* by Carol F. Karlsen; and *Everyday Life in the Massachusetts Bay Colony* by George Francis

Dow. If you are interested in learning more about the Salem Witch Trials, these books are highly recommended.

Some of Samuel Parris' language, as well as some of the language of other real-life players such as Rebecca Nurse and Sarah Good, come from primary sources. I have taken poetic license in the sharing of such texts. The portrayal of these real-life figures is completely of my own imaginings. While my intention is to remain true to the history, in historical fiction the story must always come first. As Mark Twain said, "Truth is stranger than fiction, but it is because Fiction is obliged to stick to possibilities; Truth isn't."

Thank you, as always, to my readers all over the world. You make bringing the Wentworths to life a joy.

ABOUT THE AUTHOR

Meredith Allard is an award-winning author known for the bestselling *Loving Husband Trilogy* and the Victorian novel *When It Rained at Hembry Castle*, which IndieReader named a Best Historical Novel. Her prequel, *Down Salem Way*, earned the B.R.A.G. Medallion and was a semi-finalist for the Chaucer Award in Early Historical Fiction.

A recognized authority on the craft, Meredith is the author of *Painting the Past: A Guide for Writing Historical Fiction*, a #1 Amazon New Release in Authorship and Creativity Self-Help. For over twenty years, she has mentored writers of all ages, helping them find their voices while honing her own signature blend of meticulous research and haunting prose.

When she isn't unearthing the secrets of the past, she can be found in the hills of Southern Nevada with her cats and a cup of coffee.

Join Meredith online at www.meredithallard.com for her weekly blog posts and monthly newsletter.

BOOKS BY MEREDITH ALLARD

And Shadows Will Fall

Christmas at Hembry Castle

Down Salem Way

The Duchess of Idaho

Her Dear & Loving Husband

Her Loving Husband's Curse

Her Loving Husband's Return

Painting the Past: A Guide for Writing Historical Fiction

The Professor of Eventide

The Swirl and Swing of Words: Embracing the Writing Life

Victory Garden

When It Rained at Hembry Castle

Woman of Stones